D1560285

Dear OwlCrate Reader,

I'm absolutely thrilled to be part of this month's OwlCrate! Writing *The Scorpion Queen* has been a deeply rewarding journey, allowing me—and now you, dear reader—to immerse ourselves in the rich and often overlooked world of medieval West Africa. The idea for this novel began during my final semester of graduate school when I took a seminar on fairy tales that inspired me to read folktale anthologies from across the globe. Among them, I discovered a fairy tale from the Western Sahel about a ruler who set deadly trials for his daughter's suitors that became the seed from which *The Scorpion Queen* grew.

At first glance, this novel is about sixteen-year-old Aminata Aait, a salt merchant's daughter whose comfortable life is shattered when she is falsely accused of her sister's crime. But beneath the surface of Amie's story lies an even darker tale about Princess Mariama of Mali's desperation to prevent her father, the emperor, from boiling her suitors alive when they fail the impossible trials he has devised. When she initially arrives at the imperial court, Amie believes she can trust the princess, but as she slowly uncovers Mariama's true intentions, she finds herself lost in a world of perilous desert journeys, trickster gods, and spells strong enough to bend iron and break hearts.

I'm excited to invite you to step into the medieval city of Timbuktu, a bustling center of trade where merchants dealt in salt, gold, and ivory while emperors fought for control over the Saharan trade routes that brought the city its fabled wealth.

I hope you enjoy this journey as much as I enjoyed creating it.

— Mina Fears

The Scorpion Queen

Mina Fears

...

This signed edition was printed exclusively for OwlCrate

THE
SCORPION
QUEEN

THE
SCORPION
QUEEN

Mina Fears

FLATIRON
BOOKS
NEW YORK

This is a work of fiction. All the characters, organizations, and events portrayed in this novel are either products of the author's imagination or used fictitiously.

THE SCORPION QUEEN. Copyright © 2024 by Fears Author Corp. All rights reserved. Printed in China. For information, address Flatiron Books, 120 Broadway, New York, NY 10271.

www.flatironbooks.com

Designed by Susan Walsh

Library of Congress Cataloging-in-Publication Data

Names: Fears, Mina, author.
Title: Scorpion queen / Mina Fears.
Description: First edition. | New York : Flatiron Books, 2025. | Audience term: Teenagers | Audience: Ages 12–18.
Identifiers: LCCN 2024029723 | ISBN 9781250392350 (hardcover) | ISBN 9781250852946 (stained edge hardcover) | ISBN 9781250852953 (ebook)
Subjects: CYAC: Princesses—Fiction. | Courts and courtiers—Fiction. | Household employees—Fiction. | Tombouctou (Mali)—Fiction. | Fantasy. | LCGFT: Fantasy fiction. | Novels.
Classification: LCC PZ7.1.F416 Sc 2025 | DDC [Fic]—dc23
LC record available at https://lccn.loc.gov/2024029723

Our books may be purchased in bulk for promotional, educational, or business use. Please contact your local bookseller or the Macmillan Corporate and Premium Sales Department at 1-800-221-7945, extension 5442, or by email at MacmillanSpecialMarkets@macmillan.com.

First Edition: 2025

10 9 8 7 6 5 4 3 2 1

To my parents, with love

IMPERIAL MALI
1359

1

A girl of my age was to be like the dawn.

Blooming and bright, at sixteen I was supposed to be at a beginning, looking with hopeful impatience toward my future—marriage and motherhood and the warmth of a home.

But not me.

Ruined, my parents told me, again and again. *So young, and your life is already over.*

When my father and mother said I was ruined, I knew that what they really meant was polluted, or poisoned. I was a disappointment through and through—a sickly animal that must be cast out for the sake of the herd, a dead branch to be pruned.

In their desperation to be rid of me, they sent me away to work in the emperor's court, and my very first day in the palace was an execution day. I couldn't help but see it as a bad omen, further proof of my parents' conviction that I was a blight who would always sour her surroundings. That day I was busy, with many tasks to distract me from my dark thoughts. I had spent the morning in the palace with the other servants, preparing the emperor's daughter, Mariama Keita, for the day's events by plaiting her hair into a dozen waist-length braids, darkening her lips with red ochre, and tracing her eyelids with kohl.

Upon the princess's cheeks and forehead, we dabbed small quantities of date oil.

"For the improvement of Her Highness's skin," explained Penda, another chambermaid. Then we dressed her in a wrapper of indigo brocade and fastened a series of carnelian bracelets around her wrists.

You are going to be different here, I reminded myself as we worked. *Braver. Bolder. The sort of person willing to bend the rules to get what she wants.*

All my life, I had obediently done whatever my parents asked of me, hoping to one day make them proud. For all my sixteen years, I had been timid and compliant and eager to please. But that had never earned me my parents' love. I was never their favored daughter—that privilege had always belonged to my older sister, Haddy.

I couldn't deny the prickles of envy that accompanied growing up alongside a sibling who moved so easily through life, her good looks and quick wits never failing to make our parents shine with pride. Although Haddy was more outspoken and less obedient than a daughter should be, her natural charm endeared her to them far more than my obedience ever had. But hidden beneath the surface of my sister's charm was a duplicitous streak, a talent for deceit.

She could lie better than anyone I knew.

And it was one of her falsehoods that had been my undoing, that had plucked me from the comfort of our parents' house.

In my old life, I'd had a maid of my own to dress me and bathe me. Now I tried my best not to think of it as a degradation and to ignore the flashes of humiliation that passed through me as I worked. Just last month, I was Aminata Aqit, the youngest daughter of one of the most successful salt merchants in the empire. I had been poised to marry into nobility—to a boy I loved. But that was all over now, and every task I performed that morning felt like a punishment.

A serving girl should always maintain a pleasant expression for the benefit of her employer, but I felt myself scowling with indignation instead. Luckily Princess Mariama was far too distraught to take notice. Slow, silent tears slid down her face as we draped her wrapper and pinned up her braids with gold-and-ivory hair ornaments, revealing the slender curve of her neck. Penda held the princess's hand in comfort until she ceased her weeping.

When the princess crossed over to the windows to watch the crowd of spectators gathering in the market below, Jeneba, the third chambermaid, rolled her eyes. "After ninety-eight executions, it's a wonder that she still weeps at all," she whispered, her neat dark braids catching a golden triangle of late morning sunlight.

Even with her permanent smirk, Jeneba was a striking girl, with wide-set eyes, full lips, and a small and pointed chin. If she had been highborn, she might have had several eager suitors of her own. But she was only a servant, just like all the others. Just like me.

"Jen, for shame!" Penda gasped. "What if she hears you?"

Both girls turned to me expectantly, perhaps thinking I would join in their game of gently ridiculing the princess. I had met her personal attendants only that morning, but it was already clear that there was a pecking order among them. Irreverent Jeneba was the leader, while Penda, her sweet-natured friend, followed in her footsteps. An earlier me would have joked along with Jeneba, submitting to her authority just as I had always bent to the will of my parents. But I was determined to leave that person behind, and so I said nothing.

Then came a messenger to announce that it was noon, time for the three of us to escort the princess to the market square for the execution.

Upon his only daughter's thirteenth birthday, Emperor Suleyman had issued a decree that any prince or nobleman who could pass his Trials would be permitted to marry her—while all who failed were killed. The emperor had distributed his terms to every corner of the empire in hundreds of identical scrolls:

Venture into the desert for three nights with three of my best horsemen. On the third evening, you shall come across a grove of date palms with bark as blue as a summer sky. Split the largest tree with an ax, and you will see that its wood is dark red, like blood. Return to my palace, present me with three planks of this wood, and I will permit you to wed my daughter. But if you fail this first Trial, if my horsemen bring you back to the palace empty-handed, you must attempt a second Trial—a bath in boiling water. The suitor who leaves the bath with air still in his lungs and blood still in his veins may marry the princess.

The Trials seemed impossible. But that had not prevented suitors from far across the empire, even distant cities such as Mopti or Niani or Yoff by the sea, from traveling to the emperor's palace to try to win his daughter's hand.

All had failed. Of course they had.

To my knowledge, trees of sky-blue bark and bloodred wood did not exist. And even if such a specimen could be found within the vastness of the northern desert, I doubted a nobleman would be the first to discover it. My father always said that while Mali's noblemen were skilled in diplomacy and military strategy, in drawing elegant calligraphy and mapping the stars, their desert survival skills were often lacking.

It was the merchant class that knew how to carve careful paths through the Sahara on camels laden with salt, gold, kola nuts, and richly woven fabrics. Merchants knew to travel only at night, when the desert was cool and more easily navigable, but the noble suitors always set off on their journeys in the stifling heat of midmorning, doggedly determined and sweating. So when each man inevitably failed his first Trial, never finding that elusive blue grove in the dunes, the emperor's men would force him back into the city to be boiled to death before a crowd of spectators.

As a handmaiden to the emperor's daughter, it was now my responsibility to accompany her onto the executioner's platform, along with the rest of the imperial procession: the emperor, his advisers, and his three surviving wives.

I was dreading it. I had been compelled to attend executions before—and hated every moment of them—and I couldn't think of anything worse than being on the platform while it happened.

All morning the sky had been clear, but now the day was growing overcast. Thin white clouds gathered over the city, weakening our shadows as we climbed the steep stairs to the suitor's kettle. Morbid, but the name did fit: it was a white clay kettle the size of a man, and it sat upon a white stone platform high above the market square. Although I had witnessed many suitors die within it, I had never before been so close.

I had always been grateful to stand at the edge of the crowd with my mother and father and Haddy—a wave of bitterness swept through me—where the dense throngs of people created a living barrier separating us from the slaughter. In those moments, I used to struggle with feelings of revulsion and unease that lingered long after the execution had passed. It always felt strange to walk back home toward the merchants' district with my parents and their friends, who would converse gaily among themselves and seem altogether unmoved by the events that had horrified me. I could never understand their indifference.

I forced myself to continue up the stairs. When we finally reached the platform, I looked out and wondered if I would glimpse my family in the crowd. At this height, I could see the flat white rooftops of Timbuktu scattered below me like rice upon a dark table. I turned my gaze to the river, bright as molten metal in the partial sunlight, with trading canoes flitting across it like moths. I could almost hear the fishermen's oars slapping its waters.

Then I looked east, toward the universities. Scholars hurried down the main promenade, hugging pale scrolls to their chests. From my vantage point upon the platform, they all looked so small, like ants. Was Kader among them? I finally permitted myself to think of him, something I had been trying to avoid of late. The same questions had plagued me every day of our monthlong separation: *Does he miss me? Is he thinking of me? Have I been forgotten?*

Next to me, Princess Mariama, who had climbed the stairs nervously with her soft, fragile gaze darting around her, bowed gracefully to the emperor. "Good afternoon, Father," she said smoothly.

The words seemed to change her. She was no longer the sensitive girl of seventeen whose tears had flowed easily in her own chamber; she had transformed into something flat and flinty and devoid of feeling. Now she was the emperor's daughter I was accustomed to seeing at feasts and festivals and other public appearances, the girl whose cold, practiced composure never faltered.

Emperor Suleyman smiled distractedly in return. "Mariama, you look well."

The princess straightened and beckoned for me to join her at the edge of the platform. I obeyed and passed even closer by the water-filled kettle and the condemned man who stood inside it. I wish I could say I remembered his name, but the princess had so many suitors that they blurred together in my mind. Mariama was the richest prospective bride in the empire—perhaps in the entire world—and so it was only natural that many suitors desired her hand. But they rarely mentioned her father's gold before their dying moments. They preferred to speak of true love.

"Princess," said the suitor to Mariama, his voice unsteady, "your eyes are like pools of dark water, and your skin shines like polished gold in the midday sun. You are the loveliest creature I have ever seen."

I heard Mariama make a choked sound, something like a sob. For one brief moment, her mask of regal indifference slipped, and she looked as though she might burst into tears before the entire imperial court and an audience of market-going commoners. Just as quickly, she was all serenity again, her true self pushed down deep.

I marked her rigid posture, her quick and shallow breathing. Standing beside me on the platform, the princess looked equal parts graceful and miserable. People had to say she was beautiful because she was the emperor's daughter, but I suspected they would have said the same even if she were a nobody. Mariama's was a quiet beauty: her full lips guarded a narrow mouth, her dark skin was smooth as still water, and her cheekbones were high and wide, like the face of the moon. I felt a jump in my throat when her eyes, very briefly, met mine. The contact lasted only a few short moments and then she returned her gaze to the crowd, which rippled with murmurs and insults and rude little jokes, as it always did. The more I watched her, the more I pitied her. *She never asked for this*, I thought.

"Please, Your Imperial Majesty, if you have any kindness in your heart, any generosity, you will pardon me," pleaded the suitor, turning from Mariama to her father. The water he stood in made a low sloshing sound with his movement. "Let me go and I promise I will leave the city at once. I will relinquish all of my belongings to your treasury. I will give you my land, my weapons, my gold—only please do not let me die."

I cringed at the crowd's bursts of laughter. Emperor Suleyman chuckled along with them, his gaze pitiless. His eyes were as flat as if they had been carved into stone.

I hated it when the suitors begged for their lives.

Not for the first time, I felt a surge of anger as I contemplated why we allowed the emperor to do this to so many young men. Of course, I knew I should never criticize the Trials aloud. Songhai merchant families were supposed to be imperial loyalists, and mine was no exception. Ever since the late emperor Musa had peacefully annexed our city, Mali's emperors had protected our trading boats and caravans from thieves. In return, we paid our taxes on time and never spoke ill of the emperor's decisions. And Mali's noblemen were often willing to marry commoner girls like myself, provided we brought with us a sizable dowry. My parents had already secured such a match for my sister. She was now called Lady Hadiza and lived with her Malinke husband in an opulent house in the nobles' quarter, enjoying frequent visits to the palace for festivals and feasts.

Envy and frustration gnawed at me. I, too, was meant to have wedded into the nobility. I should be married by now, a noblewoman instead of an unwed servant. I should have been my parents' pride instead of their shame.

Haddy had ruined my one chance at happiness, and I would never forgive her for as long as I lived.

A sharp slapping sound interrupted my thoughts. I looked up to watch the emperor bring his hands together high above his head and clap ten times. At this signal, a foot soldier lit the kerosene-soaked planks beneath the kettle, which promptly erupted into flames.

I looked away as my body broke out in a thick sweat, the delicate skin of my face smarting from the heat.

I longed to be anywhere else.

I focused my attention instead on the wisps of steam rising

above the kettle and over the market. The gentle noon wind lifted the smoke toward the tall white arches of the imperial palace. As the pained cries of Mariama's suitor grew louder, I pretended that I was floating away over the city. I hovered like a hawk above it all, climbing through the sky until I reached the kingdom of Nyori, god of the clouds.

The suitor's screams lasted four minutes, perhaps five—and then stopped. The crowd grew bored soon after, chatting idly among themselves as his corpse boiled. It was all so terrible that I had sometimes successfully convinced my parents to let me stay home from it entirely. I did not know how Mariama had borne it so many times over.

The smell wafting over from the kettle was truly awful, but when I pinched my nose to keep from vomiting, Jeneba shoved me. "That's not the way," she whispered, her lovely face taunting.

The old me would have apologized and dropped her hands obligingly to her sides—but she was a tiresomely obedient girl. So I shoved Jeneba right back. Not hard enough to cause injury, but with just enough force to show her that I would not tolerate bullies.

Jeneba gasped just as my nostrils filled with a scent like leather tanning over a flame. It flooded my senses with the metallic stench of coagulated blood. My stomach lurched and I plugged my nose again. I tried to distract myself from my nausea by scanning the crowd for faces I recognized. I tensed when I noticed a group of merchant-caste girls I had known since infancy, huddled together at the front of the crowd.

And then I spotted my mother. She was standing with my father in the crowd. For a brief moment, we locked eyes, and I felt a painful, familiar rush of abandonment when she looked away, gazing pointedly in the opposite direction.

My father did not avert his gaze. His cold, precise stare pierced my skin as only he could. Father could take the measure of me and find me wanting without saying a single word. While Haddy and I were growing up, he had told us often that he'd have preferred sons over daughters. He'd said that if we had to have been born girls, we should at least do him the courtesy of being marriageable—skilled in languages, pleasing in appearance, and competent at the loom and other womanly arts. Haddy was always the better student in these endeavors. She was also the family beauty. We both were short and slight, with tightly coiled black hair and deep bronze complexions—but everyone remarked that Haddy's features were more harmonious than mine, her figure comelier. The skin of her face was always smooth and clear, whereas my cheeks and forehead were often dotted with pimples that my mother treated with tonics of sour milk.

My own father is ashamed of me, I thought as I watched him. *I was never good enough for him, and now that I have fallen, he wishes I were not his daughter at all.* I turned away, my throat prickling with self-loathing, when something else caught my eye. A group of nobles in blue were standing together at the center of the audience. The lords restlessly gripped the hilts of their daggers and the ladies fidgeted with their necklaces of heavy gold.

And Haddy was among them.

She looked guiltily up at me, a silent plea on her pursed lips. I had not seen my sister in more than a month, and my hands curled into fists at my sides as I noticed the amber glimmer of our mother's wedding beads at her neck. Anger rose like bile in my throat. I would never enjoy the grand wedding I had dreamed of ever since I was a little girl. Haddy had stolen that from me, too. She was the reason Kader and I could not be together, why I was now serving in a dangerous imperial court instead of married to the kind and thoughtful boy I loved.

Watching Haddy now in the crowd, I could hardly believe that there was once a time when the two of us were the best of friends. As children, we had done everything together, from splashing in the rice paddies along the riverbank to searching for jinn in abandoned houses to braiding acacia flowers into each other's hair.

Bitter tears sprang to my eyes. I wiped them away with the back of my hand—just as Haddy's husband wrapped an arm about her waist. I felt a twinge of satisfaction when she flinched. It gratified me to remember that my sister was miserable, too.

I looked away and passed my eyes over the crowd until, finally, I spotted Kader.

The sound and heat of the fire and rumblings of the crowd all fell away. I heard nothing, felt nothing, save for the pounding of my heart and my own rapid breathing. There was my love, standing so close to the platform that he must have elbowed his way to the front of the crowd so he could look upon my face.

The sight of him made me feel lightheaded. He was my only friend in the entire world. We had been apart for just a month, but he already looked different. He was taller, all flat planes and sharp angles, with new creases in his forehead that made him look older. For one dreadful moment, I wondered if he was still on my side. What if his father had managed to turn him against me?

Then—

"I love you," he mouthed.

Relief flooded my senses as I whispered back, "I love you."

Kader believed me. He still cared about me, a month after we'd been torn apart. Although his face remained drawn, his eyes tragic, he smiled up at me and pointed across the river. Our love story was not over, as I had feared.

Perhaps it was only just beginning.

2

We met half an hour later at our favorite spot along the riverbank, where the reeds were lush and thick enough to conceal us from strangers. Visiting Kader on my very first day in service to the princess meant I was not only risking my job and position but also disobeying my parents' orders never to see or speak with him ever again. But sighting him in the crowd had only increased my determination to feel his hands in mine.

After the executioner had carried the suitor's body away for burial, Penda, Jeneba, and I followed the princess down the white stone staircase and into the market below. Guards parted the crowd to allow us safe passage back to the palace. I prayed that Mariama and the others wouldn't notice as I slipped away into the vast throng, pushing through a thicket of arms and legs until I was out of sight. Although I had already resolved to see Kader at any cost, my body prickled with anxious energy.

I had never been the rebellious sort, and disobedience was not in my nature. But if my recent fall from grace had taught me anything, it was that I could not depend on anyone but myself. And after losing everything—my reputation, my inheritance, and my future—didn't I deserve to seize any crumbs of happiness within my reach? The crowd was dense, my progress was slow, and my stomach flipped with nervous anticipation with every step, but I forced myself to not turn back.

I hastened my pace as I crossed the bridge over into the fishing district. Here, the wide streets were lined with date palms, their leaves like thin green jewels against the milky sky. Although the market had been very crowded, I saw few people on this side of the river, save for servants running afternoon errands and the occasional pair of fishwives carrying barrels of entrails. Upon the waterfront, Songhai fishermen in wooden dugout canoes worked three or four to a boat, one at the oars as the others plunged their billowing nets into the waves.

My chest felt tight as I scrambled along the bank, stopping quickly to remove my sandals before I slid across the muddy beach into a secluded circle of reeds. Kader and I had chosen it as our meeting spot long ago, during our betrothal. It was considered improper for unmarried couples to spend time together unchaperoned, but we had not been worried about getting caught. Everyone in our parents' circles who might have seen us and gossiped avoided the fishing district, just as they avoided the blacksmiths' quarter, the tanneries, and every other part of the city inhabited by lower-caste workingmen. Here, Kader and I knew we could speak freely, unheard except by the industrious fishermen, who were too busy filling their nets with wriggling catfish and Nile perch to pay us any notice.

My heart leapt when I found him waiting for me where the tall reeds bobbed in the wind like courtiers bowing to a king. I drank him in breathlessly, savoring the sight of him, the smiling twist of his mouth. He looked like a king himself, darkly regal in an indigo thobe shirt and black linen trousers. Usually, noblemen half covered their faces with tagelmust scarves, but today he had left his scarf carelessly untied, revealing his long neck.

I ran to him and cried, "Kader!"

His lips parted in a broad smile when he saw me approach. He glanced around the riverbank to make sure we were alone and drew me to him. I buried my face in his chest, inhaling the familiar scent of him: soap, dried dates from his pockets, and castor oil from the lamps he used to study past sundown.

His kiss, when it came, was gentle as the breeze that tousled the stems at our feet.

I had missed him more than I realized. I smiled up at him wordlessly as we parted, feeling a little embarrassed that one kiss could make me dizzy with delight. Kader Bagayogo was the youngest son of a prominent Malinke nobleman who had been known in his youth as one of the deadliest swordsmen in the empire. All three of Kader's older brothers were military men, athletic like their father. They always seemed to be in motion, sparring with the other young officers or hunting wild animals for sport. I liked that Kader was nothing like his brothers. A student at Sankoré University, he preferred books to swords, wrote poetry in three languages, and could debate matters of law and theology like a marabout.

Other fathers might have been proud of a scholarly son, but Kader's father cared little for academic achievements. He thought him a weakling, a disappointment in the sparring pit and the hunting field, and an embarrassment next to his brothers. But that was how he and I found our commonality. We were both youngest siblings overlooked by our parents, and we bonded over this in the early days of our childhood betrothal, one that was first conceived as a business arrangement to enrich our families but eventually led to affection and, finally, love. As our devotion to each other grew, I became Kader's escape from his demanding family—especially his father—and in turn, he became mine.

He grinned down at me. "You grow lovelier each time I see you. I did not think it was possible—"

I interrupted him with another embrace. It was a proper kiss this time, the sort we had shared when we were still betrothed, before our families separated us. I felt so lucky to finally be back in his arms.

After, I watched as he rifled through the leather pouch at his waist and retrieved a stunning set of bird-shaped silver filigree earrings. "I had these made for you as a wedding gift. I tried many times to deliver them in person, but your father always turned me away at your door. He never let me see you." Then he pressed the earrings into my open palm.

My face grew hot. It did not surprise me that my father had not permitted Kader to enter our house, nor was it unusual that he had never told me about the visits. Father was furious with me and he wanted me to suffer.

But we were together now.

"How beautiful," I breathed, holding the earrings to a ray of sunlight that burned through the wool of the clouds. They were small and delicate, crafted by a skilled silversmith—Timbuktu produced some of the best silver jewelry in the world.

"What sort of birds are they?" I asked coyly, already knowing the answer.

"Fire finches, of course."

He had always said I reminded him of the small red birds. *My fire finch*, he called me, because I was small and quick and on most days reddened my lips.

"I will wear them every day," I promised, looking up at him.

"You cannot know how much I have wanted to see you," he said. His easy smile made me feel as though anything were possible. "I saw you up on the platform and I could not believe you were real. You have been such a constant fixture in my daydreams that at first I thought I had imagined you."

"Perhaps you have," I told him. I had missed him dearly, the boy who had once brought me a string of blue beads and told me they were the river goddess's tears.

His smile faltered. "But what were you doing up there with the emperor's daughter?"

"I work for her now," I said with a grimace.

"Ah." He traced a slow thumb along my temple, as if deciding what to say next. "Was that your parents' doing?"

I nodded. "Father and Mother have disinherited me." The word *disinherited* sat heavily on my tongue. Had I really lost so much, so quickly? It still felt like a trick. "Of course, *Haddy* will keep her inheritance."

"Oh." He sounded sorry for me.

"*She* should be the one wearing this, not me," I cried, gesturing at my maid's wrapper. A rush of resentment swept through me like a strong wind. "She should be the one to lose her inheritance. Instead, she gets to attend royal banquets and braid jewels into her hair!"

Kader frowned with concern. "Her husband is known through-out court as a foolish drunk. And she has two senior co-wives boss-ing her about day and night. Girls in such situations have been known to die from exhaustion."

"Have you forgotten what Haddy did to us?" I asked more sharply than I had intended. I wanted to tell him not to pity the girl who had ruined our future together. Usually, I admired Kader's compassionate nature, but when it came to Haddy, I needed him to be firmly on my side.

"I have not forgotten."

"And will your father arrange for you to marry another?" I tried to keep my voice even, but I could hear the jealousy creeping through.

There was a silence. For a long moment, I worried that I had guessed correctly.

But then Kader whispered, "How could I?" His voice grew thick with emotion. "I have thought of you every hour of every day for the past month. Father wants me to find another wife. He invites a different highborn maiden to dine with us once a week, and he always asks afterward if I would like to get to know the girl better. But I always say no—because of you."

His words brought tears to my eyes. I tried to wipe them away but still more came. "Oh," I said.

Kader drew me close and kissed my forehead. "We should run away," he said suddenly. I could feel his heartbeat against my chin, quick as a drum.

"You cannot be serious," I said, blinking up at him.

"I most certainly am." His voice rose with excitement. "We could leave this evening and stow away on a trading boat to the tropics! You would have to dress as an oarsman at first, but once we pass Niamey—"

"That would never work," I said impatiently. I could already see the cracks in his plan. "Say we managed to escape tonight undetected and your father didn't send anyone after us. Say we got as far as the river delta and the kingdom of Benin. Then what? What would we eat?"

He paused, considering. "I could hunt for you," he said finally, tangling his fingers in my curls. "I could fish."

I sighed. "My love, you know you cannot hunt for your supper any more than I can. And then there is the problem of where we might live," I added with the shrewd practicality of a merchant's daughter. "And how shall we find housing?"

"We would find work," he said stubbornly. "You could weave textiles for markets, and I could make my living as a scribe, or perhaps . . ." He trailed off, his eyes clouding over. I knew he had realized the impossibility.

Something occurred to me then. "It might not work for us to leave tonight," I said, my thoughts leaping fast as hares. "But in one year's time, I should have enough money saved from my position at court for us to flee the empire and start a new life. A life where our parents cannot touch us."

"I will help," Kader offered brightly. "I will tutor at university and charge fees. The other students are always asking me for help. And then we can finally build our little house by the sea," he told me, brushing away the last of my tears with his thumb.

We exchanged smiles. When I closed my eyes, I could see it: a little clay house with a domed roof, nestled between cliffs of sandstone. Below our house, on a distant beach, I imagined a brood of plump children with Kader's kind eyes, splashing and shouting in the waves.

I couldn't wait to raise my future children with the kindness missing from my own childhood. That my parents' love for me had often felt conditional and transactional was one of the reasons why I so badly wanted to start a family of my own.

"It is settled," I told him. "We will save our wages. I will tuck away every single cowrie I earn working for the emperor's daughter, and you will do the same with your tutoring fees. And next year, you will come to me in the palace in the dead of night. . . ."

"And I will tell you to run and we will never look back." He broke out in a smile that could put the sun to shame.

I felt better just hearing him say the words aloud. Our dream of the house by the sea seemed distant but not impossible. An hour ago, the world was lonely and chaotic, but now we had a plan.

This was not goodbye—far from it. Kader and I would be together again.

"You seem different," he told me, still smiling widely.

That is my intent, to be changed, I thought. "Do not try to visit me in the palace before then," I warned him. "It is too dangerous. My father—"

"I know what your father will do," he said darkly.

I remembered Father's rages, his flares of anger and bursts of criticism when his daughters performed anything less than perfection. "Soon, none of that will matter," I told him. "Soon, God willing, we will never have to see our parents again."

He kissed me. "God willing."

I sighed into him, feeling cautiously hopeful and more than a little astonished that he was willing to sacrifice so much for me. By running away, Kader would lose the many luxuries of his life here in Timbuktu. He would give up his title, his standing at university, his inherited lands and fortune—all because he loved me. It was shocking and impractical and undeniably romantic, a gesture as gallant as those of any of the heroes in my nurse's stories.

The nurse who helped with Haddy and me when we were children was usually unsmiling and serious, especially in our mother's presence. But she came alive at night, spinning tales for us about gods and monsters and heroes, about beautiful maidens and wicked sorcerers and tricky jinn. My favorites followed heroes who loved fiercely and would do anything to protect heroines from harm.

The distant blurry shape of a hippopotamus reminded me of the story my nurse told often, in which the hero slaughters a chimera. The strange beast was composed of monstrous parts—a great gray body like a hippopotamus, the fangs of a serpent, talons, and tails. For years, it had been attacking farmers working in their fields, but it was taller than the tallest trees and even the sharpest arrows could not pierce its skin. Yet the clever hero charged forward, his bravery shining like a beacon in the darkness. The clash of steel against scales echoed through the valley, a symphony of chaos and courage. When my nurse told this story and others like it, I always imagined myself as the girl the hero loved well enough to risk his life for. I hoped that one day I, too, would find someone who loved me so ardently that he would think nothing of battling a monster for my sake.

A warm shower began to fall, and then a crack of thunder and heavier rain forced us beneath a thicket of doom palms. Kader and I held hands, watching the last rain of the season sifting into the river.

"Promise me you will be careful, Amie," Kader murmured against my hair. "Emperor Suleyman's court is a treacherous place." He followed my gaze to the highest tower of the palace, the apartments of Princess Mariama. In the sun the towers glinted white as teeth.

3

Parting with Kader felt like losing a part of myself, but I had to return to the palace before the princess noticed my absence. It had been an enormous risk to shirk my responsibilities on my very first day at court. I did not like to think how my parents would react if I returned to them tonight, jobless. I imagined the veins in my father's forehead bulging with fury, the lines of disappointment around my mother's eyes.

I felt as if the meeting with Kader had lasted only a few moments. But my time with him must have been longer than I had perceived, because when I returned to the palace gates, it was at least three o'clock in the afternoon. In the palace yard, half a dozen servants were scrubbing the tiles with brushes coated in perfumed soap.

The gates were locked. I stared past them into the yard to make it apparent that I was waiting for someone on the palace staff to let me in, but no one noticed me. *Perhaps the princess has already become aware of my absence and dismissed me from her service in punishment,* I worried. *Perhaps I haven't any job to return to.* I inhaled deeply, listening closely to the familiar sounds of the market in the afternoon: the shouts of merchants selling their wares, the laughter of street children, the low groans of livestock.

Timbuktu had been a global center of trade for centuries, and the stalls of our famous market bustled with people buying and selling goods from all corners of the world. Fulani herdsmen sold long-horned cattle with hides as white as clouds. Berber metalsmiths sold vases and teapots and oil lamps of shining yellow brass. Trip-olitanian dressmakers sold cream-colored silk gowns. Hausa mer-chants sold beads of glass and carnelian. Ethiopian traders sold silver antimony alongside copper so bright it hurt my eyes. I found myself wishing I could be eight years old again, running through the market with Haddy, examining baubles that struck our fancy and giggling at nothing at all.

A young fruit seller with a baby strapped to her chest stopped loading purple figs into a crate to scowl in my direction. This woman was a total stranger, yet she despised me. Then she shouted some-thing quick and profane that made me gasp, for I had been raised never to use such language.

I turned my back on her, focusing my attention on the yard and hoping that the servants had not overheard. I did not want to call out for them to let me in, because I did not want rumors to follow me to court. A feeling of dread started in my stomach and crept up toward my throat, tasting of ashes. Here I was, standing at the palace gates in a servant's wrapper, but no one had unlocked them for me yet. Was it possible I really was dismissed?

An irate voice from the direction of the tanners' stalls broke in on my thoughts. "And what do we Songhai get for paying taxes to the emperor? For bowing to the conquerors and calling ourselves citizens of Mali? Death! Either a gruesome death in the suitor's ket-tle or a slower death of starvation while the Malinke nobles take our crops and livestock and sell our daughters to foreign kings. All while the emperor luxuriates in his palace!"

A young leatherworker in a faded thobe shirt and coarsely wo-ven pants had climbed atop his table of wares and was shouting to a growing group of men gathered below. He gestured up at the suitor's kettle, shouting, "Behold this instrument of death! The em-peror and his lords think they are more civilized than us. They call us backwards and barbarous for believing in the seven gods. But they are the true barbarians. Didn't you see them kill an innocent young man this morning?"

More and more of the merchants at their stalls had begun looking up at him. Some were nodding their heads in agreement, while others scowled. "I am old enough to remember life before Malinke rule, and I can tell you that Timbuktu has prospered enormously since we joined the empire," argued a white-haired man with rings on all ten of his fingers. "Even an ungrateful boy like you must be able to see that."

"Thirty years of imperial rule has all but destroyed the hearts and minds of our people!" the young man cried in response. His supporters cheered, a harsh, warlike sound that sent a shudder through my belly.

I continued to watch the tense scene unfold, mesmerized by the young man's boldness, and my fascination might have kept me there for longer, watching and listening—but I knew I could not afford further distraction. I had to reenter the palace before the others noted my absence. Urgently, I rattled the gates just as a woman's voice rang out: "Aminata, there you are!"

Hurrying toward the gates was Issatou, the emperor's head of servants, whom I had met earlier that morning. My mother had walked me to the palace gates before sunrise, and together we had waited with my little bundle of belongings while the sky grew brighter and the market square behind us began rumbling with activity. I was so unused to waking at such an early hour that I was nodding off against my mother's shoulder when I jerked awake at the brisk *tap* of Issatou's footsteps across the tiles. With a heavy heart, I parted with my mother. I imagined her trekking back to our house in the merchants' district without me under the rosy light of dawn and feeling relieved to have made her difficult daughter someone else's problem. After bidding my mother farewell, Issatou told me that she owed me a proper tour of the palace but was too busy with the execution preparations to give me one yet. Then she put me under the care of a servant who promptly led me to Mariama's chamber, where I passed the rest of the morning after depositing my belongings in the maids' room.

Like myself and all the other servants, Issatou wore a simple linen wrapper with a leather drawstring. Her mouth sagged at its corners, which made it difficult to tell if she was scowling on purpose or if she had spent so much of her life frowning that her face had settled permanently into that position. She did not acknowledge the other servants as she crossed the soapy tiles, although they bowed their heads respectfully one by one, like stones skipping water, when she passed.

"Where have you been?" she asked me sharply as she approached the gates where I stood. In the light, her dark eyes shone amber.

Flinching under the heat of her gaze, I smoothed my wrapper and met her eyes. "Begging your pardon, madam," I began, "I thought I might visit the apothecary for herbs of indigestion. I brewed them into a tea and sipped it, and now I feel improved," I finished, praying that she would believe me.

Issatou eyed me warily. "Is that so?"

For an awful moment I thought she might turn me away from the gates, but instead she lifted a key from her wrapper and unlocked them. "Well, come back in," she said. "We need to finish your training."

I could have laughed aloud with relief as I followed Issatou between the gates. Guards lounged in the palace yard, smoking from clay pipes while servants scrubbed at the tiles. They were cleaning away the dirt and drowned earthworms and other debris from the rainstorm. The yard smelled of pipe smoke and fragrant soap.

Small terra-cotta statues of the seven Songhai gods, all in a line as if standing guard over the palace, dotted the yard. Emperor Suleyman may have officially forbidden the worship of these deities, but there was no denying that many in his empire still clung to their traditional beliefs, and so he allowed these seven sculptures as a concession to the commoners. There was Dongo, god of thunder, wearing a storm cloud like a cloak. Cirey, god of wisdom and lightning, held a sharp lightning bolt in his fist. Harakoy, goddess of the Niger River, had a woman's head and the tail of a fish. Nyori, god of the clouds, pursed his lips with a gust of storm wind. Faran, the goddess of millet, pressed a ripe seed head between her palms. Nyawri, god of the hunt, rode atop his horse with a quiver of arrows strapped to his back. Finally, placed a little apart from the others, there was a statue of Hausakoy, the god of metalworking, bent over his forge with his enchanted hammer in motion, ready to strike.

My parents had always told me that the seven gods were superstitions of common folk—like the fishermen who prayed to Harakoy for a bounty of fat, healthy carp and the farmers who asked Faran for a good harvest. Upper society recognized only the one true God, who had been worshipped in Timbuktu by learned men since long before Emperor Musa annexed the city. Still, traditions were slow to fade, and even my mother whispered a secret prayer to Cirey to protect my father's annual journey to the desert salt mines.

I followed Issatou deeper into the palace yard. My eyes flicked over the shining statues of the gods, and I found myself whispering my own little prayers to each one as I passed. I prayed to Harakoy that when it came time for Kader and me to escape, her waters would sweep us far away, drawing us quickly along her torrents until we reached the sea. I asked Cirey to help me learn my chambermaid's duties quickly and perform them well enough to bring in a steady income. I implored Nyawri to embolden Kader to hunt for clients at university so he could pocket away enough tutoring fees to fund our new life together.

I struggled to keep up with Issatou—she was old yet still quick—as she rounded a corner and disappeared beneath a white archway. I snuck one last sidelong look at the yard and the market beyond it before I followed her into the palace. My breath caught in the back of my throat when I saw what had become of the rebellious young leatherworker. He was flanked on either side by imperial soldiers with silver daggers at their waists. They had stopped his mouth with what appeared to be one of his own dried animal hides, and they dragged him, stiff limbed and defiant, through the crowded market. They carried him away, past a cluster of dressmakers' stalls and finally out of sight.

I forced my face to remain neutral as I stepped across the threshold, following Issatou into a shadowy interior corridor lined with torches. I heard servants murmuring in the darkness, yet I saw little, save for the glimmer of her pale head wrap in the dark, like the sails of a capsizing ship. The floor was damp with soap and water, so I took great care not to slip as I walked—my concentration was so deep that I scarcely noticed when we had broken into the afternoon daylight.

We had entered an ornate reception area, a hexagonal courtyard with a ceiling of rosy sky. High columns outlined in gold leaf were arranged along all six of its sides. Crowning the colonnade were two tiled pavilions with golden domes. Bronze statues encircled the courtyard in the likenesses of deceased members of the imperial family, all positioned within a mosaic that illustrated their life stories across hundreds of colorful tiles.

I at once recognized the statue of the late emperor Musa. His mosaic was a deft arrangement of camels, horses, and hills of tawny sand beneath the slender white towers of the holy city. To represent his status as the wealthiest man in the world, the tall and imposing figure clutched a gold nugget in his formidable fist.

Then another figure caught my eye. It was a bronze likeness of Empress Cassi, the princess's mother. She had died of northern plague when Mariama was still very young. I grew up listening to tales of the late empress's vanity, so I knew her instantly by the small silver mirror in her hand. Her face and body had been sculpted to perfection, although her pupils were slightly too small, giving her a placid, otherworldly appearance.

I turned to the fountain at the center of the courtyard, which was less a fountain than a great bubbling jewelry box, complete with figurines of ruby-eyed fish and stallions spitting cascades of water from their golden lips. I was awestruck. I was accustomed to handling gold nuggets and blended gold jewelry, but never in my life had I seen so much treasure.

The gurgling golden fountain was nearly as loud as the chattering of the men gathered in the courtyard—marabouts and ambassadors, soldiers and bureaucrats, noblemen and scribes. Birds fluttered in and out of the fountain, their wings tracing temporary indentations in the clear water. My stomach twisted when I spotted a red bird—a fire finch! Immediately I thought of Kader. Had I really just seen him today? It already felt like a distant dream.

I followed Issatou into a second courtyard that was smaller and plainer than the first, with a stone staircase at one end. "These are the women's halls," she said as we climbed. "Only the royal women and their female attendants may enter."

"I understand." After a few minutes, I craned my neck down, trying in vain to see to the bottom of the staircase, but it was obscured in darkness.

"Maids are expected to appear clean and modest at all times." She placed extra emphasis upon the word *modest*. "If you are caught doing anything at all improper with a manservant, I will dismiss you from service. And if you are caught in a compromising position with a nobleman, I will make sure you never find work again." She turned to fix me with a stern glare, which she had undoubtedly used to subdue generations of free-spirited maids.

She is like an old horse master with a talent for breaking young mares, I thought. The old me would have cowered and shrunk before her, as I always had with my parents. But now I met Issatou's gaze with a calm defiance to let her know that I was not the sort of girl who could be easily broken.

We climbed another staircase that opened into a corridor lined with dark wooden doors. "These are the apartments of the emperor's wives, Lady Fatimata, Lady Bassira, and Lady Kadiatou," Issatou explained.

She then led me through a network of corridors and bathhouses and lush little courtyards until I grew dizzy with the size and scope of the palace. Between each series of chambers was an ascending staircase, which we climbed one after another until we were high above the city. The emperor's palace was the tallest building I had ever entered, and the views it had to offer were far more magnificent than what I could see from the roof of my parents' two-story town house. Through the palace windows I could see the beginnings of the desert, and I paused midstep to admire the subtle geometry of the dunes, triangles and trapezoids of sand against the pale, powdery sky. From this great height, the city where I had been born and raised looked like an illustration in a book.

"You will grow used to it quickly," Issatou said as she pushed open a door with a heavy iron padlock.

On the other side was a narrow tower staircase that led to my unfortunate destination. Carved into the side of the tower like an afterthought, my new home was a tiny, cave-like servants' room that contained three sleeping pallets, a low stone toilet, and very little else.

"Welcome to your living quarters," she said, turning to read my face. "I suppose you already met the other maids this morning?"

"Yes, madam," I replied as I looked around the chamber. Its low white ceiling was speckled with dark green mold, and the toilet smelled strongly of blacksoil and ash.

I sighed. I would have little privacy here. There was barely enough space for three young women to sleep comfortably. I would almost always be watched. On the night when Kader and I made our escape, we would need to take great care to not let the others see us leaving.

"They are girls around your age," Issatou said. "How old are you?"

"Sixteen, madam." My voice wobbled.

"Then they are two years your senior. Jeneba and Penda should be able to answer any of your questions about the princess's routine. She rises early, bathes, and dresses, and then she walks the gardens until noon. It is very important that you accompany her on each of those walks—"

"Why is that?"

She looked taken aback, as if it were unheard of for a new servant to ask questions. "Because the princess cannot be left alone under any circumstances."

But why? I thought, confused. The princess was seventeen years old!

"She spends her afternoons in the library with her tutors. That is when you will clean her bedchamber and change her linens. And in the evenings, she dines with her father. You will wait on her then." Issatou furrowed her wrinkled brow, as if trying to decide if I was too stupid to follow such simple instructions.

"Yes, madam."

"Well, this is where I leave you. Good luck," she added ominously.

Issatou's words sent a tremor down my spine, but before I could ask her what she meant, she had already rushed from the room. I heard the bright *clack* of her sandals against the stairs as she made her way to the bottom of the tower, and then the heavy door swung shut.

I was alone.

I took a long, despairing look around the tiny chamber that was to be my home for the next year. There were no chairs or stools—why bother wasting good furniture on serving girls? I made myself swallow the tears rising within me, instead kneeling upon my sleeping mat and beginning to arrange my possessions. I had brought a few items along with me, which I had left in the room when the servant led me there earlier that morning: a double-sided ivory comb that had been a fifteenth name-day gift from my mother, two homespun tunics, and the small cloth-and-straw doll my sister had made for me when we were children.

I pushed the doll beneath my sleeping mat, out of sight. I was not even sure why I had brought it along, except that it had felt too final to leave it at home. When I closed my eyes, I saw servants thumbing carelessly through my things and tossing my possessions into a trash heap. I wondered if my mother enjoyed erasing her disgraced daughter from her home, scrubbing me away like a stain.

"New girl!"

Penda's high voice interrupted my thoughts. I looked up to see her standing with Jeneba in the doorframe. "We were wondering when you would be back," she said.

"My sincerest apologies," I said.

Jeneba's arms were folded, although her mouth wore half of a smile. "Where were you?"

"I was feeling unwell and so sought out a tincture for indigestion." My voice trembled with the effort of the falsehood. I'd need to become a better liar here in the palace.

"Are you a medicine woman, a tinesefren?" she asked.

"No," I told her.

She narrowed her eyes. "Are you a sorceress?"

I exhaled in frustration and said, "Of course not." Everyone knew that there were no more sorcerers left in the empire. Emperor Musa had banished them all around the same time he'd annexed Timbuktu and the surrounding river lands.

"How could you have known which herbs to pick without tinesefren training?"

"I asked the apothecary," I said defensively, willing myself to come up with a biting retort, quick and clever, something Haddy might say.

"So, you took a nice, long afternoon walk to the apothecary while the two of us did your chores," Jeneba replied scornfully. "Do you think you're too good to work?"

Penda moved so that she stood between us, a shield, and smiled a sweet, gap-toothed smile. "Jen, that's enough! I am sure that the new girl has learned her lesson and will not do it again. She can help me at the loom."

Jeneba's sharp gaze pierced my back as I followed Penda up the stairs. I climbed the stone steps one by one, thinking all the while, *It is only my first day at court, and I have already made an enemy.*

4

The three of us continued our chores until sunset, time for us to go to the kitchens and help prepare the princess's evening meal. At the loom, Penda had explained that although the princess usually dined with her father and his wives in a small party of five, tonight's supper was to be grander. The emperor had invited a dozen high-ranking military men to celebrate Mali's recent victories in the southern provinces.

I had not eaten all day, so the thought of a great feast briefly cheered me, but I quickly remembered that this food was not meant for the enjoyment of servants—we were here to work.

Penda and I were tasked with peeling a mountain of yams for the emperor's noble guests. At home, cooking was rarely my responsibility, but a childhood of helping my mother prepare tigadèguèna and pounded yams on holy holidays had at least taught me how to use a peeling knife without any mishaps.

"The empire is always expanding," Penda told me as we worked together in one of the courtyard kitchens. "Emperor Suleyman hosts these supper gatherings occasionally to honor the highest-ranking members of his army and congratulate them for a job well done."

I was glad that she was warming up to me, and I chatted with her about this and that, hoping to make a friend. The more we worked, the more my thoughts were beginning to blur with hunger. Around us, the kitchen bustled with activity. Women and girls chopped vegetables, gutted fish, and tended to wide, smoking firepits. I was unused to the close, prickling heat of the cooking fires and the clouds of smoke that billowed in their wake. My lungs began to sting and I couldn't help breaking into a coughing fit.

Jeneba looked away from the pot of rice she had been stirring to frown at me. "Aminata, you must not be sick all over the emperor's supper," she said loudly, her voice dripping with condescension.

She did not have to tell me twice. Still coughing and wheezing, my eyes smarting, I left the smoky kitchen for the cool palace interior. I steadied myself against a wall until the coughs subsided and then I peered into the modest dining chamber behind me.

I stifled my gasp when I noticed the emperor within. Reclining upon a low wooden stool, he was flanked on either side by officers—lieutenants and colonels and generals. The military men all wore uniforms of leather armor, iron chain mail, tufted helmets, and ivory daggers looped into their belts. Across the chamber, the princess knelt on a blue woven rug with the military wives, drinking tea from a wrought-gold cup as she awaited her supper.

Envy twisted in my throat when I noticed my sister at the center of the cluster of lounging noblewomen. She looked every inch the fine lady in her long linen wrapper and beaded carnelian necklace. Around each wrist she wore a bracelet of copper alloy, and from her earlobes dangled gold hoops hanging with small coins. Her attendants had even plaited ribbons into her hair. Her smile dropped when she saw me. An expression passed across her face as our eyes met, a heavy look of regret that had no place on a traitor. Then she looked across the room at her husband, Lord Ayouta, a Malinke nobleman who already had two wives when she wed him at our parents' request. A retired military man of two and forty, noble-born, Haddy's husband had served as lieutenant general in the imperial army before a battle injury cost him his left leg but gained him the emperor's favor.

Two years ago, our ambitious parents had been ecstatic to see Haddy wed to a nobleman like Lord Ayouta, who had a yearly allowance of fifty thousand cowries and owned a grand house in Timbuktu in addition to several palace apartments and a great deal of land in the southern provinces. But Haddy did not want him for her husband. He was too old, and although he did not treat her unkindly in our parents' home, he was known to frequently drink himself into a stupor to distract from the pain in his leg. Also, Haddy didn't want to get married at all, not yet—she had wanted to attend university to become a scribe, but the dream was forbidden to girls.

I could still remember my sister's look of dread the night before her wedding. In the dark of her bedchamber, she had clung to me and wept into my hair, repeating, *I cannot marry him, I cannot marry him*, until her voice grew hoarse. But she was dry-eyed and brave the next day, and over the following months, she seemed to grow accustomed to the rhythms of a noble marriage. She and her co-wives split their time between the palace and their husband's house in town, and despite my initial worries that her marriage would make strangers of us, Haddy and I remained close. She belonged now to a different world from mine, a world of courtiers, banquets, and dancing, but my grand and glamorous older sister still told me everything, from court gossip to practical advice about what to expect in a marriage.

She confessed that she hated her nights with her husband—the heat of his breath on her face and the stink of his wounded flesh turned her stomach. She also told me about her flirtation with one of the young palace scribes, Tenin, who worked for several noble families, including the Ayoutas and Bagayogos.

I'd had my suspicions before then, but Haddy always swore to me that theirs was only an innocent, courtly romance. Tenin might have given her long, desirous looks in the palace corridors and written her daily poems of admiration that she burned in her oil lamp each night, but he had never kissed her, she claimed, had never even touched her hand.

Foolishly, I had believed her. Did she not have a reputation to protect? *Haddy might be unhappily married*, I had thought, *but she would never be unfaithful to her husband. She is far too clever for that, too acutely aware of the harsh punishments for ill-behaved wives.*

I learned that I was wrong when I caught them together at the spring planting festival. Everyone else had been too distracted by the feasting and dancing to notice what Haddy and Tenin were doing in the fields, but I saw their bare legs tangled against the topsoil. Not such an innocent love after all.

When I confronted her, Haddy had refused to stop seeing Tenin, even though I had begged her to end things. I told her that it was too dangerous, that noblemen had killed their wives for less. *Think of your place at court*, I had pleaded. *Think of your reputation, your safety.* But my sister was always stubborn and a bit reckless. She insisted that she loved Tenin and would do what she liked with him.

This continued for months. By day, she was Lady Hadiza Ayouta, a married noblewoman. By night, she was only Haddy, an eighteen-year-old girl in desperate love with a scribe. I did not tell anyone what I knew out of fear that her husband would punish her unfaithfulness, but still I worried for my sister's safety with Tenin. By then I was sixteen and already busy with the preparations for my own impending marriage to Kader, whom I had come to consider a true love match despite the arrangement being orchestrated by our parents. He had luminous brown eyes and a kindly disposition, and when he recited verses from scripture or classical poetry, his voice washed over me like a warm breeze that made me want to bask in it.

It all came crashing down the morning I was meant to marry. Kader's father, Lord Bagayogo, had overheard Tenin bragging to

the other scribes about his dalliance with one of the Aqit sisters. In-
censed, Lord Bagayogo had hurried across town to our house in the
merchants' district and charged into our courtyard, where Mother
and Haddy were plaiting my hair in the traditional style for Songhai
brides. He demanded to know which one of us was guilty of such
unchaste behavior.

Before I could defend myself, Haddy—that serpent!—told him
it was *me*.

The shock of her betrayal was like a blow. My face grew hot, my
breathing shallow, shallower still when my parents, the foremost
authority figures in my life and the arbiters of my fate, looked at my
sister with trust and acceptance.

I tried to convince them that she was lying. I stood there in the
courtyard with hot tears running down my face and told them
the truth until my voice grew hoarse. "It was not me, it was Haddy!"
I cried over and over again. "I would never do such a thing!"

Haddy calmly spun a tale for our parents about an Amie I did
not recognize, a two-faced, sneaking girl who had climbed down
from her bedroom window into the arms of a young scribe each
night. I listened, stunned and open-mouthed. At the time, I'd wondered if she had chosen a scribe for her lover because she had always
dreamed of attending university and becoming one herself, but the
opportunity was denied to girls. Lord Bagayogo sent for Kader, who
defended me immediately upon his arrival and hearing the claims
against me. He insisted that I was telling the truth. Still, his father
refused to believe me.

Everything happened so quickly after that. Our wedding was canceled and my reputation was destroyed overnight. Tenin was fired
from his post and banished to the provinces.

When my parents confined me to my bedchamber, I spent day
after solitary day hoping they would come to believe my word over

Haddy's. But whenever I tried to make them see the truth, they insisted I was the liar. They said I was only jealous of my sister. A braver girl would have fought harder to prove her innocence, but I had always been frightened of quarrels and soon gave up on defending myself altogether.

This cannot be happening, I thought to myself bitterly. I did not think I could stomach the humiliation of serving my sister, filling her goblet, and calling her *my lady*. I had known there was a risk of encountering her here in the palace, but I had not been prepared to face her so soon.

Haddy had already risen from the carpets, lifting her wrapper gracefully so that she would not trip on her hem. She began to approach me, her wide eyes never leaving my face. I wanted to turn and run, but I held myself still until she closed the distance between us. And then she was with me in the corridor, tugging furiously at my hand and saying, "Come with me now," in her low voice. "Come quickly to the library, where we will not be overheard."

Could these really be her first words to me in more than a month? She had not said, *I am sorry*, or *Please forgive me*, but *Come with me*. It was a lady's order to a maidservant, not a greeting for a sister!

"I have nothing at all to say to you," I said, slapping her hand away. "You ruined my life!"

"For a good reason," she countered. "There is something I must tell you, but we cannot speak here. Too many people are watching." She eyed the dining chamber, where some of the ladies had already begun to look over at us in mild curiosity.

"Unless it is an apology for what you did to me, I will not hear it," I said, feeling suddenly struck that my sister's dark eyes were so much like my own. The more I looked at her, the more I resented her. It occurred to me that between sisters, there can be no equality. One girl always wins.

"It is an apology," she replied hastily. "And a confession. Follow me, and I will explain everything."

"I cannot hear this right now," I repeated as calmly as I could manage. I knew it would be unwise to cause a scene, but still it took all my self-control not to weep or scream or punch her squarely in the stomach. "I must go. I am needed in the kitchens."

Then I turned away, ready to walk back into the dark courtyard, which bustled with throngs of workers, lit only by cooking fires and the glow of the distant moon.

She stopped me with a hand. "I lied to our parents because I wanted to end your engagement," she explained quickly. "I could not let you marry Kader. His father hurts his sons' wives. He would have harmed you, too, if you had gone through with the wedding."

I shook my head in disbelief. "You are lying," I said. "You ruined my chances of marrying Kader because you were jealous. You could not stand it that I was going to wed someone who truly loved me, while you remained trapped in a loveless marriage to an old drunk." Heat flared in my chest; I had never before spoken so harshly to my sister.

"I am telling you the honest truth," Haddy said, exasperated. "It was the only way I could think to protect you from Lord Bagayogo."

Again, my temper flared. "Was it really about protecting me? You ruined my prospects forever!"

"I'm sorry," she said earnestly. "I shouldn't have damaged your reputation. I should have thought of a better way."

"If that's true, then why didn't you just tell me what you knew about Kader's father?" I asked her. "I could have made my own decision about whether or not to marry into his family."

Her brow tightened. "If you would only come with me, I promise to explain further—"

"I will not go anywhere with you," I cried, too loudly.

A passing page boy, shocked by my outburst, stopped in his tracks to gape at me. Haddy shot him a withering look and he hurried away.

"You are very angry with me right now, I can see that," she said when he was gone. "I will return tomorrow night for the harvest festival, and we can speak then. I promise to explain everything."

"You might have told me earlier," I said coldly.

"I couldn't! Not when our parents had you confined to your room all last month. I haven't had a chance to speak with you since your wedding day. You *know* that."

"All I know is that you're a traitor," I said, scowling. Then I tore away from her and returned to the kitchen. Anything was better than an audience with my sister.

Another slow hour of peeling yams by firelight passed, and then I served the emperor's guests a torturous parade of delicious-smelling meals. There was groundnut stew, plantain cakes, spiced lamb with butternut and couscous, oily flatbread baked in garlic, and tilapia with their heads still intact, staring out of flat green eyes.

Night crept over the hall. Musicians began to arrive under moonlight, plucking their lyres and koras in time with the gentle clanging of their bracelets. I scarcely noticed the sweet melodies. My mind was filled instead with Haddy's words: *He would have harmed you, too, if you had gone through with the wedding.* I did not want to believe her, but she obviously believed it to be the truth. Why else would she have sabotaged my marriage?

I was busy refilling one of the ladies' goblets when a shout made me stop cold.

"Cheïbane," the emperor's voice boomed across the hall. "I was wondering when you would finally arrive!"

Cheïbane Bagayogo. Kader's father's given name.

I looked up, stomach dropping, as he strode into the courtyard.

Kader and his father were both tall and slender. They had similar faces, although the creases in Lord Bagayogo's forehead were far deeper, his robes were finer, and his hair was a shock of white against his dark skin. I tried to search for traces of cruelty in his features, but he looked pleasant as always and very much like his son.

"Your Imperial Majesty," Lord Bagayogo addressed the emperor, bowing deeply. "I must apologize for my lateness."

Emperor Suleyman waved an impatient hand. "None of that, please," he said. "Come and eat."

My heart started hammering as Lord Bagayogo took his seat near the emperor. I hoped he wouldn't notice me. Except for Haddy, he was the only noble in the room who could identify me by sight. This was supposed to be my clean slate: I couldn't afford for anyone in the palace to find out about my past. My face flushed and I went to turn away, but a calling of my own name stopped me in my tracks.

"Aminata!" Lord Bagayogo's unmistakable voice made my heart sink. "Is that Aminata Aqit dressed as a servant? I'd heard you had been brought quite low, my girl, but this is even worse than I imagined."

I had an urge to lift my skirts and run from the hall, but the sudden rush of panic had paralyzed me. I stood still as a stone. Out of the corner of my eye, I saw Haddy looking uneasily up at me from her place on the rug with the other ladies, her face taut.

"Your Majesty, look!" Lord Bagayogo cried, performative as a griot. "Do you know who this girl is?" Roughly, he grabbed my wrist and pulled me toward the emperor.

The pain made me yelp.

Instinctively I looked to Haddy for help. She was tense, her brow furrowed with concern, but she did nothing. That enraged me: How could she claim to have been trying to protect me from him but fail to help me when I needed her most?

The emperor watched me impassively. "Who is the girl?"

"Aminata is the daughter of the salt merchant Modibo Aqit, my old trading partner." He twisted my wrist so painfully that I cried out. "She is a liar and a harlot. I thank God each day that her true character was revealed before she could wed my son."

Now everyone in the room was staring at me: the emperor, the princess, all the lords and ladies and servants, Penda, Jeneba, and Haddy. In full view of them all, I—shamefully—began to weep. I wept because he was proving Haddy right and because I was afraid of what he might next do to me. I regretted every silent tear that rolled down my cheeks, but I found I could not stop them.

"She was betrothed to your son?" asked the emperor.

"Yes—to my youngest, the weakling," Lord Bagayogo replied disdainfully. "By humiliating him, she has insulted my entire family. I implore you to dismiss her from your service at once."

"What exactly has she done?"

"She betrayed my son with a scribe," he spat. "A loudmouthed boy in Your Majesty's service. When I overheard the scribe bragging to the secretaries about having her, I called off the wedding and demanded the return of her bride-price."

All while the men were speaking, I was telling myself, *Stop weeping. Defend yourself.* Summoning my courage, I said, "I did not do it! Your Imperial Majesty, you must believe me. I have tried so hard to clear my name, but no one—"

Lord Bagayogo struck my face. The sting of it brought tears back into my eyes. "Did I say you could speak?" he roared. His hand flew to my left ear, tugging at the silver earring Kader had given me mere hours earlier. "You might have been able to convince my soft-headed son of your innocence, my dear, but I see you for what you are. You are lucky that I only took back your bride-price. I should have had you killed!" Then he turned to the emperor. "Look at these earrings. Purest silver. You see, Suleyman, how the girl flaunts her former wealth? She was almost a lady once and still thinks she may dress as one."

"Stop, please," I protested wildly, looking desperately at Haddy. Tears as big as cowries were gathered in my sister's eyes, but she still did nothing to help me. I could see that she would not risk herself for me, not now or ever. She couldn't protect or defend me when it really mattered.

"Stop this, my lord," I said again, but Lord Bagayogo only pulled harder on my earring.

I cried out in pain, a high animal shriek that I scarcely recognized as my own. Then I heard the awful papery sound of my left earlobe splitting.

"Enough!" A girl's voice, clear as a bell. "Father, make him stop."

Blood dripped down my neck as I turned to see Princess Mariama looking furiously over at Kader's father. "Is this how civilized men treat young girls?" she asked him. "If so, we are no better than barbarians. Does not the greatness of an empire lie in its ability to protect women?"

Everyone in the room turned to the emperor. Would he take his daughter's side?

"Mariama is correct, of course. Release the girl," he said after a lengthy pause. His voice was flat, his expression unreadable. He folded his arms across his chest.

Relief warmed my limbs like sunlight. The princess was protecting me. I had no idea why, but in that moment, I was only glad to be saved. I feared how far he would have gone.

Lord Bagayogo tightened his grip on my wrist. "But Your Majesty, she is—"

"Release her at once!"

Reluctantly, Lord Bagayogo let me go.

But I knew that this would not be the end.

I brought my freed hand to my ear and found that the entire left side of my face was wet and sticky with blood. A sliver of flesh hung loose from my earlobe. I realized with a jolt of sadness that my earring was also missing. I scanned the floor with my eyes, but lamplight had cast the ground in shadows.

"Father, this girl is in urgent need of medical attention," the princess said calmly. "I have balms and bandages in my chambers. May I tend to her?"

"Of course, Mariama," said the emperor. "You and your maids are dismissed."

"Good night, Father." Mariama stepped away from the table and smoothed her wrapper. "Penda, Jeneba, Aminata, let us go."

I took one last look back at my sister before I left the chamber. Her eyes were still filled with tears, her mouth twisted. Although I remained angry with her, I knew that I would consent to speak with her tomorrow night. She had known of the darkness lurking in Kader's father's heart. I could not help but wonder what else he was hiding from me.

We climbed a series of staircases. I followed at the princess's heels, shocked and shaken, Penda and Jeneba just behind me. Knowing that an entire room of nobles had seen me humiliated made my stomach lurch, as though I would be sick. We continued through courtyards and corridors and cool, closed chambers under glowing torchlight, not one of us saying a word.

I felt my heartbeat throbbing in my ear as we rose, but I had more pressing concerns. Why had Mariama defended me? She barely knew me. I did not understand.

More than anything, I wanted to tell Kader what had just happened, but he was at home in the nobles' quarter, probably studying by lamplight. I closed my eyes for a moment, trying to picture his face. When I reopened them, Jeneba was frowning at my bloody ear with a mixture of pity and distrust, as if my bad reputation might be contagious.

The princess had stopped and held out her palm to Penda and Jeneba. "You are both dismissed for the night," she said firmly. "I would like to speak with Aminata alone."

That took me by surprise. I heard their reluctant footsteps descending and realized they were moving as slowly as possible in order to eavesdrop on my conversation with the princess. The two of them would have many questions for me later, I was sure of it.

"Come along, Aminata." Her tone clipped, her expression inscrutable, the princess led me up the final steps of the tower and crossed the threshold into her bedchamber.

5

You're still bleeding," she said once we were alone.

I nodded, unsure of how to respond. Out of nervousness, I kept glancing around her bedchamber. It was a large, circular room with lovely trimmings, entirely fitting for an emperor's daughter. The floor was covered with woven carpets, and the windows revealed perfect circles of starry sky. At the center of her chamber sat an elevated sleeping mat piled high with silken pillows. A stone bathtub and several wooden bookshelves were pushed against the wall near a silver looking glass that was nailed to the plasterwork.

I crossed over to the mirror and examined myself. The girl in the glass was flushed red, her bottom lip split from biting. Her small eyes were wide with residual terror. The dark coils of her hair had escaped their ivory pins, hovering over her scalp like clouds. Her torn earlobe trickled blood down her neck.

I saw traces of Haddy in my appearance—a similar curve of the lips, the same square jawline—and wondered over what she had told me. She claimed that she'd had a reason to lie; she said she had been trying to protect me, in her own way. But why had she told everyone that I was unchaste and relegated me to the ranks of ruined, unmarriageable women? Couldn't she have prevented my marriage in some other way?

Tomorrow's feast could not come soon enough. I needed to talk to my sister. I needed answers.

"We will clean and wrap your ear, else you risk an infection," murmured the princess, appearing behind me in the mirror. She looked kind and concerned and unquestionably regal in her wrapper of gold brocade. Her hair was tidy, her countenance calm. She smelled of date oil and acacia perfume. Just seeing us beside each other in the looking glass made me feel inadequate in comparison.

"Thank you," I said uncertainly.

Why was she being so kind to me?

"I have bandages somewhere around here. . . ." She moved and began rifling through her dresser, casually tossing her expensive possessions upon the floor. I turned to see wrappers, perfumes, and creams scattered like leaves across the twilight-dark carpets as she continued her search.

It felt wrong to stand and watch her, so I walked over to the windows. Outside, the moon was full, and the pallid moonlit sand at the horizon glowed like the inside of a shell. I missed Kader so much that it ached. Was he staring up at the moon now, too? Was he thinking of me? I wondered if he would learn of what had happened to me tonight, at his own father's hand. Was he aware of the raw violence hidden behind his father's courtly manners? Had he ever been a victim of it himself?

"Hold still!" The princess's voice at my ear made me jump. "Oh, Aminata, I did not mean to startle you."

"You may call me Amie, Your Highness," I said nervously. "Everyone does."

"Very well, Amie." I heard a smile in her voice that did not spread to her lips. "I am going to pour some medicine on your earlobe now. Fair warning—it might sting."

I yelped at the sensation of the cold liquid on my wound, biting my hand in pain as it penetrated my torn flesh.

Then she wrapped my smarting ear with a white linen bandage. "All done! Now, Amie, I believe you owe me some answers. Why would a merchant's daughter betrothed to a nobleman's son ruin her future?"

"I didn't," I murmured.

She frowned. "What was that? I did not hear you."

Gathering my courage, I said more loudly, "Tenin, the Bagayogo family's scribe—he had my *sister*. Not me. I would never have done such a thing." My voice softened. "I love Kader. Lord Bagayogo's son. I would not betray him in a thousand years."

"Go on," she said gently.

My story came flooding out of me all at once, how Kader and I had been betrothed as children but our love grew into something genuine over time. That we were meant to wed last month, before my sister ruined everything. My shock and disappointment when I discovered Haddy with Tenin at the spring festival, and why I regretted keeping my sister's secret.

"Now I know I should have told our parents immediately," I said. "But I was trying to protect Haddy from being found out and punished as an adulteress, so I told no one. I only asked her to swear an oath promising to end things with Tenin."

"Did she swear it?"

"She did not. She said she would do what she liked with him." I gave a dry chuckle. Then I told her about how when Lord Bagayogo demanded to know which of the Aqit girls had been indecent, my sister had volunteered my name first.

"But surely your family would not believe the word of one daughter over another?" the princess asked, her eyes wide with incredulity.

"They have always favored Haddy," I explained. "I tried to defend myself, of course. I begged them to see things from my point of view—why would I betray the boy I loved? And I had never even stepped foot in the palace before today! But my parents would not hear reason. They locked me in my room that night, and would not allow me out except to bathe. They had the servants send up my meals. I was a prisoner in my own home."

I tried to keep my voice steady, but recounting those memories was like experiencing the whole awful ordeal all over again. I still felt the hurt and betrayal and helplessness as keenly as if it had happened yesterday.

"Your own parents," she said, shaking her head with disbelief. "Did Kader defend you, at least?"

She is angry for me, I realized. It was a relief to know that Kader was not the only person on my side.

"He tried his best to defend me," I said. "He came to my parents' house to attempt to change their minds, but they would not hear him. And then there is the trouble of his own parents, who believe that I am treacherous and unchaste. His father clearly abhors me," I added, remembering the sight of Lord Bagayogo looming over me in the dining hall, his face twisted with hatred.

"You have been treated deplorably by your family and his," Mariama said, threading her hands with mine. My skin prickled at the shock of her small, warm fingers. "And although they may not believe you, I do."

"You do? Really?"

"Of course," she said. "I have met so many liars at court. Liars, traitors, thieves." She counted them on three fingers. "This palace is full of hateful people who do horrible things. But you are not one of them. The longer I look upon you, the more I am convinced that you are good."

"Thank you, Your Highness," I said. But I wondered: *How can she know anything about me, when we only met this morning?*

"I will offer you as much protection as I can," she said with conviction. "Not a single person will harm you, least of all Lord Baga-yogo. As long as you work for me, I will take care of you, I promise."

———————•———————

I combed the princess's hair, took her linen, and then descended the staircase alone. I missed Kader more than ever. I wanted him to touch my bandage and give me one of his smiles. He would comfort me, telling me that I had no reason to fret, that we would be together soon. I wanted to ask him if it were possible for a girl's heart to break from loneliness even after spending all day in a crowded palace.

At least now I have a friend at court, I thought, still stunned by Mariama's kindness. I knew that it was a very good thing for me to have an ally like the princess, but her behavior was bewildering. Why would she go out of her way to defend me? She had met me only that morning, and she was already treating me like a beloved friend.

I willed my stomach not to growl as I crept past the warm lamplight of our maids' chamber. I could hear Penda's and Jeneba's voices faintly through the closed door. I considered remaining in the stairway to eavesdrop but decided against it because I was so hungry. I needed to get to the kitchens before I fainted.

But when I reached the foot of the stairs and tried to open the door, it did not move. Alarmed, I pushed it again, hard, but it still would not give. I squinted through the darkness, examining the door's handle and hinges. Below the doorknob I noticed a small iron circle that glimmered in the moonlight. Upon further inspection, I saw it was a lock.

In rising panic, I realized that we had been locked in.

Penda, Jeneba, Mariama, and I were all trapped in this tower.

Perhaps it was to protect the princess. Or perhaps someone did not want her to leave.

My thoughts whirled to Lord Bagayogo. Could *he* be behind this? I heard the echo of my sister's warning.

There came a sudden thumping sound, and I forced myself to say sharply, "Who goes there? Show yourself!" Terror crept up my throat as peals of laughter bounced against the limestone walls, accompanied by fast footsteps.

And then Penda and Jeneba were standing before me, arms folded over their wrappers.

6

"hy are we locked in the tower?" I asked them. "Is this a punishment?"

"The lock is not for us. It is for the princess," Jeneba explained. She sounded as if she thought I was tiresome.

Penda must have noticed the blank look on my face because she said, "*We* lock Princess Mariama in this tower every night. It's on the emperor's orders."

"But why?" I asked, frowning.

She shrugged. "The emperor is very protective of his daughter. He has always restricted her movements."

I recalled Issatou telling me that Mariama was not allowed even to walk through the palace unaccompanied. Remembering my solitary month with displeasure, I was struck by the similarities between Mariama and myself. We were both kept under lock and key by our families for no reason at all. I sighed and said, "I need to find something to eat. Which one of you has the key?"

Slowly, Jeneba lifted an iron key from the folds of her wrapper. "You can have it—if you answer my questions," she said. "Question one: Why would you betray your engagement to a nobleman?"

"I didn't," I answered impatiently. "My sister had been sneaking away for months to see a scribe in private. She blamed her affair on me when she got caught."

"But that is horrid!" Penda gasped. "Why would she do such a thing?"

"I do not know," I said, remembering Haddy's pained look when she had approached me at supper, her hushed insistence that she had ruined me for my own good. "May I have the key now?"

"Not yet," Jeneba said, smiling. "Question two: Why are you here? You are an Aqit; it isn't as if you need to work."

I groaned inwardly, for I had no desire to tell my story again. I wanted only food and sleep. I almost rebuffed her, to say, *That is none of your business*, but I knew it would be unwise. After all, she held the key.

"I am here because my parents hate me for what they think I did," I said at last. "They want to see me humbled, even though my sister is the one who deserves to be a servant, not me."

Too late I realized my mistake. Jeneba's eyes narrowed. "What do you mean, she deserves to be a servant?"

Stupid girl. I tried to backtrack. "Of course, waiting upon an emperor's daughter is an enviable position of employment. But it isn't the life I imagined for myself, the life that I had . . . prepared for."

"And do you believe this is the life we imagined for ourselves? Do you think we dreamt during our girlhoods about scrubbing latrines?" Jeneba asked.

"Of course not." I did not know what else to say to make things right. *Haddy would have already charmed her into handing over the key*, I thought bitterly. *She would have known exactly what to say.*

"You think you're better than us, but you're not," Jeneba said coldly. "You would be Lady Bagayogo right now if you'd only behaved decently. Instead, you went and got yourself ruined."

"You don't know what you're talking about," I said sharply, raising my hand to slap her.

She watched it without interest. "You aren't going to hit me. You wouldn't dare. You've never fought anyone in your life, have you."

Fury flared in my chest, but I said nothing. Only my stomach growled. She was right. I had never hit anyone before. Not even my sister, not even when she deserved it.

"Can't fight. Can't weave. Can't clean." She listed my failures on her fingers, one by one. "Can't even inherit your family's fortune, now that you're ruined. This world is going to destroy you. You don't stand a chance."

"Jen, stop bothering her!" Quick as the wind, Penda snatched the key and inserted it into the lock.

"Why are you helping her?" Jeneba protested. "She just insulted us."

"I am quite sure she didn't mean it." Penda pushed the door and it gave way, revealing the flicker of oil lamps along a corridor and the dark, swaying foliage of a courtyard garden. "Come with me, Amie," she said, pulling me with her down the hallway. "We must find you something to eat."

I was glad to have Penda with me. She navigated the palace as naturally as an ant traversing its colony. I suspected she could have done it blindfolded. I followed her mutely through the passageways and corridors, too hungry to speak. When we reached the kitchen, she showed me to a low wooden table, where we prepared a quick meal of millet porridge unseasoned with dates or honey. My heart sank with the realization that this would be the entirety of my supper, and I admitted that I had hoped for leftovers from the banquet, yams and tilapia and flatbread.

That made her laugh. "The kitchen staff devours what's left of the emperor's supper soon after they finish serving," she explained. "They fight like pigeons over every last scrap."

"Oh," I said, taking a bite of my porridge. It was bland but satisfying.

Penda said little to me as I ate, breaking her silence only once to say, "I'm sure you're used to finer food than this."

I replied, "Yes," with my mouth full. I knew it was unladylike, but I was too overcome with hunger to care. In any case, I wasn't to be a lady any longer.

"I suppose you grew up in a fine house in the merchants' district, with servants to cook your suppers," she added dreamily. "Did you have meat with every meal?"

"Most," I admitted to appease her, but I wanted to tell her that my childhood had not been as easy as she imagined. To be a rich man's daughter was to be treated as just one of his many possessions, and my father had always made it painfully clear I would be of no use to him if I could not marry well. Instead, I asked, "What about your father? What does he do?"

Penda's expression soured. "My father was a soldier. He died a long time ago."

That's what you get for asking. "I'm so sorry for your loss," I said awkwardly. "It must have been hard on you and your mother."

"I was young, and hardly remember him," she said with a shrug. "Losing Father was hardest for my mother and brothers. I grew up idolizing him in stories, and when I was very young I used to think he deserved a statue just like Sundiata's." She pointed to the reception hall.

"He does," I said emphatically, following her gaze to the statues. The statue of Emperor Musa caught my eye. "Why shouldn't common foot soldiers be celebrated?" The space was empty and silent, save for the musical trickling of the fountain near the statues. Emperor Musa was a hero to merchants like my father and easy for me to recognize, but I struggled to name most of the other rulers depicted beside him. I knew that they must have been lesser emperors and empresses of the Keita dynasty, but the statues all looked the same to me. The women all wore fine wrappers and stern facial expressions, and the men all held scrolls or weapons and stroked their voluminous beards. After a moment, I identified the statue of Sundiata Keita, the Lion and first emperor of Mali, by his hunting attire and quiver of arrows on his back, his face grim and intimidating in the darkness. Across the hall from him, the lovely empress Cassi stared endlessly into her hand mirror. My skin crawled with the sense of their watching eyes, all those dead emperors and empresses staring at me.

"Your father should be among them," I agreed. Then, with nothing more to say, I finished my food quickly. As I ate, I had an uncanny creeping feeling that this was not a palace at all but a tomb.

After the meal, Penda led me back to our little room in the tower, where Jeneba already slept. Feeling grateful for Penda's kindness, I laid down upon my threadbare mat and gazed out our tiny window, tracing the constellations with my fingers. I had almost discovered a sleeping position that did not hurt my wounded ear when suddenly a small scorpion scurried across the windowsill, interrupting my reverie. I flinched back from it. Unsettled, I watched the creature disappear through a crack in the white stone. I had always despised insects and other creeping things and wondered if this was perhaps a sign, a warning of bad things still to come.

7

A mie!" Jeneba's voice pulled me out of my slumber. "Amie, wake up! We have much to do today."

Slowly, I began to open my eyes. "What time is it?" I murmured sleepily.

"It's very nearly dawn!" Penda exclaimed.

I saw that the sky outside the window was indeed still jet-black and that the girls were standing over me, holding heavy bundles of the princess's freshly laundered wrappers.

"Must we rise before the sun does?" I asked sulkily, but Jeneba's glare told me that slumbering further was not an option. I regretted my rudeness as I began to feel more awake, my eyes adjusting to the lamplight.

"The princess bathes and dresses at dawn," Penda said. "We will bring up her bathwater, and while we're gone, you can take up these clean wrappers and bring back what needs to be laundered." She dumped the clothes she carried unceremoniously into my lap.

Jeneba did the same, though with a bit more violence than was warranted. She leaned close and said, "Remember that your old life is over. You're one of us now, and we rise early."

She was still cross with me about what I said last night. Part of me wanted to stay quiet and avoid antagonizing her, but I was free from those expectations now, I realized. I was no longer a lump of clay to be molded into the shape of an ideal wife, sweet and pliable and pleasing. I no longer had to smile and be silent while others mistreated me.

"I live here now. Get over it," I said firmly, forcing the words out with all my strength.

Jeneba put on an incredulous look, as if to say I was being dramatic. But I didn't care what she thought of me. I seized the bundle of wrappers, pushed past her into the stairwell, and began to climb, not stopping until I reached the top of the tower.

I found the princess already awake in her bedchamber, fidgeting restlessly with the tassels of a pillow and staring out her windows at the slowly brightening landscape. Now the sky was indigo in color, purpling at its edges. A new day was indeed dawning.

"Good morning, Your Highness," I told her, bowing deeply in greeting. "I have your laundry."

She looked up. I saw that her eyes were red from weeping. "Good morning, Amie—" she started to say, but her voice broke, and she covered her lovely face with her hands.

A more experienced maidservant might have quietly excused herself, leaving the princess alone with her tears. But I took a different approach. Remembering how kind she had been to me last night, I dropped the clothes on the carpets and rushed to her side.

I placed both hands upon her shoulders and asked, "Your Highness, what is the matter?" Even as I spoke the words, I wondered if I would be dismissed for being too familiar. Perhaps she would misinterpret my concern as impertinence.

"I know that the Trials are my father's will, but I cannot stand them," she told me, meeting my gaze. "They make me a murderess."

"It is not your fault," I replied in tones meant to comfort, as calmly as I could manage. I was lying, of course, to make her feel better. "Another will soon pass your father's Trials, and then, God willing, the two of you shall be wed."

The princess fixed me with a gaze so vulnerable and forlorn that

I had to look away. "Another suitor," she said in a small, sad voice. "Do you know how many that will make?"

"No," I said quickly, but I knew the number. Everyone did.

"One hundred. Soon, I will have sent one hundred innocent men to their deaths. I am a monster." Her breathing grew shallow, her face flushed. "*Worse* than a monster."

She was surprising me. In all the years of the Trials, I had pitied the doomed suitors and their families, all those mothers and fathers and siblings left behind to mourn. But I had never imagined that the emperor's daughter would also be distraught. In fact, until yesterday, I had not given much thought to Mariama at all, except as an extension of her father. She had been less a person than a wooden, smiling thing beside the emperor, standing on a high platform, her lips carved into a permanent expression of regal serenity.

But I had been wrong about her.

"Don't say that, Your Highness." I did not know what else to say. I only knew that I had to try to repay her kindness from last night, to listen to her as earnestly as she had listened to me.

"I think about them all the time," Mariama continued, looking past me as if I had not spoken. "I remember all of their faces, see them in my dreams. I remember what each of them said to me before they died. I remember the suitors who begged. The suitors who pleaded. The stoic suitors, the suitors who tried to be brave and joked about the flames. The ones who were angry with me, for tricking them to their deaths. All gone because of me."

"Have you ever thought of asking the emperor to call off the Trials?" As soon as I asked the question, I regretted it. "Perhaps," I said hurriedly, "coming from his daughter, he might consider it. . . ."

She frowned. "What do you mean?"

Panic coursed through me. *So this is how I will lose the princess's fa-*

vor. "I meant no offense, Your Highness. I only suggest that perhaps if you plead with your father, he might call off the Trials."

"I have already tried that, of course! Do you think I enjoy watching the deaths of innocents? Father is beyond reason, and his advisers are spineless sycophants who only tell him what he wants to hear." She lifted her gaze to mine, fresh tears trickling down her chin. "I know we have only just met, but I feel as if I can trust you. I have something to tell you. But you must promise not to tell another soul."

"I promise," I said breathlessly, not understanding why she was choosing me to confide in. After all, I was a stranger.

"Father's advisers have convinced him that the Trials are the perfect method of killing off the heirs of noble families from the outer provinces. He's so paranoid that he went along with it. And of course, the advisers told their own sons and nephews never to attempt the Trials."

I gasped, startled. The Trials weren't purely a method of finding Mariama a husband. They were also designed to eliminate the emperor's rivals and ensure the longevity of the Keita dynasty. It struck me as so cruel that I could not manage a response. Again, I wondered why she had chosen to tell me about her father's strategy. My new knowledge was a secret that we now shared, binding us together as if by twine. I was not sure if I wanted to be tied to Mariama in that way.

"Father's paranoia will be the death of him one day. He locks me in at night because he's paranoid," she said. Her beauty shone through her distress as brightly as a star. "Because he thinks I'm a possession and not a person. He says it's for my own protection, but I do not believe it."

I said, "I see," feeling a twinge of sympathy. I knew well what it was like to have a father who penned me away like cattle at his whim. Still, I wondered why she was trusting me with such talk about the emperor. I was a stranger. Perhaps Mariama's sheltered upbringing had left her too trusting of others. Or perhaps because she had grown up without a mother to entrust with her innermost thoughts, she would share them with anyone who cared enough to listen.

Mariama took note of my silence. "You will not repeat this, of course?" she asked.

I said, "I wouldn't dream of it, Your Highness."

There was more that I wanted to ask, of course. I wanted to know how long she had known the truth about the Trials. And I wanted to know why she had chosen to share such a momentous secret with someone like me. But before I could open my mouth to speak, Penda and Jeneba arrived with the bathwater.

The morning sun climbed steadily as the three of us bathed her, dressed her hair, and robed her in linens. As we worked, I wondered who her next suitor would be. Whenever he arrived, he would die in that godforsaken kettle, just like all the others.

———— • ————

It was the first warm and cloudless morning of the dry season. Sweat pooled beneath my arms as we strolled the gardens. The palace was cast in a golden daylight that made even the most ordinary things—soil in the flower beds, footprints on the tile—glow.

At length, Mariama took my hand, compelling me to fall into step with her. Penda and Jeneba walked a few paces behind us. "Have you encountered Lord Bagayogo since last night?" she asked. "Is he bothering you?"

"I have heard nothing from him at all, Your Highness," I told her.

"I cannot believe he would make such a disgusting scene in front of half my father's court. Especially not on an execution day." She paused, then, raising her voice, called out, "Good morning, Fatimata," to the emperor's youngest wife, who sat reading by a fountain.

Lady Fatimata stood, set down her book, and bowed gracefully to the princess. "Good morning, Your Highness." Her blue wrapper had been let out for her stomach.

"No need to bow in your condition." Mariama touched Fatimata's rounded belly. "How fares your baby today? Has he started to kick?"

"Not yet, but he ought to any day now."

Penda, Jeneba, and I stood apart at a respectful distance, watching our betters discuss babies and breastfeeding.

"The princess is kind to take an interest," I murmured as we waited for their conversation to end. "Not every girl in her position would be so kind to a woman whose son might have the power to banish her one day."

Penda frowned. "What son?"

"Why, the child Lady Fatimata is carrying," I said carefully. "Unless she bears him a daughter."

"That child will never be emperor," said Jeneba with a snort.

"Why not?"

"Because it will never be born."

"Jen, not in front of the new girl," Penda whispered hotly.

"What do you mean, 'It will never be—'" I began, but before I could finish, the princess had returned to our side.

"It is almost noon!" She looped one arm through mine and the other through Penda's. "My tutors do not like me to be late. We must make haste."

We accompanied Mariama into the crowded reception chamber, where the soldiers and noble lords gathered there knelt reverentially as we passed. Of course, these men did not pay the three of us maids the same respect. I did not see Lord Bagayogo among them, thank God, but something told me my battle with him was not yet over.

After we dropped off the princess at the library, my thoughts returned to Jeneba's strange comment. Why wouldn't Lady Fatimata's child ever be born? It chilled me how Jeneba had spoken so calmly, as if she were commenting upon the weather.

"No time for talk, I'm afraid," Jeneba replied when I tried asking her about it. She quickened her step. "We get our wages today. We should hurry to the treasury."

"First, you must tell me!" I hastened my pace to match hers. Penda fell behind us, out of earshot. "Is Lady Fatimata sick? Is her child in danger?"

Jeneba hesitated for a moment. Then, with the obvious joy of a girl sharing a particularly juicy bit of gossip, she whispered, "Have you never wondered why the princess is an only child? Think about it. The emperor has three living wives of childbearing age, so why does he only have one daughter? He should have half a dozen sons and daughters by now."

I was glad to have been brought into Jeneba's confidence, and I glanced out a nearby window as I considered this. The day was hot and clear, the moon faintly visible against the powder-blue sky. It seemed to flicker in and out of focus, winking at me as if it, too, kept secrets. "I suppose I had not thought about it," I said.

"His wives ask Issatou for all sorts of tinctures, herbs, and potions to halt their courses. They fear becoming with child, but every once in a while, they'll pretend so as not to raise suspicion. That's what Lady Fatimata is doing. She'll probably pretend to miscarry next month."

"Issatou?" I repeated with interest. "You mean the head of servants is a tinesefren?" I had heard of the skilled female herbalists who practiced their craft using leaves, bark, and roots to alleviate women's and children's ailments, but I had never encountered one in person due to their forbidden status under Islamic law. Women like Issatou were not permitted to exercise their remarkable healing skills, which involved connecting with the seven gods and other non-Koranic spirits for divination and curative purposes. The closest I had ever come to witnessing the power of a tinesefren was through a household servant of my father's, who sometimes boasted that his great-grandmother had been a renowned local herbalist in the days before Mali's emperors annexed Timbuktu.

Jeneba stopped walking to scowl at me, realizing too late that she had told me more than I was meant to know. "Do not repeat that to outsiders," she warned me, and I wondered if she had formed a sort of begrudging trust in me. She did not seem terribly concerned that I would tattle. "Issatou's gifts are known only to the women of court. If the devout common folk knew that Emperor Suleyman knowingly harbors a pagan herbalist, they would call him a hypocrite—or, worse, an unbeliever."

"I will not breathe a word of it to anyone," I promised. I felt a twinge of sympathy for all the women and children in Timbuktu who were unable to receive the care that only a skilled herbalist could provide. The tinesefren and their practices were now deemed unholy and officially banned by the imperial regime, but apparently Emperor Suleyman held himself to a different standard. He allowed Issatou, a wondrous resource possessing important medicinal gifts, to reside in his palace and serve his royal women, yet he denied ordinary subjects access to her healing wisdom. Having an available tinesefren was just another of the countless luxuries enjoyed by nobility and not commoners.

We resumed walking, turning a corner down a long, narrow

corridor, as I recalled Issatou's stern, scowling face yesterday morning. Then I had another question. "But Lady Fatimata certainly *looked* like she was with child. How?"

Jeneba rolled her eyes, as if I were an imbecile for even having to ask. "She uses a silk cushion."

I was genuinely perplexed. "Is it not an honor to bear an emperor's child?"

"It would only be honorable if the emperor made the mother of his heir the new empress, but he refuses to do so out of respect for Mariama's mother."

"Is he so in love with the late empress that he refuses to let a living woman take her place?" I asked, turning the idea over in my mind.

It was sad but romantic. His love for his late wife was the immortal, death-defying love of the heroes and heroines in my nurse's stories, like Musa Nyame's love for the maiden Meynsata, like Emperor Sundiata's love for the first empress of Mali. *Like Kader's love for me.*

Penda caught up and fell into step with us, saying, "Isn't it ridiculous? The empress has been dead for thirteen years. A ruler cannot be in mourning for so long. It's impractical! He must have an heir, a proper heir, a son. The line of succession depends on it."

"I cannot say that I blame Lady Fatimata for her deception," said Jeneba thoughtfully. "I don't think I'd give the emperor a baby after what happened to Binta."

"Who is Binta?" I asked, looking between the two of them without understanding.

Penda elbowed her in the ribs. "Jen, you always say too much!"

Something in the atmosphere had shifted. The air around us seemed suddenly thinner.

"Who is Binta?" I said again, lowering my voice. "You can tell me."

Taking my hands, Penda pulled me to the side. "Amie, you must swear that you will not repeat her name. Not now, nor ever, or there'll be hell to pay." The sudden severity of her words made me flinch.

"I swear it," I said. "I will not say a word."

Penda released my hands and gave an almost imperceptible nod to Jeneba, who began in a hushed voice, "Binta was a commoner who became Emperor Suleyman's mistress twenty-odd years ago. Most accounts say their affair began around the same time the empress began to grow with child. When his wife gave birth to Princess Mariama, the emperor should have held a joyous celebration for his healthy infant girl, but he would not even acknowledge her. For months, he neglected the empress and princess while boasting to everyone who would listen that Binta was his only love. He gave her wrappers and jewels and even built her family a grand house in the nobles' district. The empress prayed to God that her husband's infatuation with Binta would wane, but over the next five years, he grew increasingly besotted with his mistress and remained uninterested in his wife and child. Eventually, the empress died of heartbreak."

Penda snorted. "The empress absolutely did not die of heartbreak, Jen. She died of northern plague."

"The plague only killed her because her husband's betrayal weakened her spirit," said Jeneba defensively. "One cannot battle disease with a broken heart."

"What happened to Binta after the empress died?" I asked, a knot growing in my stomach. I had often heard stories like these when my aunts came over to gossip: these situations rarely ended well for the other woman.

"The emperor went mad with grief," Penda told me. "He realized that he'd made a terrible mistake by neglecting his wife and child in favor of his mistress. Empress Cassi had truly loved him, while Binta had only ever wanted his power. By that time, Binta was heavy with child, about to give birth. It was a difficult pregnancy, and she was always falling into ill humor because of it. She complained to her handmaidens about everything—from the weather to her aches and pains to the emperor himself. Word reached the emperor that she found him to be a dull and weak-willed ruler. That was the end for her."

I toyed listlessly with my remaining earring, trying to process this information. "What do you mean, it was the end?"

"Oh, for God's sake," said Jeneba suddenly. "No need to speak so delicately. It isn't as if there's a lady present." She brought her face so close to mine that her warm breath dampened my forehead. "The emperor took Binta out into the desert as punishment. He chained her to a rock and left her there to die. The skeletons of both mother and child were found months later."

"But that's awful," I whispered.

Thanks to the Trials, I had already known that the emperor was capable of great cruelty, but to murder his own mistress and unborn child? Only a monster would do such a thing. No wonder the people of his court followed his whims so obediently—he might do the same to them! A strange, creeping feeling spread through my hands like pins and needles. Kader was right. The emperor's court was indeed a treacherous place. I looked forward to leaving the palace in one year's time and never again returning.

———————•———————

We waited for what felt like hours standing in a queue of servants, soldiers, and bureaucrats. All were impatient for their weekly wages. I found myself trembling with excitement, for soon I would hold the first real earnings of my life in my hands. Penda had explained that the payment for chambermaids was ten cowries a day. It was not a lot of money, especially compared to my family's fortune, but it would be all mine.

My anticipation mounted as I watched the palace employees receive their wages. One by one, they stepped into a dim little room at the end of the hall, announced their name and position to the secretaries of the treasury, and emerged a few seconds later with a handful of cowries. Penda and Jeneba went before me—and then, at long last, it was my turn.

"Name and occupation?" asked one of the secretaries when I entered.

"Aminata Aqit al-Sanhaji al-Timbukti," I told him. "I work for the princess."

"Ah, there you are." He squinted at the page. "That's strange. . . ."

My heartbeat quickened. "What is the matter?"

"It says here that I must not give you wages," he said regretfully. "I'm to read you this note instead."

Pinpricks of dread crept up my neck. "What do you mean, you must not?"

"The note is from someone called Modibo Aqit," he said. "It reads: *Aminata, I have sent notice to the treasury that they are to withhold your wages and bring them directly to me instead. The preparations for your wedding cost your mother and me twelve thousand cowries, and you will work until you have repaid every bit of your debt.*"

No, I thought. *It cannot be.* "Let me see the note!" I demanded.

He gave it to me. To my dismay, it was just as he had said. My parents were robbing me as further punishment for my so-called scandal. "Twelve thousand cowries!" My voice rang with despair. "How long will it take to repay it?" The cold realization washed over me in waves. I remembered just yesterday at the riverbank, when a rain shower fell over the two of us and it had been easy to feel hopeful. Kader and I had thought we could escape in less than a year and start our new lives together.

Now that would be impossible.

"At a rate of ten cowries per day . . ." The secretary paused to work at his abacus. "Just over three years," he told me.

"No," I whispered. "You are wrong. My father would never . . ." I trailed off. Of course he would. Without another word, I turned and fled the treasury.

I pushed past the servants waiting in line and tore down the hall, not stopping until I reached a secluded corridor where I hoped no one would notice me. There, I sank into a crouch against the wall and willed myself not to scream aloud in frustration.

Three years of unpaid servitude in the emperor's court stretched out before me like a long shadow. The thought of being away from Kader filled me with disappointment. I did not want to be kept from him anymore. I did not want to keep waiting for us to live together as man and wife. I knew that the ache of being parted from him would grow unbearable, but it seemed I had no other choice. I hoped that Kader would make a great deal of money of his own by tutoring the other boys at university. If I could not fund our escape from my work here in the palace, then the responsibility would fall upon him, or else we would never be able to leave together at all.

8

I spent the rest of the afternoon in a haze of chores, following orders while my insides churned with distress. As I worked, I cursed my father for taking my wages away. I cursed my sister, too. Haddy had said that she would explain everything tonight at the feast, but I was skeptical.

What explanation could possibly make up for what she had done? She had already explained why she had sabotaged my wedding, and the proof of Lord Bagayogo's violence was in my bandaged left ear. But I still did not understand why she had blamed her own romantic indiscretions on me when she had *known* I would be ruined. Couldn't Haddy have found a way to protect me without turning our parents against me in the process?

These were my thoughts as I helped the other servants flood the reflecting pools and scrub the floor tiles. We polished the golden colonnades until they gleamed. We filled the fountain at the center of the reception hall with floating candles and covered the floor tiles in yellow petals to symbolize the golden millet of a good harvest. I searched the floor for my lost earring as I worked, but it had disappeared as completely as my future.

The sun was starting to sink when I was sent to help in one of the courtyard kitchens. There, girls and women worked at hearths and grinding stones, and the fragrant evening air was heavy with their gossip about me. It seemed that word spread quickly here in the palace, especially among servants. I knelt before the pile of yams I'd been tasked with peeling and overheard snatches of their conversations:

*Salt merchant's daughter . . . Shameful . . . Almost married Lord Bagayogo's
youngest . . . Disinherited . . . Absolutely ruined.*

Every callous comment was like citrus juice rubbed into a cut.
It was only my second day in the palace and I was already being
shunned like an outcast. How could I survive three years of this
kind of treatment? I glanced up at the sunset-stained sky over the
courtyard, feeling a wave of dread wash over me with the approaching evening.

I did not want to hear Haddy's explanations tonight. She was a
lady, and with my new knowledge of my circumstances, seeing her
flaunt her riches might feel unbearable. I didn't want to talk to her at
all, and part of me was tempted to avoid her entirely, but it was becoming clearer to me by the moment that I was in need of her husband's money. Kader and I *needed* it—how else could we run away
together? Surely Haddy's husband would be too drunk to notice if
some of his wives' jewelry had been taken, or if two hundred cowries vanished from his purse. My thoughts kept turning as I lifted
another yam from the stack before me and pierced it with the little
knife one of the other servants had given me. Slicing open its orange
flesh, I decided to ask Haddy for money tonight. I would tell her
that Father was taking my wages and then I'd ask her for help—she
owed me after such a betrayal. Quickly, I finished peeling the yam,
feeling pleasantly surprised at my speed, my skill, and the fact that
I still hadn't yet accidentally cut myself. Smiling to myself, I sat on
my haunches and glanced around the kitchen. Off to the side, one
of several hearth fires was lit, burning brightly against the darkening
courtyard, and a woman busied herself over its heat, carefully adjusting the handle of a slender black skillet. Between the hearths was a
series of smaller cooking fires over which bubbled and simmered
pots and pans, filling the air with the aromas of rice and grilled meat.
I noticed that some of the other kitchen girls were occupied with

tasks like gutting fish and plucking chickens, their activities attracting a steady trickle of bluebottle flies, and I thanked my luck that I had not been assigned to either of those unappealing chores.

I pulled another soil-dusted yam from the stack to reveal a flash of green between its companions, a leathery object that I initially mistook for leaves. On closer inspection, I saw that it was a manuscript bound in green leather, like one of my father's trade route atlases. Surprised, I pulled it carefully from the pile and examined it under the fading daylight. What was a book doing here, amid dirty yams and servants who couldn't read?

"Is this yours?" I asked the young woman who knelt a few paces away from me, grinding yams into a fine orange paste with her pestle and mortar. She was older than me, but not by very much, and when I saw from the way she tied her wrapper that she was a married woman, I felt a lurch of envy.

"No," she said, her teeth drawn back from her lips in disgust, as if she could not believe I had dared to speak to her.

"It isn't mine either," I replied, undeterred. "Do you know who it might belong to?"

But the girl only returned to her work.

I turned the book over in my hands. Its well-worn leather felt soft and comforting against my skin. Sunset dimmed the courtyard, but still I paged quickly through the volume under the waning daylight, astonished to see that the paper within was stiff and pale, newer than its exterior had led me to believe.

I came across a sketch of Harakoy, the goddess of the river, and another when a few pages later I read an inscription praising Cirey, the great god of lightning. I let out a gasp: this was a heretical manuscript, a tapestry of tales of the seven Songhai gods written in a clear, neat hand—not at all something the devout emperor Suleyman would allow in his palace. What was it doing here? Curiosity made me tuck it under my wrapper for safekeeping as I continued working by twilight until, finally, it was time for the feast to begin.

——— • ———

In the feasting hall, Haddy and her husband were noticeably absent, but serving kept me so busy that I could not dwell on it. Foremost in my mind were the ache of being on my feet all evening, the heavy platters of food in my arms, and the ceaseless orders from servants and guests alike.

At the center of all this confusion was Issatou. She kept pacing between the kitchens and the reception hall, squawking out her commands. *She is a tinesefren*, I reminded myself when her gaze fell upon me. I wondered what skills she might have. Could she stop an infant's fever? Could she create a tincture that eases the pain of childbirth? Could she develop a love potion to ensure that Kader never forgot about me as I toiled in the palace, to make certain that his dedication to me never faltered?

I was bringing a new platter into the hall when I was stopped in my tracks: Kader's father had arrived. The sight of him filled me with cold fear. He did not even attempt to speak with me, although he still watched me from afar with an intensity that set my nerves on edge. I tried my best to avoid him, which was easy with the guests eating so much. Almost everyone asked me for second and third helpings, and I was happy to run back to the kitchens and oblige them if it kept me away from Lord Bagayogo.

The only person who did not appear to be gorging herself was Mariama. She sat upon her feasting couch and picked at her food, looking down at her smoked fish and yams as if they were a miniature terra-cotta sculpture carved to resemble a meal. Although the ladies Fatimata, Bassira, and Kadiatou spoke animatedly and laughed frequently with one another, none of them spoke to her. Mariama was as unnoticed and unseen as a ghost.

Not for the first time, I observed her beauty. She may have seemed lonely and bored, but still she looked lovelier pushing a clump of rice around her plate than most girls did at their own weddings. She was almost too perfect to be real. Her dark almond eyes were captivating, and she wore her midnight-blue wrapper as naturally as if it were her own skin.

When Mariama caught my eye, I felt a flush of embarrassment and looked away. New guests were arriving by the dozens as the evening turned into true night, a parade of nobles making their glittering way into the feast. The noblemen wore black cloaks and flashing rings, and the noblewomen wore heavy earrings and long wrappers in the colors of the harvest.

I noticed a nobleman in silver mail being led over the threshold and recognized him immediately as Haddy's husband. He was leaning heavily on his walking stick. His wooden left leg struck the tiles irregularly, kicking up petals in little gold bursts. His left leg was missing, and he covered the stump of it with pale strips of cloth, carefully wound. One of the ladies escorting him frowned up at him, concerned, tilting her face to the lamplight. I saw with a jolt that she was Haddy. My sister was dressed just as opulently as I'd feared she would be, but when she met my eye, I felt a twinge of that old affection between us. I continued to hold myself aloof.

The feasting hall narrowed, closing in on me like a tide as Haddy made her way over to me. Dread pooled in my stomach, but I forced myself to hold her gaze as she approached. Whether I liked it or not, it was time to speak with my sister.

———•———

Haddy led me through the palace under torchlight, her long wrapper trailing elegantly behind her. I worried at first that someone might stop us and ask where we were going, but everyone of status was at the harvest feast. Servants and guards still flitted across the halls, but none of them paid us any mind.

My sister did not speak to me until we entered the emperor's library and closed the doors. As she had predicted, we were entirely alone. It was quiet here. All the sounds of the feast had fallen away, the clatter of knives against boards and the laughter of the emperor's guests muffled as if by a thick blanket. The flicker of castor-oil lamps illuminated the vast chamber, which was filled with rows upon rows of books and scrolls that were stacked in piles as tall as men.

"Amie, your ear!" Haddy suddenly cried out, touching my bandage with concern. "Does it hurt?"

"Only a little," I told her. "Kader had these earrings made for me as a wedding gift. They are birds—fire finches," I added, remembering his innocent excitement as he'd presented them to me by the river, his earnest desire to please me. "I lost one of them when his father attacked me."

My fire finch. Perhaps the endearment did not fit me, not anymore. Fire finches were agile and clever birds, adaptable and quick. They could soar high above the treetops just as easily as they could flit between lily pads, feasting on the mosquitoes and other insects that thrived in the river marshes. I was not like that. Tonight, I felt more like a flightless bird: trapped and waddling to the slaughter.

"Beautiful silverwork," Haddy said. Then she did something that made me wrinkle my brow in confusion. She removed a silver ring from her index finger and placed it onto the floor of the library, staring at it intently. "*Tóndikidòw,*" she said, a strange word that dripped as easily as nectar from her lips.

"What are you doing?" I asked, bewildered.

But she ignored me.

"*Tòndikídòw*," she said again, louder this time.

She was addressing the ring, I realized. My sister was speaking to a lump of silver. I was about to tell her to stop behaving like a madwoman when the air over the ground grew dark and clouded. The sight was unsettling, as though the library had become a tinderbox that might burst into smoke and flames.

When the air stilled again, the ring was changed. What had been a small silver sphere was now a silver fire finch earring that was identical to the one that still dangled from my unharmed ear.

"For when you heal," Haddy said, looking up at me cautiously. Her eyes were nervous, but her mouth wore a faint smile. I could tell she was pleased with herself, and she had also wanted to impress me with the demonstration.

"How have you done that?" I whispered. My gaze darted involuntarily between the transformed earring and my sister's face. I felt puzzled, tricked. It seemed as if the entire expanse of the library were rushing in on me, crushing my chest.

"I am a sorceress," she said plainly.

I was shocked into silence. I could not have laughed if I had tried. I was a little girl again, and she was my older sister, larger and faster than me, so many steps ahead.

"But there are no more sorcerers left in the empire," I finally managed. "Emperor Musa exiled them more than thirty years ago." My tongue felt heavy and numb, and I did not fully believe what I was saying. Hadn't Jeneba just told me that Issatou was a tinesefren? If there were still tinesefren in the empire despite official discouragement, perhaps the same could be said for banished sorcerers. And hadn't my sister just done something impossible, something that could be explained only by magic?

"Only he did not exile all of them," Haddy told me softly, pressing the earring into my palm. "Not the ones like me, because we take our power from the gods."

Her words were blasphemy. I wanted to remind her that our parents always taught us that there was only one God. According to their religion, the seven gods were just ancient lore, better left to the past. But my words died in my throat; I could only listen to my sister in fascination as she continued.

"Each of us serves a patron god, one of the seven, who awards us our abilities," she said. "By the god of smithing, I may manipulate metal—I can twist any piece of jewelry, any coin, any blade."

Her mention of the seven gods reminded me of the book tucked beneath my wrapper. I thought of showing it to her and asking if she knew anything about it, but instead I felt my forehead wrinkle with disbelief and more than a little jealousy. If my sister could perform sorcery . . . could I?

"First, of course, we must pray and make offerings to the god, and study under the tutelage of a priest," she added.

"Who taught you this?"

"Tenin did, all of those nights I was away from my husband," she said, her expression darkening as soon as she spoke his name. "At first, he was only training me."

"Tenin the scribe was a sorcerer, too?" My mind swam with images of the night I found him with my sister at the planting festival— the starry sky, the millet stalks twisting in the wind, their bare and tangled feet.

"Yes. Tenin's family is one of many who have been practicing magic in secret these past three decades, training and waiting, preparing to oust the Malinke invaders," she said. "We call ourselves the Scorpion Order, and we hate Emperor Suleyman as we hated Emperor Musa before him. For decades, Mali's leaders have overtaxed our villages, draining our crops and livestock. Soon, there will be nothing left. That is why the leaders are preparing an insurrection."

It was easy to recognize the young leatherworker's rhetoric on Haddy's tongue. My sister was a rebel, just as he had been. I hoped she would not be arrested, too—a hope that surprised me, because I knew I shouldn't have cared what happened to my traitor sister.

"I was seated near Tenin at a banquet," Haddy continued to explain, "and he tried to amuse me with his gift for metal magic by transforming a coin. We met in secret many times after that, and he began teaching me the spells he learned from his father and grandfather before him."

"And then he betrayed you," I pointed out. "He told his friends about what the two of you had done, knowing it would humiliate you."

She looked down regretfully at her hands. "I was foolish to trust him," she admitted. "But I had just wed a man I disliked, and my co-wives pecked at me like crows. It was a comfort to have a boy my own age saying that I had a talent for magic and that he cared for me."

"Why did he do it?"

She shook her head. "I cannot know for sure. I believe he began to grow jealous of me when my abilities surpassed his, despite my training period being so much shorter than his own. I have no love left for Tenin now, not after what he did to us. I am only glad that he taught me what he knew of sorcery before he was banished. I cannot imagine how my life would have gone had I never met him. I would be just another young noblewoman without magic, I would be—"

"You would have the life I have always dreamt of, the life you stole from me," I said softly.

"I owe you an explanation," Haddy said.

"I don't want an explanation. I want money." I told her what I had learned at the treasury that afternoon, that our father was planning to steal my wages until I worked off the debt of my canceled wedding.

The longer I spoke, the more I realized that I was enjoying this, forcing her to listen and making her feel guilty. It felt good to lash out at her directly after so many days locked in my bedchamber, raging as my parents confined me for my supposed wrongdoings. Days of lonely isolation had nearly driven me to the edge of my wits. It had been almost a relief when my parents told me they were sending me to court—anything was better than staring at the walls of my room all day.

"I am sorry, Amie," Haddy said. Her lips were pressed into a tight line. "For what I did to you, and that I do not have any money to give you."

Anger bubbled up in me, rising like the river in flood season. How could she lie to me so blatantly? "Of course you do!" I protested, my voice absorbed by rows and rows of dry old scrolls. "Your husband is one of the emperor's favorites, surely he has at least—"

"My husband spends his income on wine and remedies for pain," she said. "He drinks all day and night to dull the ache in his leg."

"But I don't need your husband's entire income," I pointed out desperately. "Just a few hundred cowries, or an object worth as much, so I can leave here forever."

"You want to leave Timbuktu?" She seemed to grow panicked. "You cannot do that. Stay here!"

I heard the desperation in her voice and felt a twinge of satisfaction. "Why do you care whether I stay or go? And couldn't you misplace one of your husband's jeweled daggers or swords? It sounds as though he'd be too intoxicated to notice."

"My co-wives keep a strict inventory." She paused, then added, "He is not as rich as our father hoped. Truthfully . . . he is in debt."

"Lord Ayouta is in debt?" I asked, surprised. Our father had often spoken of the wealth of the Malinke nobles and the endless supply of gold they mined from the western mountains. I had always thought of my father as an authority on commerce and trade.

"I have learned much about Malinke noblemen over two years of marriage," she continued. "Father was wrong to revere them so much. What Lord Bagayogo did to you last night is nothing compared to how he treats his daughters-in-law. He whips those girls within an inch of their lives for the slightest infractions, and he encourages his sons to follow suit. I have grown close to one of them, Lady Salimata, who showed me her many bruises." Her face drew in with sorrow. "Now do you understand, sister?"

I fell silent. I had expected lies but saw none written on her face. There was only guilt and sorrow and an elder sister's protectiveness. And although I did not want to believe that my sister's husband had no money to spare, what she had said was plausible. Alcohol could not be produced in the empire due to our religious laws, and although palm wine could be imported, it was taxed heavily and therefore not cheap. Haddy's husband may very well have spent his entire fortune on wine.

"Why did Kader never warn me about his father?" I asked her. "He always tells me everything."

"Kader lives in a world of books," Haddy said dismissively. "He studies all day and writes poems all night. He is not the type to notice much of anything. I'd be twice the student he is if the universities accepted women." That was a sore spot for her. She had always wanted to be educated at Sankoré University like our male relatives.

I must have looked shocked by her harsh assessment of Kader, because she added diplomatically, "I know that you care for him, but I could not let you marry him. He would have buried himself in his studies while his father made your life unbearable."

No! I wanted to shout. *Kader loves me, he would do anything to protect me! Why can't you see that?* But aloud I only said, "You ruined my life. How could you do it?"

Haddy took a deep breath and said, "I know what I've done to you is unforgivable. You're suffering because of me and my stupid infatuation with Tenin. I'm the one who put you into this terrible position, and I am truly sorry."

The words had been building up in me for more than a month, and now they poured out of me. "But why did you make me unmarriageable? I cannot inherit. I will die alone and destitute. . . ." I suddenly could not breathe. Tears began to trickle down my cheeks, and then I was sobbing into my sister's neck like we were children again.

She wrapped her arms around me as I wept, saying, "I should have been cleverer. I should have invented a way to end your engagement without jeopardizing your future, but I panicked in the moment and could not think to do anything else. Father had his heart set on marrying you into the Bagayogo family. I told him about what was happening to Lady Salimata, but he did not care. He still wanted to sell you like a goat so he could boast that both of his daughters married into Malinke nobility. And now that you are ruined—"

"Now that you've ruined me," I corrected. "It's your fault."

"You're right, it's my fault that you are ruined. And I'm sorry for it." She looked down at her hands, then back up at me, her eyes bright with a remorse I wasn't yet ready to accept. "But Amie, did you ever wonder how you came to be in service of the princess? It isn't often that the imperial staff hires a girl with a reputation like yours."

Her words surprised me. I held her gaze, digesting what she'd said. I had assumed that our parents made the arrangements for me to enter the palace, but now I saw it was Haddy's doing. "So, you asked the princess to hire me?" I asked finally.

She nodded. "I asked around at court for empty positions, and one of the ladies put me in touch with Issatou. At first, she said she did not want you because you lack experience, but I convinced her that you'd be a great companion to the emperor's daughter. I wanted you to have a chance to leave home, get away from Father and Mother. I knew they would keep you confined in your room forever otherwise."

It was indeed thoughtful of her to find me a job in the palace, but I wasn't in the mood to tell her that. "Am I supposed to thank you for the opportunity to rot here at court instead of rotting at home? I'm not meant to be here at all! I should be living with Kader as his wife. All I have ever wanted is to marry someone I loved," I shot back. My chest felt tight. "I had one dream, and you took it away."

"It was wrong of me to blame you publicly for my own indiscretions with Tenin. And, again, I am very sorry for it. This doesn't justify my actions, but the Order would have expelled me if I'd been the one caught. It was you or me, and so I chose you, and that wasn't right, but it's the choice I made. And I'm sorry," she said again, only infuriating me further.

I would not respond. I did not care about Tenin or the Scorpion Order or even the fact that the seven gods were not just part of the past, that their power was still alive and well. All that mattered was that Haddy had stolen my future.

"Please, try to forgive me," Haddy said in a voice that was thick with regret and sorrow. And then it was her turn to cry, her eyes shining.

Crocodile tears, I thought as she wept. I did not try to comfort her, even though I could see that she was apologetic. Apologies simply weren't enough; I wanted her to go further, to tell everyone the truth and clear my name. Her apology had not changed anything. It had not been accompanied by an offer to make things right. And if she did tell our parents the truth about her relationship with Tenin, would they restore my inheritance? I doubted it.

Through her tears, Haddy said, "I could teach you metal magic, if you want to learn. I can show you how to pray to Hausakoy for the gift of sorcery, to memorize smithing spells."

My anger flared, the flames of it licking my skin. I stood up so quickly that I grew dizzy. "I do not want to learn anything from you," I said, looking down my nose at her. "What would I gain but entry to a group of doomed rebels? Surely by now you understand that the emperor does not allow those who resist him to survive. You and your friends would all be executed within a fortnight if you made your political allegiances known. I hope for your sake that you are wise enough to keep your distance from these people from now on."

For a moment we watched each other, both of us bruised, missing the sister we remembered and unable to recognize the stranger before us. My hands were clenched so tightly into fists that my fingernails dug into my palms. It was just like my stubborn sister to support a cause she had to know would fail.

I needed to place as much distance between us as possible.

I tore out of the library and hurried down a succession of torchlit corridors until I was breathless. I followed the sounds of the feast.

Angry tears blurring my vision, I arrived at the kitchens.

A scowling Jeneba asked, "Where have you been?" when she saw me.

She gave me a heavy brass pitcher filled with mint tea. I carried it to the center of the feast, where the princess knelt silent and alone, an isolated island in a sea of happily chattering guests. When I re-filled her cup, she smiled up at me and my face grew warm with the weight of her gaze. My heartbeat quickened behind my ribs as, haltingly, I returned her smile. It was not appropriate conduct for a server to linger upon one guest, but for a long moment, I let myself look at her openly, drinking in her loveliness like honeyed wine.

9

Midnight. I lay undressed on my sleeping mat, the book I'd discovered next to me on my discarded wrapper. I had looked at it briefly, until Jeneba extinguished my oil lamp, and the stories I'd seen had heroes and giants and monsters, reminding me of my childhood. Although I was exhausted after being on my feet all evening, I found myself unable to fall asleep. I was consumed with thoughts of Haddy. She could perform *sorcery*, had studied strange skills under a league of rebel sorcerers who meant to one day take up arms against the emperor. I still did not forgive her, but she was my sister, and I worried over her choice to align herself with the Scorpion Order.

If the Trials were impossible, then the dream of seceding from the empire was even worse, the errand of a madman. My parents had been wrong about many things, but I knew that their allegiance to imperial Mali was not one of them. Loyalism was the shrewd choice, the sensible choice. Rebellion meant death.

I intended to stay alive.

I changed positions on my sleeping mat, trying to make myself more comfortable, but the floor was hard and my mat was thin. And I could not stop thinking, *Haddy is a sorceress. Haddy is a sorceress.* Curiosity rose in my throat like smoke. The little silver bird she had created for me was proof that my sister had magic. Could I have it, too? Could I use it to shorten my period of servitude in the palace or to do away with it entirely? Perhaps there was a spell that could make my father forget I owed him any debt. Perhaps there was a spell that could trick the dockworkers into allowing Kader and me onto their dugouts without paying any fare or tolls. Using the right magic, I imagined with excitement that I could get myself out of this trap and back into Kader's arms.

"Tomikido," I whispered into the dark, trying to replicate her spell, but nothing happened. Couldn't the gods hear me? I had always thought of them as stories and superstitions, but after the encounter with my sister, I was beginning to understand that they were very, very real. I glanced over at Penda, who was staring sleeplessly at the ceiling. If she heard me rustling, she did not show it.

Next to her, Jeneba lay coiled upon her mat like a snake. Her black hair glistened with perspiration in the lamplight. I wondered what she and Penda thought of having to share their chamber. Did they pity me, hate me?

I shut my eyes determinedly, trying to forget about my sister's magic, my father stealing my wages, and the sharp stone floor at my back. I was close to falling asleep out of sheer will when a sudden scream pierced the air. I flinched up from my mat, startled.

Penda already stood at attention, her eyes wide.

Jeneba leapt to her feet, too. "Come along, new girl," she said sleepily, pulling me into the stairwell with her hard grip. It felt reassuring to hold her hand, and the fact that she'd been the one to initiate it put to rest my fears that she might hate me.

I had followed them halfway up the stairs when another cry, louder than the first, made me drop Jeneba's hand to cover my ears. Under my palms, I felt Kader's earring on one side and Mariama's bandage on the other. The pain of pressure on my damaged ear made me wince.

When the three of us burst into Mariama's chamber, we found her weeping into the carpets. We had undressed her for sleep just an hour earlier, cleansing her eyelids of the kohl she had worn at the feast and loosening her hair. She looked fragile in the white wrapper she wore to bed.

We tried everything we could to calm her.

Penda rubbed her shoulders and I held her hand while Jeneba stroked her hair and asked, "Are you unwell, Your Highness? Shall we fetch the physician?"

Mariama shook her head rapidly. She tried several times to speak, but her tears kept coming, as did her gasps, her hiccuping sobs. "Thank—thank God you have come," she finally managed to say.

"What did you dream of this time?" asked Penda.

"Scarabs," Mariama whispered. "Scarabs and spiders."

Under the oily light I saw that her eyes were wide. I wondered why she was so frightened. She had little cause for it: her father was the most powerful man in the empire. *She has a tender heart*, I thought as we lit the dozen lamps in her bedchamber.

We kept trying different things to help her sleep. Penda fetched tea from the kitchen, and Jeneba sang lullabies—I was surprised by her clear, bright soprano. But none of this calmed the princess. Despite our best efforts, she continued to shiver like a plague victim.

I grew sleepier by the hour, teetering on the edge of a deep and dreamless slumber.

"Let's play a game," Penda suggested at one point, with a forced cheer that was utterly incongruous with the exhaustion in her voice.

"What sort of game?" asked Jeneba drowsily.

"Growing up, my brothers and I would play the wishing game until we fell asleep," Penda said. "First, everyone has to say the name of something they wish they had in their pocket."

Jeneba gave a groan that made me suspect she had played this game several times before and had not enjoyed it.

"I'll start," Penda added brightly. "I wish I had a pocketful of honey to sweeten my tea."

"I wish I had a pocketful of kola nuts to keep me awake," said Jeneba with a yawn. "Your Highness, what do you wish for?"

Of course, Mariama still wept and did not respond. Her back expanded and collapsed with shaky breaths as she darkened her pillow with tears.

"I wish I had a pocketful of jewels to sell at market," I said instinctively, wincing a little at my honesty. After all, the princess's bedchamber was filled with rare jewels, deep blue sapphires and yellow riverbed topaz and blood-colored rubies. The last thing I wanted was to seem like the sort of servant who would steal.

Penda's long silence told me that this was indeed the wrong answer. "Thank you, Amie," she said finally, a note of exasperation in her voice. "Next, let's all name something we wish for that's very big. Perhaps it isn't an object at all, but a desire. The grandest desire of your heart."

"Aren't you bored of this yet?" Jeneba asked impatiently.

"It's only a game," Penda said, looking wounded.

"I can start," I said, overcome with a sudden urge to defend Penda. "The greatest and grandest desire of my heart is to be with the person I love."

"The greatest and grandest desire of my heart is to be a noble-woman," Jeneba said suddenly, surprising all of us.

Even the princess lifted her tearstained face to look at her.

"Of course, I know it is not possible," Jeneba added self-consciously. "But so long as we're playing a children's game, I might as well speak childishly."

A silence fell over the room, longer and heavier than the last. It made me uncomfortable to see Jeneba so vulnerable, so painfully honest. I almost preferred her spite to this. Because she was right, of course—Songhai society had always been divided by caste. No Songhai could improve upon the caste of their birth without marrying out; one could only sink lower, as I had done.

"I've always admired noblewomen. I've always liked their fine clothes, their heavy jewelry, the graceful way they carry themselves. . . . Even as a little girl, I wanted to be more like them." Jeneba smiled wistfully, adding, "Whenever foreign nobles came to shelter in my village—I'm from an oasis town, so it happened frequently enough—I would wake before dawn to see their caravans arrive and note what the noblewomen were wearing. I loved to watch the ladies dismounting from their camels and horses that were decorated with more beads and fabric than my family could buy in a dozen years."

"You didn't grow up here? When did you come to Timbuktu?" I asked, curious. I had not known where she was from.

"I came here when one of those visitors brought plague to my village. It devastated us. My parents and siblings died, and my surviving relatives did not want to care for me, so they took me to Timbuktu to wed my uncle's friend—a fisherman."

Penda added in low, horrified tones, "She was ten years old, and he was nearly twenty."

"You did not marry him?" I cried, aghast. "Not at ten years old, surely!"

"I had no choice." Jeneba smiled mirthlessly. "Everything between the ages of ten and fifteen, I try not to remember. He died right before I turned sixteen, and I've worked in the palace ever since."

For the first time since I met Jeneba, I suddenly felt that I understood her. She had built up a fantasy for all those years because the reality of her circumstances was too painful to endure. I saw her now for who she was: a survivor.

"The greatest and grandest desire of my heart is to see my brothers again," said Penda suddenly, interrupting my thoughts. She gave a sad attempt at a smile that hurt my heart.

"What happened to your brothers?" I asked. I'd thought it was only her father who was missing. I remembered her lying awake and wondered if it was her missing brothers on her anxious mind.

At first, she would not elaborate. But with some coaxing, we eventually convinced Penda to tell us about her older brothers. Their names were Yazzal and Ousmane, they were twins, and their father, a soldier, had died in battle with the Mossi invaders. Like many widows, Penda's mother took in washing and weaving to support her family. Then came the happy day she secured a position in the empress's household. She moved her sons and daughters into the palace that same night.

Penda told us that her brothers never completely accepted the fact that their father was dead. "They joined Emperor Suleyman's army as soon as they came of age," she said. "That was three years ago, and nobody has seen them since. The generals stationed my brothers' unit in Agadez for ten months, and less than half of them have ever returned. The army claims that the remaining soldiers have chosen not to return to Timbuktu after taking local wives."

"So your brothers married Agadezien women and stayed with their brides' families?" I asked her.

"No," said Penda firmly. "Yazzal and Ousmane would never leave me and Mother all alone in the world without so much as a note."

Her story unnerved me. Healthy young men could not simply disappear.

Then Jeneba asked the princess, "What's the greatest and grandest desire of your heart?"

I do not think any of us expected an answer, but she replied softly, "To stop my father. To end the Trials."

We all looked over at her, startled. These were the first words she had spoken in hours.

"I do not care what happens to me," she said in a voice that was thick with tears. "I just want to stop more deaths."

Eyeing Mariama's tearful face, Jeneba sent me to fetch more of Mariama's tea. The palace was silent so late at night, and only a few of the lamps upon the walls remained lit. In the kitchen, I tended the firepit and waited for the black iron pot to start bubbling. All the while, I felt as though someone—or something—was watching me. Even after I had snuffed out the fire, poured hot water into the terra-cotta teapot Penda had given me, and crushed in dry mint leaves, I still felt invisible eyes upon me, heavy as weights.

Terror stricken, I rushed away from the courtyard kitchen and back into the corridors, my fingers trembling around the teapot as I went. Lamplight flickered along the walls. I quickened my pace, fixing my eyes upon the narrow stairway a short distance away that would lead me back to the women's quarters. I was so focused on that lamplit stair that I barely noticed the figure of someone in my way.

Someone was blocking the corridor, a stout, robed figure turning its shadowy face toward me—

My breath caught as I nearly collided with Issatou. In the semi-darkness, I thought I saw her brow furrowed with disapproval at the sight of me. How strange, I thought, that she was wandering around the palace late at night! Perhaps she had been gathering herbs and medicinal barks by moonlight.

"Why are you awake and outside?" she asked hoarsely, her voice like rustling leaves. "Are you returning from a lover's bed? I'd been warned that you were difficult, but to be so brazen on your very first week of service is a very poor choice indeed."

I stepped back from her without speaking, my heartbeat heavy against my ribs. I felt certain she meant to punish me.

Her tone grew impatient. "Are you going to answer?"

"The princess cannot sleep, so I was sent for tea," I told her as steadily as I could manage.

Issatou's eyes narrowed. She looked at the teapot in my arms and muttered, "My sweet Mariama is always having nightmares. She cannot blame the executions for it, either. She's been this way since long before her father put the Trials into place. Did you know I was once her night nurse? And I was her mother's, too. The late empress Cassi was a calm, easy child, but the princess was such a fitful little girl that she needed an army of us to get her to sleep through the night. Do you want my advice?"

Relieved, I said, "Yes, madam," trying to imagine Issatou as Empress Cassi's nursemaid. How many years ago had the empress been a child? Issatou seemed to have been in the employ of the palace for decades.

"When she was a child, I would often lull Her Highness to sleep by telling her stories," she said. "Just a suggestion."

"Thank you, madam," I said.

When she finally left me, I held the teapot against my chest, enjoying its warmth as I retraced my steps back toward Mariama's tower, walking as quickly as I could without spilling her tea. I wondered how long I had been gone, and if Jeneba would scold me for dawdling when I arrived. But I knew it was worth it to try everything to help Mariama to sleep.

It must have been nearing dawn, because the palace was no longer silent. Some of the earliest-rising servants were beginning to light the wall lamps that had faded overnight, and I heard the heavy footsteps of guards making their morning rounds. But it was not yet daybreak—each window I passed revealed a sky that was still black and full of stars. As I unlocked the tower, I decided that I could not have been away for more than half an hour.

The situation in the princess's chamber seemed unchanged.

Jeneba huffed in annoyance at the sight of me, grabbed the teapot from my hands impatiently, and demanded, "What took you so long?" She poured a cup for the princess and placed it gently at her side.

I did not respond. Mariama took a single disinterested sip and bent her face over the cup, weeping silently. I watched her with pity and sat with her on the carpets. Then, in a fit of inspiration, I remembered the book that was still tucked beneath my wrapper on my sleeping mat. Hoping the stories within would be enough of a distraction to mitigate the princess's distress, I ran down to the maids' room and then back up the stairs with the book.

After opening to a story I'd glimpsed earlier, I began to read aloud. "It was late in a long dry season," I narrated hoarsely. "The crops were yellow with drought when Hausakoy, god of smithing, left his forge house to seek a mortal bride."

It was a story I had heard before. In it, the divine blacksmith realizes he is lonely at his forge beneath the desert, so he looks for a wife. First, he takes the form of a man and approaches a young girl in the daytime. He asks her to be his bride, but the shy girl declines and runs into her father's house to hide. The god Hausakoy waits until nightfall. He assumes the form of a giant scorpion with golden armor and a sharp hooked tail as long as a man. As the mighty scorpion, he kills the girl's father with his grasping pincers and wounds her brothers near fatally. Then he kidnaps his bride. He takes her into the desert, burrowing with her under the dunes until they reach his forge house. He keeps her trapped with him for many years, until she grows old. Then, he returns her to her home, but none of the villagers remember her after so many years, not even her brothers—who are all old men now with children and grandchildren of their own.

"Hausakoy's bride died of sadness, lonely and without kin. Her sorrowful story reached the god of the clouds, who took pity upon her and vowed to avenge her death by sending Hausakoy into permanent exile. He pursed his lips and exhaled a gust of hurricane wind that blew Hausakoy to the ends of the earth. He wanders the wastelands to this day, alone and undying, and his forge house remains empty," I finished, glancing over at Mariama to see if the story had calmed her.

To my delight, she was no longer weeping, although her eyes remained red. "Amie, I didn't know you could read," she said.

"Yes, Your Highness." I felt Jeneba's gaze on me as I spoke. "And I can write, too," I added.

"Where is that book from?" Mariama asked.

"I brought it from home," I lied.

"I believe I am quite recovered," said Mariama. A faint smile tugged at the corners of her mouth. "You may leave."

I felt triumphant. *Sleep, at last!* I followed the others to the door.

"Amie," she called out suddenly. "You will stay."

I obeyed, but my heart sank. I wanted only to sleep.

"You have had a difficult two days," she told me once Jeneba and Penda were gone. "You deserve proper rest. Would you like to sleep in my chamber?"

"Your Highness," I began, looking uncertainly at her thick sleeping mat, the complex embroidery on her carpets. I wanted nothing more than to bury my face in one of those pillows and fall into slumber. "I accept, so long as I will not be a bother to you."

"No bother at all." Mariama smiled, and then almost as an afterthought, she added, "I did not really dream about spiders. I never do."

Her words surprised me. "What do you mean?"

For a long moment, she did not answer. From somewhere on the street below, I heard the lurch and shudder of nocturnal music, the strings of a kora plucked expertly. The tune was so familiar that I felt certain I had heard it before.

She did not respond. And then she leaned slowly toward me until her cheek was pressed to my shoulder. Her heavy head rested against my collarbone, and I found myself inhaling the sweet scent of her hair.

"That is what my dreams are about," she said in a voice as smooth as butter. "I dream of my dead suitors. Sometimes I think I must be cursed, for I have been surrounded by so much death ever since I was a child." I could feel the vibrations of her words against my skin.

"You mustn't blame yourself, Your Highness," I said, trying not to sound as nervous as I felt. But in truth, the closeness of her face to mine, the confidences she had shared . . . all of it had sent my insides into a panic.

I was not sure what to make of this feeling, so I began to read aloud again, this time a tale of Dongo, god of thunder, and another of Nyawri, god of the hunt. I had grown up hearing these stories from my nurse, so they were not anything new, but it was thrilling to revisit them with the knowledge that the seven gods were not just superstition. My sister's words swam through my mind—*Each of us serves a patron god, one of the seven, who awards us our abilities.* I wondered if this book was written by a sorcerer.

Would Haddy recognize this book? Would she know who wrote it? Part of me wanted to find her tomorrow and ask her as many questions as I could think of about how she harnessed the magic of the gods. But I was still angry with Haddy, and I did not want her to interpret another visit as forgiveness. I didn't think I could ever forgive her.

A soft snore broke through my thoughts. Mariama was finally sleeping.

I stopped reading aloud midsentence, feeling victorious. Carefully, trying my best not to make a sound, I lowered the book to the floor and looked down at Mariama through the lamplight. Even in her sleep, she looked so unhappy. The sight of her made my heart ache.

10

My body gave a start and I found myself awake, roused not by any sound but by a strip of morning sunlight that had fallen over my eyes. It was late, I realized. Perhaps an hour before noon. Mariama and I had slept in. So had Jeneba and Penda, otherwise they would be with us already in the chamber, pouring bathwater and stirring tea.

I was glad. Serving girls worked hard and rested little. They deserved the rare pleasure of sleeping late.

Next to me, Mariama still slept, snoring quietly. She was lucky to be the sort of girl who looked lovely at all times, even in slumber. I smiled, satisfied, as I remembered that after our desperate efforts last night, I had been the one who had finally gotten the princess to sleep. Not Penda, not Jeneba—*me*. I was pleased that Mariama seemed to like me; I liked her, too. It was also dawning on me that gaining the emperor's daughter as a friend could be an invaluable asset. Maybe she could reduce the cost of the journey Kader and I would be making by getting us one of her father's dugouts so that we wouldn't have to hire one ourselves when we left Timbuktu. I understood then that I was making a very useful ally in the princess, and that was a magic all its own. Not as impressive as Haddy's spells, perhaps, but at least it was mine.

The book of the seven gods was still on the floor. I picked it up and paged through it, studying the stories one by one. Instead of lingering over the book, I should have begun fetching Mariama's bathwater before she woke and asked for it. But the stories were so diverting that I ended up reading for longer than I meant to. I was midway through a tale about the millet goddess transforming dead crops into vibrant ones when I turned a page that peeled soundlessly away, detaching itself from the book as if by its own will.

I watched in surprise as it fluttered softly to the carpet.

Startled, I examined the page. It had been flat just moments earlier, I was sure of it. But now it was curled into a neat little scroll that reminded me of the letters my father mailed to trading partners who lived far away. I leaned down to pick it up. The scroll grew larger and larger as I unrolled it, and then spread out before me was an enormous map, big enough to half cover the carpet at my feet. It curled up stubbornly at its edges, as though it had been rolled for many years.

Sighing with the realization that sorcery—magic—was the only answer, I stretched my neck and looked more closely at the map. It depicted the empire and its surrounding kingdoms, from the western mountains to the northern sea. The mapmaker had placed an illustration of Timbuktu at its center, complete with a sketch of the late emperor Musa holding a golden nugget to his lips. To the west were the villages of Aoudaghost and Mopti and Dakar by the ocean. To the immediate north was the vast desert, dotted with oasis towns such as Ghadames and the salt-mining centers of Taghaza and Taoudenni. Even farther north sat the ancient cities of Marrakech and Tripoli and the grand pyramids of Cairo, all bordering the bright blue Mediterranean Sea, which they said was filled with monsters. To the south I saw the cities Kano and Djenné-Djenno, their names written in an especially elegant script.

It was a lovely map, and I had seen one or two similar to it in my father's possession. But I did not think it had always belonged in this book. It was not a story; it did not fit. I traced the curve of the continent across the map's surface and with a strange creeping sensation began to realize that someone had deliberately hidden it in this book. But why would a map need to be hidden in the first place? And why had it just dropped like a fruit into my lap?

I looked up to the sound of doors opening. The other handmaidens came into the room looking drowsy. Poor bleary-eyed Penda even rested her head sleepily upon the pile of laundry in her arms. I supposed they hadn't slept in after all.

Across the room, the princess was beginning to stir. "Girls, what is the matter?" she asked, rubbing her eyes. Then she stood, crossed over to us, and peered curiously at the map, then over at me. "Where did you find this, Amie?"

"It fell out of the book we read together last night," I said.

Penda gasped, "Look, Your Highness!"

I turned back to see that the illustrations on the map were changing, growing more and more lifelike with each moment. The dark green foliage of the southern kingdoms sharpened into focus. The ink-and-dye oceans rolled with steady, crashing waves as tiny sketched seagulls flew in circles overhead. The desert cities of Cairo and Marrakech shimmered with sand on the wind. Miniature lions and gazelles chased one another across the distant savanna. Tall, long-necked giraffes chewed at the tops of baobab trees. Illustrated caravans moved along Saharan trade routes, led by minuscule merchants in fluttering blue robes.

A small sketch of the Moorish sultan of Granada waved to the sketch of Emperor Musa, who raised his golden goblet in a toast of friendship. I could almost hear their voices, the cries of gulls along the Spanish coast. But no, I really was hearing something—a low buzzing that grew steadily into a hum.

"Do you hear that?" Penda asked us quietly. "It's like the whispering of jinn."

Mariama grabbed my hand. "If this is the work of some unholy creature, then may God protect us all."

Watching the map made me feel the same nervous fascination that had flowed through me when Haddy cast her spell in the library. The low hums emanating from the map reminded me of that strange spell-tongue she had spoken; was it the language of sorcerers?

Penda tugged at my sleeve. "Amie, what does it say?"

New words were forming in the margins of the map, as if written by an invisible hand. I saw the letters *h* and *e*, and then a full sentence: *Hello, Aminata Aqit al-Sanhaji al-Timbukti.* My stomach dropped. The sorcerer who had created this map knew exactly who I was.

Mariama turned her frightened gaze upon me. "How have you done that?"

"I do not know," I admitted. I could hear my heartbeat in my ears. "Truly, I have no idea how this is happening."

"Are you quite certain . . . ," began Mariama, but she stopped at the sight of a new illustration appearing on the map, larger and brighter than all the others.

Behold the forge house of Hausakoy, god of blacksmiths, wrote the map in its elegant calligraphy. My mouth went dry as I remembered last night's tale about Hausakoy stealing his bride. Had the map been listening to us?

Beneath the words, a dwelling of white adobe and limestone rose like bread. The structure looked so real that I wanted to pass my hands over it. Then a golden light flickered from its center, bathing all four of us in its glow. I could not turn my eyes away from that light. It flowed like a liquid, pulsing as rhythmically as the blood in my body.

New words began to bloom across the map. *Mariama Keita. Penda*

Diallo. Jeneba Sangaré. Aminata Aqit. Our names were together there on the parchment, next to the illustration of the palace.

A chill passed through me. *The map knows where we are.* I wondered if it could see us, too.

"How is it *moving* like that?" Jeneba's voice was a small, horrified squeak. "And what do those words say?"

"The map knows our names, and it shows us *here*—" I pointed at the illustrated palace, then dragged my finger across the map, into the blank space that indicated desert. "And it says that *this* is the forge house of the god Hausakoy," I explained as a furnished interior began to take shape within its walls, complete with ceilings and staircases. The rooms started to grow new details and embellishments—an anvil, a smoking hearth, a bellows of wood and leather—until the house really did look like what I'd imagined for the home of an immortal blacksmith.

I spotted an orange hammer by the hearth, glowing like a firefly. "Hausakoy's hammer," I murmured without drawing my eyes away from it.

The stories said that Hausakoy had an enchanted hammer that could turn you into stone for as long as you held it. One young hero, after learning that Hausakoy's forge house had been empty ever since his exile, decided to break into the god's dwelling. He wanted to steal the enchanted hammer for the sake of his beloved wife—she had lately been imprisoned by a demon in a fiery cell. With Hausakoy's hammer clutched tightly in his hand, the hero stepped through a wall of fire and rescued his wife. So long as he held the hammer, he was made of cold stone instead of flesh, so he did not burn to death. After saving his wife from her prison of flames, he dropped the hammer, immediately transforming from stone back into flesh. The hero and his wife lived well forever after.

The idea came to me slowly at first, and then quickly, like the first drops of rain thickening into a downpour. The idea filled me to bursting, the pressure of it increasing until I called out almost involuntarily, "Your Highness, this is how you can end the Trials!"

She looked blankly at me, not understanding. Perhaps because she was a Malinke princess, she was unfamiliar with Songhai folklore. "What do you mean?"

"Hausakoy's hammer turns men into stone temporarily," I explained. "There is an old story about a man who used it to pass unharmed through a wall of fire. Perhaps one of your suitors could use the same trick to survive the kettle."

Slow relief spread across Mariama's face. "You mean if we manage to find this hammer, we could end the Trials forever?" she whispered. I could see in her eyes that she was afraid of hoping. The Trials had been a constant fixture of her life since she was just thirteen years old. Perhaps she had resigned herself to the idea that they might never end at all.

I wanted to give her what she longed for.

"If the stories are true . . . I believe so," I said, feeling suddenly aware of the other girls' eyes on me.

Penda watched me nervously.

Jeneba looked at me as if she had just decided I was even more of an idiot than she had previously thought. "Hausakoy isn't *real*," she said. "Didn't your costly education teach you that? There is only one God, and everything else is just old wives' tales." Still, she couldn't help but turn her awestruck gaze back to the enchanted map with its shifting illustrations and buttery-golden light.

"Believe what you want," I told her. I had already decided what I believed: I believed in Hausakoy the smith, Faran the planter, Harakoy the river goddess, and Nyori the ruler of clouds—how could I not, with everything I saw before me? I chose to trust instead in the magic I'd seen in my sister's hands, the magic I saw now in this map.

And then I fell silent, remembering something else about the god Hausakoy. He was *rich*. Because he worked with precious metals, his house was filled with objects of silver and gold. My old nurse used to sing me a song about his wealth. I could still recall her soft voice, singing: *Gold are his goblets, silver his chairs. Gold thread for his carpets, gold wood for his stairs.*

Once, I would have dismissed it as a rhyme for children, but today I wondered if it held any truth. If the gods were real, then at least some of the stories about them must be true. I had witnessed two separate acts of magic since arriving in the palace—my sister's sorcery with the silver ring and now this map—and there was not much room left in me for skepticism or doubt. This was a treasure map. Anyone who followed it to its destination and managed to retrieve even a small portion of the smithing god's riches would become incredibly wealthy.

The realization came over me in a wave of relief. I understood that I held a map that would lead me not only to a treasure that would end the Trials but also to a liberation from all the ills that currently plagued me. There would be no more slow waiting for my maid's wages to repay my debt to my father. And there would no longer be any need for Kader to pocket his tutoring fees to fund our future together. I had already worked out how much we'd need to live on and had gone over the figures until I knew them by heart. I'd thought it would take us years to earn, but now I saw myself leaving Hausakoy's forge house with enough riches to support Kader and me a dozen times over for the rest of our natural lives.

When I returned home, everything would be different—for the better this time. I would quit my job at the palace. I would pay my father back for the costs of my canceled wedding and never need to see him ever again. Kader and I would use our newfound riches to hire our own private dugout downriver, then pay local guides to help us trek the Bambouk Mountains at the western edge of the empire. We'd make our way to the Atlantic and begin a life for ourselves in one of those seaside kingdoms outside Mali's jurisdiction, where Kader's father and mine would not be able to reach us. Hope flared in me as I imagined it.

"Dearest Amie!" Mariama cried abruptly, throwing her arms around me with as much enthusiasm as I currently felt bubbling within me. "You wonderful girl! You have found the key to ending this, once and for all. Now we have everything in our power to put a stop to the Trials. The next suitor to come to the palace is the man I will marry," she said determinedly. "I will help him win the Trials, no matter what. With this map, I will *make* him win."

Mariama's clear dark skin glimmered above the golden light of the sorcerer's map. Her eyes were huge and her eyelashes thick with tears. Still, I do not think it was only her beauty that won us over. It was also her voice. She had a voice that was thrilling, captivating, triumphant. It commanded our attention and made us want to be loyal to her. If she were a general in her father's army and we were her lieutenants, we might have pledged fealty on the spot.

"When I am wed," she declared, "I will see to it that my father does not harm anyone else ever again. I have ninety-nine dead suitors. There will not be a hundredth."

"Yes, Your Highness," the three of us said, almost in unison.

We were quite in awe of her. I do not believe we could have managed anything else.

———————— • ————————

Mariama did not go to her tutors that afternoon. Penda, Jeneba, and I did not clean her room or fetch her linens. From this moment on we were no longer just her chambermaids, we were also her co-conspirators, her acolytes, her spies. We transformed the princess's chamber into our own private quarters to plan and strategize. We were intoxicated with the knowledge that the four of us had the power to end the Trials.

We pored over the enchanted map, memorizing it until we could see it reflected back at us when we closed our eyes: the Sahara, the savanna, the pulsating forge house at its center. When it grew dark outside, Mariama did not take supper with her father and his wives. Instead, she ordered her meal to her room after sending word through a servant that she was feeling unwell and needed rest.

In truth, Mariama was better than I had ever seen her. The promise of the map had positively filled her with a hopeful energy. She began to speak of the grand imperial wedding her father had promised her, of bridal fashions and the dancing and feasting that would linger for days after she was wed.

She told us she would like to have the suitor's kettle destroyed as a wedding gift. "I hate the wretched thing," she said. "Perhaps, after my wedding, we shall go to it in the dead of night and smash it to bits with hammers. The Trials end soon, girls. No more suitors will die for me. I will be married and the four of us will go on a great tour of the empire and enjoy everything it has to offer. Penda, you are our lookout," she instructed. "Keep your ear to the ground for the arrival of my next suitor. I must know about him as soon as he reaches the palace."

"Yes, Your Highness," Penda said obediently.

"And then Jeneba will slip him a note during his welcome feast," Mariama said.

Jeneba frowned. "But how will I manage it?"

"Oh, just do what you always do. Flirt." Mariama performed a nearly perfect imitation of the coquettish smile Jeneba reserved for noblemen, causing all four of us to dissolve into giggles. "Amie will write the note," she added, and kissed my cheek so suddenly that I jumped.

"Thank you," I murmured, looking away. My cheek felt hot where her soft lips had touched it.

"The note will say, *Follow me, Your Lordship*, or some other nonsense that will lure him down to the grain storeroom, where Amie will be waiting with the map." The princess went on, assigning us tasks based on the qualities that made us useful: Penda's watchfulness and knowledge of all the goings-on at court, my aristocratic education, Jeneba's quick wits and distracting beauty.

Later, once we lured the new suitor down to the storeroom, I was to explain to him that no man would ever survive the suitor's kettle without help from the gods. I would explain that the only way to win the Trials was to become impervious to heat and pain, and then I would show him the map to Hausakoy's forge. I would tell the suitor that if he stole the god's hammer, he could use it to win the Trials by turning himself temporarily to stone.

If the suitor asked me for the map, I was to refuse him. Mariama said she could not trust a man she had never met with such a valuable object. She wanted one of us to accompany him on his journey into the desert to make sure that he did not run off with the map or sell it for gold.

But the rules of the Trials were strict when it came to who would be permitted to accompany each suitor on his journey into the desert. There were always three horsemen who had been handpicked by the emperor, three strong horses, and no one else, certainly not unauthorized maids. We spent a long time debating how we should manage it before Mariama suggested that one of us conceal ourself in the suitor's saddlebags and ride into the desert, unseen by the emperor's horsemen.

"Which one of us should do it?" asked Jeneba.

"Whichever of you wants Hausakoy's gold the most, I suppose," Mariama replied.

The idea of following the map into the Sahara until I reached the uninhabited house of a banished god struck me as both thrilling and terrifying. There was much that could go wrong with this plan and with desert travel. I knew from my father's stories that we might run out of water or get kidnapped by smugglers. We might perish from snakebite or suffocate in a sandstorm. I feared all those possibilities, but my desire to escape my life here and to be with Kader was far stronger than my caution.

A plan began forming in my mind: this was a way for me to be with Kader. I had hoped for a solution to the problem of my parents stealing my wages, and it had arrived in the form of a map. Just a fraction of the god's gold would keep Kader and myself fed and housed for many years, perhaps for the rest of our lives. We could comfortably flee the empire and make a home for ourselves far away from our families. If we succeeded in stealing Hausakoy's hammer and ending the Trials, both Mariama and I would get what we wanted. I would escape Timbuktu and be with Kader, and she would stop the senseless killings of suitors that haunted all her days and nights. *Kader and I will soon be together, our love story is not over—*

"I want to go," Penda said, her voice breaking through my thoughts. "I'd like to use Hausakoy's gold to hire a search party to find my brothers."

"You're not going," Jeneba told her. She sounded angry. "And Amie can't go, either! She doesn't need the money like I do."

We bickered until Mariama conceded that all three of us would go with her suitor into the desert. "It is probably for the best," she said thoughtfully. "It cannot be safe for just one of you to travel alone at night with four men, not to mention all the dangers of the desert. The three of you must protect one another."

"But how will all three of us fit into one saddlebag?" Jeneba asked quite sensibly.

"We'll ask Issatou for an enchanted thread for roomier saddle-bags," replied Penda as matter-of-factly as anyone. She explained that her mother the laundress sometimes washed Issatou's purses and waterskins, which were much larger on the inside than they were on the outside. "One for each of us. There are three horse-men, after all."

"And you won't need to hide for very long," Mariama chimed in. "Only until the sleeping potion kicks in, and it is safe to reveal yourselves."

She told us in low, excited tones of the plan she'd concocted for us to dose the breakfast of the emperor's horsemen with an elixir that could induce enchanted sleep. Issatou made one and had used it to help the babies of court sleep, including Mariama herself, once upon a time. And it would not take long—with the right dosage, the horsemen would slip into a sudden slumber within only a few hours of desert travel. After that, we could ride on unobserved toward the forge house.

By then it was close to midnight, and we were all lightheaded with hunger and exhaustion and the thrill of our shared secret and plans. Penda, Jeneba, and I whispered jokes as we went without the princess to a courtyard kitchen to fix ourselves a late meal, occasion-ally covering one another's mouths to stifle our riotous laughter. It was as if the tension between us were melting away.

Back in the tower, we ate and plotted and joked and ended up falling asleep together in a damp, tangled heap on the carpets. When morning arrived, we rose early with the red sun.

It was the dawn of a new day, for all of us.

11

The next evening's task was for me to get the sleeping potion from Issatou. I knocked at her chamber three times, quick as a thief. After a rattle of locks, the door creaked open. In the dim lamplight I saw only her pale teeth (it occurred to me, distantly, that I'd never seen a woman so old with all her teeth), her white head wrap, and the whites of her eyes. The rest of her face was obscured in shadow. I would not have known her if she hadn't spoken.

"Aminata, is that you?" Issatou asked, surprised. "Why've you come at this hour?"

"Please, you must help me." I made my voice desperate, as Mariama had coached me to do. "I haven't been able to sleep for days."

Seeing what she supposed was sleepless desperation upon my face, Issatou led me inside. Her room was dim and, curiously, windowless, and the shelves along her walls were covered in strange, irregular lumps. Upon closer inspection, some of the lumps were hollowed-out drinking gourds; others were the horned skulls of animals. The sight made me shiver.

The room grew brighter as she saw about lighting the oil lamps, muttering, "You say that you cannot sleep?"

"I do not know what is wrong with me," I said in a whimper. "Only that I have been distraught ever since my father disinherited me, and lately I cannot sleep at all."

Issatou lifted her hands and massaged her white-haired temples. "I have what you need," she said. "But you must promise to follow my instructions very faithfully. I used to give this to Empress Cassi as a little girl." She launched into a lengthy explanation, telling me that just half a spoonful of the potent mixture was enough for a good night's sleep. She claimed that those who ingested more than one spoonful would enter a sleep both dreamless and deathless, rendering the sleepers unable to die of hunger, exposure, or thirst so long as they still slumbered. The only way to revive them was with a dense, ink-dark paste made from a crushed flower that grew only on the slopes of a distant mountain near the western sea. Issatou had this antidote already on hand, and she sold it to me for an additional sixty cowries given to me by Mariama.

From one of her shelves, she pulled a gourd that had been hollowed out. I watched as she placed a little wooden funnel over a water pouch and poured the contents of the gourd, a pale syrup, inside. The liquid was slow and thick and made not a sound.

———— • ————

At last, our plan was prepared. All we had to do was wait for Mariama's next suitor to arrive, and we could spring into action. But no suitor came. The weeks passed slowly, and we walked through our days in a half-cheerful, half-nervous reverie, with small, secretive smiles on our faces.

Sometimes we passed Lord Bagayogo on our morning turns through the gardens, and he would fix me with a hard gaze. But he no longer frightened me as he once did. *Soon, I will be wealthy again, rich with Hausakoy's gold*, I would think, returning his glare with a defiant smile. *Soon, I will run far away with your son, and there will be nothing you can do about it.*

I briefly considered sending word to Kader about the map and our plan to end the Trials with Hausakoy's gold, but I decided against it. I did not want him to worry. He would not like to think of me riding for three days into the desert, as he would understand the danger it entailed and try to stop me. I wanted to use the god's gold for the both of us and make a life together far away from everything I had ever known. But I did send him a message that I missed him and that my father was taking my wages, so that he would understand why I couldn't contribute my wages to our plan.

Many nights, I slept next to Mariama in her bedchamber. She said that the only way to chase away her nightmares was to drown them with tales, which calmed and distracted her. So we would read aloud to each other from the book of stories until we both fell asleep. Our friendship grew steadily with each passing evening, like the waxing of the crescent moon. Before, I had imagined that the emperor's daughter would be devout and studious, that her days would consist of scripture and prayer. But I had long since learned the truth: when Mariama was not studying with her tutors and marabouts, she enjoyed a life of leisure that bordered on boredom, with little to occupy her time besides reading scripture, dressing herself in the latest fashions, and taking long walks through the palace courtyards.

Mariama quickly afforded me new privileges that were far beyond those I had come to understand were given to chamber attendants. As the days passed, I became something closer to a lady-in-waiting. Mariama shared her perfumes and face creams with me. She allowed me to wear her jewelry. She even let me sit with her at dinner and insisted the kitchen girls serve me as if I were a noblewoman. They did as they were commanded, though they looked contemptuously down at me as they heaped my platter high with goat stew and rice.

I noticed then that I had changed: the opinions of other servants had ceased to matter to me. They were as inconsequential as flies buzzing around my head, and Mariama was like the sun. I was also beginning to dress like a noblewoman, for Mariama encouraged me to wear her clothes. It was obvious to everyone in the palace that I was the princess's favorite. One day we might spend thumbing through scrolls in the palace library. Another we might spend dressing and undressing ourselves at our leisure, arranging beautiful outfits from her extensive finery: blue wrappers of dyed cotton from the indigo pits of Kano, white gowns of Egyptian linen, and carnelian bracelets. And as we read aloud to each other from scrolls, or trailed our fingers through the courtyard fountains, or braided each other's hair into tall, elaborate styles, a feeling began to grow within me. It was a wave of affection that was almost overwhelming.

Sometimes when she fell asleep against my shoulder, I felt overcome with the weight of her beauty and her intoxicating proximity. At other times I sensed something else, a hungry, incomplete feeling that felt like a sneeze that would not arrive or the rumblings in my stomach before a meal. It was a sort of greediness, I supposed, to have her near, or else a protective instinct to keep her close.

"We look alike, don't you think?" Mariama asked me one night as we stood side by side in front of her mirror.

She was wearing a wrapper the color of hibiscus, while I wore a borrowed wrapper of the palest gray, like storm clouds. She had braided my hair in her favorite style, traced henna along my hands and feet, reddened my lips with root pigment, and smudged my eyelids with kohl. And she was so very close to me, her breath warm on my face and her hands placed gently on my shoulders. Each time our eyes met, I felt a flush of embarrassment.

"We do look a little bit alike, yes," I answered, because I knew it would please her.

In truth, Mariama and I did not even faintly resemble each other. She was taller than me, with darker and smoother skin. My complexion was oily and prone to blemishes. Her nose was small and rounded, her eyes liquid and huge. I'd always thought my nose was too long for my face and my eyes were set together too closely. People had given me mild compliments on my looks over the years, but Mariama was a true, and distinct, beauty. I caught myself staring at her more and more each day. It was almost a relief to be apart from her when she studied with her tutors, because at least then she could not distract me with her lovely face.

Penda, Jeneba, and I began to spend those afternoons in the princess's chamber, working at the looms. We were weaving three saddlebags out of the coarse and gleaming thread that Penda had purchased from Issatou. Thanks to the magical thread, the bags would be large enough for a girl of our size to fit comfortably within. But still no suitor arrived.

In the meantime, the three of us used our indolent afternoons to try on Mariama's jewelry, sing songs, and teach one another the latest dances. We had the princess's favor and were taking advantage of it by relaxing while we could, much to Issatou's chagrin. We confessed our hopes for the future, our fantasies, our fears. Penda told us more about her brothers, how they had always admired soldiers, the season they spent teaching her to fence with a wooden sword when she was a little girl. She was quite determined to find them, and she had even decided upon the mercenaries she would hire to help with her search once she was rich with the god's gold.

Jeneba told us often about the grand lifestyle she would live when Hausakoy made her a wealthy woman. "I'm going to be the most elegant lady Timbuktu society has ever seen," she said one afternoon while we were at the loom, working on the saddlebags. "I'll wear the latest fashions and travel in a covered palanquin carried by half a dozen strong young men. And I'll toss out golden nuggets to beggars as I pass, like Emperor Musa did on his pilgrimage."

Another week passed, and still no suitor came. The rainy season was decidedly over. The air grew hotter and dusty. The sun swelled like a melon against colorless skies. When the tower grew warmer than the three of us could stand, we hauled buckets of water up from the drinking wells and took turns emptying them over our heads.

On one especially hot day, I peered out of the tower and spotted something unusual down in the market square. A cluster of spectators had gathered around two young men. Both of them waved their arms and shouted, exciting the crowd.

I called Jeneba over to watch with me, and we stood together at the window looking down into the dusty market below. We were too high up in the palace to hear what the men were saying, but their voices were passionate, and they were inciting shouts and sighs from the throngs that encircled them. We were still watching when a fleet of the emperor's soldiers marched into the square. Shoppers scattered and screamed while the soldiers held down the two young men and slit their throats.

I jumped back from the window with my heart pounding.

Jeneba sighed. "Rebels, poor fools," she said, and shook her head.

Later that night I lay awake, still haunted by the image of the two rebels, their blood mingling with the dust. I hoped my sister would hear of what had happened and cut ties with the rebellion, for her own sake. As much as I tried my best not to think about her, that was more difficult now that I was permitted to dine with the princess and an ever-changing gaggle of visiting noblewomen, which sometimes included Haddy.

During one of these evening banquets, my sister sidled up next to me and whispered into my ear that she needed to speak with me privately. She tugged insistently at my hand like we were children and attempted to lead me out of the dining hall and into the emperor's library.

I told her coolly that I did not wish to speak with her. Of course, a curious part of me *did* want to talk to Haddy. I wanted to ask her a thousand questions about sorcery and rebellion and the seven gods and the Scorpion Order. But another, more spiteful part of me still wanted nothing to do with her, even if she might be able to help me. In the end, my bitterness won over my curiosity, and I successfully ignored Haddy for the rest of the week.

By then, my ear was nearly healed. One afternoon, I found myself alone in Mariama's bedchamber standing before the looking glass. I unwrapped my bandage slowly and slipped in the silver bird earring my sister had sung into existence with her strange spell. Then I examined myself in the mirror, staring at my reflection and wondering if I looked like a girl who could survive the desert.

For one brief moment, I thought I saw a finger tracing the surface of the glass—but when I blinked, the phantom digit was gone. Cold fear gripped me and I looked closer, bending my face to the mirror and pressing my fingers against it as if gesturing for the ghostly hand to return. The room was bright with midday sun and the air was thick with heat, but the silver felt cool against my fingertips, crisp and refreshing as rain on a sultry day. The girl in the mirror was looking at me with startled disbelief, her full lips parted in an O of shock.

I was telling myself I had only imagined it when Penda burst through the doors, breathing hard, as if she had climbed the steps of the tower as fast as she possibly could.

"A new suitor has come for the princess," she said in a rush, barely looking at me. "Come quickly. His welcome feast is already underway!"

I took her arm and hurried with her to the dining hall, feeling hopeful and excited. *Our plan is finally in motion.* The servants had decorated the chamber lavishly for the welcome feast. The marble colonnades gleamed in the lamplight, the reflecting pool was filled with floating lanterns, and noble guests danced about the courtyard to the soft plucking of koras. The emperor sat at his stool with his wives, and advisers knelt upon their feasting couches, taking small sips from nearby goblets.

Mariama was among them, wearing a wrapper of midnight blue and shivering despite the heat. I had not seen her looking so anxious since before we had found the map. *Something is wrong*, I thought.

She caught my eye and mouthed, "I am sorry."

I watched her without comprehending. The guilt in her eyes should have made me wary, but all I could feel was confusion, mixed with a bewilderment that pricked my mouth like fish bones. My mind swarmed with questions, one after another in painful succession. *Why is she sorry? What could she possibly have to apologize for?*

That was when I saw that a young man was sitting on a stool opposite the emperor, the seat of the guest of honor, looking grim and brave.

A coldness slid into my veins, creeping toward my heart. It was Kader.

12

"Your Imperial Majesty, I formally present to you my son for the Trials!" Lord Bagayogo cried, lifting his goblet in triumph. He wore a smile so broad it seemed his face might split. "I know he will win them, wed your daughter, and make us all very proud."

For one long, horrible moment, my mind went blank. My body felt numb, and I itched all over, as if a colony of termites had taken up residence beneath my skin.

Sharp panic coiled like twine around my ribs, and I felt myself taking fast gulps of air, as though I had just come up from a swim in very cold and deep water.

The realization washed over me in waves. Kader was Mariama's newest suitor. *Kader.* Yesterday he had been mine alone, but today he was the princess's long-awaited one hundredth suitor, the man who would steal from a god's house and finally win the Trials. Alarmed as I was by this knowledge, a knot of certainty in my stomach assured me that he was not here by choice. Other noblemen might choose the Trials willingly, lured by their thirst for power and the magnetic pull of Mariama's gold, but Kader was not like them.

Someone else had made this choice for him.

Mariama told me that the Trials were her father's strategy to reduce his enemies by killing their sons. She said every young noble who died in the suitor's kettle was like a brick in the wall guarding the empire. Perhaps the emperor was displeased with Lord Bagayogo and meant to punish him by condemning his youngest son to death. But neither Emperor Suleyman nor Lord Bagayogo looked to be in an ill humor. If anything, they seemed amused.

I watched them from the shadows as servants rustled and whispered around me.

Kader prostrated himself before the emperor, respectfully sprinkling dust upon his head as he did so. "I shall make Her Highness my bride, or else die trying," he said solemnly, repeating the words of ninety-nine suitors before him.

Anguish washed through me when I thought about all those dead young men. What would happen to Kader if the map turned out to be useless and we never reached the forge house? What would happen if he returned to Timbuktu empty-handed like all the other suitors? Who was to say that Kader would not join them in their awful fate?

I looked helplessly about the feasting hall, understanding the cold significance of everything I saw. Platters heaped with dates and plantains and Nile perch and goat cheese. Overturned cushions. Palm leaves draped ceremoniously across the tiles. Noble supper guests with their clatter of stools and the rattle of amber beads at their necks. Was it a festive celebration? Or was it Kader's funeral?

It took everything in me to keep my composure, to force myself not to cry out in front of all the court. I wanted to shout, *It cannot be him! Find another suitor to sacrifice!* I heard myself let loose a sick little laugh instead, like a jackal. I tasted angry tears on my tongue; the salt of them stung my skin.

I remained in the shadows while Jeneba swept through the feasting hall, weaving as easily as a water serpent through the flocks of lords and marabouts and kings until, finally, she reached her target: Kader.

Under the pretense of refilling his goblet, she pressed a folded paper square into his hand. I knew what the note would say. I had written it myself. He would follow its instructions and slip away from the feast, descending staircase after staircase into the bowels of the palace, where storerooms held the emperor's abundance of oil, grain, and gold. There, he would find me, and I was to show him the map and explain how it could help him win the Trials.

In the morning, he would journey with the horsemen, Penda, Jeneba, and myself into the desert, our horses traveling swiftly toward the forge house of a god. I had worried over our plan for weeks, but it had never unsettled me so much as now, with the understanding that *Kader* would be the suitor to attempt this dangerous mission. He was not some stranger who was trying to win the princess's hand. He was *my love*, and anything that jeopardized his safety was unacceptable.

A while later, I waited for Kader in the dark of the grain storeroom, my mind racing. Even if everything went according to plan and Kader used the god's hammer to survive the kettle and win the Trials, he would be wed to Mariama and not to me. He would be someone else's husband. This would not, could not, end well. I began to feel sick. My heartbeat was ringing so loudly in my ears that I scarcely heard his descent upon the stairs.

And then Kader was so near me that I could catch the familiar scent of him: soap and ink and castor oil. "Amie, I can explain," he said, closing the gap between us in three fast strides and pulling me clumsily into his arms. "This was not my choice, it was my father's. He does not want the two of us to marry. That is why he is making me attempt the Trials, even though he knows they are a death sentence. He would rather see me dead than wed to you."

"Your father made you do it," I repeated breathlessly. My relief gave way to an anger at Lord Bagayogo that seared my insides. How could he condemn his own son to death?

Kader nodded without dropping his gaze from mine. "Last night, Father brought over a nobleman's daughter he thought would make a suitable bride for me. When I told her that my heart already belonged to another, Father exploded with anger and said he would rather me dead than still in love with you." His eyes lit up with a sudden burst of excitement and urgency. "Amie, if we are to leave, we must do it now. There will be turmoil when my father and the emperor discover that we are gone, so we have to escape as soon as possible to acquire a strong start. Everything is at the ready. I have hired a riverboat and paid off the dockmen. We must make haste."

I wrung my hands, feeling uneasy. "What? How did you pay them?"

"With my tutoring money."

No. "And how much do you have left?"

"Just two hundred cowries," he admitted, wincing. "But do not worry, I can make more!"

My pulse hissed loudly in my ears as I thought of what would happen if I ran away with Kader tonight. Two hundred cowries was only enough to keep our bellies full for a fortnight, and a riverboat journey could take months. I envisioned our pockets emptying as the waters pulled us south to the rainforests by the sea. When we reached our destination, he and I would be in a distant coastal land without any food or gold.

I took a deep breath and said, "We cannot go."

Confusion swept across his face. "But we *must* go, otherwise I will die!" he protested. "No one has ever survived the Trials."

"Not yet," I said. "But you could be the first."

He looked at me strangely, so I told him everything as quickly as I could. I showed him the enchanted map and explained that it led to Hausakoy's home in the desert. Inside the forge house was the god's enchanted hammer, which would enable Kader to survive the suitor's kettle.

"But Hausakoy's hammer is the least of his treasures, is it not? Isn't he also richer than any mortal king?" he asked when I had finished.

At first, I was simply surprised that a boy like Kader, from a family of Malinke nobles, knew so much about the Songhai gods. Then I realized what he was suggesting. "Kader! You have no intention of ever stepping into the suitor's kettle, do you." My breath caught in my throat. "You want to follow the map, take Hausakoy's riches for yourself—for *ourselves*—and flee the empire."

"We do not really have a choice," he pointed out. "If we return to Timbuktu, I will have to marry the princess."

My stomach twisted with guilt—because he was right. We could never return, not if we wanted to stay together. By choosing him, I would have to betray Mariama and the others, too. But I knew I would choose him. I would choose *us*.

It was crucial for Penda and Jeneba to believe that Kader intended to return to Timbuktu for the suitor's kettle and the wedding. If they suspected otherwise, they would try to stop us.

Shame sat thickly in my throat, making it difficult to say the words that came next. "We cannot rob the forge house and then just abandon Penda and Jeneba in the desert," I began. "We must give them food and water and horses first. And we will leave the map with them, so they can return it to Mariama. That way, they can give it to the next suitor." My mind worked quickly, my thoughts turning and revolving like a spindle. "I will write her a note of explanation—something like *I am sorry to prolong the Trials, but Kader cannot marry you. Although I cannot tell you exactly where we are, please know that we are safe.* She will be livid, of course. She wants to end the Trials more than anything, and she will not like that we have delayed things. But she'll have to understand eventually."

He turned to me, dark eyes filled with surprise. "She really hates the Trials that much?" His features seemed sharper than usual under the unsteady glimmer of the storeroom's oil lamps.

"She absolutely despises them. You should see her, she's a wreck before and after the executions. She has terrible nightmares about them." I paused, remembering how distraught Mariama had seemed on my first day in the palace, her kohl-darkened tears before the execution. Even though I had not yet known her, I had still felt a desire to comfort her.

Now I felt an intense protectiveness toward Mariama, mixed with a feeling I was afraid to name aloud. It was a strange longing that made my breath quicken.

"The princess is a good person," I said. "She is nothing like her father."

"It seems that she and I have that in common, anyway," he said bitterly.

I began to tell Kader about the plan for the morning, scarcely believing how quickly everything had changed. "Now, my love, you must listen to this next part carefully," I said. "Tomorrow at dawn, the other maids and I will serve you breakfast, and then we will climb into the three charmed saddlebags we have weaved. Take care to strap our bags to your horse very tightly, so that we do not fall out. And once the horsemen have fallen asleep and the four of us are alone in the desert, you and I must put on a great show of not being in love to throw the girls off our scent. Oh! And you must remember not to eat your breakfast."

He raised his thick eyebrows. "Why not?"

"Because it will be dosed with sleeping potion for the emperor's men," I reminded him. "Haven't you been listening?"

"I apologize," he said with a sigh. "It is just that this is a complicated plan. What if something goes wrong?"

"Nothing will go wrong," I told him as confidently as I could manage. "I will not allow it."

———•———

Penda, Jeneba, and Mariama were waiting for me in the princess's chamber. They had been sitting together on the carpets, but they all climbed to their feet as I entered. Penda and Jeneba wore identical expressions of anticipation on their faces, and Mariama chewed nervously at her lower lip.

"Well?" asked Jeneba as soon as she saw me. "What did His Lordship say?"

"His Lordship?" I was confused.

"Yes, the young lord Bagayogo," she said impatiently. "Is he quite aligned with our plan?"

"Oh. Yes, yes, he is," I said. I had never referred to Kader as *His Lordship*. It sounded strange.

"Good. He looked positively perplexed when I gave him the note at supper," Jeneba said with a sigh. "I've never met a man so oblivious to my charms."

It was silly, but her words filled me with relief. Kader wanted only me, and even beautiful creatures like Jeneba and Mariama were beneath his notice.

"Issatou says that this potion is incredibly powerful," I told them, thrusting a stoppered bottle into Mariama's hands. The liquid within was pale as goat's milk, but it moved slowly, like sap. "No more than one spoonful in their porridge tomorrow morning, else their sleep will never end."

She whispered into my ear, "I am so, so sorry. Kader is yours. He has always been yours. I promise that when we are wed, I will not touch him. I will be his wife in name only. I will not even—"

"I understand, Your Highness," I said. I could not stand to keep talking about what would happen after she married Kader, because I knew it would never happen. She had no idea that he and I were not coming back.

"Really, Amie, he is yours," she insisted. "Please know that I only intend to marry him to save him from death and to end the Trials."

"I know." I felt suddenly overcome with guilt and exhaustion. I did not want to look into the three girls' faces and think about how I was going to betray them all.

While they talked breathlessly among themselves and practiced hiding within the enchanted saddlebags, I dragged a blanket to the corner of Mariama's bedchamber, blocked out the lamplight with a cushion, and fell asleep immediately. I imagine I slept only two or three hours, perhaps less, because the lamps were still burning and the moon had barely changed position in the sky when Mariama shook me awake.

"Amie, you cannot go," she whispered. Although her voice was steady, she wore an expression of pure terror.

"Cannot go where?" I sat up, glancing around the chamber in alarm.

I could not for the life of me imagine what had so frightened Mariama. There was nothing at all threatening in her room. Penda and Jeneba slept by the door, one of them steadily snoring.

"You cannot go into the desert," she said. "It is not safe."

I blinked up at her, confused. Of *course* desert travel was not safe—but we had all agreed that the benefits of such a journey outweighed the dangers.

"But it is not safe for them, either," I protested, pointing at Penda and Jeneba, who were still lost in slumber.

"We are not speaking of them, we are speaking of you," she said coldly.

What was this really about? I had a rising suspicion that Mariama had somehow discovered my plan to run away with Kader, and she was trying to make me stay.

My temper flared along with my guilt. "But I *have* to go! We have been preparing for weeks."

"You forget yourself." Mariama's hands balled into fists. "I am the emperor's daughter. You would do well not to cross me."

I took a deep breath and tried a new tack. "Forgive me, Your Highness, but I must go with the others. If you are to wed him at the end of all this, I cannot bear to be away from Kader for another moment. To be apart from him any longer would surely be torture, you must understand—"

"I forbid you to leave me!" she said sharply. Then her mouth began to tremble, and her eyes filled with tears. "Amie, you must have noticed by now how terribly lonely my life is. I never had a friend before you came to the palace. If you leave, I will have no one."

Her display of vulnerability made my breath catch in my throat. "I will only be away a few days," I lied.

"Promise you will remain with me at court." She moved almost imperceptibly closer to me and whispered, "I need you here."

Now I could smell the sweetness of her, soap and oil and perfume and, beneath that, the heady scent of her sweat.

I heard myself whisper, "I promise," before I could stop myself.

Her face lit up. "Do you?"

I nodded slowly. "I promise I will stay here with you."

Of course, I intended to do nothing of the sort, but I had to placate her now.

Mariama really did look terrified at the notion of being in the palace without me, and I felt awful for telling her the falsehood. My guilt ripened like fruit when she reached out and took my hand. I could feel the warmth of her breath on my fingers as she pressed her lips gently to my palm, holding eye contact as she did it.

"Kader is yours," she said with her mouth against my hand. Her eyes were black as the night sky. Her voice shook. I could already imagine her despair when she found out about my betrayal.

How could I do this to a girl so kindhearted?

"Yes, Your Highness. I understand," I whispered. "Thank you."

I tried to think of Kader, of our life together. But in truth, being so close to Mariama had almost made me forget our plans for the future. I could hear my breathing coming out raspy and ragged. I sensed prickling heat where her leg pressed against mine. My head was spinning.

She looked at me from under her eyelashes, half-taunting, half-fearful, as if to say, I dare you.

But she only asked, "You'll really stay here with me?"

"Of course I'll stay," I said. Despite how I felt about her, it was still a lie.

13

I awoke at dawn filled with a strange, restless energy. Mariama still slept beside me, her thick-lashed eyes closed. I studied her quietly, the red beams of early sunlight tossed about her body and her black hair tumbled about her sleeping form.

I needed to leave. Last night, it had been easier to tell her false-hoods, promising that I would stay with her at court and never leave her side. The night sky had cloaked my guilt as I'd looked into her eyes and lied to her directly. But I feared I could not keep up my pretense in the light of morning. If Mariama asked me again, I would have to tell her the truth: that I was leaving forever. I had to choose—and I chose Kader.

I knew I was being cowardly by not being honest with Mariama. My heart was heavy. I was still the same girl who lacked the strength to speak up when it counted. When Penda and Jeneba left with the morning linen, I followed them out of Mariama's bedchamber and quietly made my way around to the other side of the tower and down the narrow staircase.

The palace was cast in rivulets of pink and golden light as we walked to the courtyard kitchens. The stillness of dawn gradually gave way to a burst of morning activity: the pounding of millet, the chopping of firewood, the milking of goats, the rattle of sandals upon tiles. Many servants thronged the kitchen, working so intently that they scarcely paid the three of us any attention as we prepared porridge for Kader and the emperor's horsemen.

Jeneba and I watched as Penda stirred three careful spoonfuls of the sleeping draught into the bubbling pot. The potion was odorless and clear as water. It must have been tasteless, too, because the emperor's horsemen consumed their porridge quickly when we served it to them, never giving any indication that it tasted of poison. Each man demanded second helpings—all except for Kader, who remembered what I'd told him and feigned a stomachache.

I stole quick glances at him when I could, savoring the sight of him, and he in turn took every opportunity to stare into my eyes when the others were not looking. *You are making the right choice*, I told myself. *He is your future.*

Kader's presence made me feel warm, even as I watched the unsuspecting horsemen consume Issatou's potion. If everything went according to our plan, the emperor's soldiers would fall asleep after journeying a few hours into the desert. Then Kader would signal for Penda, Jeneba, and me to emerge from our saddlebags. We would leave the horsemen to their enchanted slumber, driving their horses on toward the house of the blacksmith god while the sleeping men stayed behind, blanketed by the sands. It was a terrible thing, but we planned to return to the soldiers one or two days later, on our way back to the palace. We would give them the antidote then, and they would awaken and return to the city, not remembering the days they had lost.

This had seemed like a solid, if not impenetrable, plan when we had first devised it. But now that it was all really happening, the cracks were beginning to show. What would happen if the sleeping draught was ineffective and the emperor's men never fell asleep? Or what if the potion was all too effective and the horsemen slept on forever, unable to be revived? What would happen if they were attacked in their slumber by bandits or a pack of wild animals? Would the "deathless, dreamless" sleep Issatou had promised protect the horsemen from violent deaths such as these?

As I watched those three young men shovel porridge into their mouths, their lips shining, I knew that I would not be able to forgive myself if any harm came to them on my account. Their deaths would remain forever on my conscience. But I knew, too, that I would not let Kader die in the suitor's kettle. We had to proceed with the plan.

After breakfast, I snuck off to the stables to help conceal Penda, who held the enchanted map, and Jeneba, who had the sleeping draught and antidote, within the saddlebags. We had woven them well, and the bags' insides were so spacious that both girls could conceal themselves with ease. I was preparing to climb into my own bag when Mariama appeared suddenly in the doorway, flanked by grooms.

My body went rigid, frozen with the realization that I had been caught. I could not hide in a saddlebag, not now. Not with the princess watching us.

Her eyes found mine, and she sighed heavily. "There you are," she cried, running to me and grasping my hands. "Where have you been all morning?"

"Helping with breakfast," I said truthfully.

The grooms and stable hands worked quickly around us, fastening Kader's bags onto a gray riding mare and passing the reins to one of the horsemen we had just drugged. I watched helplessly as a stout young groom heaved away the saddlebag into which I had been about to climb. I would have to find another method of following Kader and the others into the desert.

Mariama tightened her grip on my hands. "Oh, Amie, I am so glad you are staying here with me." Her eyes were wide, and I could see the relief and gratitude within them.

My heart lurched. "Of course I am staying!" I said through gritted teeth. I felt torn between my guilt over abandoning her and my annoyance that escaping was proving more difficult than I had anticipated.

"I know you want to go with Kader," she said. "But I need you to remain with me at court. Why don't you take the afternoon off and try on some of my clothes? You can wear anything you like—my jewels, too."

"I would like that," I said softly. Guilt bloomed in the back of my chest.

"Are the girls in their saddlebags?" she asked.

"Yes." I pointed at their hiding places.

I suspected that Penda and Jeneba could hear our current exchange, and I wondered what they thought of it. It was not as if they could poke their heads out of their saddlebags and tell me, not in front of the stable hands. Were they confused? Surprised? Perhaps not, for they had long known that I was Mariama's favorite. Perhaps they already understood that she could not bear to be parted from me.

"Come with me," she urged, her eyes darting between me and the stables, a tremor in her voice betraying her unease. It was a command, but she did not sound commanding.

Reluctantly, I followed Mariama away from the stables, past the pens of braying, stinking livestock. Now hand in hand, the princess and I made our silent way through the windowless halls of the imperial armory with its rows and rows of shelves full of bronze and silver weapons: swords, arrows, spears, shields, and daggers. When I asked Mariama why she was taking me this way, she said she didn't want us to be found. I was not sure what she meant by it. And I had never before visited this part of the palace, which was off-limits to maidservants, and I was shocked at the sheer scope of weaponry in the emperor's possession. He had enough military supplies for an army of fifty thousand men. Perhaps Emperor Suleyman was more worried about the threat of rebellion than he let on. It looked as if he were preparing for a war.

We walked those uninhabited corridors for several minutes, our footsteps a whisper against the tiles. Mariama led me, knowing the palace far better than I did. I was unable to recognize my surroundings until we passed under an archway and found ourselves enveloped in white-and-yellow daylight.

I blinked, my eyes adjusting to the sight of the palace yard and the seven terra-cotta statues of the gods that dotted its length. Kader, the horsemen, his father, and Emperor Suleyman all waited by the gates alongside a group of blue-robed noblemen and their wives. Seeing Kader and Mariama standing so close to each other threw my mind into disarray. I wanted to be loyal to them both at once but knew it was impossible. I wanted to throw myself into his arms. I was choosing him, but I felt guilty for betraying her. She had been so kind to me during my time at court, defending me against Lord Bagayogo and treating me like a noblewoman even though I was just a maid. I wondered if I'd ever see her again.

The day was hot. Some of the women were soaking their feet in the reflecting pool, which shone like a mirror under the direct sunlight. In the market, a crowd was gathering. Merchants and other commoners jostled by the gates, knocking against one another and peering up into the palace yard. All were eager to set eyes upon the new suitor.

If Kader felt uncomfortable before the droves of market-goers and their insistent stares, he did not show it. He stood tall with his shoulders back, his face handsome and serious. His dark eyes were fixed steadily on mine, regarding me with bewilderment—he did not understand why I was not hidden in his saddlebags. I wondered if he thought I had changed my mind about accompanying him into the desert. Did he think I was capable of breaking my promises to him?

I was not. Although I couldn't deny that Mariama had captured a part of my heart over the past weeks, I needed to escape Timbuktu in order to secure my future with Kader. As soon as I could find an excuse to leave, I planned to make my way to the edge of the city and find a horse to follow his caravan into the desert. He had my loyalty, now and always. I wanted to pull him aside and explain that the princess had prevented me from hiding in his luggage with the others, but for the moment, I could do nothing to mitigate his fears. I tried to communicate with my eyes that he had nothing to worry about.

Mariama noticed me staring at him. "Kader has not eaten any of the porridge, has he?" She squeezed my hand tightly, as if she feared I'd float away.

"No. He did not even touch his breakfast," I assured her.

There came a loud clattering of hooves from behind us. I turned to see the emperor's horsemen leading four luggage-laden riding mounts out into the sunlit yard. I knew it would take hours for the sleeping draught to absorb fully into their blood. For now, the horsemen were as spry and alert as ever as they helped Kader mount his gray mare and then climbed atop their own horses. The emperor said a quick and solemn prayer of encouragement, as he always did. Sneering, Lord Bagayogo wished his son luck. The crowd roared in approval, a thunderous sound that made my mouth go dry.

With that, the horsemen began to ride out of the yard and away from the palace. Kader, following several paces behind them, twisted back in his saddle to look at me. His heavy eyebrows were crumpled with alarm and disbelief.

I wanted to run after him, to cry out that I was coming for him, that we would soon be together. But I stayed silent, squeezing Mariama's hand with frustration as the horsemen continued on through the crowded market. We watched the caravan snake along the riverbank, drawing ever closer to the sandy scrubland at the city's northern edge.

Soon, the emperor went back inside. The nobles quickly followed, glad for an excuse to escape the noonday heat. Lord Bagayogo—my almost father-in-law, my tormentor—smiled mockingly as he passed me. I watched him walk into the palace and vanish behind the archway. I reminded myself that once I escaped, I would never have to see him again. *Good riddance.*

Gradually, the rest of the crowd dispersed. The servants closed the gates and went back inside. The palace yard was empty, save for myself and Mariama. Holding hands, we watched Kader's caravan grow smaller and smaller against the enormity of the desert. Soon, his horse would only be a distant speck upon the horizon, fading before my eyes. The thought filled me with dread. What if the wind washed his footsteps from the sand and I found myself unable to follow his trail?

Mariama, sensing that his departure made me miserable, wrapped an arm around me in consolation. Guilt bloomed at the back of my throat. She cared for me. I cared for her. And now I was going to abandon her. Still, part of me was painfully aware that every second I spent with her increased the distance between me and Kader. If I were ever to catch up to him, I needed to sneak away from her, and soon. But how would I do it? What excuse could I give that would not make her suspicious?

I searched for words, but nothing came to me. I was beginning to despair when a familiar voice called out, "Aminata! There you are."

I looked up to see my parents rushing over, their eyes wild. A lump formed in my throat when I saw that my father's robes were improperly tied and my mother's hair was undone, her fingers bare of their usual rings. That was how I knew it was an emergency. My parents had always been preoccupied with appearances, and they would never go out in public looking less than their best unless it was a crisis.

I noted the rare anxiety in my father's voice as he addressed the princess. "Pardon us, Your Highness," was his greeting to her when they reached the gates. "But might we have a moment alone with our daughter?"

"These are your parents?" Mariama looked closely at them, as if trying to find my features behind theirs. Then she started back toward the palace, a small half smile on her face. "Hurry back," she told me as she stepped through the doors.

She was gone before I could respond. I realized I was free of her, and in a perfect position to follow Kader into the desert—with one exception, my visibly distressed parents.

My mother seized my shoulders with a viselike grip. "Where on earth have you hidden your sister?"

I frowned, not sure what to make of this. "Is she not with her husband?"

"Of course she is not!" Her voice was thick with desperation. "He is the one who declared her missing!"

Father said tightly, "Aminata, you would do well to be honest with us. We will not punish you for hiding her, we only want to know where she is."

Mother's tone was more accusatory. "How much did Haddy bribe you to shut her up in the palace?" she demanded. "Did she offer to pay your debt to us?'" Her eyes bored into mine, searching for any sign of deception.

"She didn't bribe me," I told her, looking away. I couldn't believe she thought that. As if I could be bought. As if I would allow my sister to buy me!

And if Haddy really was missing, did her disappearance have something to do with the Scorpion Order? Regret wrapped its hands around my throat. She had asked me for a private audience and I had refused her. Perhaps if I had swallowed my pride and spoken with her, she might have told me about her plan to leave her husband for an insurgency of sorcerers.

All at once, I wondered if she had run away at all. She might have been arrested instead. Ugly images scurried across my mind. Haddy, chained and bruised. Haddy, pacing her desert cell like a caged animal. Haddy, suspected of treason and sentenced to death without a trial.

But I could not believe that she was imprisoned or dead. Though the emperor had no trouble punishing lowborn rebels like the bold-tongued leatherworkers his soldiers had executed at market, he would not arrest a noblewoman—at least, not without telling her husband and family first.

She must have run away of her own accord.

"Wherever Haddy has gone, I am quite certain that she will be able to fend for herself," I told my parents. She was a sorceress, after all. Her spells could bend metal and sharpen knives, and I did not doubt she could use her magic in self-defense if she needed to. My parents might not have understood this, but I did.

My mother shouted, "Tell us where she is!" Then she slapped me.

The sting of it sent aftershocks through my skull. I had been leaning against the palace gates as if in a trance, letting my parents interrogate me. But when I felt the burn of my mother's palm upon my cheek, I started away from her, my temper rising.

"Why would I help her run away from her husband after what she's done to me?" I shouted. "Why would I help her with anything at all? And where could I hide her where her husband could not reach her? Certainly not in the palace with its hundreds of spies!"

"Not so loud," said my father tensely, eyes darting.

I followed his nervous gaze to the market, where some of the younger, poorer merchants were watching us and giggling. I recognized the panicked look in his eye—he did not want to draw attention to our conversation.

"Damn you both," I said, not bothering to lower my voice. "I promise I have nothing to do with her disappearance, but it serves you right that she's gone. It serves you both right for marrying off a girl of sixteen to an old drunkard like Lord Ayouta!"

I reeled back, surprised by the words I had just spoken. I was not at all accustomed to talking back to my parents, not even after a lifetime of their snide comments and blatant favoritism.

"We have looked everywhere," my father said, his eyes filling with tears. "His Lordship is threatening to take back her bride-price if we cannot find her."

So it is all about money, I thought bitterly. Of course. For a moment, I had thought that Haddy's disappearance could move my father to tears. But he was, as always, primarily concerned with his treasury.

"You must help us find her," insisted my mother. Under the harsh sunlight she looked tired, and the lines around her mouth seemed deeper than I remembered.

"I will do nothing of the sort," I said, a new lightness settling into my limbs. When had I ever denied them? The feeling was intoxicating. "You didn't believe me when I said I'd been faithful to Kader. You locked me away for more than a month, and then you sent me here to earn back the expense of my canceled wedding. But I owe you no such debt!"

My mother started back, as if my words had been a physical blow.

Taking a deep breath, I added, "As for Haddy, I would not worry too much about her. She is bound to turn up eventually."

My father whispered, "Amie, for shame."

"Go and find your favorite," I told them.

Then I fled.

I tore past the palace gates and into the market, running faster than I ever had in my life. I raced like a madwoman through the crowded streets until I reached the end of the city, at the herdsmen's compounds in that desolate stretch of scrubland that separated Timbuktu from the desert.

Here lived some of the most impoverished people in the empire. Between their thatched-roof huts were sandy little gardens set with broken sticks for climbing vines and stretches of rope for laundry. They subsisted on livestock—goats, hens, spotted pigs—and the most well-off among them sold larger pack animals. I hoped to persuade one of them to sell me a horse so that I could follow after Kader's caravan.

Sweat streamed down my face as I appraised the huts and pens, trying to catch my breath. I noticed a group of young herdsmen—boys, really, yet unable to grow hair on their faces—gathered by an ancient-looking wooden stable. I felt them watching me, which made me nervous, but I so longed to be reunited with Kader and away from this city that I wished that kind Penda and bold Jeneba were with me as I approached the young herdsmen. I forced myself to be courageous and approach them alone.

"I need to buy a riding horse," I told one of the boys in as confident a tone as I could muster. My voice was hoarse from shouting at my parents, and my borrowed blue wrapper clung to my sweat-slick skin.

"Why—yes, my lady." He and the other boys exchanged smirks. "But it'll cost you one hundred cowries."

My lady. One hundred cowries. He thought I was a noblewoman, no doubt because I was still wearing Mariama's fine clothes.

"I am afraid that I haven't any money with me," I admitted, inwardly cursing my stupidity. Why hadn't I stolen some of Mariama's cowries or jewelry when I had had the chance?

"Fine, then," he replied. "You can get out of here."

"No, wait!" My hands flew to my ears. "What about these earrings? They are pure silver, and worth far more than one hundred cowries. Can they buy me a riding horse?" I unfastened the silver fire finch earring that Kader had gifted me on my first day in the palace, along with the perfect replica that Haddy had carved with her magic spell. I thrust them into his hands.

He frowned doubtfully, considering the earrings. "Are they really silver?" he asked finally.

"Yes, pure silver, I promise," I said. I did not want to give away Kader's gift, or Haddy's, but it seemed I had no choice. "I wager you could exchange them for two or three new horses at market."

The boy gave an uninterpretable grunt, pocketed my earrings, and disappeared into the stables. He was gone for such a long time that I began to worry he would not return. I tried my best to ignore the talk of the other herdsmen while I waited, but it was difficult, especially when so much of their conversation centered on the curve of my breasts and the spread of my hips beneath my borrowed wrapper.

It was a relief when the first boy finally returned, leading a young Barb stallion with a mane like yellow silk. "The stable master agreed that the earrings were worth it. This is the best one we've got," he explained tersely. "Who's to ride it? Your husband?"

"I will ride it myself," I replied, taking the reins from him.

He widened his eyes, and the other herdsmen hooted in laughter. I had shocked them. Of course I had—it was seen as improper for a young girl to ride on horseback. The only reason my father had taught me and Haddy to ride was that he had always wanted sons.

I tried to ignore the feeling of so many eyes upon me as I carefully mounted the horse. Quick as I could manage, I urged it on to a trot and then a gallop, treading over sandy scrubland toward the two roads leading out of the city. I knew that one of the roads led northwest to Marrakech, while the other snaked northeast to Ghadames and Tripoli. I followed the northeastern trading road, as Kader had, because all the previous suitors had started out on this route. I said a little prayer under my breath that I would soon catch up to his caravan. And then I was alone in the desert and heard no sounds at all, save for the quick hoofbeats and the faint wind and my own shallow breathing.

14

I rode on, following the hoofprints in the sand thankfully still left by Kader's caravan. The farther I ventured from the city, the more unfamiliar the landscape became. The soil grew gradually looser, the shrubs and doom palms disappeared, and I soon found myself surrounded by rippling dunes with shadowy valleys and peaks as tall as trees. All was quiet: I heard no birdsongs, nor the buzz and croak of insects.

I had passed all sixteen years of my life in Timbuktu, with its crowds and its markets and its streets filled with man-made goods. The city I called home had been carved and hammered to precision by generations of skilled workmen, and I had grown accustomed to the comforting sensation of roads beneath my feet.

Until now, I had not realized how much I relied upon the reassuring presence of houses, temples, banks, and the many other stone buildings dotting my city. The soft, yielding desert terrain made me feel unmoored and unsteady. Everything was sand in all directions, an ocean of brown-gold sediment interrupted only by the occasional rock formation or cluster of dried reeds.

I traveled all afternoon through that unsettling silence and heat, my father's warnings about the dreadful desert creatures that could cause harm to an unaccompanied traveler ringing loudly in my ears: *Sand vipers. Smugglers. Scorpions. Marauders. Wild dogs.* My newly purchased stallion had a stubborn temperament and jerked his head with every step, tugging my arms forward with the reins until my upper body grew sore. I became hotter and thirstier as the hours wore on and cursed myself for not stopping at a well and filling a waterskin or two before I rode into the desert. I should have brought a shawl along, too. The sky was cloudless, and the midafternoon sun burned the skin of my neck and face.

It was not a pleasant journey, but at least my path was straightforward. The trading road was easily followed and well maintained, and the weak wind had done little to obscure the hoofprints Kader's caravan had made as they followed it deeper into the desert. My mind ran in anxious circles as the sun sank lower and lower against the reddening sky and the sand began to glow gold. I did not fret about getting lost since the path was clear. I trusted I would find Kader by nightfall. Instead, my worries were elsewhere.

Had Mariama yet noticed my absence? What would happen when she did? *I forbid you to leave me*, she'd said, and it had been impossible for me to ignore the pain in her eyes in that moment. When she found out I was gone, would she be angry? Would she send someone to retrieve me?

The sky grew darker, and I began to consider for the first time the terrifying possibility of having to spend the night alone in the desert. I really had to catch up to them before nightfall. If they moved off the trading route, I might not be able to pick up their trail in the morning.

I urged my horse ahead faster. A girl like me could come to a lot of trouble in this place. Smugglers regularly crossed these roads, transporting young women across the Sahara to the slave markets of Morocco, Algiers, and Tripoli. Teens were especially desired as domestic slaves and concubines, and I worried that I'd be taken by a caravan tonight if I was unlucky. The desert was also full of dangerous wildlife; during my father's trips to the salt mines of Taoudenni, members of his caravans sometimes died of snakebites and wild animal attacks. And then there was the threat of death from exposure to the cold. . . .

So when I finally came upon Kader's caravan, I almost wept with relief. At first, he didn't notice me approach. I shouted his name and urged my horse to go faster. "Thank the gods I've found you!" I cried as I raced toward him, my horse's hooves pounding against the sand. I kept my speed until I could make out the whites of Kader's eyes; only then did I slow the horse to a trot.

Kader rushed over to help me dismount. The feeling of his hands on my waist as he lifted me down to the sand filled me with comfort and clarity. My conscience was still heavy with how I'd left the princess, but I knew in my heart that Kader was the right choice. From this moment forward, I would be devoted only to Kader. Looking at him now, I felt my heart swell with loyalty.

"Why weren't you hidden in the saddlebags with the others?" he asked in a rush.

"My parents crept up on me right before I stepped into the saddlebags," I replied breathlessly, gazing up at him. "They wanted to know where Haddy has gone."

Kader looked up, stunned. "What do you mean? Gone where?"

"All I know is she ran away from her husband and now no one can find her." I shook my head. "My parents came to the palace just to interrogate me about it. As if I could know her whereabouts!"

"Aren't you worried about her?"

"No. Perhaps a bit," I admitted with a sigh. And then I told him about Haddy's sympathy for the rebels and her gift for sorcery, expecting him to balk or tell me I was speaking nonsense. But as always, he believed me wholeheartedly.

I told him next about how I had subsequently found my way to the herdsmen's compounds and successfully bartered my earrings for a riding horse. "I am sorry to have given away your gift," I finished.

He waved away my words. "I will buy you other pairs of

earrings—and necklaces and bracelets and strings of amber beads. We will be richer than royalty after we leave Hausakoy's forge house. And you will live like a queen every day for the rest of your life in our cottage by the sea."

I felt a burst of tenderness for him. He was so unlike his father, so kind and respectful.

He looked well—as handsome as ever, positively brimming with vitality. He smelled of ink and dust and sweat. I wanted to press my nose into his neck and breathe him in, and restrained myself only because we had planned to pretend mutual disinterest for Penda and Jeneba's benefit. If they realized we were still in love, even after our arranged marriage was canceled, they might suspect that we planned to run away with Hausakoy's treasures. I could not let that happen.

I wished I could embrace him, but I knew it would not be possible in full view of Penda and Jeneba, who were sitting tall in their saddles and looking down their noses at me.

But no, they were not looking down at me, I realized as Kader and I drew nearer. Their eyes were fixed instead upon three low blue lumps strewn across the ground.

All at once, I understood that the blue shapes were the emperor's three best horsemen, still in their sky-blue riding robes. They were sleeping, cushioned against the sand.

I called out to Penda, "The sleeping draught worked, then?"

She nodded, and I could not read her expression. "They collapsed about an hour ago," she told me.

Jeneba pointed over at them. "Enchanted slumber. I've never seen anything like it."

Neither have I, I thought as I looked closer at the sleeping horsemen. First, I hovered my hand over one man's lips and felt the heat of his breath. Then I pressed my ear to another man's chest and heard the slowed thump of his heartbeat. They were still living—that was good, for I had worried that they might be killed by the sleeping draught. I noticed that the horsemen did not sleep as people typically do, with their eyes closed and limbs in drowsy disarray. Instead, they lay stiff as wooden planks, their wide-open eyes unblinking.

Kader told me how it had happened. The horsemen had ridden steadily on all that afternoon, not showing any symptoms of intoxication. As evening approached, they had slowed their mounts in wordless unison and come to an abrupt halt. Then they'd dismounted, sunk sleepily to their knees, and—still without saying a word, as if their tongues had been cut out—stretched themselves out against the sand. Kader's words made me cringe. We had done something truly terrible to these three innocent men. I would never wish such a sleep upon anyone, not even an enemy.

An argument followed over what we should do with the slumbering horsemen. Jeneba and Kader wanted to honor our original plan to leave them sleeping in the desert and come back for them after we had returned from the forge house. Penda said it would not be right to abandon these men—they had done no wrong besides following the emperor's orders. She wanted to bring them with us on our journey, and after some thought, I agreed.

When I spoke my assent, Kader offered to help us conceal the heavy men in the charmed saddlebags and lift them up to be fastened against the horses. It was clumsy work, and although my arms ached with the effort, the worst part by far was having to feel their staring, empty eyes on us as we pushed their heavy bodies into the sacks.

I wondered if they could see their surroundings. Could they feel what was happening to them?

When Haddy and I were younger, we spent many long, cheerful afternoons building sandcastles and fortresses for our straw dolls. I would never again be able to recall those afternoons with fondness,

for now I understood how the dolls must have felt: lifeless and helpless, unable to defend themselves, unable even to scream.

———————•———————

We rode a few more hours after sundown until we found a suitable spot to camp for the night. Then we dismounted, took the
tack off the horses, and fed them. We kept the drugged horsemen
in their saddlebags, which were still affixed to the horses, and I
tried my best not to think of the terror those poor men might be
feeling, paralyzed and muffled in the darkness. We pitched a tent
and built a nearby fire over which we had our own little supper.
It was not small for lack of supplies, because the emperor's servants had packed us several days' provisions for four adult men:
gourds of water, clay pots, wicker baskets for steaming millet, flatbread crackers, dates, tea leaves, goat cheese, salt-cured meat, and
smoked fish. We might have feasted if we desired, but the unnatural slumber of the emperor's horsemen had turned our stomachs,
and so we ate little.

"I understand that Your Lordship was once engaged to Amie,"
Jeneba said, turning her attention to Kader. "Was it an affectionate
betrothal?"

"Not at all," I interrupted quickly before cursing my awkward-
ness. *Let her not discover our plan.*

Kader came to my rescue. "Our fathers are trading partners, but
Amie and I hardly knew each other," he said evenly. "I barely recognized her when she met me last night in the storeroom."

This response seemed to satisfy Jeneba, and she fell silent.

Then Penda asked, "Begging your pardon, but why has Your
Lordship decided to attempt the Trials in the first place? You're not
a foreigner, you live in Timbuktu. So surely you've seen what happens to men like you in the suitor's kettle."

"It was not my decision," said Kader, pain in his voice. "I know that the Trials are a death sentence, but my father forced me to compete. I have no other choice."

"Why would he do that?" Penda sounded appalled.

Kader made no response.

It is because of me, because Lord Bagayogo hates me more than he loves his son.

Kader set up his sleeping mat alongside the fire while the girls and I retired to our tent. I did not want to go with them, but I knew that I had to. Jeneba had already asked if my betrothal had been one of affection, and it would only confirm her suspicions if I stayed up late with him by the fire.

I waited for the others to fall asleep. The cold made me tired, and I soon found myself counting the stars through a hole in the tent's cloth ceiling in an effort to stay awake. I thought I had already known the night sky, but here in the desert, the sight was something else entirely. My view of the stars and planets through the hole in the tent's cloth ceiling was very clear, hundreds of thousands of white and gold pinpricks set against the black blanket of the sky.

Penda's shallow breath came out of the darkness. It struck my ear. "Amie," she whispered.

"What is it?"

She said sleepily, "You betrayed Her Highness's trust. Why?"

Because I have to be with Kader, I thought. *Because the two of us are going to run away with as much of Hausakoy's gold as we can carry.* I did not say that, of course. What I said instead was, "It made no sense for me to remain at court with the princess. Our plan was for all three of us to go. I cannot say why Mariama insisted on my staying behind at the last minute."

A vision came suddenly into my mind of the princess alone in her bedchamber, perhaps sleeping, perhaps restless. The image filled me with dull guilt and a sudden surge of longing to see her one more time. She deserved a true goodbye.

"The princess has never been at court without us, you know," Penda said. "Her father doesn't allow it. He wants us to accompany her everywhere because he's so controlling. . . ." She trailed off, and her breathing grew slow and rhythmic.

Beside her, Jeneba began very faintly to snore. I waited another hour or more, just to be sure that both girls truly slept, and then I crept out of the tent. Kader was waiting for me by the dying fire, faithful as ever.

"Are they sleeping?" he asked as I approached. He had removed his shirt for the night, and in the firelight the dark coils of his hair glowed like coals.

"I believe so," I said, standing over him. It was a nothing sort of response, but I could not improve upon it—all I could focus on was the way Kader's arms rippled as he pulled himself up from the sand to face me. Despite the difficulty of the day, I felt elated. He was perfect, and he was mine. "I imagine that the princess is very unhappy with me indeed," I offered, changing the subject. "She wanted me to remain with her at court, and I disobeyed her. What's worse, she believes you shall return to Timbuktu in two days' time, clutching Hausakoy's hammer in your hand so that you survive the suitor's kettle. She has no idea that she will never see you again."

"Why do you care what the princess thinks?" Kader said, wrinkling his nose.

"Because I care very much for Mari—for the princess," I amended. I did not want him to know how close I had grown to her during my time at court. I did not want him to learn about the nights I had spent curled up next to her on a mountain of silk pillows, our hands intertwined loosely as we slept. I wasn't telling him the full truth of my experience in the palace, but how could I explain what had happened between me and Mariama? "She has a kind soul. It felt awful to betray her trust."

"She is the emperor's daughter," he said with a shrug.

"What does that have to do with anything?"

"Don't you see? The imperial family cannot be trusted. They will praise your loyalty in one breath and sentence you to an early death in the next." His hands shook. "My father would rather see me boiled alive than wed to you. He prefers a dead son to a happy one. My father, the emperor, and all their ilk are the same—changeable and cruel, concerned with power above all else."

"Your father ripped my earlobe," I said. I had been debating whether to tell him.

He looked taken aback. "What? When?"

"At my first banquet in the palace. He said it was a disgrace that I'd humiliated you. He called me the most unthinkable names."

"Curse him," Kader spat. "I'm so sorry for it. You didn't deserve that treatment. My father can be monstrous." Then he reached over, touching my earlobe gingerly. "Does this hurt?"

I shook my head. "It is nearly healed."

He sighed. "He's a coward and a bully, attacking you. I cannot believe that I used to want to impress him. I used to want to be a soldier like my brothers so that he would like me better. I used to dream that I'd achieve a victory in battle and be promoted to lieutenant general and earn the emperor's favor, maybe be given a principality or a chiefdom in the western provinces. Father wants nothing more than for the emperor to hold his sons in high esteem; he wants us all to be war heroes and to be awarded land and titles. But I don't care about that anymore," he said with conviction. "I don't want what he wanted for me. I only want you."

"You really never cared about winning land or property?" I asked him, pleasantly surprised. It seemed that land and power were every nobleman's desire—but then again, Kader was different. He was *better*, and I loved him for it. "What if you were such an asset to the emperor's military that he made you a prince of Bambouk province?" Bambouk in the western mountains was known for its gold fields.

"I never wanted to join the military. I could never kill another person, not for all the gold in the mountains. Of course, my father hates that about me. He thinks I'm weak. People with power have no consciences, they're all without humanity, from my father to Lord Ayouta to the emperor and his daughter—"

"The princess is not like them," I interrupted, thinking of the gentle way she had bandaged my ear on my first night in the palace, the cool touch of her fingers on my face. She had defended me against Lord Bagayogo without knowing me, simply because it was the right thing to do. What came later . . .

He chuckled dryly. "I confess I do not know the girl, but do you really believe that the emperor of Mali sired a kindhearted daughter? Whatever motives she had for trying to keep you with her at court, they cannot have been all good."

I wanted to argue further, but I knew that it would be of no use. Kader could be stubborn, and it was often difficult to change his opinions once he had set his mind on something. He was of noble Malinke blood, just like Mariama, so I did not understand why he was so wary of her. Why did Kader think she was so different from himself? Actually, the more I thought about it, the more I realized that the two of them had something in common. Kader and Mariama had both endured horrors at the hands of their fathers. And the lack of wages in my pocket even after weeks in the palace reminded me that I, too, was a member of this sad club.

I watched in silence as Kader stood and began to rummage within one of the small pouches that hung from his mare. That was when I realized that all his bags had been refastened and tied to the still sleeping horses. "You—you've packed!" I exclaimed. "Why?"

"Hush, or the girls will hear you," he said, retrieving a waterskin from his pouch and then gently leading me to my own yellow stallion. "We must leave them."

A wave of disapproval and reproach swept through me as I realized the cruel trick he meant to play on the others. "But what of Penda and Jeneba?" I protested. "We cannot simply leave them here."

He looked at me as if I had grown a second head. "Why, of course we can."

"My love, we cannot abandon two girls of eighteen in the desert. They might be set upon in the night!"

"We are not too far from the city," he said with a shrug. "We shall leave them two horses and enough food and water for their journey back to the palace."

"But I thought . . ." I trailed off, distressed. "I thought we would remain with them until we reached the forge house, at least."

"What is the point of taking the girls with us? They will only slow us down, and what would we do with them once we got there?"

"Penda needs money so that she can hire someone to track down her missing brothers," I explained. "And Jeneba is an orphan—a share of the gold would change her life forever."

He watched me speak without taking his eyes off my lips.

Despite myself, I knew that he was right. Our travels would indeed be far more efficient without the girls. But I had already abandoned Mariama. I could not leave Penda and Jeneba, too. We were becoming friends, and my conscience would not allow it.

"We cannot leave them," I insisted, holding his gaze defiantly.

"Very well, fire finch," he conceded with only a note of reluctance in his voice. "We will sleep here tonight. We will not leave the others quite yet."

"Thank you."

I felt a tremor of satisfaction as I watched him remove the supply bags and pouches. The rest of the bags he left tied to the horses.

"You look beautiful tonight," he said when he was finished. "Your wrapper becomes you."

My face grew warm from his gaze—and from guilt. "It is not mine. It belongs to the princess." *One more thing I have taken from her.*

Kader did not seem to notice. He only smiled and asked, "May I kiss you?"

When I nodded, he lifted me up into his arms and set me down gently by the fire, our backs turned against the warmth of the flames. The two of us remained there under the stars for hours, kissing and whispering until I nearly burst with desire. My lips felt swollen and bruised, and my skin thrilled with the sensation of his hands on me.

Kader's thin arms were surprisingly strong, and although I loved when he wrapped them around me, there always lingered in the back of my mind an uneasy understanding that, if he wanted to, he could crush my rib cage as easily as I could snap a twig. I felt the press of him against me and found myself sorely tempted to let him undress me as if it were our wedding night. But he saw the battle raging beneath my skin and released me.

We sat facing each other, both of us breathing hard. The stars seemed closer and brighter than ever.

Then came a harsh animal whine from somewhere in the darkness, beyond our camp.

15

I stiffened with fear. "What was that?" I whispered.

The darkness whined again, followed by a chorus of high-pitched yips and barks. The sound brought a rush of blood to my head.

"Those will be jackals," said Kader nervously. "Or perhaps a pack of wild dogs. My brothers and I often encountered them on Father's trading expeditions."

I squinted into the darkness, searching for the creature that had made the noise. We had camped at the base of a tall dune that stood alone upon an otherwise flat plain. I glanced up the dune but saw no lion perched atop its peak, ready to scamper down the sand and claw out our throats. Then I looked down the dark expanse of sand to my right, but still I saw nothing, save for the silhouettes of the tent and our five sleeping horses. I was beginning to think I had imagined the growl entirely when I noticed a pair of eyes beyond our fire.

Two eyes, small and round and yellow as lanterns.

Cold horror passed over me in waves until my arms were numb and lifeless as rubber. I tried to pick up my feet, but they felt rooted into the ground like stems, unmoving. I felt Kader tense next to me. All I could do was hold myself very still as the yellow-eyed beast crept toward us. I marked the hunch of its back, the wild tufts of hair over its ears. Sand made the creature noiseless on its feet, but still I heard its rapid, heavy breathing. There was a stench of death on its breath, hot and sharp and metallic—not at all dissimilar to the smell of the suitor's kettle.

Then, finally, the beast stepped into the firelight, and I could see it clearly. It looked very much like a large dog with pointed ears and a thick, muscular body, but it was covered in spots like a leopard's. Between its thin black lips, I spotted a row of teeth so long and sharp that I had no doubt this creature could decapitate me with just one well-placed bite to my neck. Its mouth widened, gaping, and I thought it was going to lunge at me—but it only bared every tooth in its head and laughed, a shrill mechanical chattering that made my blood run cold.

It was a hyena. I had never seen one so close, but I had some-times heard their eerie laughter echoing from my bedroom window at night. Hyenas did not often venture into the city, but when they did, they were known to maul whoever happened to be sleeping outside—elderly beggars or the orphaned children who lived on the streets of Timbuktu. Because hyenas traveled in packs, I knew that wherever there was one, its brethren could not be very far behind. My face grew wet with frightened tears.

"Hyena," I whimpered. "Over—over there. What should we do?"

"I do not know," Kader whispered, his eyes alert with terror.

Across from us, the hyena whined. The sound made my stomach tighten.

"What do you mean, you do not know?" I pleaded, my voice cracking. "Did you and your brothers not encounter hyenas on your father's caravans?"

"Yes, but Father always had men to scare them away," he admit-ted, sounding just as frightened as I felt. "Servants and guards and the like. Perhaps—"

Before Kader could finish his sentence, the hyena leapt at us, quick as an arrow. It landed upon him and sank its fangs deep into his thigh, gripping and chewing as he bellowed, "It's trying to kill me!"

What happened next occurred so quickly that I scarcely realized what I was doing. I had no time at all to think, I could only act. I knelt and grabbed a glowing red log from the fire, letting loose an involuntary scream of pain as the heat of it burned my hands. But I held tight to the log, refusing to drop it no matter how much agony it caused me. And then I took two quick steps toward Kader and brought the log down hard upon the hyena's skull.

The beast rounded on me, snapping and snarling. I heard myself cry out in fear and alarm as it jumped up onto its hind legs and pressed its sharp claws into my ribs, piercing the fabric of my wrapper. With another shriek of pain, I took the glowing log and plunged it as hard as I could between the hyena's forelegs, striking its heart.

The animal whined. The tufts of spotted fur upon its belly caught fire, smoking and sizzling.

Behind me, I heard Kader gasp, "Amie . . ."

Ignoring him, I struck again, harder, and finally managed to draw blood. With a pained bark, the hyena tumbled backward into the fire. Then came an awful, confused moment like the start of a nightmare. My vision shrank into a tunnel so narrow that I could no longer see Kader or the tent or the dunes or even the stars. The world had become smoke and fur and blood and the gnashing of teeth. I continued to strike the hyena with more force and violence than I had known myself capable of, even as its fur became enveloped in flames.

And then I found that Kader had pulled me back from the fire, and the beast lay dying in the ashes. "You can drop it," he told me.

"Drop what?" I asked in a daze. The feeling of the kill fizzed like venom through my blood, numbing me to my surroundings. It took a few seconds for me to realize that I still held the burning log tightly in my hands. I gave a yelp of delayed pain and dropped it unceremoniously to the sand.

"That was amazing," he whispered incredulously. "You saved my life."

I felt a surge of pride. I was not a hunter, nor was I a soldier. I was only a merchant's daughter without a single day of combat training, and yet I had managed to defend myself and Kader from a bloodthirsty beast. I was like Nana Miriam from my nurse's stories: with her charmed spear, Nana Miriam fought a shape-shifting hippopotamus and saved her village.

My fingers and palms were slightly burned, red and raw to the touch, and I knew that later they would blister and leave behind scars. Mother would be in an absolute state over the damage done to my hands, saying that the scars were unladylike. But I had saved us. A triumphant smile stretched my lips, wide as a mask—and then it faded as I thought of Jeneba and Penda. I prayed that they were safe inside the tent.

An eruption of high-pitched barks and frightened whinnies forced my attention to the horses. All five of them were awake, stamping and snorting in terror as several hyenas began to charge at them. Dread throbbed in my throat as I realized that in order to keep our horses, we would have to fight off the entire pack.

I shouted, "We have to save them!" and tugged at Kader's hand.

One hyena charged toward a horse and bit its leg. The others quickly followed, and soon the air was filled with the wet, squelching sound of teeth tearing through horse flesh.

We scrambled over to the gruesome scene as my yellow stallion reared up on his hind legs in surprise and terror.

"Whoa," Kader cried, grappling desperately for its reins.

But the horse was spooked and could not be calmed. He reared up again, the whites of his eyes rolling in panic, and kicked Kader swiftly in the chest.

He fell to the ground, limp as a doll.

I cried out, "No!" as my horse began to gallop at breakneck speed away from our camp with two hyenas in hot pursuit. Our other four horses bolted away, one by one, in an easterly direction, galloping across the moonlit plain. The rest of the hyenas followed, barking and squealing.

I knelt with Kader upon the sand, cradling him in my arms. "Say something," I pleaded.

"My fire finch," he whispered. His chest was bruised, and his eyes fluttered like moths' wings, but he smiled weakly up at me. He was still alive, thank the gods.

"Yes, my love?" I traced the purple bruise spreading across the spot on his chest where my horse had kicked him.

"We cannot lose the horses," he said faintly. "You must chase after them."

I did not want to leave his side. My nerves were in an awful uproar, and my body felt as numb and stiff as ice. But I knew we needed horses if we were ever to make it to Hausakoy's forge house.

So I forced myself to my feet and hurried off after the animals, screaming, "Stop, stop!" as I ran, as if they could understand me. I did my best to pursue them, but the horses were so very fast and the sand beneath my feet was so frustratingly slippery that I soon knew it would be impossible for me to catch them.

In the end, I watched helplessly as the galloping horses and pursuant hyenas swept like a wave over the sands, their brown-and-yellow hides glistening in the starlight. The distant end of the plain was covered in a silvery mist like muslin fabric that made the outline of the animals grow blurrier and blurrier the closer they drew to the horizon. Finally, they were gone, lost to the mist.

I allowed myself a quick scream of frustration and returned to the place where Kader lay wounded. He seemed to have grown even weaker in my absence. I wondered if he was losing blood. I felt no wetness when I touched his chest, but I thought perhaps he might be bleeding beneath his skin. I had heard of soldiers sustaining such internal wounds, which were as undetectable as they were deadly.

"The horses left," I told him regretfully. "I could not stop them."

"Amie, my fire finch." His eyelids fluttered.

"Stay with me," I begged, my voice shaking. "You must not die. I *command* you not to die!"

"Amie . . ."

Just then the girls' screams rose from the tent, accompanied by the barking of hyenas. I heard Penda's voice, high and frightened, and Jeneba grunting with exertion. My heartbeat quickened. I'd thought we had seen the last of the beasts, but it seemed that their brothers were lingering.

"Help!" shrieked Penda. "Help us, please!"

I knelt and dug through the sand at Kader's feet, praying to the gods that I would come upon something sharp enough to use as a weapon—an arrowhead, perhaps, or a rusty old knife left by some long-dead caravanner. But I felt nothing useful, only dry, loose sand and flat stones that were smooth to the touch. In the tent, one of the hyenas snarled, a high, awful sound.

I had to make do with what I already had. I wrapped my fingers around the largest of the stones and tugged. But it seemed sewn into the sand and would not move. I pulled it harder, with so much force that the sting of rock against the raw burns on my palms made me cry out in pain.

"Kader, you must not die," I said again. "Promise me that you will not die."

He only grunted in response. His eyes drooped closed.

With new tears streaming down my face, I pulled again at the stone. Finally, it sprang free, along with a burst of sand that flew directly into my mouth. Coughing and sputtering, I rushed over to the tent and pulled back the flap.

Inside, it was so dim that I could just barely make out the outline of Jeneba being pursued by a massive spotted hyena. One of its pack mates had thrown itself upon Penda, who stood stock-still in terror. The creature perched on its hind legs, snapping and snarling, its front paws pressed against Penda's rib cage. If it were just a few inches taller, it could have torn out her throat, but it was too small for that and could only chomp up at the tips of her braids.

"It's going to kill me," Penda cried. Her dark eyes were huge with fear.

I did not feel very brave. In truth, I felt as though I were going to be sick. But that made no difference in what I knew I must do. Gathering all my courage, I turned toward the hyena that was attacking Penda and tried to crush its skull with my stone. The last time I had attempted this maneuver, it had taken many tries to strike the creature dead. But this time my aim was clumsy, and I missed the mark.

The hyena looked at me, sizing me up. Its yellow eyes flamed and its triangular teeth were exposed in a grotesque grin. Then, as if deciding I was not worth the effort, it turned away and sank its fangs into Penda's armpit. She gave a cry of pain that fell upon my ears like glass.

I was going to strike at the hyena again when a new pair of jaws fastened themselves around one of my sandals and tugged, tripping me. I thudded upon the ground with a sudden surge of pain that made me gasp. The hyena with its teeth on my shoe was larger than all the others, and its yellow eyes stared into my own with a cold intelligence. Desperation twisted knots into my stomach.

"Amie, watch out!" Jeneba's warning echoed out from somewhere

in the darkness of the tent, several seconds too late. Penda still struggled with the hyena at her arm.

I tried to scramble away, but the hyena was already lunging at
me. I raised my pathetic little stone, brandishing it like a dagger, and
tried again to smash the beast's skull. Again I missed, and the hyena
erupted into squeals.

It was mocking me. I felt its breath, hot and rancid upon my face.

Rage pooled beneath my skin. I stabbed uselessly at the hyena's
flank with my stone. It snarled and bit my right arm. I cried out in
pain and terror as it bit me again—deeper, this time. And then I understood that the beast meant to devour me, eating me while I still
lived. It shifted so that the weight of its body pinned my arm in place,
rendering me powerless to fight back. I gave a wordless shriek of fear
and frustration as I realized that in the confusion of the fight, I had
lost the stone that was my only weapon. The hyena snarled in response, its bloodshot eyes rolling up toward mine. But no, it was not
looking at my eyes.

Its gaze was sinking lower.

I realized with horror that it was staring at my exposed throat. If
I did not act fast, it would go in for the kill. It would sever my head
from my body in a few quick bites. My arms were sticky with my
blood, but I tried to ignore my fear and pain.

Think, Amie, I told myself desperately. *Think quickly, or you will
die.* I had to act fast, save myself—but what could I do? I had no real
weapons, nothing sharp that I could use to defend myself. I did not
even have a stone anymore.

In a surge of inspiration, I pushed my thumb deep into one of
the hyena's eyes, pressing as hard as I could manage until I felt the
wetness of its blood. It whined in shock, taking one step back, and
then another, until my pinned arm was free. I pressed even harder

as its head bent back and blood from its eyeball burst around my fingers, warm and sticky and disgusting.

The beast lunged again, trying to bite my throat, but my partial blinding caused it to miss. With triumph coursing through my veins, I turned the hyena over and straddled its back like a horse trainer, clamping my hands tightly around its throat.

I squeezed with both hands. It tried to run away, but I hung on. Squeezed even harder.

Finally, I heard the death rattle. The hyena's head drooped. I let go. It fell away.

Across from me, Penda screamed.

"Amie, get out of the way!" cried Kader from behind me.

I whirled around, breathing hard. He stood above me, coldly beautiful in the starlight, his pale robes dark with animal blood. He held a metal tentpole high over his head like a spear. He shouted wordlessly and then charged at the hyena that was attacking Penda. The round, blunt end struck its back with a metallic *thunk* that made the beast arch in pain.

He brought down the tentpole again, harder this time. It was a death blow. The hyena staggered and collapsed against Penda's chest.

"Help me get it off of her," Kader grunted.

Jeneba and I rushed to his side, and together we lifted the hyena and rolled it away. It was even heavier than it had looked.

Penda's dress was torn, and her limbs were covered in cuts and gashes. "Thank you for saving my life," she murmured, but her voice was flat, her eyes empty. She had retreated into herself during the attack. She had gone somewhere else. I could not blame her for it.

More footfalls came from behind us. We turned, ready to lunge at the final surviving hyena, but it seemed to sense that we were not worth fighting. It whined and retreated, tail between its legs, and disappeared into the dark dunes. We watched in uneasy silence as it grew smaller and smaller until, finally, it blended with the mist and could no longer be seen.

"Is that all of them?" Kader asked when it was gone.

I looked nervously about the camp. One hyena lay dead in the fire. Another two were slain and still at our feet. Our tent was ruined, our horses were gone. The odor of blood and smoke and raw meat permeated the air and made us cough. But I could not see any more of the spotted hyenas, and that was what mattered.

I said, "I think we have killed them all." I was trying to sound confident, but my voice was trembling.

"Have all the horses run away?" asked Penda, frowning.

Kader nodded regretfully. "The hyenas spooked them."

Jeneba asked, "And the horsemen?"

"Still in their saddlebags," he said. "I hope that the horses are taking them back to the city."

I hoped so, too, but I knew that without the antidote those men were lost to the world. Nothing could awaken them from their cursed slumber.

"But how shall we reach the forge house without our horses?" asked Penda.

"We'll have to walk," said Jeneba.

Penda insisted that we try to track down our horses, but Jeneba and Kader warned that it would be useless. After a while, I stopped listening, turning my attention to our ruined campsite and the dead bodies of hyenas, two of which I had killed myself. What other dangers awaited us here in the desert? Would I be as brave as Nana Miriam the next time a threat came around?

We gathered around the fire and tended to one another's wounds. We washed the cuts, scrapes, and bites, applied medicinal herbs that we had brought along, and wrapped the wounds with strips of cloth to keep them clean.

Afterward, the girls went back to the tent to try to sleep, and Kader laid down to rest out by the fire. For the rest of that night, I found myself gasping at every sound, even the faintest whistling of the wind.

16

I slept very poorly, but still I dreamed—though my dreams were odd and scattered, a quick succession of scenes, each stranger than the next. First, I was trapped alone in Mariama's tower with an invading army at the door picking the heavy lock. Next, I dreamed that Haddy and I were children again attending one of our father's banquets for visiting merchants. His guests hailed from a far-off country and spoke a language I had never heard before. My sister spoke it fluently and our parents praised her for it while shaking their heads at me in disappointment. Finally, I dreamed Kader and I were living as husband and wife in a great clay house by the western sea, raising four small children together. When we took our children for a walk along the beach, they tossed themselves into the waves and promptly drowned.

The shock and grief of the final dream woke me up.

I opened my eyes into the loveliest dawn that I had ever seen. Roseate light made everything about our ravaged campsite seem beautiful—from our destroyed tent to the saddlebag and supplies strewn across the ground. Even the bluebottle flies that buzzed about the corpses of slain hyenas glowed like sapphires under the rising sun.

The others were already awake. Jeneba and Kader were breaking their fast with flatbread and goat cheese, while Penda, apparently lacking an appetite, knelt poring over the map. I sat by her side, following her gaze to the dancing illustrations upon its surface. For a long moment, we both were lost in the spell of the map and the warm liquid light that emanated from its depths.

Hausakoy's forge house remained at the center, shining with the promise of unguarded gold within. I noticed Mariama's name was etched near the illustration of Timbuktu—she was still in the palace, evidently—while the rest of our names were clustered together in the blank desert expanse between the palace and the god's house. *Penda Diallo. Jeneba Sangaré. Aminata Aqit. Kader Bagayogo.*

"How does it know our names?" Kader asked us suddenly. He was still chewing his flatbread, but his attention, like mine and Penda's, was fully focused on the map, his eyes wide with awe. His voice was hoarse, and when I looked at him more closely, I saw that his rib cage was still badly bruised from the night before.

"I don't know," I told him. More than anything, I wanted to touch his injured skin and tell him that I loved him, that I was glad he had survived. But I could not allow myself to display affection for him in full view of the others. So instead of telling Kader that I adored him or praising his bravery in the face of danger, I turned to Penda and asked, "How many days' journey do you think it will take for us to reach the tomb, now that we have lost our horses?"

"It is difficult to tell just by looking at the map," she replied. "But based on how far we've come, I would wager at least two days, perhaps three."

"Two more days!" Kader sighed. "May the gods protect us."

Jeneba looked up from her flatbread to frown at Kader, but she said nothing.

Perhaps she suspects us, I thought anxiously. *I would do well to be less friendly.* So I squinted in performative exasperation and forced myself to turn a cold shoulder to him as I prepared our morning tea. We drank it in silence, took down what was left of our tent, and then gathered our luggage as best we could.

We set off into the morning, walking in a straight line, a caravan without camels or horses. Kader was at the head of our procession, leading us, and the girls and I plodded behind him. Our sandals were slippery against the sand, making our progress difficult, and soon my thighs began to ache with the effort.

Penda had carried the map with her yesterday, but today she relinquished it into my hands, because I was the only one besides Kader who could read its instructions. I held up the map, watching the slow progress of our names through the illustrated desert and calling out directions as necessary—"We must turn east, my lord!" "Continue on straight past that grove of doom palms, my lord." "Sharp right, my lord, through the little valley."

It was strange to address Kader as "my lord" instead of "my love," but I knew we must pretend at such formalities, feigning indifference for the sake of our future together. And he, in turn, kept his voice cold and devoid of affection whenever he responded. His act was so convincing that a small, paranoid corner of my mind began to wonder if Kader really had lost his affection for me, just as Tenin had stopped loving my sister. Couldn't what had happened to Haddy happen to me?

I tried to distract myself from these anxious thoughts by listening for birdcalls, but there were none. We were entering a silent section of the Sahara, a lifeless world without even the humming of insects in our ears. There were no sounds, save for our grunts of effort from walking on unsteady sand and the faint hiss of the wind. The quiet made me shiver, despite the growing heat—for the sun was rising quickly overhead, shrinking our shadows, and the sky was transforming from a rosy pink to a deep and cloudless blue. By midmorning, the sun had begun to burn my face, and I had to borrow one of Penda's veils to fend off the hot columns of sunlight that pricked my skin like needles. My feet grew blistered and sore, and my aching muscles slickened with sweat.

But the worst of the heat arrived in the early afternoon, when the air became so hot that it seemed to ripple and quiver before my eyes. I knew it to be an illusion of the heat, but still the sight made me uneasy.

Penda felt it, too. "That's a bad omen," she murmured. "Issatou says when the air dances with heat, the wrath of the gods is never far behind." She handed over one of our waterskins, from which Jeneba drank greedily.

We traveled another hour on high, level ground, where the gentle winds wrinkled the sand. On either side of us stretched a great empty expanse of treeless desert that glowed white as freshwater pearls in the afternoon sun. Thin, flat clouds were beginning to gather upon the horizon, too distant to blanket us from the harsh glare overhead.

The ache in my legs worsened with each step, but I tried to ignore the pain. All that mattered was that Kader and I would soon reach the forge house, seize the exiled god's gold, and escape forever. I told myself that I must not care about anything else—not the heat, not my pain, and certainly not the silence of the Sahara.

"Look!" cried Jeneba, pointing at the sky.

I looked up to see three vultures circling above us, their outstretched wings casting wheeling shadows in the sand. They were the first living creatures we had encountered since leaving camp that morning.

"Another bad omen," said Jeneba sarcastically. "Eh, Penda?"

"Can't you be quiet?" Penda's voice, usually soft and sweet, was sharper than I had ever heard it.

We watched the vultures soar higher and higher until, finally, they vanished entirely. As if on cue, the wind began to pick up speed. The air grew rough and choppy, uprooting the sand in gusts, and a cascade of sediment tore a dozen tiny cuts into my cheeks.

"The horizon!" cried Penda, shouting over the wind. Her innocent face was contorted with terror.

When I followed her gaze, I saw that the skyline had darkened from blue to a hazy reddish brown. The horizon was concealed with fast-moving clouds that were growing closer by the second.

Dread coiled in my throat. "What *is* that?" I asked the others, tucking the map into the folds of my wrapper to protect it from the violent winds.

But I already knew in my gut that it was a sandstorm.

Despite its proximity to the desert, Timbuktu was rarely struck by such phenomena. I remembered that once, when I was six years old and Haddy was eight, we were playing together in the courtyard as a great pillar of dust rose over the city. My mother had shouted for us to hurry inside. I remembered shrinking away in fear when the storm blocked out the sun. I had not liked the sudden darkness at midday and the awful roar of the wind.

Now a sudden gust of hot wind made our clothes billow and filled our mouths with sand. For a long moment, we could only cough and sputter while red clouds rolled across the sky, creeping toward us. The wall of the storm grew taller, looming over us like a wave. I was beginning to panic in spite of myself. My mind swam with all the warnings my father had given about desert storms— that they could bury entire caravans with ease, the sand suffocating men and beasts alike. That no one would find you until your skeleton resurfaced centuries later.

We began to walk again, this time with our backs to the wind. The ground beneath us began to tremor, a scratching, rumbling sound that joined the low roar of the storm. The red clouds on the

horizon rushed toward us at a gathering speed. Whirlpools of sand
and dust formed around us, as if invisible jinn were turning the air
with their crude hands. Plumes and pillars of wind turned at our
feet, threatening to topple us over. The loose sand in the air grew
thicker and heavier until it blotted out the sun, the sky, and even the
faces of my companions. It began to smell like smoke, although I
saw no fire.

In moments, the afternoon sky darkened to an inky indigo and
then to black—a false nightfall.

"I cannot see anything!" shouted Jeneba. Her usual calm, sarcastic
demeanor had vanished, and now she sounded panicked.

"Neither can I," came Penda's frightened voice through the dark.

We formed a chain with our hands so as not to lose one another,
then continued to walk through that awful darkness, coughing and
sputtering all the while. Try as I might, I could not help but inhale
sand with each breath. It gathered in my mouth, coating my throat
and tongue, and when I gritted my teeth I heard the *click* of sand
grains splitting.

At length, the blasts of hot wind grew so forceful that we could
no longer walk. We were forced to crawl for what felt like an eternity. The winds lashed at us with an unbearable force, and the air
was black as ink. In the corners of my eyes shifted large and indis-
tinct shapes that seemed to pounce and gallop like animals, and
above the howling of the storm I heard strange wails that sounded
like they came not from men or beasts but from something else
entirely.

Perhaps Jeneba was right, I thought with growing horror. *The vultures were indeed a bad omen, and now we are being pursued by some
spirit or unearthly creature that sent this storm to bury us alive.* I grew
dizzy with fear, the speed of the wind continued to increase, and
the gravel and sand in the air tore at my skin like thorns, but still

I crawled on until, without warning, I began tumbling away from the others from the peak of what must have been a very tall dune.

And then I was falling.

I screamed as I fell but was soon silenced by a wave of sand pouring into my mouth. When I finally collapsed, blind and spitting, at the bottom of the dune, my head collided with something hard. Pain vibrated through my skull. I saw watery red and tasted my own blood. The skin at the crown of my head felt raw, and I wondered if I was wounded. I tried to call out to the others for help, but my throat was still full of sand and I could only croak wordlessly.

Around me, the storm raged on. The air remained as dark as midnight. I turned against the wind, coughing weakly. I felt tired and frail and began to wonder if I was dying. Part of me wished I *would* die, just to end my torment. I felt tempted to give up, to let my body go limp. I imagined allowing myself to lie there in that valley of swirling wind until sand stole the breath from my lungs. Would it really be so terrible to be buried alive, to suffocate? Perhaps it would only feel like slipping into a slumber. . . .

No. I could not let this be the end. I reached deep inside myself for the strength I thought I had long since expended and forced myself to crawl back up the dune. My arms and legs were burning with exhaustion, and I felt myself flickering in and out of consciousness, but I scaled the mountain of sand in a feat of sheer will.

"Kader!" I shouted into the wind. "Penda? Jeneba? Can any of you hear me?"

Silence was the only reply.

I screamed at the top of my lungs in pure frustration. All I had ever wanted was to live a happy life with a husband who loved and cared for me, but I wondered now if I would ever get that chance. Perhaps I had been painfully naive, and now I would perish for it.

17

All at once, the storm began to retreat. The wind slowed and slowed and then, finally, came to a halt, as if it knew it had overexerted itself. There followed an eerie stillness in which the evening-dark air was gradually pierced by beams of yellow sunlight. Over the next several minutes, the clouds of sand fell steadily away, replaced by a thin layer of russet dust that lingered in the air like bloodstained pollen.

I watched in a daze, the top of my skull still throbbing, as the sun slowly penetrated the dust and turned the world to copper and gold.

"Amie! Where are you?" Kader's voice fell out of the silence—distant and faint, but unmistakably his own.

"I am over here!" I cried. "I cannot see you. . . ." And then I spotted a tall, distant silhouette moving toward me through the dwindling dust. The figure called out my name in Kader's voice, and my heart leapt. "I am here, my love!"

My love. The words had slipped from my lips by accident. I knew in the back of my mind that I must not refer to him with so much affection in front of the others, but in that moment, I was too drained and depleted to care what anyone else thought. I only wanted him.

The air was growing lighter. The copper dust continued to dissipate in its battle against the afternoon sun. The distance remained dark and blurry, but the foreground became clearer with each passing moment.

I looked up to see him hurtling toward me, his long legs in urgent motion. The joy in his eyes fell over me like rain. Penda and Jeneba followed behind him, both looking tired and disheveled but undeniably glad to see me. And I was happy and relieved to see them, too.

He reached me first. To my surprise, he swept me up in his strong arms and kissed me, right in front of the others. I kissed him back. I could not stop myself; I was helpless.

I wondered dimly how Jeneba and Penda might react to our admission, but all that mattered for the moment was that Kader's lips were on mine and I could feel his rapid heartbeat against my chest. We had survived our hateful families, the start of the Trials, a wild animal attack, and a deadly sandstorm—and still our love held fast.

"You're alive!" He stroked my face lovingly. "I was so afraid I had lost you. My fire finch, my love."

I pulled back from him and glanced around at my surroundings. I had not noticed it before, but I saw now that the landscape was very much changed. When the sandstorm had first begun, we had stood upon great flat plains, but now we found ourselves at the edge of a small mountain range, a plateau of sandstone and granite hills that cast shadows as long and deep as rivers.

Recognition sparked within me. "I saw these mountains on the map," I told the others in an excited rush. "We have been traveling in the right direction. We are closer to the forge house than ever before!"

Jeneba did not share my enthusiasm. "I knew something was going on with the pair of you," she said coldly. Her lips were pressed together in a tight line, her arms folded across her chest with disdain.

Kader and I exchanged a look.

"It is true," I admitted. "We are in love. We have been for a very long time, but—"

"You're never returning to the palace, are you." Jeneba's accusation was an ugly thing, uglier still because she spoke the truth. "And His Lordship has no intention of ever wedding Mariama. You're going to abandon us."

"Jeneba, you must understand . . . ," I began to reply, but guilt stopped my throat and I found myself unable to speak another word.

"Amie, is it true?" Penda's lips quivered with the shock of my betrayal.

A wave of cold shame made me drop my gaze to the ground. I chewed at the sand in my mouth, feeling uneasy.

Taking my hand, Kader said, "Amie's place is with me. Although our families object to our union, we are quite determined to marry. I intend to use Hausakoy's gold to travel far away from the empire and make her my wife."

Jeneba made a sharp sound of exasperation. "But the emperor's daughter is expecting your return," she insisted. "She is relying on you to find Hausakoy's hammer, survive the suitor's kettle, and end the Trials. Does loyalty mean nothing to you?"

"I promise that when we reach the forge house, I will locate the hammer and give it to you for safekeeping," he told her. "And when you return to the palace, you can pass the hammer on to the princess. Tell her to give it to her next suitor, so that he will win the Trials."

An image moved through my mind, a vision of Mariama alone in her bedchamber, furious at me for leaving. She had only ever treated me with kindness and affection.

I tightened my grip on Kader's sweat-slick hand and said, "We have no other choice if we want to be together. If we returned to Timbuktu, he would have to wed the princess."

"And why shouldn't he marry her?" Jeneba snorted. She turned to Kader. "Your Lordship, why would you want to be with Amie when you could wed an emperor's daughter and acquire her fortune? And when Emperor Suleyman dies, you and your sons would take the throne. You would hold all the wealth of Mali in your hands. How can you decline that opportunity? Ninety-nine men have died trying to win the princess's hand, and you would toss her away like a sack of grain?" She seemed genuinely perplexed, as if she could not understand why anyone would ever reject money and power in the name of love.

It occurred to me then that Kader was turning down everything she had longed for all her life: safety, status, and affluence. If Jeneba were in his position, she would discard me in a heartbeat. But I could not judge her for it: she'd had a short and difficult life, being orphaned and married at ten years old and then widowed six years later.

"But I don't want any of that," he said with a reassuring squeeze of my fingers. "I only want Amie."

I wrung his hand like a wet rag, feeling uneasy. I was of course glad to hear that Kader was choosing me over a princess, but I also felt guilty over betraying the trust of the girls I had begun to call my friends. Although he grimaced in discomfort, he did not release himself from my kneading grip.

"You'd really give up the chance to rule Mali for the love of a commoner with a tarnished reputation?" Jeneba asked finally. "Then you're even less intelligent than I thought."

Her words stung like a slap, even though I knew that I deserved them. I met her gaze and said through tight lips, "Perhaps a love like ours is not something you are capable of comprehending, Jen, but it is a beautiful thing, far more important than wealth or station."

She shook her head in mock disgust. "You two deserve one another. And maybe I am a little jealous." She smiled and gave my other hand a little squeeze.

Penda spoke for the first time in a long while. "I should like to see the map again, please," she said calmly. Grains of sand from the storm still clung to the sweat on her cheeks.

"Please, Penda—" I began.

"Give me the map at once!" Her voice rose to a shriek that echoed against the mountains.

I handed her the map quickly out of shock. I wondered when sweet-natured Penda had acquired such a temper. Her eyes shifted across the parchment with slow conviction.

The sun slipped behind one of the mountains as she examined the map, plunging our group into shadow. Finally, she asked, "These four lines of text here—they represent the four of us, correct?"

"Yes, they are our names," I said softly. I wondered what it felt like to live in a world with so many indecipherable symbols, surrounded by a code that she could not understand.

"And the house beneath the sand belongs to the god of the blacksmiths?"

I nodded.

"In that case, I think we're here," she said.

"What? No, it is too soon." I sucked in a sharp breath, tasted dust. "The last time I checked, we were more than a day's journey away."

"Not anymore," said Penda confidently. "It seems that we've arrived."

"But that cannot be," I protested. "Do you *see* a house? There is nothing here!"

But when I squinted over at the map in disbelief, I realized with a chill that she was right. All four of our names were now positioned within the forge house.

A knot began to form in my stomach. Something was wrong.

"Let me see." Kader took the map and studied it. "This has to be some kind of trick," he muttered.

"It's not a trick," said Penda in a strange voice. She pointed with one trembling finger at the base of the summit. "Look! Over there!"

The mountain, which had previously been a perfectly ordinary wall of solid stone, now possessed what appeared to be a door. Carved into the rock as if it had always been there was a narrow rectangular opening, so small that only one of us could pass through it at a time. The door was topped with a delicate archway that reminded me of the sloping domes in the palace, and it glowed with the same dazzling golden light that emanated from the map. When the sun sank behind the mountain, the four of us had been cast in shadow, but now we found ourselves bathed in a yellow luminescence that made our skin sparkle.

We had arrived at the dwelling of a god.

On the other side of that door stood the chambers of Hausakoy, the immortal blacksmith whose legendary hammer held the power to end the Trials forever. Although I knew he had not lived here since his exile many centuries ago, now that we had arrived, the thought of entering a god's residence without his permission made me uneasy.

It dawned on me that we were probably not the first group of mortals to attempt a break-in. If other maps like ours existed, then perhaps earlier adventurers had been lured here by tales of the god's treasure and the hammer that transformed flesh into stone. Perhaps Hausakoy, who was known to be wily and clever, had filled his forge house with false passageways and deadly traps to deter thieves. Or perhaps his home was already occupied by bandits who wanted his fortune for themselves and would kill the four of us without remorse.

Next to me, Kader was beginning to look worried. I gave him a small smile to assure him that everything was going to be all right, although of course none of us could guess what dangers were on the other side of that door.

But we had come all this way. We had risked far too much to be here.

We had to go inside.

Jeneba gave us a hard look. "Penda and I will go first," she said decisively. "You two may follow ten paces behind, and don't try anything strange."

I took Kader's hand and watched the girls disappear beneath the archway, one by one, like ducklings diving into a pond. I still considered them my friends, but I knew in my heart that they would never trust me as they had before. There was no going back. I counted under my breath, and when I reached ten, I squeezed his fingers.

"Let's go," I said, still hoping for happiness ever after with him but fearing the worst.

Holding hands, we walked into the mountain.

We soon stood inside a hollowed-out stone chamber far smaller than I had expected, with low, rough ceilings. There were no candles here, or torches. Still, the room was alight with an eerie yellow glow, and a humming seemed to come from the air itself. I saw no furniture or carpets. The place was bare and empty, save for a thick layer of dust that coated almost every surface.

I exhaled softly. If living bandits lurked within, we would be able to see their footprints in the dust, but there were none. I guessed that we were the only visitors who had come here in a very long time.

I noticed that Penda was pressing her small hands against the rough sandstone walls. She grunted with effort. "Come now," she muttered. "Why won't it move?"

"Because that's solid rock. It would take an army of workers to move it." Jeneba tucked a black braid behind her ear.

"Is this really the forge house?" I glanced about the chamber in disbelief. There was no treasure whatsoever. "Why, there's nothing here."

"The map shows that this is only the antechamber," said Penda, sounding strained and breathless with exertion. "Hausakoy's living quarters include several circular rooms that are stacked around one another like a honeycomb, and the hammer is at the center. There should be a trapdoor somewhere along this wall, but you'll have to help me push."

I took a quick look at the map to confirm what she had just said. Then I felt a surge of pride on her behalf. Penda could not read or write, but her impressive ability to navigate the twists and turns of the palace had prepared her for this house of tricks. She had a knack for direction.

For the next half hour or so, the four of us busied ourselves searching for the secret door. In the end, we found nothing. Disappointed and tired, we sat upon the dusty stone floor and looked again at the map. There could be no mistake that we had arrived at Hausakoy's forge house—but where was his hammer? Where were his weapons and jewelry?

"This entire journey was a waste," said Jeneba unhappily. "The blasted map has led us to a dead end."

I found myself nodding in silent agreement. I had betrayed Mariama, traveled out into the desert, and risked my life battling hyenas and a sandstorm. All for what? An empty room at the base of a mountain? I should have listened to Kader on my first day in the palace. If we had run away together that very night, none of this would have happened.

"At least we can safely make camp here tonight," said Kader, ever the optimist. "I doubt the hyenas will follow us inside."

"But what will we do in the morning?" I whispered.

Penda sighed. "I suppose we'll have to go home."

"Home?" I repeated angrily. "Kader and I cannot go back to Timbuktu, you know that."

"What I meant is that *Jeneba and I* will head home," she corrected herself. "I don't know what the two of you will do."

I was preparing my reply when I felt a sudden tremor beneath my feet. The quake lasted only two or three seconds, and then it ceased.

"What was that?" asked Kader in a small voice.

No one answered.

"We shouldn't sleep here tonight." Penda wrung her hands. "I don't think this mountain wants us inside."

Jeneba sighed. "Pen, don't be ridiculous. It's just a big rock, it doesn't have feelings."

As if in disagreement, the chamber shook again, much more violently this time. All four of us exclaimed in surprise. I clung to Kader, frightened, as the floor began to lurch up and down like the choppy surface of a river. The walls bubbled around us like water boiling for tea.

We watched in horror as the narrow doorway yawned itself closed. It made an awful choking sound and then it shuddered— once, twice. It throbbed and hiccuped like a throat, and suddenly it was a doorway no more, only another smooth stone wall.

We were trapped.

Then there came a rending, tearing sound. The floor beneath us was splitting, cracking open like an egg. We all tried our best to cling to the walls for safety, but the fissure at our feet widened quickly into a chasm until there was no floor left at all, only a great pit that was dark and hungry and ready to swallow us up. *Penda's trapdoor*, I thought distantly.

With a hoarse scream, I slipped inside. The others tumbled after me.

The sudden rush into space overwhelmed my senses so that I could hardly think. I braced myself to bash my head on a rock or be smothered by sand, but instead I found myself tumbling down a sort of well.

In stark contrast to the desert, the well's chute was lush with green moss and blooming vines. Water trickled down its sides, illuminated by colorful flowers unlike any I had ever seen before—their petals throbbed with internal light.

But the flowers did not hold my attention for long, for I noticed a circle of molten metal at the bottom of the tunnel, glowing red as pomegranate seeds. Was this the trap Hausakoy had devised for intruders?

The pool of liquid alloy grew larger as we plummeted toward it. I tried to grab at the sides of the well as I descended, hoping for a vine to grip or a jutting cliff—anything to save me from the fiery death below. But the walls shrank back like a living thing when I tried to touch them, like a throat expanding, and the flowers seemed to blink at me like eyes.

The air grew hotter. I smelled sulfur and began to cough. The red molten river came rising up at me.

I shut my eyes tightly, hoping for a swift and painless death.

18

When I opened my eyes again, I was in another world entirely.

I had prepared myself for an impact that never came. In the last moment I remembered, I had been a hair's width away from colliding with molten metal—but now I found myself settled upon something . . . soft. I was lying on the earthen floor of a long limestone corridor. Its white walls and low ceiling were covered in a crisscrossing pattern of vines.

I thought I must have been unconscious for several hours because my mind felt foggy and I was aware of dried bits of sleep in the corners of my eyes. I rubbed my eyelids and looked more closely at my surroundings. Along the vines flickered flowers in blue and purple and pale yellow, all of them glowing like oil lamps in the semidarkness. I was suddenly overcome by a strong desire to pluck a flower, and I chose one with petals of iridescent violet.

But when I tugged at it, the flower shuddered and struggled like an animal in pain.

It gave me a shock, but of all the magical objects I had encountered of late, a bloom that fought back was perhaps the least surprising. My determination to possess it only increased, and I pulled harder. When it finally sprang free, a thick, sticky liquid trickled from its stem. At first, I assumed it was sap, but the color was all wrong.

My breath caught in my throat when I realized it was blood. Horror made me drop the bloom.

Perhaps I am dead, I thought in a panic. *Dead, or else dreaming.*

Memories of the past few days swarmed my mind like flies. Holding Mariama by lamplight. Being accused by my parents of assisting in Haddy's disappearance the next morning. Bargaining for a horse so I could follow the caravan into the desert. Kissing Kader by starlight. The hyena attack. The sandstorm. The look of betrayal on poor Penda's face. The vitriol in Jeneba's words: *You'd really give up the chance to rule Mali for the love of a commoner with a tarnished reputation?*

Where was Jeneba? Where were the others? Had they left me while I was still sleeping? It was through this tangle of panicked thoughts that I first heard the sound, dry and distant and mechanical: *Clink. Clink. Clink.*

I backed against the nearest wall, startled. The flowers behind me crumpled under the pressure of my back and whined softly as if in pain, a sound that made my stomach turn. And although the corridor had the appearance of being carved from white limestone, when I pressed my hand against a wall, it did not feel like stone at all. I had never known stone to be so moist and yielding, like rice.

I pulled away so quickly that I tripped on the hem of my wrapper. Disoriented, I stumbled and glanced up the corridor. The stretch of hall before me was as long as a river. It went on in a straight line—so far that I imagined I could sprint across it at full speed for several minutes and still not reach its end—and then curved abruptly to the right, out of sight.

Behind me was nothing at all.

How could that be? There had been two directions to the corridor, I was sure of it. Moments earlier, there had been a pathway behind me—but the path had silently caved in or else disappeared. And now there was only a wall at my back, white as moonlight and covered with flowers that groaned and bled at my touch.

Cold panic trickled through my chest. I looked at the wall, and looked again, not wanting to believe what I was seeing. Where *was* I?

My heart pounding, I took a closer look at the wall behind me. I realized with a start that it was . . . *expanding?* The white substance of the corridor was rising like bread dough, like a living thing taking a slow and endless breath. It seemed to grow a hand's width each second, shrinking the air around me, closing me in.

I understood in a corner of my panicked mind that the wall would keep growing indefinitely. It meant to flatten me. I had to escape. *Perhaps that is what happened to Kader and the others*, I thought in a blur of fear. *Perhaps the flowering walls have already crushed them, one by one.* What if I was the last one of us left?

I prayed to all the gods that this was not the case. I hoped to find Penda and Jeneba and Kader somewhere along the length of this hallway, together and frightened but alive. I began my walk. *Please, wherever they are—let them be safe.*

Moving through that corridor was an acutely disorienting experience. The length of it shrank behind me as I walked, which made me feel as though I had not made any forward progress. The wall at my back inflated like a lung, growing and expanding until the path behind me had become so narrow that only a small child could have retraced my steps.

Turning back was no longer an option.

So forward I went, taking slow and cautious steps down the corridor. I had passed the long and straight portion of the hall, and now my path wound and twisted like a thicket. I held my breath each time I rounded a corner, worried I would encounter another smooth blank wall—a dead end. I would be penned in like an animal, trapped. Even worse than the thought of finding myself stuck down here was the idea that I might come around a bend and find myself face-to-face with someone who wished me ill. Those strange flowers were unlikely to be the only monsters that awaited me.

Every ten paces or so, the metallic *clink clink clink* echoed again, making me jump. And after what seemed like half an hour of walking, I heard another noise, a sound that made my blood run cold. It was like a man's cough, followed by the low grunt of a beast.

I stopped in my tracks, paralyzed by fear. I did not want to keep walking along this corridor only to be consumed by whatever creature lurked at its end. But what choice did I have? I took a deep breath, tried to push the fear out of my mind, and went around another corner—where I nearly stepped on a body. Its small limbs were sprawled out against the floor, unmoving.

Shock ran through me when I realized it was Penda. She was stretched out along the ground next to Jeneba, their legs intertwined, both looking like soldiers fallen in battle. My heart sank into my stomach. I feared they might be dead until Penda's eyelids began to flutter.

Relieved, I knelt and felt for her heartbeat. She was alive—and so was Jeneba, thank the gods. "Penda, can you hear me?" I scooped her up in my arms and gave her a gentle shake. "Please, wake up."

For one long, horrible moment, she lay limp against me, and I began to worry that she was hurt on the inside, in ways I couldn't see. But then she gave a soft groan and asked, "Where are we? Are we in the forge house?"

It was such a relief to hear her voice that happy tears sprang to my eyes. "I do not know," I told her, wiping them away. "But I do not believe so." I heard the panic in my voice as I finally allowed myself to speak aloud the concern that had plagued me ever since I had awoken alone under the flowering vines. "But I fear that we were *never* headed toward Hausakoy's house. I think the map lied to us."

A map that told lies. The idea was perplexing—but the girls only looked solemnly back at me. They saw it now, too. They under-stood how foolish we had been, following an enchanted map that I'd found in a heap of yams. Such sorcerous objects were known to be untrustworthy, but we had wanted to believe so badly.

"Where is the map?" Jeneba narrowed her eyes. "Have you sto-len that, too?"

I remembered foggily that she and I had quarreled. It felt like a very long time ago. "No, of course not," I told her. "Last I remem-ber, we had spread the map out against the floor of that room in the mountain, but then the ground split open, and—"

"I remember," Penda said in a small, frightened voice. "I remem-ber looking at the map, and then falling. It fell with us, I think." She searched the ground, frowning. "But I don't see it now."

"So we're even more lost than we were before," said Jeneba with a sigh. She extended her hand to me so that I could help her to her feet and asked as if it were an afterthought, "Where is His Lord-ship?"

"I wish I knew." Fear pooled in my stomach as I imagined the worst. What *had* happened to Kader? What if he was dead, or close to it? But no, I could not allow myself to think of his death or I would go mad.

If the three of us are still breathing, I tried to reassure myself, *then so is he. He* must *be*—

Another *clink clink clink* interrupted my thoughts.

"What's that sound?" cried Jeneba, frightened.

"I think it is a person," I said. *Hopefully.*

"The corridor is shrinking!" Penda's eyes went wide.

"Be careful," I said. "I am just as afraid of this place as you are."

The living corridor forced us to continue our slow march. We moved in silence, holding hands, all three of us trembling with fear. I pried a loose stone from the wall to defend myself, although to my horror, it did not feel at all like stone. It was warm and moist and seemed to breathe.

Whatever is at the end of this hall, I thought, *it will not kill us without a fight.*

The clinking sound and accompanying grunts grew louder as we walked, until finally we turned a corner and they stopped. Everything was quiet as we found ourselves on a cliff overlooking an enormous subterranean cave. The surface of it was like nothing I had ever seen before—rough, grainy white like limestone and cut through with thousands of streaks of turquoise and amber and deep azurite blue. The blue-and-white ceiling was sharp and uneven, the green-and-amber walls round and smooth, as if they had been eroded by centuries of rushing water.

Every inch of the cave, from the roof to the walls to the pale green stalactites and stalagmites that jutted out like incisors, was covered in those flowering vines. Hundreds of thousands of petals glowed in gemstone hues of jade and rose quartz and topaz and amber, all of them positively throbbing with light. The cave had no need of sunlight or oil lamps with these bright blooms. The air smelled pleasantly damp, like the breezes off the river Niger, and the flowers emitted a savory scent, rich as spice.

"Look down!" cried Jeneba.

I followed her awestruck gaze to the floor of the cave, where one hundred feet below us there was a beach of rocky gold. On its shores lapped the tongues of a silvery lake, which narrowed into a river that turned a sharp corner into darkness at the far edge of the cave. Dugouts of gilded wood crossed the gray-and-blue wave tops, pilotless and completely empty. I saw that the oars moved unassisted, as if powered by ghostly rowers. The sight made my heart lurch.

"If only we could climb down and reach one of the boats," I told

the others, trying to hide my fright. "We might escape to . . . ." I trailed
off, unsure of how to finish. Where exactly would the boats take us?

"I'm not getting in a riverboat unless I know who's rowing,"
Jeneba said stubbornly.

"We may not have a choice," I pointed out.

"Is that His Lordship?" Penda called.

"You see Kader?" I scanned the boats with excitement. "Where
is he?"

"There." She nudged me. "By the river bend."

Kader was seated in one of the pilotless dugouts. He looked
about the cave with wide, bewildered eyes. His knees were drawn
up against his chin as if the boat were crowded, although it looked
completely empty. The oars moved rhythmically without his assistance, slicing the water with invisible strength.

The sight of him made me dizzy with relief. He was alive and
well—thank the gods. But where was he going?

I waved my arms and cried, "Kader! Kader, look up! Please look
up, it is me! It is Amie!"

But the cave was vast and the waves were loud, and he could not
hear me. He only frowned down at the water as his canoe turned
around the river bend. And then I could no longer see him. He was
lost to me once again.

I grew faint, sensing a rush of warmth to my temples, the blood
quickening in my brow, and stumbled. I think Penda caught me.

Behind us, Jeneba said in a voice more startled than afraid, "Oh!
Our apologies, sir, we did not mean to interrupt."

At first I thought she was talking to Kader, but she usually called
him *my lord*, not *sir*. Then I thought, *We are not alone.*

I turned and was quite relieved to see, instead of the monster I
had been imagining, an elderly man, small and frail, with slightly
stooped shoulders.

He appraised us without even a glimmer of surprise. "Has my lady sent you?" he asked mildly.

"Your lady?" I said in bewilderment.

"Begging your pardon, sir," began Penda in her sweet and halting way, "but are we in the house of the god of smiths?"

"I'll ask you again." Frowning, the man flung his arms outward toward the gemstone cliffside and the crystalline lake below. "Has my lady sent you here?"

"No one sent us," she said quickly. "We're lost. Please, can you tell us where we are?"

I forced myself to speak, adding, "We have traveled a very long way. We would like to know where we have landed."

He passed his hands over his sparse and graying hair. "I cannot answer your questions," he said. "My lady will not allow it."

The manner in which he said *my lady* struck me as odd. Why did he sound so fearful, so reverent?

"Which lady do you serve?" asked Jeneba impatiently.

He frowned. "I cannot tell you her name. She forbids it."

I could feel my annoyance growing as I told him, "We have our own lady to report to, you see—Princess Mariama, daughter of Emperor Suleyman of Mali. She sent us on a mission of great importance, and we are running out of time. If you could just tell us where we are and how we might leave this place so that we can continue on our journey, the three of us would be forever in your debt."

"I cannot answer your questions."

Although I had already guessed he would respond in this vague and unsatisfying manner, I still heard myself exhale sharply in exasperation. "If you cannot answer us, who *can*?" I asked through gritted teeth.

"My lady, of course," he said matter-of-factly.

"Can you take us to your lady, then?" I had finally realized that this man would be of no use to us. He was a servant, and the only person who could help us was his employer.

"Why, yes, of course!" Without another word, he turned his back to us and started down a flower-lined cliffside path.

After a brief hesitation, the three of us followed him. We walked in a single-file line like schoolchildren, all of us exchanging uncertain glances, trying to decide which of us should speak first. Ahead, the old man trod so very close to the cliff's edge that I half expected him to slip and fall to his death, but his steps were practiced and he never once lost his footing. He walked with a jaunty, balanced athleticism that I would have expected from a hunter or a soldier, not a frail and hunched manservant.

Who is he? I wondered as we walked, but I knew it would be useless to ask any further questions. His mistress, whoever she was, had instructed him to be tight-lipped.

"Your lady has a beautiful home," said Penda carefully. The sound of waves crashing against the cliff had grown louder, and she had to project her usually soft voice in order to be heard.

"I built this place for her," he said, a hint of bitterness creeping into his voice.

His words surprised me. I had taken him for a servant, not an architect. Perhaps he was both.

The man's pace was brisk, and keeping up with him was tiring.

"You built all of this?" Jeneba asked through shallow breaths.

"My lady is used to luxury. She asked me to replicate all the comforts of her former home. I did as she bade me, although now I see that I should have refused. That is what love will do. Makes you a fool."

"Who is your lady?" I asked, knowing already that he would not answer.

The man stopped walking and fixed me with a hard stare. I

noticed with disbelief that his hair had grown thicker, his skin younger and smoother. Even his shoulders seemed to have straightened and grown broader. My stomach clenched. Was this the same man we had met moments earlier?

"I gave her everything she wanted," he said finally. "And look how my lady has repaid me." He lifted a leg from under his tunic, revealing a long gash on his muscular thigh. Maggots as pale as ivory writhed in the rotten flesh.

Jeneba and I shrank away in disgust.

Penda said with great pity, "What a cruel lady. She did this to you?"

"Ages ago. Ages and ages ago."

"Is it painful?" she asked.

He nodded. "But not as painful as my love for my lady. She was so sad when I found her. Utterly despondent and yet beautiful. I knew that I had to give her a better life. She deserved so much more than what they had given her. . . ." For a moment, he looked as if he were going to weep, but he swallowed his tears and, after smoothing his tunic, resumed his walk. He grew younger and more vigorous with every step. In a matter of minutes, he had become a sturdy young man who would not have seemed out of place in the imperial army.

We followed him hesitantly, exchanging confused looks behind his back. Our uncertainty was caused not solely by his transformation—although it was undoubtedly bizarre to witness an old man metamorphose himself into a young one—but also by his strange speech about the lady. Who was she? The way he had spoken of her made me wonder if she was his lover, his employer, his jailer, or some combination of the three.

I could not understand who the lady was to him, but it was clear that she held enough power for him to find her fearsome. I began to think that perhaps she was a sorceress, or not a woman at all but a goddess. Or it could be that she was a monster, some sort of female chimera. As we walked, my mind conjured an image of the lady as an ogre with a woman's body and five scaly, serpentine heads. Fear wrapped its cold hands around my throat. Five sets of fangs swam in my vision, five forked tongues. . . .

The man rounded a corner, bringing us onto a little rocky peninsula that jutted out over the cliff's edge. A pale cluster of stalactites marbled with swirling turquoise and gold dangled over the promontory, casting it in shadow. Here, he stopped walking.

I was glad to be able to catch my breath after what had felt like half an hour's hasty journey. Penda steadied herself against me, breathing hard. Perspiration had collected on the curve of Jeneba's forehead. For a long moment, the only sounds were the licking of waves against the shore and three weary girls gasping for breath.

In contrast, the man did not betray any signs of fatigue. He held himself still in the dimness, his carriage perfectly erect. His broad chest did not undulate with panting and wheezing, and his skin was as dry as paper. After such a journey, even the most athletic of young men would be tired, but he did not seem to need to breathe at all. He frightened me, and I was glad for Penda and Jeneba by my side. It would have been truly awful to be alone with him.

Squinting at him through the shadows, I wondered if he was a sorcerer.

As my eyes adjusted to the gloom, a spherical object began to take shape behind him. It was a great clay cauldron, its surface a mottled gray shot through with flecks of green and brown that reminded me of bruises.

I had always imagined that the suitor's kettle at the market of Timbuktu was the only one of its kind. I had always been told that Emperor Suleyman had constructed the largest fireclay pot in the world in which to torture his daughter's suitors. It was a unique monstrosity, an irreplaceable instrument of death.

But here was its duplicate, its subterranean sibling. It was the same size and shape as the suitor's kettle, and it stood upon a white stone platform that was identical to the one that towered above the market square. It was even filled with the same murky river water. The only discernible difference between the suitor's kettle in Timbuktu and the clay cauldron before me was that this one was encircled with flowering vines that wound themselves around its exterior like twine.

Jeneba saw it, too. She whispered, "Doesn't that look just like the suitor's kettle?"

I nodded, but something else had caught my attention—a wide, stiff vine that appeared to be floating on the surface of the water within the kettle. I stepped closer, scrutinizing it. This vine was not at all like the others. It was a deep, earthy brown instead of green, it carried no flowers, and five short tendrils floated at its end, bobbing like lily pads—

I stifled a scream.

They were five *fingers*. I was looking at a human hand. What I had taken for a vine was actually an arm, a wet and swollen severed limb. It remained afloat in the facsimile of the suitor's kettle, bloodless and buoyant as a fish. My mind went blank with shock.

Penda made a soft sound of revulsion and horror. "What *is* that?" she asked, wrinkling her nose at the cauldron.

"It is a replica spirit," the man replied. It had been a long while since he had spoken, and I flinched again at the low, youthful boom of his new voice, so unlike the weak quavering of his old one. "My lady requires replicas of the comforts to which she is accustomed: chefs, servants, scribes."

I did not know how to respond. Neither did Jeneba or Penda.

The three of us watched in perplexed silence as he gestured to the kettle.

"This is my workstation," he told us. "I was here earlier, but then I heard you talking and thought I ought to come and say hello. I really must return to my labors, or else my lady will be displeased."

As he spoke, a fire began to grow out of the cliffside. The flames were controlled, concentrated at the center of a flat brick-and-stone hearth that rose from the ground like impossibly fast-growing grass. It reminded me of the forges used by the blacksmiths in Timbuktu, complete with a great black anvil, an oxhide bellows, a clay pipe, and glowing red coals. A wave of heat passed over me, and my armpits prickled with moisture. Upon a low stone table gleamed a metalsmith's various tools—chisels, hammers, axes, tongs. Wrought iron smoldered hotly in a nearby mold.

He is not a sorcerer, I thought. *He is something else, something far more powerful.*

Penda said, "Our sincerest apologies for distracting you, sir." Her eyes were wide with bewilderment, but her servant's training had made her unfailingly polite.

In response, he made a low sound like a dog's grunt, as if he could not be bothered to converse with us any longer. He took his seat at the forge that he had apparently conjured out of thin air. We watched in silence as he heated a long flat sword against the coals. When at last he lifted his hammer and began to strike it, he made the loud, echoing sounds that I recognized as the same clinks I had heard when first I awoke.

A realization passed over me. The map had not led us astray after all. The journey had brought us to a grand house where what I now recognized as an immortal being stood before me, gripping a hammer in his hand. The longer I watched him, the more certain I felt that he was the smithing god. Could this be his favorite hammer, the one that could turn a man to stone, just like in the stories? Or perhaps it was another hammer, elsewhere, that had the power to end the Trials?

We were exactly where we needed to be.

19

Summoning my courage, I said, "You are Hausakoy, god of the blacksmiths."

I shrank back instinctively as I said the words, thinking Hausakoy might strike me with his hammer. But he did not harm me. He only smiled down at his foundry, his face blurry from the smoke.

Then he said, "I'm glad you know who I am. You've traveled such a long way to find me."

The harsh, dissonant sound that came from his throat made the cliff tremble beneath our feet. His words clattered and croaked, the scrape of them like iron against stone.

Next to me, I heard Jeneba take a deep breath. "Divine god of the forge, of iron and armories, patron of smiths and farriers," she began, "we apologize for disturbing the peace of your home. Please have mercy upon us. All the legends say that you were exiled, so we had hoped . . ." She trailed off, looking shaken.

"You hoped to steal my hammer, was that it?" He fixed her with a look that made the hairs along my arms stand up straight.

"We would not—not—we weren't going to—to steal from you," she stammered out. Her usual haughtiness had been replaced by a palpable panic. I had never seen Jeneba so flustered. "We only needed your hammer to—to end the Trials. You see, Emperor Suleyman has decreed that the only man who may marry his daughter—"

"I know of your Trials," he said impassively.

"How is that possible?" Penda asked.

I thought he might answer. Instead, he brought his ear close to a flower on a nearby vine, bending toward it as if listening. He sat motionless for a long moment, watching us with blank eyes.

Then he said, very calmly, "My lady has asked me to kill you."

"Come again?" Jeneba said.

"My lady has instructed me to bash your skulls in with this hammer," he replied.

For a god like Hausakoy, the task of ending three mortal girls would be as easy as wringing a hen's neck for supper.

Everything in me was screaming to run. I sensed the same impulse to flee in the other girls. Penda was shaking, and Jeneba kept glancing desperately down the cliff, as if weighing our odds of surviving a hundred-foot jump to the stony shore.

I knew it would be of no use. The immortal gods were known to be far stronger and faster than humans, and they could even, in some stories, fly. We could not escape him by running or jumping.

Hausakoy lifted his tunic and ran his fingers self-consciously over a scar on his thigh. It was an absent, involuntary gesture, startlingly humanlike. I was surprised to learn that immortals fidgeted. It also struck me as extraordinary that a god could be punctured and pierced, and that the resulting laceration would scab and scar just like my own. I began to think that perhaps the gods and goddesses were not so very different from mortal men and women. Perhaps they were capable of illness and madness, if not death.

Perhaps they could even be tricked.

A plan was beginning to form in my mind.

"Great god, kill us if you must." I forced myself to use my calmest voice, trying to convey the impression that I was a woman of poise and composure, someone who confronted death threats with equanimity. I refused to let him see my fear. "But first, I should ask—why do you love a lady who disrespects you? A woman who cut a wound into your flesh?"

"The woman I love has commanded me to put you to death," Hausakoy replied. "That is your only concern. I think I'll kill you first. Or should I begin with your lovely friend?" He peered over at Jeneba, who pulled Penda's hand as she started back in fear.

My stomach dropped at the thought of something happening to Jeneba. "You love this lady," I said carefully. "But are you certain that she returns your affection?"

He paused, considering my words. Then he said, "She is my own lawful wife. I suffered for centuries before I knew the happiness of holding her in my arms. You are intruders in our home. I must protect her." His voice rang with his famous pride, reverberating through the ground and sending vibrations up through my feet.

Awe flickered through me. He really was the smithing god.

My own lawful wife was what he had called her. All the stories said that Hausakoy was a bachelor, with the exception of the bride he had stolen and returned a very long time ago.

"You could kill us," I told him. "You could do as your lady wife bids, as you have for many years. Or you could disobey her. You are an immortal god, and her husband. There is no higher authority. Who is she, a woman, to give orders to you? Let us live, sir, and remind the lady of her place. Let us live, and you may have this token of my gratitude."

I fished Issatou's sleeping draught out of Jeneba's pouch and held it to the thin red light of the forge. Under the flickering flames the clear liquid seemed to dance in its vial. "See? Medicine created by the careful fingers of an experienced sorceress for the relief of pain. I can see that the wound on your thigh is still painful. I purchased this medicine from Emperor Suleyman's head of servants, a healer of undeniable talent, said to be the best in the empire. But you must be careful—in incorrect dosages, it will make you very sick." I heard myself beginning to lose my composure. I knew I sounded desperate, like a merchant trying too hard to close a sale.

Around me, the flowers prickled and twitched upon their vines, as if insulted.

Hausakoy asked, very slowly, "If I spare your life, will you show me how to use the medicine?" A flicker of pain crossed his face as he shifted his weight, and I saw then the deep gash along his side.

"Yes," I said. *And then, hopefully, you will fall asleep long enough for us to escape.*

The god gave me a long, searching look. He was wary but undoubtedly interested. "Very well," he said finally. "Hand it over."

I gave him Issatou's potion, hoping he would succumb to slumber more quickly than the emperor's horsemen. My desire to find Kader, to save him, had grown into an ache—and every moment placed even more distance between us. What if deadly creatures—sharks or eels or sharp-toothed cichlids—swam in the cave water? I glanced down at the pilotless dugouts gliding along the lake. They all seemed to be moving in the same direction, borne swiftly toward wherever Kader had disappeared off to. I longed to throw myself into one of those rowboats and follow him. What if his canoe capsized and he drowned?

Trying not to let my worries show on my face, I said, "You must not take this medicine all at once." I spoke in the calmest and most knowledgeable tone of voice that I could manage, although of course I was making everything up as I went along. "Follow my instructions carefully. You will take one sip from the vial and then wait ten minutes. Then take your second sip, and wait ten more minutes. Continue until your tenth sip, and the pain of your wound will be dulled."

Penda gave me a secret congratulatory smile as I spoke. Even Jeneba looked pleased with me. They understood that I was buying us time.

"Ten sips, you say?" asked the god in a rasp like shattered pottery.

"Yes, exactly," I said. "Now you must promise not to harm us, as was our bargain."

"Sure, sure," he murmured without lifting his gaze from the sleeping draught. Hunger shone from his eyes. He placed his hands against one white wall and pushed. It gave way to a narrow shaft lit with the pigments of flowering vines. I was glad to notice the thin wooden rungs of a ladder within.

"This will take you safely to the beach," he told us. "Make haste. I cannot protect you from my lady once she discovers I have let you live."

Jeneba looked cautiously over at me, as if to ask, *Should we trust him?*

I shrugged to say, *We have no choice.*

The three of us began to lower ourselves down the ladder. Hausakoy turned his back to our descent, his broad hands already uncorking the vial. Soon we could see him no longer, and we were alone in the darkness of the shaft.

Our only lamps were the luminescent cave flowers. The farther we descended, the more certain I became that the flowers sensed as organs did, like noses or ears. I had a sneaking suspicion that they could smell us or listen to our voices. They extended petals like soft fingers and stroked our skin.

"Who do you think his wife could be?" asked Penda in a small, scared murmur once we were decidedly out of Hausakoy's earshot.

"I cannot guess," I told her. "But I think she may be able to hear us."

We continued down the ladder in tense, careful silence. It was a long way down, and the rungs were slick with dew. Each passing moment was an exercise in balance and concentration—a single misstep could spell death for all three of us. At long last, we heard a new sound below us, the distant lapping of water against a shore. Feeling encouraged, we hastened our climb, growing clumsy in our desperation to reach the beach.

Finally, the tunnel with the ladder ended. We lowered ourselves onto a pebbled bank and waded hesitantly into the water. Dozens of invisible oarsmen pulled wooden boats across the lakes. The dugouts darted as quickly as shadows, their noses gliding gracefully through the waves. All were moving swiftly away from us in the same direction. All except one.

One of the boats was perched curiously in the muddy shallows, as if it had been placed there for us. I moved toward it on impulse.

"Amie, don't," Penda said. "It's a trap."

"Whose trap?" I asked, swinging a leg into the canoe. It shuddered and bobbed under my weight and then grew still. "Hausakoy's? His lady, whoever she might be? We have no time to worry. We must escape while we still have the chance." *And I need to find my way back to Kader.*

Jeneba agreed to climb into the boat with me, but Penda refused. She did not trust the boats. She only watched as Jeneba and I used our combined strength to try to disentangle it from the net of muddy reeds that held it in place. But the boat was heavier than it looked, and it was stuck in a thick layer of muck, knots of pale seaweed coiled around its belly.

We pushed and pushed, but it would not move.

"Help us, Penda," we begged, just as Hausakoy roared like a hailstorm from the cliff above.

"This is not true medicine," he cried. "The three of you are trying to poison me!"

No. Penda joined us as we shoved the dugout again in a panic, but this time it moved even less than it had on our first try, as if we had grown weaker.

"Accursed thing!" I pushed again. That time it did not move at all.

There was a thud behind me. I turned to look, my insides screaming.

Hausakoy had thrown himself from the cliffside, and now he was with us on the beach.

The hundred-foot drop down from his foundry to the rocky shore had left him unscathed. He wielded a hammer in one hand and a golden longsword in the other. He vaulted toward us on sinewy legs, shouting, "You gave me poison! I shall end you for it."

Swinging his sword, he sliced at Penda, who still remained on the shore.

She dove away, shrieking. He lunged at her again, this time with his hammer, but she stumbled out of his path, splashing frantically as she rushed deeper and deeper into the water.

And then she was at our side, helping us push the boat. We worked desperately, the three of us pressing against its wooden hull with as much force as we could.

A metallic stench filled my nostrils. I turned to it on instinct.

What I saw then nearly stopped my heartbeat.

Hausakoy was mere meters away, looming over us, his thin mouth wide with anticipation of the kill. His hammer had quadrupled in size and glowed orange with searing heat. I tried to imagine the pain of being clubbed with it, the agony of hot metal upon my flesh. There was a lethal gleam in the smithing god's eyes as he raised it over his head, gathering momentum for our slaughter.

My panicked mind worked quickly. I saw three paths, three equally perilous fates. We could play run-and-chase with a god on that rocky little beach until he eventually caught and butchered us.

We could continue our futile efforts to untangle the immobile dug-out until he sliced us into ribbons of muscle and blood.

Or we could swim.

"Forget the boat! There is no time," I cried, grabbing the girls' hands and hurrying with them into the water.

We were wading, and then we were paddling, and finally we were swimming with the current. Twice I looked back at the shore, certain that Hausakoy would swim after us, plummeting into the waves with his weapons at the ready.

But he did not even attempt to pursue us. He stood motionless on the beach, his mouth closed, his sword limp and useless in the sand. Could he not swim? He watched us with a strange expression on his face.

He was frightened, I realized as I swam. That was why he had not followed us. Fear of what, though? I did not know, and for the time being, I did not care. All that mattered in that moment was survival.

Penda paddled in front of me, growing ever closer to the throngs of wooden boats that represented our escape. One boat was racing toward us, its narrow nose pointed in our direction. We avoided a collision only by holding our breath and ducking beneath it. The water was not cold, but the salt stung my tightly closed eyes. Once the dugout had passed, we all three came up for air, gasping and panting. A childhood on the river Niger had made me a strong swimmer, but now my lungs were screaming for respite.

"I can't tread water for much longer," said Jeneba, coughing.

Another boat was headed in our direction, its broad wooden oars moving unassisted. This time, instead of diving below it, I made a desperate grab at its edge. Jeneba soon caught my meaning and helped me to hold the dugout in place. It swam against our weight like a horse straining at its reins, but we managed to force it to stay still until all three of us had climbed inside.

And then we were flat on our backs in the boat's plank-wood belly, wheezing and sputtering and coughing up water. Hausakoy remained a small figure on the distant shore, his hammer flickering like a star. Relief and exhaustion fell over me in a deluge. We had escaped an angry god. We were safe—for now, at least. The boat bore us along, bobbing against the waves, moving through the subterranean lake on a path known only to itself. The shore receded and disappeared.

Next to me, I heard Penda groan softly. "Did he get me?" she asked. Her voice was small and scared.

I turned. She held her hands at her stomach and slumped forward, her chin resting on the boat's wooden edge. She was wounded.

Jeneba wrapped her arms about her. "Pen, did he strike you?"

"I don't know," Penda murmured. Her eyelids fluttered, and I wondered if she might faint. Her wet wrapper was as dark as the wood of the dugout, making it difficult to tell if the god had stabbed or merely struck her. But at last she lifted a small hand from her wrapper and held it before her face.

I bit back a scream when I saw that the underside of her palm was dark with blood.

"Gods save us," Penda said, and collapsed against the bottom of the boat.

"Pen, you'll be all right." Jeneba's eyes filled with rare tears. "Amie, help me turn her over."

"Just keep breathing, Penda," I said in a small voice, my throat tight.

The two of us lifted her as gently as we could. We turned her so that her back was pressed to the floor of the boat, and then Jeneba bade me rip the fabric over Penda's stomach. She said we needed to see how deep the puncture went.

Penda's wrapper had acted as a sort of bandage, for as soon as we tore it open there came a sudden spurt of blood from her abdomen, right below her navel. I had never seen someone bleed so freely. Her blood struck the boat, our hands, our clothes. It pooled at her stomach and soaked into the wood, where it mingled with water from the lake.

My nostrils filled with the iron scent of my friend's blood. All at once, I felt sick. I vomited over the side of the dugout. The lake was narrowing into a river with surging white rapids, and the meager contents of my stomach were soon lost to the frothing water below.

"Help me put pressure on the wound," Jeneba instructed me.

We pressed our palms to Penda's abdomen. For a few blessed moments, this slowed her bleeding. But then her crimson blood began to bubble up around our fingers like a spring.

Her eyelids drooped; her head lolled weakly from side to side. "Oh, gods," she said with a shuddering groan that made my heart ache. "Gods, I'm dying."

"You're not going to die," said Jeneba sharply, as if she could forbid it.

"Tell my mother goodbye, will you?" Penda's voice grew very soft and clear, like a child's. "And tell my brothers—tell my brothers I'm sorry I never found them."

"You're not going to die. You're going to find your brothers yourself," Jeneba said. There was a desperation in her voice that sent me into a panic. I wanted so badly for Jeneba's words to be true, for Penda to recover. But there was so very much blood. I heard my heartbeat ringing in my ears.

"Yazzal and Ousmane are still out there, somewhere," Penda

told us with another groan. "You have to find them. Promise me you'll find them."

"I promise," Jeneba said.

"I promise," I whispered.

I could not deny her final wish, although I had not the faintest idea how I might find Penda's brothers. But I would try.

The river narrowed and quickened. The ceiling of the cave grew lower. Stalactites in emerald and sapphire hues whistled past us like arrows. A stony underpass gaped at us, sucking us toward its dark jaws, but I no longer wondered who was piloting us and where our final destination might be. I could think only of Penda. Her eyes shifted rapidly between me and Jeneba, but her gaze was weak and unfocused, as if she could no longer see us at all.

Our boat rushed on. The opening of the passage drew nearer, a shadowy mouth ready to swallow us whole. I saw the waves leaping over its rocky lips.

"No," Penda said—to whom, I was not sure. "Please, no."

The dugout gave another lurch, and then we were plunged into darkness.

I do not know how long we journeyed through that black passageway. It might have been minutes or only seconds. The boat moved so swiftly and sharply that I worried we would crash into a wall and be thrown into the dark water below. I think I screamed.

Finally, thankfully, the currents began to slow. We glided smoothly through the brightening tunnel until a river bend brought us back into the light. Not daylight—we were not yet so lucky—but the spectral glow of the cave flowers.

"Amie," whispered Jeneba. "Amie . . ."

I knew even before I turned to see her that Penda was dead. Her eyes had fluttered closed, and upon her lips was a soft, horrible smile. There was so much blood in the boat that the air smelled of metal. My fingernails were caked in it.

Jeneba began to weep. "No!" she cried, wrapping her arms around Penda's body and burying her face in her shoulder.

For a long moment, I held Jeneba through her sobs. Shock sent me deeper into my shell, separate and detached from the bloody scene around me. I could not believe that Penda was truly gone. It felt impossible to be in this maddening place with the dead body of my friend; it did not seem real. None of this did—not the cave, not our conversation with the god of blacksmiths, not this strange boat that moved on its own, rushing us through silvery rapids to who knew where. It was all like some horrid nightmare.

I closed my eyes tightly and prayed that it really *was* all a dream. *Please, let this not be real. Let me wake up. Let me open my eyes and find myself back in the palace. Let Penda be safe and alive at my side.*

But when I reopened my eyes, I was still in a ghostly little boat thick with the scent of salt water and blood. Jeneba was still sobbing in my arms, and Penda was still dead. Sweet, constant Penda, the laundress's daughter and my first friend among the servants at the palace. She looked so small, so frail. Dead at eighteen, forever suspended in the prime of her youth, never to see her family again.

Something in me broke like a weak bit of thread. I fell to the floor of the boat, weeping, my tears mixing with Penda's spent blood. Guilt multiplied my grief. If only I had never found that map, she would still be alive. Everything in this cave might have been trying to kill us, but I was the reason we were down here in the first place.

Her death was my fault. It was as if I had killed her myself.

"She is d-dead because of me," I stammered out through my tears. "B-because I found that s-stupid map."

Jeneba wrapped her sticky hands around my face, holding me still. "It's not your fault," she told me gently. "You couldn't have foreseen that Hausakoy would be waiting for us. You couldn't have known."

I looked up at her, my face a mask of regret. "I killed her," I said. My voice was trembling. "I am the reason we are all here. I led her to her death."

"No." Jeneba took my hands in hers. "You mustn't say that, Amie. Don't even *think* it."

Her voice was stern, but the firm reassurance in her eyes surprised me.

Our bodies tensed as our dugout joined a long line of empty, identical boats, all headed in the same direction, all moving with purpose, like bees returning to their hive.

"They're slowing down," Jeneba said, squeezing my hands for emphasis.

"Where are they taking us?" I wondered aloud. The timbre of tears lingered in my voice.

Slowly, the line of dugouts rounded a corner that brought us within sight of a sandy bank. There, each dugout would stop for a short moment and then continue on out of sight, where—and of this I felt certain—the whole system would go in a large semicircle and take us back to Hausakoy, who would kill us on sight. This notion was lodged so firmly in my mind that when we reached the shore, I scrambled out quickly, dragging a still-weeping Jeneba with me.

We left Penda in the boat. I knew I would never forget the sight of her drifting away, her slight body submerged in blood. We watched from the shore as the dugout bore away what remained of our friend, joining the other empty boats and heading back toward the silvery rapids. We watched until we could no longer see the dugout carrying her body.

On the beach, Jeneba clung to me so tightly I feared she would bruise my ribs. "When I came to the palace, I was a sixteen-year-old widow. I had nothing and no one," she said through her tears. "Penda made my new life in the palace bearable. For an orphan like me, she became something like an adopted sister. And now she's gone. . . ."

I wrapped my arms around her, stroking her hair and sensing that the two of us were not alone. Although I could see no one else on the beach, only the vines and the glowing flowers, I could not shake the feeling that something was watching us or listening.

My suspicions were confirmed when the blooms on the beach slowly began to swivel in our direction, bending their stalks toward us as we walked.

The flowers could hear us. They were Hausakoy's ears. Or his wife's.

"It's not safe here," I told Jeneba. "We have to keep moving."

Hand in hand, we walked down the rocky shoreline, which narrowed into another stone passageway that was long and white and covered in blooming vines. We started down it and had walked for perhaps ten minutes when in the dim light we saw a small lump sitting in the middle of the hall.

Fear leapt up my spine and set my nerves on end, for at first I thought it was Hausakoy, returned to kill us at last.

Jeneba tightened her grip on my hand, saying, "Don't fret, Amie. He's only a little boy."

I looked closer. Indeed, there was a child of five or six years kneeling before us on the floor, playing a game with large glass beads. He wore the blue robes of the nobility, but whose child was he?

Then I remembered that the gods could cast illusions, and I felt my stomach clench with dread. "Jen, you do not know what he really is," I warned her. "Perhaps he only looks like a child, it could be a trap—"

But Jeneba was already walking over to him. He barely seemed to notice her, he was so focused on his game with the beads, until she knelt with him and asked, in a voice more motherly than I had ever heard from her, "Child, are you lost?"

"I do not think we should speak to him," I said nervously.

She ignored me. "Where have your parents gone?" she asked him.

"My parents live in the daylight," said the child with an easy smile. "They do not dare venture here."

His words chilled me to the bone.

"We should go," I said, taking Jeneba's hand and trying to lead her away.

"Don't go yet," the child protested, still smiling up at Jeneba.

I looked uncertainly down at his plump little face. He looked very much like the children who played barefoot on the riverbanks—but still there was something frighteningly unchildlike about the way he watched us. For a second, I swore I saw his eyes go entirely white.

"I'm sorry, we cannot stay," I told him in the most apologetic tone I could muster. Clutching Jeneba's hand tightly in mine, I began to walk away.

"You are Aminata Aqit," said the boy. Hearing my name on his lips made my stomach lurch. "You are sixteen years old and a salt merchant's daughter."

I felt my eyes widen with disbelief and turned to face him. "How do you know who I am?"

"Your companion is called Jeneba," he continued. "She is low-born, and you think you are better than her. Whenever she is rude to you, you comfort yourself by remembering that you are cleverer than her, more ladylike and respectable. You see her as unwashed and uneducated. After all, she cannot even read."

Jeneba fixed her gaze on me, wounded. "Amie, is this true?"

"Not at all," I said, my face burning. "Do not listen, he spins lies."

But I remembered harboring secret feelings of superiority when I had first met Jeneba, when the palace was vast and frightening and she was my tormentor, my bully. All the times she had made me feel like nothing, some shameful part of me had imagined myself above her. And I had enjoyed all the ways in which Mariama treated me specially. She had given me wrappers and jewelry, a place at her side during banquets, a cushion for me in her bed. Earning the friendship of a princess had only strengthened my shameful secret belief that I deserved more than the other handmaidens because of my education, my caste, and my name.

"You two are not truly friends," said the boy. His pupils had fallen away, and now his eyes were flat and white and full of hunger. "You do not even know *how* to be a friend, Aminata. Look at what happened to Penda. Everyone close to you suffers at one time or another. Perhaps Kader will be next."

Hot anger passed through me. How could he dare to speak Kader's name? Or Penda's? I ought to have continued down the corridor. I ought not to have reacted as I did. But I was not in my right mind. I was still reeling from Penda's death and this child had struck a nerve.

In a fury, I held him very tightly in place, with one hand on either side of his head as if I were going to box his ears. "Apologize, right now," I cried. "Or by the gods, I will thrash you."

"Stop it," he said, seemingly a child once more. His lower lip trembled. "You are scaring me."

"Amie, calm down," Jeneba scolded. "He's only a little boy."

"He is nothing of the sort! He is some sort of creature placed here by Hausakoy to make us distrust each other."

"You're petrifying the poor child." Jeneba tried to pry my hands off him, but my anger made me stronger than her in that moment.

"Apologize to us, now," I demanded. "I will not say it again."

The boy screwed up his face and howled, "Mama! Mama, come quick!" Then he began to screech. It was not a child's scream at all, it erupted from his lips with a sound like rolling thunder, so loud I thought it would burst my eardrums.

The force of it made the walls tremble and the ground shake.

Beside me, Jeneba tugged my arm and shouted something, but I could not hear her over his screams. I assumed she meant for us to run. We sprinted down the corridor as quickly as we could, but the child's great scream had caused an earthquake that made bits of the ceiling crumble and drop along our path like a hailstorm.

"Hurry!" I screamed at Jeneba.

We ran for our lives, our breathing rapid with exertion and terror. Jeneba's long legs made her faster than me, but my fear propelled me so that I was right on her heels, both of us dodging divots of rocks and collapsing stalactites that pierced the air like knives. The corridor was long and pin straight, with no spirals or turns. The deafening screams receded into the distance behind us, but still we hurried on, too frightened to stop.

"Gracious, what is that smell?" Jeneba said, breathing hard.

"What smell?" I asked, slowing to a jog. The boy's cries were far behind us, and this part of the corridor was free of rubble, as if the earthquake had never happened. After a few seconds, I smelled it, too. It was a good scent, suspiciously pleasant. A supper dish with spices and oil and meat cooked over a flame. I had not eaten in more than a day and realized all at once that I was very hungry.

"Perhaps it's a trap," said Jeneba.

But I felt so famished that I did not care. Although we slowed to a walk to catch our breath, still we continued forward because we had no other choice. Behind us was an immortal blacksmith and that screeching, truth-telling child, and before us was . . . something else.

The unknown was at least preferable to what lurked behind us.

We pressed on in silence. I did not feel much like talking, and apparently Jeneba didn't either. Perhaps she was thinking of Penda again, as I was. I could not shake the image of her bleeding into the boat, smiling blindly, her body as still as a stone.

The child's voice echoed in my mind as we walked: *Everyone close to you suffers at one time or another.*

Penda was dead. Kader was missing, perhaps also dead. I hadn't wanted to think that Kader could be dead, had tried not to let my mind drift in that direction. But now I could not stop it. Strangely enough, I started to notice that I was missing Mariama more than I missed Kader. What if I really was a poison that infected everything I touched? Perhaps that was the true reason my parents sent me away. Perhaps they had seen the venom inside me before I did.

"Look!" cried Jeneba.

I looked. I had been so preoccupied with my thoughts that I had scarcely noticed that the end of the corridor had finally come into focus. Now I could see a circle of light ahead as yellow as the yolk of an egg. And the delicious scent had grown stronger, the colorful and intoxicating odor of a great feast. My mouth began to water.

"I don't think we should keep going," Jeneba said nervously. "I don't trust whatever's out there."

"I do not trust it either," I replied. "But I don't think we have much of a choice."

Together we walked cautiously out into the light.

We stepped into the grandest dining hall I had ever seen. Once I had been stunned by the splendor of the imperial palace, but this room put all of that to shame. This hall was so wide and deep that it seemed to go on forever, as if one thousand people could be seated and served at the same time. The floor was layered with dark blue carpets embroidered in golden thread, and there was a long wooden table with golden crossrails, hundreds of platters of food with jewel-encrusted goblets and silver utensils. And above our heads, a high, golden-domed ceiling hung with copper lanterns, which swayed in their cages.

I wondered if we had finally found the god's treasures—it had certainly taken us long enough. What could I pocket now, quickly, that was of value?

"I cannot believe it," Jeneba gasped.

I followed her awed gaze to a reflecting pool at the far end of the hall. The water was pale green, its surface dotted with floating candles and lily pads, and beside it—dangling her feet in the water and gazing into its smooth, flat surface but turning as she heard our steps, blinking—was Empress Cassi Keita, Mariama's mother, who had been dead for thirteen years.

20

The bronze statue of the empress in the palace in Timbuktu had made me think Empress Cassi had been tall and imposing. But she was not—at least, I did not think so as I studied her now. I found her small and rather sweet faced.

Her features were remarkably similar to Mariama's: wide cheekbones, plump lips before a narrow mouth, a rounded jaw, and a straight nose. The empress was shorter than her daughter, and her eyes were light brown, like amber, while Mariama's were dark enough to see your reflection in.

And she looked young. People at court often said the princess had an innocent demeanor, a maiden with the mannerisms of a child. I should have liked to know what they thought of the empress, for if Princess Mariama appeared innocent, then Empress Cassi was like a newborn lamb. She seemed so fragile that I was almost reluctant to breathe on her, for fear she might crumble.

"Your Imperial Majesty," I said in awe, tightening my hand around Jeneba's.

Jeneba bowed deeply, touching her forehead to the ground and sprinkling dust over herself in the traditional gesture of deference to an emperor's wife. I followed suit, my mind buzzing with questions. How could Mariama's mother still be alive after all these years? Or was this just another of Hausakoy's cruel tricks, like the unnatural child in the hall?

I had to admit that she did not look dead. Quite the contrary: her young skin was dewy with health, the whites of her eyes were luminous, and her fingertips were rosy. She seemed to be at the very peak of vigor and salubrity. How could that be?

The empress took one step toward us, and then she hesitated, clasping her hands neatly over her wrapper instead. Her pale blue wrapper stretched tightly across her hips in the fashion of twenty years earlier, and her high neckline showed a pattern of curling golden thread. Her bare arms wore thin golden bands, and her forehead was encircled in a metal hoop with long links of gold and silver coins. Her dark hair was half covered by an indigo veil, and on her feet were sandals of blue leather.

The empress said, "Your name is Aminata Aqit. May I call you Amie? And you must be Jeneba Sangaré. Both of you work in the palace in service of my daughter, if I am correct?" She spoke in soft, honeyed tones but hardly looked at us. "Mariama thinks the world of you both. Although she seems especially infatuated with *you*, Amie."

I felt a rush of embarrassment as her words brought back a memory of my last night in the palace. I recalled Mariama's warm lips upon my hand and her desperate plea: *I forbid you to leave me.*

"But she is a kindhearted and sentimental girl, as I am sure you are aware," continued the empress. "She develops attachments easily."

"We thought you were dead," Jeneba said, her voice full of disbelief.

"The whole empire thinks that." The empress smiled and tilted her pretty head.

She had a lovely smile, I thought. Such kind eyes! Such neat and milky teeth.

Still, something about her unsettled me. I stepped back involuntarily, and must have looked frightened as I did it, because the empress cried, "Dear girls! Only please take a seat, and I will explain everything. You are both very hungry, I am sure?"

Jeneba and I looked longingly at the fragrant feast upon the table, but we did not move.

"You need not fear your supper, girls," the empress said, as if
reading our minds. "It was prepared in the style of the palace chefs.
I have sorely missed their cooking in my exile."

"Were you only exiled? I thought you died of northern plague."
My words escaped callously, without the sensitivity an empress deserved. I felt a flush of shame, but my curiosity was strong and I did
not take the question back.

"You are incorrect. I was killed," she replied, her eyes downcast.
"The emperor grew bored with me in the early days of our marriage. He took a commoner for a mistress and lavished upon her
every earthly luxury all while neglecting me, his empress and lawful
wife. I bore Suleyman a healthy daughter, a princess of his blood,
and still he would not visit my chambers. It was as if I no longer
existed.

"And then there was a small rebellion among the Songhai in the
eastern provinces. One of their governors refused to pay tribute to
Mali, and so Suleyman did what any emperor would—he killed the
obstinate governor and his family and sent the empire's soldiers to
burn the crops of the surrounding villages. Word spread quickly
among the Songhai people, and tales of the emperor's cruelty in
the provinces traveled to Timbuktu, where rebels who despised the
imperial monarchy had begun to outnumber loyalists. Suleyman
learned from his advisers that the rebels were planning an assassination attempt." She chuckled, a watery chime that set my teeth
on edge.

"But this never happened," Jeneba said, her eyebrows knitted
with confusion. "If someone had attempted to assassinate the emperor, people would speak of it."

There *had* been rumors of an assassination attempt in the past and whispers of a coming insurrection. The seeds of rebellion had been planted long ago; the demonstrations I had seen at market were only the first rain droplets in a storm a long time coming.

"You are correct," said the empress. "Those who wanted to seize power from Mali were stripped of their weapons by the gods, stopping the uprising before it could begin. Suleyman consulted often in those days with sorcerers. He put on a show of being a God-fearing Muslim, of hating paganism in all its forms. But one of his advisers was a sorcerer who drew his magic from the god Hausakoy, and it was through him that Suleyman struck his divine bargain. Hausakoy agreed to end the rebellion, seizing the insurgents' weapons and delivering them to the imperial armory."

I frowned in concentration, remembering my walk through the military storerooms with Mariama on the morning I left her. There had been enough swords and daggers and spears to outfit a great army. How many of those weapons had Emperor Suleyman commandeered from the rebel forces with the assistance of a great god?

The empress continued. "Of course, the gods do not aid mortals for free. Hausakoy expected payment. Suleyman offered him gold and slaves, but Hausakoy refused to accept any compensation besides a wife. He wanted to take me for a bride. I am afraid that all the stories about him are true; he prefers mortal women to goddesses, and he has been known to kidnap young girls from their fathers' houses and take them to his home beneath the sands. So Suleyman gave me to him in exchange for quelling the rebellion. His advisers forced me to drink a potion that ended my life in the mortal world and gave me a new life in Hausakoy's palace in the desert. I wed Hausakoy here in this cave on the very same day of my funeral procession in Timbuktu."

"You are Hausakoy's wife?" I gasped out.

"*You* gave the order for our deaths?" Jeneba's voice was sharp.

"Is that what he told you? That it was *my* idea to have you killed? Girls, this has been his plan all along. Three deaths for his hammer," she said matter-of-factly. "Penda's death, Aminata's death, and your death in exchange for his hammer and the end of the Trials. I told you that the gods do not aid mortals without payment in kind."

A horrible sinking feeling caught hold in my chest. "No," I tried to whisper, but my mouth had grown so dry that my voice came out in a weak, inaudible croak.

"Do not look so aghast," said the empress. "That is simply how the gods operate. I have been trying to make my daughter understand this for years. 'Mariama, if you really want to end the Trials,' I told her, 'you will need to send me your next suitor, along with three people who will not be missed. Then you will have Hausakoy's hammer.' But she is softhearted, and it took a very long time for me to convince her of what must be done."

"You speak with the princess," I whispered. "How is that possible?"

"I left her my favorite hand mirror before I died. When I married Hausakoy, I asked him to build me a mirror of my own, so that I could watch my daughter grow up. He constructed this reflecting pool with an enchantment that allows for communication with mortals. I did not often speak with Mariama when she was a young girl, but as she grew older, I began to show myself to her."

I remembered the little looking glass on Mariama's wall, the phantasmic fingers brushing the surface of the glass. I had not imagined them after all.

"When Suleyman started those awful Trials, my daughter asked me to help her end them," explained the empress. "I consulted with my husband, and he told me that he could help a suitor survive the kettle—in exchange for a blood sacrifice."

Finally, I could guess why Mariama had ordered me so adamantly to stay with her at court. She had been trying to spare my life. Now it all made sense: her bad dreams, her lingering guilty glances, her tears.

"So she *knew* she was sending the three of us to our deaths?" I asked numbly. I did not want to believe it, but I could not deny the story. I felt a flush of disgust: she had not even tried to prevent Penda or Jeneba from following the map out into the desert like fish swimming into a net. To Mariama, they were simply not worth rescuing.

How could I care for a girl so callous as that? Her conscience was as dead as the men who had perished in her name.

"The princess was in on it from the start?" asked Jeneba, voice shaking. "She was talking to you? Taking *your* orders?"

"I am her mother," the empress said plainly. "Of course she obeys me."

"What about the map that led us here?" Jeneba pressed. "Where did it come from?"

The empress looked amusedly between the two of us. She asked, "Well, where do you think it came from?" with a condescending smile on her lips, as if wondering which of us would be the first to solve the riddle.

My mind worked rapidly, trying to put things in order. Had Mariama and her mother set a trap for us by planting the map where I was likely to find it one day?

"*You* made the map, in order to lure us here," I said numbly. The princess and empress had tricked us into thinking the desert journey was our own idea when really we were falling right into their plan.

"Close guess," said the empress. "My husband made the map, actually, and delivered it to my old nursemaid, Issatou, who has remained very loyal to me for all these years. She hid the map in a book where she knew you would find it while you were cooking."

I could not manage a response. The depth of Mariama's betrayal shocked me, snatching the words from my throat and leaving me lightheaded. A memory moved through me, cutting me like glass—Mariama smiling down into her teacup and wiping away her tears as I read aloud the story of the scorpion's bride. I realized now that it wasn't a coincidence that her crying fits had ended when I discovered the book she and her mother had wanted me to find. She was a talented little performer, I had to admit. Had her night terrors even been real? Or were they mere fictions, just another method of getting others to do her slippery bidding? I wondered how close Mariama was with Issatou. She had been her nursemaid, and her mother's, too, but I had rarely seen them interact. Still, it was likely that Issatou had been a part of the plan and ready to provide the potion and antidote when I came to her.

I had believed myself so lucky for finding a treasure trove of stories to chase Mariama's bad dreams away. But it hadn't been a treasure after all. It was a trap.

"Curse you," Jeneba hissed. "Curse you and your daughter both!"

Something caught my eye then, a dark blue shape at the far end of the feasting table. For a moment, I thought it was an animal, perhaps a bird with indigo plumage. But I had seen no birds here, or any other living things, save for the cave flowers.

I looked closer. A young man in blue robes was slumped forward, his head pillowed on his folded arms. His back rose and fell with the slow, even breathing of someone in a deep slumber. The sight of him made me bring my hands to my mouth in surprise and whisper, "Do you see him?" in Jeneba's ear. My breath came out hotly between my trembling fingers.

Jeneba looked just as startled as I felt. "Has he been here the whole time?" she asked, too quietly for us to be overheard.

The empress was frowning like a schoolmistress who disapproved of her pupils conversing. "What are you two whispering about?"

Instead of answering, I turned my attention to the man sleeping upon the table. His face remained hidden, buried in folds of indigo cloth, but I could hear his gentle breathing. And then I saw the silver pendant at his neck and at once I knew. "Kader!" I cried, no longer caring if the empress heard me. "Here, help me to wake him."

Jeneba rushed over and propped him up against her shoulder while I shook him and begged him to wake up. But to our horror, he did not stir. I forced his eyelids open in a panic. They rolled backward into his head.

Jeneba said, "He is ill, or drugged!"

I turned to the empress, fury building in my stomach. "What have you done to him?"

She did not like to see us in such a state of alarm. "You girls don't need to worry," she said reassuringly. "He will be fine."

"Fine?" I repeated incredulously. "He is half-dead! You must revive him at once."

She looked at us blankly, her lips a tight line. "And why should I?"

"Because he and I are going to be wed." I felt my heartbeat in my throat. "Because we are in love."

"Love!" The empress laughed, a pretty, tinkling sound that reminded me of coins. "Love, love, love. I was once enamored with Suleyman, but he preferred his mistress. I should have listened to my nursemaid, Issatou, when she warned me about him. As things turned out, it was my love for him that killed me and sent me to this infernal prison beneath the dunes. Let me offer you girls some advice: love only your blood relations. It will save you a great deal of heartache."

"You must revive him *now*," I insisted. My voice was shaking, but

I had to speak up for Kader. "Whatever draughts you have fed him, whatever venom you have dripped into his veins, you must provide an antidote. Wake him at once!"

"He has not been poisoned, you dimwit." The empress rolled her eyes as though it were perfectly obvious that he was in no real danger. "Far from it, he is only resting. I wanted to look upon my future son-in-law, and give him a farewell meal. He has a very long journey ahead of him."

Kader's eyes began to flutter open, the whites of them trembling like moths' wings. Relief flooding my senses, I said, "You are awake!"

He blinked up at me, sleepy and uncomprehending. "Amie," he said softly. "Where am I? What has happened?"

"It is not safe here," I told him. "We have to go."

Jeneba asked, "Can you stand?"

The empress watched, apparently bemused, as the two of us placed our hands under Kader's arms and tried to help him up. But he was heavy as lead and could not be lifted.

"Kader, we have to go," I pleaded. "That woman is evil. She means to hurt us."

"Which woman?" He looked lazily about the chamber as if in a trance. Then he smiled, very slowly. "Oh, you mean the lady? She wouldn't hurt us. She's lovely."

"The empress has confused his mind," breathed Jeneba over my shoulder. "She has placed him under an enchantment."

"My love, we have to go *now*." I spoke clearly and loudly, as if instructing a child. Kader's eyes had grown dull and glassy. All the usual intelligence had dropped from his gaze, replaced by a blankness that filled me with worry. What if he stayed like this forever?

But Kader would not move. He only looked at us with that strange smile upon his lips.

Jeneba shook her head sadly. "He doesn't understand anything."

"He will not go anywhere with you," said the empress without emotion. She stepped around the table, trailing her fingers along its wooden leg as she moved. Her gait was graceful, and as she drew nearer, I could smell spices on her breath. "I have made sure of it. He will not leave this cave with anyone other than my husband, the god. Hausakoy will give him his hammer and lead him safely through the desert and back to Timbuktu. Kader will survive the suitor's kettle, and then he will marry my daughter. It has been decided."

I ignored her. "Stand," I told Kader determinedly. "You are coming with us."

For a moment, I thought I had pierced the cloud of enchantment and reached his mind. He frowned briefly, and something like understanding stirred behind his eyes.

But then it was gone, and he was smiling blankly at me once again. "I am not permitted to go with you," he said. "I must wait for the great god to give me his hammer and take me back to the palace."

The empress nodded approvingly. "Good! Now you must share with Aminata and Jeneba what you were just telling me before you fell asleep. Explain to them that you would very much like to be emperor one day."

My heart dropped. "Kader? Is that true? You have never said anything like that to me before."

"I would make a good ruler," he said, still smiling. "I would not be like Emperor Suleyman. I would be the emperor that Mali deserves."

His words sent a pang of disappointment reverberating through my chest like a drum. I had always held Kader in high regard, his kindness and generosity shaping my perception of him decidedly in his favor. Yet the shadows of doubt had begun to creep in ever since he had suggested abandoning Penda and Jeneba that night in the desert. My admiration for him waned further still with his swift surrender to the empress's enchantments, replaced by a disillusionment that made my mouth taste bitter.

I wished Kader were strong enough to resist her sorcery, but I had to admit that he was not strong. Perhaps he had never been. In contrast, Mariama had been cunning enough to trick me and determined enough to sacrifice her maids' lives to end the Trials. She was stronger than him, a strength I couldn't help but begrudgingly respect.

"Tell the girls that the great god has asked for a sacrifice of three deaths in exchange for his enchanted hammer," urged the empress, pulling me out of my thoughts. "Tell them that they must die so that you can win the Trials."

"Your Lordship?" Jeneba's voice trembled.

The fog of his enchantment seemed to thin. He stopped smiling and grew agitated. "Oh, Amie, you do not know what it is like!" he said suddenly. "You cannot fathom the pain of being an outcast in your own home. But if I win the Trials, my father will finally respect me as he does my brothers. With a path to become emperor, I'll be greater than all of them."

No. "Kader, this is not you," I said. Perhaps it was the god's enchantment speaking, not Kader. He would never say such a thing.

Or would he? Perhaps Kader presented one image of himself to the world while suppressing his larger ambitions because he thought his likelihood of achieving them was so low. I did not want to believe it, but part of me worried that the empress's spell craft had only drawn out the truth.

"I will have Princess Mariama for a wife," he said. "And one day, I will be emperor of Mali, and my father will boast of me to all who will listen."

The empress beamed at him like a proud mother. "Very good!"

"Enchanted or not, he's a traitor," Jeneba scoffed.

"Those are not his true feelings," I said, trying to convince myself as much as Jeneba. "The enchantment is speaking for him."

"Amie, I care for you very deeply. I wish it did not have to end like this. But you must understand that this is an opportunity I cannot ignore." Kader spoke in a soft, dazed voice, not his own. Still, I could feel my heart breaking with his every word.

"You would let us die down here?" I asked him. Now my tears flowed freely, and I did not bother to brush them away. "You'd let us perish, all so you could win this contest?"

Kader gave no reply. His eyes went completely vacant.

"My husband approaches, we must make haste," said the empress. "Kader, should you like to win the Trials?"

After a brief hesitation, he nodded. "Yes."

I knew then that I had lost him. How was he any different from Mariama? One had tried to save me from death and the other would allow my death for the opportunity to one day rule Mali. I felt sick and confused.

The empress looked expectantly up at the doorway, and suddenly Hausakoy was moving toward us. He looked just as he had on the beach, holding his golden longsword and the hammer that would allow Kader to survive the suitor's kettle.

"Hello again, girls," he said.

Fear made my mind go empty. I wanted to run, but my limbs felt dead as firewood. I wanted to scream, but terror clogged my throat. I could only watch as the god who meant to end our lives drew closer.

"No, no," Jeneba whimpered.

She could not move, either. It was as if we had both been enchanted, but I knew in my heart that the paralyzing element was not magic. We were numb with terror, stupefied, like animals gone into shock.

Hausakoy put his hammer into Kader's hands and whispered to him in a tongue I could not decipher, a serpent's hiss. Kader looked down at the hammer. For a moment, I thought I saw his skin go gray as stone. And then they were gone—mortal and immortal both. Not even so much as the scent of them lingered on the air.

Panicked, I rushed around the room, turning over furniture, as if I might bring Kader back by making a loud commotion. "Where has he gone?" I asked, rounding on the empress. I was breathless, my chest rising and falling rapidly against the front of my wrapper.

"Up," she said simply. "Up to the desert, and then on to Timbuktu, where he will try his luck in the suitor's kettle. With the hammer, I am sure he will survive."

"And then he'll wed Mariama," finished Jeneba bitterly. "Meanwhile, the two of us will remain down here, dead and forgotten, just like Penda."

"But he will come back for me," I said. My voice sounded small and strange. "Right? He would not leave me here to fend for myself. He loves me. He would not leave me here to die. He wouldn't . . ." I faltered. New tears welled in my eyes and traveled down my cheeks.

Jeneba held me. "We'll find a way out of this," she whispered. "I promise." I returned the embrace tightly in thanks and hope. We were all we had left.

Through the gauze of my tears, I felt the empress staring at us. It was not a cruel look, only curious. She looked very much like her daughter when she was thinking intently about something. I imagined Mariama wearing that same look when Kader stepped out of the suitor's kettle entirely unscathed. In my mind's eye, I sketched the two of them dancing together at their wedding, together on their first night as husband and wife. I shuddered, pushing the images away.

The empress asked, "You thought he loved you?"

"He does love me," I replied through great, hiccuping sobs. "He does love me, or he did, until your husband poisoned him against me with his magic."

"Men often lie," the empress said with a shrug. "I could fill this room with the lies my mortal husband told me about that chit of a girl, Binta. She is long dead, and good riddance. I was nothing but loyal to Suleyman. I gave him a beautiful daughter. And how did he repay me? By taking a lowborn mistress. What scum!"

All along the walls, the flowers seemed to blush and grow more vibrant in agreement.

"When do you intend to kill us?" Jeneba blurted.

"Kill you?" repeated the empress, apparently confused.

"In order for Kader to win the Trials, Jen and I must die." My voice trembled. "That is what you said, was it not? Three deaths in exchange for Hausakoy's hammer?"

"Why—yes, eventually," the empress said, offhand. "But first, you must tell me more about your time with my daughter. Do the people like her? How is she perceived among the nobility? Does she have a talent for courtly affairs?"

Jeneba and I looked at each other for a long moment. "We cannot trust her," I whispered.

"This is another trap," she whispered back.

But if the empress was planning to kill us anyway, we might as well delay the inevitable for as long as we could. Glad for the gift of borrowed time, we let her lead us to the bathing pool. I examined its sweet-smelling turquoise surface, still and smooth as a mirror, and my red-eyed reflection gazed wearily back at me. Watching myself in the bath, I noticed a bruise Kader had left upon my collarbone on the night of the hyenas when he kissed me too hard. Shame swept through me like a hot wind at the memory.

"I have always wished to know what my daughter is like at court," said the empress. She stepped delicately into the warm, scented water. "You must tell me how she is spoken about in society. I want her to rule Mali one day, and an empress needs many supporters."

"Mariama is well-liked by nobles and commoners both," I responded, lowering my foot into the bath. The heat of it made me gasp. "Please, tell us more about how you speak to your daughter."

"My divine husband built this pool as the mirror image of my daughter's looking glass," she told me. "It allows me to watch her from afar or be pulled into her dreams."

"Oh," I said, stunned. Anger swelled in me as I thought of Mariama's supposed night terrors. I understood now that she and her mother had conspired together in those dreams, thinking of ways to end the Trials and planning our murders. The rotten fruit had not fallen far from its tree.

I hated to remember those tiresome nights when I had pitied her and wiped away her tears. I wished I could take it all back.

"So the princess's nightmares . . . ," Jeneba said slowly. Rage was building in her dark eyes. "They were in fact conversations—"

"Conversations with me, yes. But do not tell me that my daughter calls our talks nightmares!" The empress's hand flew to her smiling mouth in mock horror. "I admit that I sometimes speak with her harshly, but it is always for her own good and for that of the empire. Her father is far too paranoid to ever end those odious Trials. I'm sure he thought it would bring him peace, to boil the sons of his enemies, but it will have only caused the nobility to dislike him. Suleyman would be so distracted by the sport and spectacle of the Trials that he'd fail to notice the insurrection gathering beneath his nose."

She looked at me again, drawing me in with her sharp amber gaze. "You should have heard her the night before you left. She said, 'Mother, we cannot send Amie into the desert with the others. I love her, and I want her to live.' It was such a disappointment to learn that my daughter would ruin months of careful planning for some silly flirtation with her maid. When she becomes an empress, she will learn not to be so softhearted."

My heartbeat hastened despite myself. I tried to imagine Mariama and Cassi's conversation through the silver looking glass. Mariama had knowingly sent Jeneba and Penda to their deaths, but she had tried to save me. A flush climbed up my cheeks as I recalled my final night at court, the lamplit glow of her bedchamber, the crush of her skin against mine. I found myself wondering what would have happened if I had stayed behind. If she had known all along that three lives must be given in exchange for ending the Trials with the great god's hammer, who did she expect would die in my place? Perhaps she would have sent another servant out into the desert whose blood would replace mine when it came time to pay Hausakoy's divine debt.

"Show us how you enter your daughter's dreams," I said.

"Very well," she said. "I will show you how it is done, by the grace of my divine husband. First, you must look into the water. Then speak the name of the man or woman you wish to converse with in their dreams."

I peered cautiously into the pool, examining my reflection. My eyes were filled with a mixture of worry and determination. "Hadiza Aqit," I breathed out, taken aback by the sudden and unwavering conviction in my words. My sister's whereabouts remained elusive, and I needed to know if she was okay. But it was more than that—I also wanted her help in finding a way out of my current situation. I hoped that her knowledge of magic would allow her to advise us how to escape.

Almost immediately after I had spoken my sister's name, the pool began to glow. The water burbled softly, as if summoning me to its depths. Soon, shafts of golden light rose from it like steam, and a vision of a great sweeping scrubland had replaced my reflection in the water. I could make out a dry riverbed lined on either side with doom palms. Tents leaned against trees, and livestock wandered between little thatched-roof houses.

At first I saw no one, but I then noticed two young women kneeling together upon the bank. Their backs were turned to me and I could not see their faces, only the dark linen of their wrappers. Looking closer, I saw that they were crushing dried herbs into a terra-cotta bowl. I watched in fascination as one of them set aside her mortar and began to pour water over the herbs as if she were brewing tea. The other started stirring fistfuls of sand into the same bowl. Both young women worked quickly and expertly, and in a few short moments they had created what appeared to be some sort of medicinal paste.

At last, one of them climbed to her feet, took the bowl in her hands, and rushed into a tent. Someone within it must have been sick or injured, and she had been ordered to create a remedy. I could just barely see her companion peering over anxiously at the tent; it was not until she jutted out her chin and shouted through cupped hands that I finally glimpsed the girl's face. As soon as I looked upon her properly, I knew that she was Haddy.

My relief rose and crested like a wave. I had found my missing sister. It put me at ease to see her alive and well. Although I'd guessed she'd run away from home willingly, part of me had still worried that the emperor's soldiers had arrested her in secret, quietly locking her away as punishment for her treasonous association with rebel forces. I'd imagined her being interrogated about the Scorpion Order.

Seeing her safe was a blessing, but I was wary of trusting my eyes. "Is that really Hadiza?" I thought to ask. "Or are you trying to trick me?" I knew that the empress was under no obligation to tell the truth.

"I promise to not deceive you further," she said. "This is not a trick. My pool is showing us your sister's true whereabouts, and the only reason you cannot enter her dreams is because she is not presently sleeping."

All this time, Jeneba had been watching the water with bewilderment. "Where are they?" she asked suddenly. "I don't recognize the landscape."

"I do not know," said the empress with a shrug.

Jeneba turned her confused gaze upon me. "Amie, I thought your sister was married to Lord Ayouta. What was she doing with those herbs? And who was the other girl?"

"I have no idea," I said, remembering the evening in the emperor's library when Haddy first told me that she was a sorceress. She had said that her leaders at the Scorpion Order were preparing an insurrection. I wondered if perhaps the other girl was also a member of the Order. Was she a sorceress, too?

I needed to see more, needed to understand.

But now the vision was beginning to fade. Haddy's face rippled out of view, the sandy riverbed disappeared . . . and then I was looking at my own reflection once again.

"I must retire," said the empress with a yawn. "My husband will be back by morning. I shall leave it to him to kill you then." She spoke in a relaxed, informal manner, as if she had not just spoken of ending our lives.

My stomach twisted. I thought, *You villain*, but I did not speak. I was too angry and too frightened.

Next to me, Jeneba's face was rigid with terror. She took my hand silently and I squeezed it. It was a comfort to know that I would not be alone, at least, for my last night among the living.

I wondered if we had any chance of escape. I did not think Jeneba and I could fight a great god and win, but Hausakoy was away in Timbuktu. Perhaps there was a way for the two of us to get out of this cave before his return. Might we smash in some window and find ourselves in a passageway that led to the desert? Or could we climb into one of the enchanted canoes and try to steer ourselves to safety?

The empress clapped her hands and two manservants entered the hall. Both of them were tall and broad shouldered and appeared to be male, but in truth they did not look like any man I had ever met. Their forms were lumpy and misshapen, like a child's smudged sketches, and their faces were sunken and pulpy, their skin like petals of flowers and their eyes and noses melting into each other like wax. But the most unsettling thing about them were their hands, split into two great pincers like a scorpion's.

When one servant placed his clawed hands upon Jeneba's shoulders, she shrank back from him with a look of revulsion. "What's this?" she asked in a panic. "I thought you were going to let us live until the morning!"

The empress let loose her beautiful, tinkling laugh. "Do not worry about the spirits. They cannot harm you. They've barely the wits to follow simple instructions."

I whirled around to see if they had taken offense, but they only looked at us blankly, without recognition. *I suppose she's right about their wits. Or else they don't let her know what they're thinking*, I thought, trying to put pieces together. I remembered the great cauldron at Hausakoy's forge on the cliffside. It resembled the suitor's kettle almost exactly and even had a human hand floating within. The god had called it a *replica spirit*. He had said his wife liked him to duplicate the comforts to which she had become accustomed: chefs, servants, scribes. I was beginning to wonder if the spirits were Mariama's suitors, brought halfway back to life to serve the empress. I didn't doubt that Hausakoy could breathe new life into dead men.

"Take the girls to their chamber, will you?" Empress Cassi said to the spirits. "Do not let them out of your sight."

21

The spirits led us down several bone-white corridors until we arrived at the small, plain chamber where we were meant to spend our final night. The room was large and circular; all its walls were streaked with vines, and the air was thick with the sweet, heady scent of those strange flowers. Jeneba and I glanced fearfully around the chamber, looking for shackles or chains, and gripped each other's hands tightly.

But the spirits did not fetter us or put our legs in irons. They did not even lock us in our cell. They only waited outside the door like guards, holding us captive on behalf of our jailer, the empress. They did not speak, and although we listened for their breathing, we heard nothing at all.

I felt like a woman condemned. *Penda is dead*, I thought numbly, still holding Jeneba's hand. *Jen and I will die in the morning, and it is all my own fault for finding that dreadful map.*

"This is the end for us, isn't it." Jeneba sank to the floor, panicked tears forming in her eyes. "This is to be the very last night of our lives."

I could have comforted her, but instead I found myself beginning to pace the chamber and trying desperately to think of a plan, a means of escape. But no schemes came to me. I saw no windows to smash or staircases to climb. Earlier, I had hoped Jeneba and I would be able to find our way back to the cave lake and sail away to safety in one of those unmanned, unnatural canoes, but now I doubted we could manage it. I knew that the spirits would not permit us to leave until the morning, when the great god of the blacksmiths returned to put us to death.

Then I thought of Kader. I wondered where he was right now—had Hausakoy already flown with him all the way back to the city? How long was the journey taking them? Not long, I supposed, for I knew that the gods could travel faster than mortals. I also began to wonder what sort of enchantment the empress had placed Kader under, and if there had been any truth in his words when he said he wanted to make his father proud. Did he really still crave Lord Bagayogo's approval after everything the man had done? What sort of father would send his son to certain death in a kettle of stone? Part of me was worried that he was not put under an enchantment after all, that he had decided to be loyal to his father and not to me without any magical intervention.

I had no way of knowing. Kader was lost to me forever. I knew that I would never see him again, nor would I ever be reunited with my sister or my parents or even Mariama. I was ashamed to think that I had once been so proud to be the princess's favorite, wearing her clothes and perfumes and jewelry like badges of honor when, really, they were bribes. Now I understood why she had defended me against Lord Bagayogo on my first night in the palace. It had not been kindness at all. Mariama's affection for me, our so-called friendship—it had all been part of her mother's plan to find a third victim, a third soul to exchange for her one hundredth suitor's survival. I imagined she and her mother had already decided that Penda and Jeneba would have to die, and they needed a third person whom no one would miss. Who better than a merchant's disgraced daughter?

And yet Mariama had tried to save me, in the end. Was I supposed to be grateful that she had meant to spare my life, even though she had not attempted to rescue Penda or Jeneba? Or should I despise her for plotting to put two innocent girls to death?

It was not lost on me that if I had done what Mariama asked of me and stayed with her at court, I would be safe right now. I would not be pacing my cell beneath the desert, waiting for death to come in the morning. I had thought that disobeying the princess was an act of rebellion, that following Kader into the desert was a sign that I was becoming bolder and more defiant; but in reality, I had walked directly into a trap.

The flowers tilted their faces at me as I walked up and down the room. I saw their petals and stems twisting left to right, right to left, following my every movement. *The empress is watching*, I thought. That unnerved me, and finally I grew still.

"What are you thinking about?" Jeneba was looking up at me, her face as despondent as I had ever seen it.

"I thought I was becoming a new person," I said bitterly. "Instead, I led us to our deaths."

I've never stopped following orders.

At last, I sat down on the floor with Jeneba and wept. I sobbed into the blue folds of my skirts until I remembered that I still wore Mariama's borrowed wrapper and not my own. Then I started up, brushed furiously at my tears, and forced myself to think. *Hurry and come up with a plan of escape*, I told myself. *You must do it not just for yourself but also for Jeneba's sake. You cannot let her die down here. You owe her that much.*

She was still watching me, her eyes wide with terror. It was that look that saved me. Her look gave me back my future—for in the second of starting up from the floor, wiping away my tears, and meeting her gaze, my fear and confusion began to slip away and I devised a plan. It came to me fully formed in a sudden rush of clarity.

It was a desperate plan, but it would have to work.

I wanted to explain it to Jeneba, but I worried the flowers would overhear us and report back to the empress. So instead, I took her hands in mine and whispered, "I am going to do something now. Something risky. But I cannot put it into words just yet, so you will have to trust me."

She frowned up at me. "What are you talking about?"

"I am going to get us out of here, I promise," I whispered, so that the flowers would not overhear. And then I brought my lips to the door, knowing that the spirits were listening on the other side, and asked, "Can you come in?"

Jeneba frowned at me with horrified disbelief. "You're inviting them in? Those monsters?"

"Trust me," I said again.

The door gave a shudder. Then it swung open, revealing one of the spirits—his companion had apparently vanished—looking at us with a stare so vacant that I wondered again if he was a deceased man brought back to life by Hausakoy's cauldron. I searched the spirit's face, hoping to recognize the features of one of Mariama's suitors, but his countenance was entirely distorted and malformed. In truth, I found him very frightening.

"Jeneba and I are thirsty," I announced, trying my best not to look at him directly.

At first, he only gaped at me. Frustrated, I pantomimed drinking a glass of water. When that failed to produce any response, I said, "Take us to the empress's dining chamber, so that we may drink."

That worked, I thought as he bowed and gestured for us to follow him. I supposed that the spirits required very specific instructions. We walked through a maze of corridors until finally we reached the empress's empty hall. He led us to the edge of the bathing pool and looked at us proudly, as if to say, *See! I found water.*

"Thank you," I said. "You are dismissed."

This was wishful thinking on my part. He had been commanded to guard us, and he would not leave. I felt his dull gaze upon me as I bent to the water and whispered, "Hadiza Aqit."

"You're going to try to visit your sister?" Jeneba said, grabbing my hand.

"We both are," I said, thinking, *My sister is a trained sorceress. If anyone can save us now, it will be Haddy.*

The two of us watched the water expectantly. I had hoped it might glow and shift as it had when the empress showed us how to use it. But the water remained dark and still. That made me nervous.

"Amie, are you sure you're doing it right?" Jeneba asked anxiously.

Louder, with a note of fear in my voice, I repeated, "Hadiza Aqit. Show me Hadiza Aqit al-Sanhaji al-Timbukti."

This time felt different. A cold throb started behind my eyebrows, and my legs began to shake. The blooming vines on the walls seemed to tremble, and the petals of the flowers leaned toward me as if I were the sun. My head felt heavy, and my limbs grew slack. I thought I heard someone say distant, murky words, but I didn't know what they were.

Then I started back from the pool, dizzy and stumbling.

Jeneba watched me nervously. "What's happening to you?"

I parted my lips but found I could not answer her. My voice felt far away. I could only watch her terrified face as the cold dark wood of the floor came rushing up at me, followed by impact.

———•———

I dreamed of my sister. But no, I was there *with* her, kneeling over her sleeping mat in a large tent filled with slumbering women and girls. Some seemed as young as eleven or twelve years old, while others looked to be in their thirties. All of them slept with their weapons, and in Haddy's tightly closed fist, I saw the jeweled hilt of a dagger.

"Haddy," I whispered, looking nervously about the tent to see if the others could hear me. None of them stirred. "Haddy, wake up," I said more loudly.

At last, her eyelids fluttered open. When she saw me, she gave a hoarse cry of delight and embraced me, pulling me down with her to the mat. "Amie! What are you doing here?"

"I do not think I *am* here," I said into her hair. "If I were really here, the others would see me, or hear me. I think we are dreaming."

She pulled back, frowning. "How—how have you entered my dreams?" she asked.

"I do not know," I admitted. "Mariama's mother, the empress, has imprisoned me underground."

Haddy exclaimed softly, "Amie, have you gone mad? The empress died years ago."

"She is now wife to the god Hausakoy. It seems she is still alive. Or half-alive. Oh, I don't know!" My voice wavered with my mounting fear. "The great god has already murdered our friend Penda, and he is going to kill me and my other friend Jeneba in the morning. Our three lives were to be given in exchange for the smithing god's hammer so that the next suitor can survive the kettle and the Trials can end. You have to save us."

"I will come for you, right away," she promised. "I will not let anything bad happen to you, ever again. You have my word."

I nodded distractedly, noticing an opening at the edge of the tent through which I could see a slim crescent of scrubland and stars. "Where are we?" I asked, hoping to guess how close she was to the forge house.

"We're about a day's journey northeast of Timbuktu. But where are you? How do I find you?" she asked in a worried rush, leading me past the rows of sleeping women and out of the tent. We stepped out onto a dark plain dotted with tents. Smoke rose in thin plumes from several campfires, blurring the flat-topped silhouettes of nearby acacia trees. Young men and women in leather and metal armor strode confidently between the firepits, jostling one another and laughing.

Above it all was the luminous evening sky. Never before had I seen so many stars.

"We were about two days' journey north of the city when the great god took us underground," I said, wishing I could show her the map. It frustrated me that I couldn't give her more accurate directions. "What's around here? Any landmarks? How close are you to the trading roads?"

"We're not near the roads. The Scorpion Order has been using these training grounds for decades. We cannot risk being found out by caravanners," my sister explained. She directed my attention to the red emblem of a scorpion on the side of her tent. "Do you see, now, why I was asking to converse privately? I already knew that I was going to leave my husband for the Order, and I wanted to bring you with me."

"I . . . understand," I murmured. But in truth I was only half listening, looking at my surroundings and realizing that very few of the other dwellings were labeled with scorpions. Most of the perhaps fifty tents in the campsite were plain sheepskin. I felt a low buzzing in my stomach and a sudden surge of respect for Haddy's resolve.

"I will bring weapons and armor to help you survive the great god's wrath," she told me. "This campsite was built upon an ancient quarry, and the ground is rich with iron ore. I can make you a sword and shield and suit of armor within the hour, and then bring a small search party northbound—"

A new voice interrupted her, a saccharine singsong murmur that made my stomach drop. "*Amie, wake up.*" I knew at once that it was the empress speaking. A frigid wind picked up. It was so cold that Haddy and I had to cling to each other for warmth. The tents around us rippled violently, their metal tentpoles groaning as if in a storm.

"What is happening?" Haddy cried over the wind.

"The empress has found us," I shouted back. "We do not have much time!"

"I will not let her take you," she cried, and tightened her grip on my shoulders.

A creeping red mist was beginning to pierce its way between Haddy and me, tearing through us like a knife. I felt myself being pried away from her by the red fog, and I shouted, "Help me!"

"*Amie, wake up,*" said the empress again. Her voice seemed to come from the wind itself.

The cold red mist had thickened so that I could no longer see Haddy, or anything at all. It seemed to grow into a living being and speak: "*Amie, wake up. Wake up.*" The mist began to sting my eyes like smoke from a cooking fire. I rubbed at them furiously.

When I opened them again, I was back in the empress's dining hall. Jeneba was holding me in her trembling arms and the spirit who had been watching us was gone. In his place stood the empress, looking as young and lovely as ever. "Amie, you must wake up," she said again firmly.

I started away from her and stumbled back into the wall, fear and fury coursing through my veins. I had been so close to helping Haddy find the forge house, and now it seemed like it would be impossible for her to come rescue us from this wretched place beneath the sand. My frustration bubbled up and I punched the wall, my knuckles sinking into the soft petals of cave flowers, which hissed and crackled at my touch. The empress winced. I had already thought that those strange blossoms were in some way connected to her, and now I was sure she could feel what they felt. I began to wonder if she could be truly harmed through them. If I killed them, would I kill her, too?

That gave me an idea. While the empress was distracted by the pain, I secretly slipped two of the knives from the dining table into my pocket. Then I took a deep breath and said with as much confidence as I could muster, "You will let us go now."

"I cannot let you go," the empress said with a sigh. "Have you not been listening? My immortal husband requires three deaths in exchange for ending the Trials."

"You are going to let us go," I repeated. "You will lead us out of this place unharmed, and in return, we will spare your life."

That made her laugh. Her laughter sounded so very much like her daughter's that I flinched. "*You*, spare my life?" she asked, still chortling in astonishment. "How could you girls possibly harm me? You are mortals and commoners."

By way of response, I pushed my hand against the gummy, sticky white wall and pulled at one of the flowering vines.

"What are you doing?" Jeneba asked, bewildered.

Ignoring her, I tugged harder, using my full strength until the blossoms shuddered and snapped on the vine.

Across from us, the empress gave a hoarse little scream. "Stop that at once!" she said sharply.

That encouraged me, and I pulled harder at the stem. As I tugged, it made a faint whistling sound and clung like a cobweb to my hand. Finally, the section of vine popped free from the wall.

As I had hoped, the vine began to bleed. The empress came rushing toward me, her face contorted with contempt, but I put my foot out to trip her. She stumbled and fell clumsily to the ground. For a long moment, she stayed sprawled where she had fallen. After I gave Jeneba the knife in my pocket, she and I seized the opportunity to rapidly tug and saw at the thick stems of the surrounding vines. We worked until they were all bleeding. The floor became a river of gluey liquid lapping at our feet, the blood black as oil under the glow of the hanging lanterns.

"I knew it," I said triumphantly, more to myself than to the empress. I pulled at another vine and she grunted in pain. She scrambled up from the ground where she had fallen and began to walk unsteadily over to me. I knew I had weakened her because her slow steps were clumsy and made her wince. My suspicion had been correct: the flowering vines were the empress's veins and arteries. They kept her alive.

She cried, "I will end you myself!" and then swung at me, but she was frail and I evaded her with ease.

"The vines are keeping her alive," I told Jeneba as I tore up another from its roots.

Jeneba nodded. Her face went taut with concentration as she ripped a vine away from the floor tiles. That made the empress scream again, a high, sorrowful wail that turned my stomach.

"Let us go, and we will stop," I told the empress.

She grimaced. "I cannot. I could never do that to my daughter."

I said, "Suit yourself," and pulled another stem.

And another, and another. Jeneba and I were rushing about the room, tearing the vines down one by one. The flowers hissed in protest and the vines made our hands slick with blood, but still the two of us persisted. We pulled out vine after vine after vine.

"It's working," Jeneba whispered as we worked. "She's growing weaker."

Indeed, each vine we uprooted seemed to incapacitate the empress and make her cry out. It was as if we had been ripping out her veins, one by one. She had lost so much blood that now she slumped weakly against the floor tiles, unable even to lift her head.

"Stop, please . . . ," she croaked.

"You are wounded and vulnerable," Jeneba told her matter-of-factly. "The two of us could put you to death easily, but we will spare your life if you show us the way out of this cave."

We both looked to the empress, hoping she would agree to lead us to safety. But she only sighed and said, "I shall not let you out of my sight until my husband returns." Then she began to cough, a horrible, rasping sound. A death rattle.

"She's dying," Jeneba breathed.

All around us, the blooms on the vines were beginning to perish. They curled and wilted with an unnatural quickness, and soon the air was thick with the odor of decomposition and decay. The empress lay still upon the ground, unmoving, as if rooted to the spot. Her eyes fluttered closed. She did not stir again.

For a moment, Jeneba and I could only look at each other. Perhaps both of us were afraid to speak. Finally, she broke the silence. "The empress is dead, but her husband will be back soon. Now's our chance to run."

I nodded slowly, in a kind of daze. I could not take my eyes away from the empress, or what was left of her, here in this cave beneath the desert. Lying there upon the bloodstained tiles, her eyes closed, she looked so very much like her daughter that my heart ached.

Jeneba tugged impatiently at my hand. "Amie, let's go!"

The sharpness of her voice tore me from my stupor. I followed her across the room, the two of us clambering quickly over torn vines and pools of viscous blood until we reached the doorway. It led to a corridor that was longer and darker than I remembered, stretching out for perhaps half a league before curving abruptly out of sight. I glanced down it warily.

My breath caught when I realized that this passageway did not at all resemble the one that led us to the empress. Its stone walls were as black as polished obsidian, whereas the other hall had been pale as chalk.

The empress may have been dead, but this place was still playing its tricks on us.

I asked Jeneba, "Does this hallway seem different to you?"

Her eyes grew wide. "I scarcely recognize it."

"This is the empress's doing," I said. My voice was trembling. "She has concealed the exits and rearranged the corridors to prevent our escape. Even in death, she will not let us leave."

Jeneba said, "We will find our way out, I know we will," and squeezed my hand reassuringly.

Just then, the shadows along the corridor began shifting, tumbling over one another like leaves in the wind. Low whispers grew with the shadows, hissing and chanting, *"Avenge the empress. Avenge the empress. Avenge the empress. . . ."*

"Look!" Jeneba cried, her fingernails digging into my palm.

The shadows were brightening from black to an unsteady blue, moving toward us in a thick, dark current that threatened to pull us under. The whispers grew louder, vibrating from the walls, the ceiling, even the great dining chamber behind us. *"Avenge the empress. Avenge the empress. . . ."*

Panic fell upon me. I was overcome with an urgent need to run—but run where? Down the unfamiliar corridor? It hardly seemed safe. But I also did not want to retrace my steps back to the empress's dining room, where her corpse lay. Which way would lead us to safety?

A gravelly voice called out, "Lost, are you?"

The two of us tensed with alarm, preparing to fight for our lives. But we saw no one and nothing, save for the twisting of shadows along the obsidian corridor. The darkly shifting silhouettes grew taller and more detailed with each passing moment until, finally, they became a sturdy, broad-shouldered young man. I recognized him immediately, and when he stepped forward, Jeneba and I recoiled.

"You murdered my wife," he said, smiling hideously. "You will both die for it."

Hausakoy, god of the blacksmiths, had returned to put us to death.

22

I held Jeneba's hand ever more tightly. "Please, have mercy upon us. Let us live."

"Your lives have already been pledged to me," Hausakoy said, stepping closer. I gagged as the fiery smell of him filled my nostrils. "And why would I spare you after what you've just done to my wife?"

"We are so, so sorry," I began, but dread stopped the words in my throat.

"We were only defending ourselves," Jeneba said stubbornly.

"Can't you see that you shall never escape this place?" he asked us. "Your three lives have belonged to me ever since you first laid hands upon my map."

When he said *three lives*, I thought of Penda and flinched. I glared up at him and said, "Kader escaped."

"You are right, he did. But that was only because I showed him the way out. I would never extend the same courtesy to the two of you, who murdered my wife."

"You call her your wife, but you owe her nothing," Jeneba told him. "She never returned your love. She was forced to come here and be your wife because of your deal with the emperor. Why should you avenge her death? Great god, if you only let us go, we will be forever grateful. We will leave daily offerings upon your shrine for the rest of our lives."

Whatever effect she had hoped her words would have upon

Hausakoy, they appeared to have the opposite. He only smiled at her and said, "Such defiance. And from such a beautiful girl, too."

Then he brought his hands to her face, stroking her cheek. She recoiled.

"Do not touch her!" I cried.

He turned his attention to me. "Would you like to die first, is that it?" he asked. "You want me to kill you before I kill your pretty friend? I am happy to oblige."

He clapped his hands twice.

At his signal, spirits began to shuffle in from the corridor, blank-faced and glassy-eyed as fish. There were dozens of them, all like poor sketches of men. But now the petals of their skin had begun to wilt and curl, revealing the spongy, bloodless flesh beneath.

With the empress gone, what might have been the remains of Mariama's suitors were rotting before my eyes. The stench of it made me swallow back vomit.

"Would you still like to die first?" Hausakoy asked me. "Well, I shall not give you the satisfaction."

He nodded pointedly, and two of the spirits grabbed hold of Jeneba, tearing her away from me.

"Wait!" I cried. An idea came to me, a desperate one. "What about your loneliness? You will kill us quickly and then grow solitary and bored, without even the empress to keep you company."

Hausakoy signaled for the spirits to release Jeneba. *Good.* "What are you suggesting?" he asked me, still smiling.

"I propose some entertainment."

He smiled wider still. "And how will you entertain me?"

"With a hunt," I said, sounding braver than I felt. All the stories said he liked to chase mortal women, that he enjoyed a pursuit, and so I hoped he would be excited by my suggestion. A hunt meant a chase, which meant time and space to escape—gods willing.

Hausakoy brought his face so close to mine that he might have kissed my lips. The scent of iron upon his breath was difficult to bear.

"Interesting," he said, considering it. "Yes, a hunt would be just the thing. . . ."

"What are you doing?" Jeneba asked me quietly. Her eyes were a desperate warning.

"Trying to save us," I whispered.

"I accept, although I must warn you that the spirits and I are very good hunters. We can smell humans from several leagues away." Hausakoy pointed down the corridor. "This cave has many hallways, all branching out in different directions. Only one of them will lead you up into the desert."

I swallowed hard. "Which one?"

He chuckled. "I can hardly tell you, can I? That would ruin the hunt."

Jeneba asked, "So if we find our way out of the cave, you will let us live?"

"Of course. *If* you find your way out. Perhaps you will. Perhaps not." He began to fidget absentmindedly with his iron chisel, effortlessly rotating it by the handle. It was a disconcertingly human gesture that reminded me of a child playing with a spinning toy.

I said, "We will," and looked down the hallway with bitter resignation. The cave was a vast network of tunnels and pathways that could evidently collapse and rearrange themselves at the great god's will. It would be difficult, but I was determined to find the way out.

"It is time for the hunt," he said suddenly. "Run along. My spirits and I will give you a start, but then we're coming after you."

Jeneba and I did not need to be told twice. We bounded down the passageway as quickly as our legs would carry us.

The obsidian floors and ceilings were dark and glasslike, and now that we had left the empress's dining hall, there were no lamps or torches to light our way. Without the jeweled glow of the cave flowers, our path forward was very dim. After what felt like several minutes of running, the corridor had grown so dark that I could no longer see Jeneba. I could only hear her footsteps beside me, her quick and frightened breathing.

We soon came up against a damp earthen wall, nearly colliding with it in the darkness.

"It's a dead end!" Jeneba cried.

"Perhaps not, perhaps there is a door we cannot see," I said. "Help me feel for one."

Together, we clawed at the wall in the darkness. Loose dirt showered our faces as we ran our hands blindly over it, hoping to find a door. But we found nothing.

I was about to suggest that we abandon this route for another one when distant footsteps *tap-tap-tapping* along the corridor behind us made Jeneba whisper, "It's too late. They're coming after us."

"We must burrow into the wall, then," I said, trying my best to conceal my fear. "We'll dig ourselves a hiding place so that the great god cannot find us."

The footsteps were growing closer. Then I saw a fiery blur that illuminated the walls as it approached. It was Hausakoy, rushing toward us with immortal speed. He led the charge, his skin glowing like molten metal in the darkness, and the spirits followed him like soldiers following a general into battle.

I had never been so afraid in my life. I scrambled desperately against the wall, tunneling into the dirt like a rodent, desperate for a hatch, a door, an escape.

"Bad luck, girls!" Hausakoy cried as he neared us, his footsteps heavy upon the ground. His incandescent skin burned so brightly that the entire corridor was bathed in his red-hot glow. He raised his longsword over his head and swung it in front of him, ready to kill us both.

"Amie, look!" cried Jeneba, pointing to the stretch of earthen wall where she had been digging.

I looked—and almost fainted from relief.

Her efforts had revealed the wooden rungs of what looked like an ancient ladder, hidden within the wall. Under the flashes of fiery light I could see that it led upward, to a small opening in the ceiling. *We are saved*, I thought.

"We have to climb!" I shouted, pushing her to the ladder. "Climb, climb now!"

Jeneba and I ascended the ladder as quickly as we could. Loose soil rained down on us as we climbed, accompanied by falling beetles and dirt grubs and inchworms that wrapped themselves around our fingers like thread.

I heard her cry out in disgust, "There's something on my face!" Then she stopped on the ladder, slapping desperately at her skin in order to dislodge the clinging insect.

Behind us, Hausakoy cried, "Hurry, girls! We're going to catch you."

He and his army of spirits were a mere stone's throw away. His flesh flamed and burned like embers. His sword glowed white-hot, as if he had just forged it. Watching him made my eyes water from heat.

"Keep climbing, Jen!" I pushed her forward with all my might, forcing her up the ladder and into the hole in the ceiling. "Go, go now!"

She turned to help me up, but the dirt around the opening crumbled at her touch. I felt in danger of falling into Hausakoy's open arms. He was inches beneath me, slicing up at my dangling feet with his sword. He could have severed my toes.

"Help me, Jen!" I cried, holding on to her with all my might. I felt the clammy hands of one of the spirits upon my ankle, pulling me down. "Help, please!" I screamed, trying to kick the spirit away, but he only tightened his grip.

I gasped in pain and desperation.

With a grunt, Jeneba heaved me up through the hole. Relief and disappointment battled within me as I realized we had found ourselves once again on the beach at the edge of the cave lake, watching dugouts glide unassisted across the green-and-silver rapids.

It was brighter on the beach than it had been in the tunnel, and now I could see her face properly. Jeneba's cheeks were covered in dirt and clinging worms—so, probably, were mine, but for the moment, I did not care. I kept looking down at the hole we had just climbed from. It pulsed with a blazing light that grew brighter and redder by the moment. The air that rushed from its opening felt hot.

Hausakoy is following us, I thought. *He will be upon us soon, unless we act quickly.*

I looked over at Jeneba and saw that she had begun to weep. "We're right back where we started," she said through her tears. "We'll never find a way out of here."

"Yes, we will," I told her determinedly. "We have to plug the gap in the sand first." I was still feeling frightened and just as disappointed to find ourselves right back where we'd started, but I kept my voice steady.

The two of us worked quickly, packing driftwood, sand, and clay into the top of the hole and creating a cap, which we covered with rocks. For one brief, hopeful moment, I thought we had made a barrier to delay our pursuers. But then the gap began to glow crimson, and two great dark pincers sprang out, grasping and tearing through our hastily built wall.

Fear coursed through me at the sight of the god Hausakoy lifting himself through the opening. He looked half-transformed into his other configuration, the colossal armored scorpion of the old stories. He still retained the form and visage of a man, but his hands now resembled a scorpion's pincers and his skin had begun to sprout scales that were an iridescent yellow, the color of dying leaves.

"Run, girls!" Hausakoy called out excitedly as he scrambled up through the reopened hole. "Run quickly!"

Jeneba and I did not need further encouragement. We rushed to the water's edge.

"The great god is too strong for whatever barriers we put up," I shouted to her as we ran. My legs were numb, and my heart was pounding more loudly than I had ever heard it. "We should just run!"

"But run where?" she asked breathlessly. "Up the cliff?"

"Into the water," I said with a sudden surge of inspiration, remembering that Hausakoy had refused to follow us into the water when he'd first tried to kill us on the beach. "Come with me!"

Before she could protest, I took her hand and leapt with her into the lake.

The salt water was cold and stung my eyes. I forced them open anyway. The water was so clear that I could see the swift shadows of boats moving along the surface.

Next to me, Jeneba paddled and splashed. Her cheeks were distended from holding her breath. And below us—very, very far below—at the bottom of the lake, I saw the mouth of an underwater tunnel that was bright with golden sunlight.

Daylight, I thought with a sudden giddiness. *We are saved.*

I pulled Jeneba again to the surface, both of us panting and gasping. "The way out is at the bottom of the lake!" I told her in a rush. "We have to dive all the way down."

"I cannot swim very well," shouted Jeneba, her eyes wide with fear.

"Just follow me," I reassured her, grasping her hand again. "Take a deep, deep breath, and follow me down."

We inhaled together and prepared to plunge into the watery depths—when we heard the great god calling after us. He and his army of spirits were crawling out from the hole in the beach, and he was shouting across the sand in a voice like fire and gravel.

"Kader never loved you, Aminata!" he rasped, his voice echoing above the crashing of the waves, growing closer, closer still. "It was so easy to convince him to abandon you. We hardly had to enchant him at all. He was already halfway there."

At that moment, I had been preparing to dive to safety. I was about to swim down into the underwater passage, but a sudden surge of anger and resentment made me hesitate and shout back, "You do not know what you are speaking of! He has pledged himself to me already."

"He *never loved you!*" cried the god again, so loudly that the ground tremored.

"Don't listen to him," Jeneba begged. "We must go underwater; we must go now before he catches us."

She was right. Hausakoy was taunting me because he knew we had seen the sunlit tunnel and discovered the way out. He was trying to distract us. We could not let that happen.

"Plug your nose," I told Jeneba grimly.

We plunged beneath the surface. I took the lead, diving as quickly as I could manage with Jeneba clinging desperately to my hand. We descended deeper and deeper, closer and closer to the light at the bottom of the lake. There was a stitch in my side and my lungs ached, but still we swam on, spurred forward by the memory of the great god glowing red as iron in a hearth as he chased us, his pincers poised to strike.

Finally, we entered a little waterlogged tunnel that was bright with daylight. *Yes*, I thought. *Thank the gods.*

Abruptly, Jeneba tugged at my hand. I paddled around to face her, my lungs close to bursting. In the sunlit water I could see that her eyes were bulging, her cheeks puffed out. She pointed upward in desperation, and I caught her meaning.

She could not hold her breath any longer. She needed to go to the surface and take another gulp of air, or else she would drown. I shook my head *no*. The great god was waiting for us at the shore. We had to keep swimming.

I turned and paddled wildly at the water, trying to force Jeneba to swim with me, but she pried herself away with a sudden force. And then she was shooting upward, up to the surface on a search for fresh air. The sight made my heart sink.

No. I could not keep going without Jeneba. I had to bring her with me. I tugged at her ankle—but she was frantic and accidentally kicked me so sharply in the face that my nose released a red cloud of blood in the water.

I reeled away in shock and pain. Panicked, I gave up on following her and started swimming as fast as I could in the other direction, desperately seeking the mouth of the underwater tunnel that was the source of daylight. The water brightened as I swam, from blue to yellow to pink to orange as the dawn.

And then I was breaking through, gasping for air, coughing up salt water on the wet sand. I was outside. *Finally*, I was outside. Here was yellow sand and blue-gold sky. Here was fresh air, a warm breeze on my face.

I pulled myself out of the water and onto the dry land, laughing aloud with relief. I could hardly believe that I was finally back in the desert.

"I found it!" I called to no one in particular. My throat was sore, my voice exhausted. "I've found the way out!"

Before me, the red sun rose against the golden dunes. Behind me was the watery tunnel from which I had emerged. I waited a long moment, hoping to see Jeneba's head surface and hear her gasping for air. But more moments passed, and she still did not come. I had hoped that she would follow me, eventually—where was she? Had the great god caught her?

I have to go back, I thought in a rising panic. *I have to save her.*

I took another deep breath and prepared to plunge myself back into the tunnel—but suddenly, the water started to recede and the dark entrance along with it. The evaporated earth clamped around my legs, dry and tight as quicksand.

The tunnel was closing. My one chance to rescue Jeneba, my only way back into the cave, was disappearing before my eyes. I made a low, terrified noise and tried my best to swim down into the sand, but the water was gone. There were no traces of moisture to be found anywhere at all. Even my wrapper, which had been soaking wet just seconds earlier, now felt dry as grain. Where there had been a watery tunnel was now only sand, waves and waves of rippling dunes that stretched out as far as I could see in every direction.

This is the great god's doing, I thought helplessly. *He has separated Jeneba and me forever.* Where was she? I hoped that she would somehow manage to find another way to escape. Perhaps there was another tunnel, another exit, and she could find it.

"Congratulations, Aminata," came a soft voice at my ear. "You have won."

I almost jumped out of my skin and spun around.

There was the great god Hausakoy—not in his half-scorpion

form, red and clawed and frightening, but in the frail and aging human blacksmith's body in which he'd first appeared to us. He reached toward me with wide arms, as if to embrace me in congratulations. I darted away from his grasp. Although this form was far less frightening than the molten monster that had been chasing me down the tunnel just moments earlier, I still did not want to be anywhere near him.

"Where is Jeneba?" I asked. "What have you done with her?"

"She will remain with me," he said.

Rage blurred my vision. "No, she will not," I insisted. "We won! We found our way out, and now you must let us go."

"I have to let *you* go," he corrected me. "But your friend never made her escape."

"No! No, you have to let us *both* go."

He shook his head. "Only you found the way out. Jeneba failed, so she shall stay with me."

I asked, "Are you going to kill her?" My throat felt tight.

The great god smiled thoughtfully. "Not immediately, no," he said. "Your game has inspired me. I have decided to kill your friend slowly. I will make great sport out of her, hunting her for many days and nights until she goes mad."

"No," I whispered. "You cannot." My mind swam with images of a desperate Jeneba, trapped and pursued and close to death. My chest tightened.

"I can, and I will."

My lungs were stinging, but I still managed to gasp out, "Did you really take Kader back to the city?"

"I did as the empress commanded," he said. "I gave him my hammer and, with it, the ability to turn into stone and to survive being boiled. Then I flew him back to the kettle at market square."

I wanted to retort, but I suddenly found that I could not speak.

The great god had turned my entire body as stiff and still as a statue, my tongue included.

"Tongue-tied?" asked Hausakoy in mocking sympathy. "How inconvenient for you."

I tried to ask, *What have you done to me?* But my mouth felt as if it had been filled with cotton wool, my lips sealed with palm sap. I could only groan wordlessly like an animal. *I won the game, but that does not matter to him,* I thought in a panic. *The great god is going to kill me anyway. He never intended to let either of us survive. . . .*

Hausakoy pulled my chin to his so that I felt his curiously cold breath on my face and said, "Aminata Aqit al-Sanhaji al-Timbukti, youngest daughter of Modibo Aqit the salt merchant, you have surprised me with your courage and daring. Not every mortal would have proposed a hunt. You are now free to leave this place."

Then let me go! I wanted nothing more than to pick up my skirts and run. But of course, I could not move at all. The great god pressed his palm to my forehead. I heard a distant echoing *click*, and then the world went black.

I found myself in a perfectly suffocating darkness that felt as warm and dry as a blanket. Nothing marred its surface, unlike the colorful floating shapes that often blemished the darkness behind one's eyelids. That frightened me, and I tried my best to scream for help. The sound was muffled, as if a hand covered my mouth.

Then the great god's gravelly voice was in my ear. "Steady, girl," he said. "It is almost over. You are nearly saved."

I turned sharply but did not see him. I realized with relief that I could move my body again. I took one tentative step toward the source of the voice, and then another, but he did not speak again. There was only silence, the all-consuming darkness, and the slow sound of my own breathing.

Over many long moments, my surroundings began to soften to

a deep storm-cloud gray. I was in a long slate tunnel. At the far end of it, I spied a circle of rosy-gold light.

"Hurry along," said Hausakoy.

His voice seemed to come from the tunnel itself. It was a deep, resonant sound that vibrated through the soles of my feet and rattled my teeth. I felt it in every part of me. Slowly, cautiously, I made my way toward the light, not stopping until I tasted fresh air again.

I was in a different part of the desert, rockier, with more shrubs and small, anemic palm trees that lined a great road. I recognized it immediately as the one that led from Timbuktu to Tripoli.

I called out, but thankfully Hausakoy was nowhere to be found. It was a relief to be free of him, to be alone in the desert once again. I looked up at the sky. All the stars and planets were fading away against the insistent march of the rising sun. I looked and looked, grief and exhaustion building in my stomach as somewhere behind me, the earth yawned closed.

23

I followed the road south toward Timbuktu. I should have been frightened—after all, I was walking alone on a road notoriously populated by kidnappers and bandits—but after nearly dying at the hands of a great god, mortal criminals seemed unthreatening and mundane.

My body shook with anguish and sorrow as I walked. Penda was dead because of me. Jeneba was alone and afraid and would be dead soon, too. I should have tried harder to save her, acted more quickly. Every time I closed my eyes, I saw her as I had last glimpsed her in the cave water, half-drowned and desperate for air. I thought of her still in the forge house with Hausakoy, trapped and terrified.

He said he would kill her slowly. He said it would be more diverting that way.

I imagined her crying out in pain and fear as the great god's pincers tightened around her slender neck. I imagined him slicing her throat with a slow-moving knife. Her body went limp in my mind. Her blood ran in torrents down the front of her wrapper.

My vision grew red with the stain of my friend's sacrificed flesh, and I felt as if I were going to be sick. The dirt of the road and the sand of the dunes turned red as wine.

"I will come back for her," I whispered to myself. "I swear it. I will find some way back to the god's forge house, and I will rescue her." I took several deep breaths, looking around me at the desert. I had a feeling like waking from the edge of sleep as I followed the road, watching my feet tread sand in their sandals and the blue hem of my wrapper flutter in the dry wind. *Not my wrapper*, I remembered. *Mariama's.* One of many she had loaned me when I lived with her in the palace, when we spent a few short weeks together as companions and confidantes.

My memories of that final night with Mariama filled me with rage and confusion, mixed with a longing that throbbed about my temples like a fever. A longing to see her again, to confront her and understand why she did what she did. I knew that her scheme was not her own, that the empress had put her up to it. But she had still deliberately sent two innocent girls to their deaths. And why had she tried to save me from that fate? I needed to speak with her.

I needed to see Kader again, too. I had to know how much of his betrayal had been enchantment and how much had been real. I was going back to Timbuktu, and then—I had not quite figured out the details, but I was determined to make it happen—I would ask for an audience with them both. How much time had passed? Perhaps Kader had already won the Trials and the two of them would be wed by the time I arrived at the palace, and I would have to greet them as man and wife. The idea of the princess taking Kader for her prince consort filled me with unexpected jealousy that propelled me forward so surely that, for a long while, I almost did not notice the heat. But desert travel is harsh, and by midafternoon I was so weak with thirst that my rage faded into bitterness and my bitterness turned to determination. I needed to rescue Jeneba. I could not live with myself if I didn't at least try to return to Hausakoy's forge house and save her.

The landscape had begun to change. The rocky dunes gave way to a plain that was spotted with low shrubs and trees. It became so

hot that I grew dizzy and had to kneel in the shadow of a roadside
acacia to catch my breath. Once I sat down, I found I did not have the
strength to stand up again. And I was tired, so tired after my sleepless
night in Hausakoy's cave. I willed myself not to fall asleep out in the
open, but I failed.

It felt as though I had slept only a few short moments. In truth,
I must have slept for several hours, because when I next opened
my eyes, the sun was already setting and there was a din of voices
and the nickering of horses. I tried to move toward the sound, but
something was wrong—I felt weaker than ever, unable to move, so
weak that I could only incline my head to the source of the noise
very slowly and somewhat painfully. Finally, I saw a small riding
party assembled on horseback. Divots of sand flew out from their
mounts' hooves as they trotted toward me, and men's murmuring
voices, broken by the occasional laugh or shout, fell upon my ears
like rain. One young man at the front of the pack was incredibly
tall, with an elegant bearing and a wariness in his gaze. Behind him
were about half a dozen others. I tried to sit up and see them more
closely, but I found I was too weak to even lift my head. Panic set
over me as the riders drew closer, until I noticed with relief that my
sister was among them, riding a small, nimble Arabian the color of
gingerroot.

The sight of Haddy filled me with a gladness that made my
eyes sting. She sat easily in the saddle, her face tight with concentration, her leather armor dark against the brilliant red of
her wrapper. Her dark coils were arranged in two plaits, and her
eyebrows, frowning against the sun, framed a face that was very
much like my own. Just a few weeks earlier, seeing my older sister
would have filled me with anger, but looking at her now, I felt only
affection. Affection and urgency. I thought, *I am saved, but only if
Haddy notices me.* I tried to call out for help, but my voice was so

hoarse that I could only croak. It took the last of my energy to lift a single hand skyward with the hope that she'd notice me dying of thirst and exhaustion in a heap on the sand.

At first, she did not see me. Her dark eyes were trained determinedly on the horizon.

But one of the other riders stood high in his saddle and cried out, "Hadiza, look!"

My sister finally met my gaze. "Amie," she said, looking frantically in my direction. I tried to call out *Haddy!* but my throat was dry as paper, and I gave only a croak like a frog's. I wanted to run and greet her, but exhaustion prevented me from doing anything except collapsing farther into the sandy road.

"We've found her," she told the rider, who signaled the others to gather around, their horses circling. Twenty pairs of eyes took me in, some of them frowning while others seemed uninterested. Everyone except my sister stayed on their horses, but Haddy dismounted and hurried over to me, trying to scoop me into her arms. "Thank the gods you're alive, Amie," she choked out in a voice that was full of emotion and regret. "I thought I was going to lose you."

Her familiar scent made me want to cry. But when I tried to speak, my throat was so parched that it came out only as a whisper. "Haddy . . . ," I murmured, too quietly for her to hear. My dizziness and dehydration threatened to take me away.

My vision was blurring. I felt as though I were going to faint. I could only watch uselessly as my sister mounted her horse again and circled the others, her mouth held in a grim line.

"We need to move quickly," she said with authority. "We'll take Amie to the physician."

What about Jeneba? I wanted to ask, but I was too weak.

The riders made small murmurs of agreement. Two of them dismounted and pulled me to my feet, and although I saw their lips moving, their voices sounded distant and echoed as if they were at the bottom of a well. And with every passing moment, I found it more difficult to see Haddy properly. It was not only her: *all* my surroundings were growing blurrier by the minute.

I was tired, so tired.

24

I dreamed of Jeneba as I had last seen her, treading water in the depths of Hausakoy's house, a look of panic and exhaustion on her flushed face as she fought against drowning. Although I tried to reach out for her, the churning waters swallowed her whole. Horror climbing my throat, I watched her sink beneath the surface. Soon, she was only a few weak bubbles rising, and I felt the guilt and regret of losing her all over again.

The pain of my loss was so real that I awoke with a start. "No," I heard myself say aloud. Then I looked sleepily about my unfamiliar surroundings, still thinking about Jeneba in the smithing god's trap as my dream fell away.

I must rescue Jeneba, I told myself with steely determination. *Where am I?*

Sunlight slanted into the tent from strategic slats along its roof, casting pink and gold triangles on the silken walls. I had never seen a tent of silk before, let alone one of such a lovely—but clearly impractical—cream color.

I stood slowly and rubbed my eyes, trying to recall what happened yesterday after Haddy rescued me. I remembered walking the road to Timbuktu until my legs gave out from exhaustion. I remembered being lifted into a saddle and traveling on horseback as the sun sank lower in the sky. Mariama's blue wrapper was gone now, replaced by the same linen uniform worn by my sister and the other women of the Order. I looked down at my legs: thick linen covered them both, and when I lifted my wrapper, I could see the bruised and irritated skin beneath.

Upon the floor sprawled pale carpets and imported goods that I deemed with the educated eye of a merchant's daughter to be expensive indeed: a dark leather shoulder bag, a terra-cotta figurine, a ceramic vase. Small oil lamps flickered in the corners, all carved with intricate patterns and made of bronze or gold. A nearby table was almost completely covered in bound books and loose scrolls, with only a bit of empty space left for a quill and inkwell. Beside it, someone had left me a meal of millet porridge and dates, which I began to eat hastily.

As I ate, I remained distracted by thoughts of Jeneba. In my mind bloomed awful images of Hausakoy tormenting her in his dwelling beneath the desert. I knew I owed it to her to try to set her free, but imagining what might be happening to her at that very moment made my breathing shallower, and so I put a hand to my chest to calm myself. There, I felt hard leather—*armor*, I realized. Whoever had dressed and fed me had also decided I needed protection.

I heard approaching footsteps outside the tent. There was a silken rustle as someone opened the flap and closed it again. Then came my sister's voice.

"Good morning, Amie," she said. "I trust you liked your breakfast?"

"Haddy!" The sight of her made my heart race. I wrapped myself around her with ease. She even smelled familiar, and I buried my face in her shoulder to take in her scent. "You saved my life," I said into her hair. My breath hitched in my throat when she hugged me back.

I felt stronger after eating and resting, with enough newfound energy to spend the next half hour explaining to Haddy in detail the trick that the princess and her mother had played on me. I told her everything: the false promise of the map, the sandstorm and hyena attacks, the horrors of the smithing god's forge house, Kader's enchantment and his destiny in the suitor's kettle. As I spoke, my sister watched me with a combination of concern and admiration—I recognized that same look of hesitant pride from those long-ago days of our shared girlhood, all those times she had smiled at me when I'd finally mastered a new stitch at the loom or achieved some other minor accomplishment. Her gaze was fixed upon me as she listened, her imagination bringing to life my descriptions of the god Hausakoy and the deceased empress Cassi. I told her what had happened to Penda, explaining that she had bled to death at the center of that boat. Tears gathered in the corners of my eyes. Retelling these events made me feel like a stringed instrument pulled too tightly, rigid and tense. How had I survived such an ordeal? Why had I been able to escape that place when the others had not? And then my sister had saved me from the elements when I was stranded in the desert, weak enough to die . . . how had I been so lucky? I did not always feel that I deserved my survival.

By the time I had finished recounting all that had happened, Haddy was breathless with astonishment. "So, the great god of smiths took the empress for a bride a very long time ago," she said in a hushed, awestruck tone. "And she conspired with the princess to lure you and two serving girls to his home, all with the intention of exchanging your lives for Kader's, so that he wins the Trials. Am I understanding it?"

I nodded.

She continued, "And then you and the other girl killed the empress by pulling upon ropes—"

"Vines," I corrected her gently, remembering the scene with disgust: the blood caking beneath my fingers as I pried each flower from its place, the empress growing weaker and collapsing.

"You say you traveled with two girls, and Hausakoy killed one of them in the caves. What happened to the other one?"

"I cannot know what happened to Jeneba," I said. "I'd found the way out of the cave, and we were swimming together toward the exit when she ran out of breath and swam to the surface. She might still be alive in there," I added, recalling the force of Jeneba prying herself away from me, the sight of my blood clouding the sunlit water when she accidentally kicked me in the nose. "I keep thinking about her, and although I cannot know for sure what became of her, I have this gnawing feeling that if she's still living, then I owe her a rescue."

Worry spasmed over Haddy's features. "A rescue? What do you mean?"

My insides tightened. I knew that Haddy would not like to hear what I had to say next, but I pushed on for Jeneba's sake. "I'm going back to Hausakoy's forge house," I told her. "If I do not go back for Jeneba, who will?"

Fear warred with frustration in her expression. "You're speaking nonsense," she said with furrowed brows. "I cannot let you endanger yourself for someone you only met a few weeks ago. And that is what you would be doing, Amie—endangering yourself—if indeed you did find your way back to Hausakoy."

"I know it will be dangerous, but I've already made up my mind," I said resolutely. "Jeneba and I took care of each other, back in the caves. We helped one another survive. And over the short time I've known her she has proven herself worth rescuing a thousand times over."

"But Hausakoy is a most wicked god—you know this first-hand!" Her voice grew shrill. "Even those of us at the Order who owe him our sorcery admit that we fear him. How can you think to encounter him again? And how can you be so sure that Jeneba is still alive?"

I sighed. "Sister, you will never talk me out of it. And I cannot know what has become of Jeneba, but that's exactly why I must try to find her."

"Then I will go with you," Haddy said firmly. She stood, her bright uniform rippling like a river over her steady legs. "I cannot let you do this alone!"

"Thank you," I said, standing so that we were of a height. I don't know if I'd hoped for this response from my sister, but I was grateful that she had offered to accompany me. If I were to brave Hausakoy's cave once again, it would be prudent to do so with a trained sorceress at my side. And then I threw my arms around her, and she held me tightly for a long moment. Tears of relief gathered in my eyes. When we finally separated, I saw that she was also beginning to weep.

"I don't think we should do this," my sister said. "I think it is foolhardy and unsafe. But I see the determination in your eyes when you speak of Jeneba, and if you want to save her, then I owe you my support." She chewed her full bottom lip as she always did when she was thinking. "After all, I am responsible for this entire situation. If I had not betrayed you when it mattered most, if I had not ruined your chances at happiness with Kader, then you would have never met the princess in the first place, and she could never have lured you toward danger." Her arms tightened around me, her cheek pressed so closely to mine that I could feel her breath. "I have failed as your sister," she said in low tones. "I'm meant to protect you."

"You did protect me. You found me on the road when I was half-dead from the heat and thirst," I pointed out, still a little in awe of how quickly she'd come to my aid. Once, I had doubted her love for me, but when I had needed her most, she'd pulled through.

She brushed a tear from her cheek, saying, "I was wrong for what I did to you."

I almost couldn't believe it. Haddy was finally apologizing to me.
My proud, self-assured sister was actually admitting her wrongs.
"I forgive you," I told her, realizing that I'd already done so. As I
looked into her eyes—meeting her gaze, which was both apologetic
and proud—my heart ached with the understanding that, yes, she
had done wrong by me, but at my core, I had also known she had
always been there for me when I needed her. What mattered most
was that my sister and I were finally reunited. In my darkest hour,
she had come for me.

"Tell me how I can help you," Haddy said earnestly. "Whatever
you need. I will do my best to assist!"

"I'm not sure," I admitted. "I'm still planning. But I don't think
we'll be able to find Hausakoy's cave on our own," I told her. "At
least, not without the map."

Haddy frowned, considering. "What happened to your map
from before?"

"I lost it when I was underground. But I believe there may be
others," I said, thinking about how Mariama and Issatou must have
worked together, hiding the map for me to find in a book of stories
concealed within a pile of yams. I wished I'd never found it. "The
princess might have other maps to Hausakoy's forge house," I continued. "And even if she doesn't, I think the empress must have told
her something about his whereabouts. We need to interrogate her,
find out what she knows. She's the only one who can lead us back
to Jeneba."

Haddy said thoughtfully, "It's a risky idea, interrogating a princess, but I could help you. Of course, we would need to ensure she
answers your questions truthfully—a blade to the throat motivates
most people. I could fashion you a dagger."

I tried to envision myself holding a dagger to Mariama's neck
while I asked her how to find Hausakoy's caves. Could I do such a

thing? I had no talent for violent threats, but Haddy's advice rang true. Physical intimidation might be the only way to get Mariama to tell me what I needed to know to find Jeneba. And there were a half dozen other questions I planned to ask the princess, like how much she had known about what the empress was putting her up to. I did not think she was innocent in any way—to me it was only a matter of determining how complicit she had really been. Just like I needed to understand how complicit Kader was in his betrayal of me. I hoped that it was all the fault of the empress's enchantment. I hoped that she had seized hold of his mind and turned him unnaturally against me, because that was a matter of magic, and magic, I was learning, could be reversed.

I hoped for a future where Kader could be returned again to his right mind and could choose me. But what if my worst fears were true? What if the empress's enchantment had only revealed the true Kader, who cared more about impressing his father and brothers than building a life with me? It made my heart hurt to imagine that this was his true nature. How could I have been so blind to who he really was?

I told Haddy, "If you give me a dagger for it, I won't deny you. I'll hold the blade to her throat, without question. But I don't want to kill her. I just want answers—from her and from Kader, too. I need to know what he's really thinking." Something else was occurring to me. "What if Mariama screams while I'm threatening her? What if she wakes the guards and they come to her aid? They'd see me taking a dagger to the emperor's daughter and strike me down instantly!"

Haddy waved my concerns away with a hand. "That is the least of our problems. I'll sing a spell to thicken the walls of her chamber, muffling the sounds so that her guards do not hear a thing. You'll see, later—I'll show you how I do it."

"I should like to learn," I said. Admiration rippled through me at the thought of my sister using sorcery to help me reach my goals. "But now I'm realizing I don't have the faintest idea of how to get into the palace besides through the front gates."

"The Order has members at court who can let us in," Haddy told me. "One of Ousmane's friends works as a palace guard, but he is loyal to our cause."

"Who is Ousmane?" I inquired, struggling to recall where I had heard the name before. It held a note of familiarity.

"He serves the Order as a lieutenant general," she said with a note of deference in her voice that betrayed her feelings for him. I recognized the same dreaminess from when she used to talk about Tenin.

I blinked at her, still unsure about what he had to do with anything.

"We are in his tent," she explained.

"Oh," I said slowly. "I thought this was yours."

"I *wish* it were mine." Haddy sighed. "I still sleep in the women's tent with the others."

"Your sister is the most talented young sorceress I have ever met, and the Order has offered her more fitting accommodations about a hundred times," said a voice from outside, soft and deep and preternaturally confident. "She always refuses. She thinks she has not yet earned them."

With a whisper of silk, the tent opened again, overwhelming my eyes with bright morning sunlight. A young man of about twenty stepped inside. Tall and sturdily built, he wore a soldier's uniform of deep red robes and a tagelmust scarf that was a rich shade of blood. A leather belt at his broad waist held several weapons—two swords in iron hilts, short and long daggers—and upon his back he wore a quiver of arrows. He held all this weaponry so easily on his solid frame that I knew he was accustomed to it.

Something about him felt immediately familiar. Although I was certain that I had never met him before, I recognized his smile—thin lips, a wide mouth, a considerable gap between his front teeth. It was a warm smile, the sort that put you instantly at ease.

Haddy's eyes lit up when she saw him. "Ousmane! You've been listening!"

"Only for a few moments," he told her.

"It is impolite."

"Half of the camp has been eavesdropping," he said with a sigh.

"Did Liya put them up to it?" Haddy scrambled to her feet. "She never knows when to stop—"

"Aren't you going to introduce me to your sister?" he interrupted. Although the smile never left his face, he regarded me with a combination of wariness and curiosity. *He has Penda's smile*, I realized as I watched him. I thought of Penda's missing brothers, the twins who had joined the imperial army three years ago and hadn't been seen since. Their unit had been stationed in the town of Agadez, where they supposedly decided to stay after taking local wives. Before she died, Penda had been determined to find her brothers. I found myself wondering if we were in Agadez, or at least near it. It occurred to me then that I had not the slightest idea where this camp was located.

"This is Aminata," Haddy told Ousmane.

"You are one of Penda Diallo's brothers," I started cautiously. How lucky I was to have found him. How strange, in fact. "Are you not?"

He seemed taken aback, and the smile faded from his face. "How did you know that?"

"I have something to tell you," I began slowly. "Something terrible."

I had never told someone about the death of their kin.

Ousmane was still as stone as I recounted his sister's last moments. I tried to omit the more painful details—the way she'd coughed and sputtered a mixture of cave water and blood, the blind, terrible smile that had remained on her lips even after she was gone. Instead, I tried to paint a picture of Penda as a sweet and courageous girl, a girl whose determination to find her brothers had never faltered, even with her dying breath. Because that was who she was until the end.

When I had finished, Ousmane's face took on the quality of a mask. He was a soldier, and I knew he was likely doing his utmost not to show any emotion. I could see him holding back tears as he murmured, "My Penda. Little Penda. . . ."

A silence fell over the tent, long and mournful. Ousmane's grief was a blow; it felt like watching his sister die all over again. I avoided his eyes, unsure what I could possibly say to make this moment better. Haddy gently placed her hand upon his, and he tensed.

"I am very sorry for your loss," I told him finally. "If I had known what I know now, I would never have let your sister follow that map."

"It isn't your fault. The princess tricked her into it. She tricked you, too." Ousmane shook his head, clearly enraged. "Soon, we will avenge Penda's death," he said in a voice so filled with conviction that I lifted my gaze to his. I did not think I had ever seen a man so unflinchingly determined. "We're going to make the imperialists pay for what they've done to my little sister. And for what they did to my brother."

"The Scorpion Order grows stronger by the day," Haddy said, turning to me. "Five hundred fighting men, seventy sorcerers, and three dozen sorceresses have so far pledged themselves to our cause. We've even received recruits from the palace guard." She lifted open the tent flap to show me the rows and rows of tents on the plain.

There were too many to count. Open fires dotted the sandy ground, surrounded by small groups of soldiers in red uniforms. The scents of steamed rice and millet porridge drifted up to me, smells that reminded me of breakfast in my parents' home. Rising smoke swirled around the morning mist that still lingered in the air.

The sight rendered me momentarily speechless. I could never have imagined all this from our parents' home in Timbuktu. I drank in the fresh air, feeling awestruck. Part of me was inclined to watch it all dumbly, but my practical side took over and I found myself asking her, "What is all of this for?"

"For war," she said simply, and I felt a chill pass over me. "Once our numbers reach one thousand, we will finally take up arms against the emperor. And speaking of taking up arms . . . Amie, come with me. I'll work with the other armory sorceresses to make you a fresh dagger to the exact size and shape of your hand," she continued, leading us out of the tent. Ousmane was at her heels, looking at her steadily—he was clearly smitten with my sister.

"Thank you," I said, and followed behind them, stepping into the thick of the campsite. Soldiers thronged the grassy rows, all dressed in the same uniform I wore, and I felt glad to blend in here, in such an unfamiliar place. We walked in silence past several campfires and dozens of tents before I asked Haddy, "And then what? Surely your aim is not anarchy."

"Of course not," she said a little breathlessly as we trekked the campsite. "We only want the Songhai people to be once again governed by a ruler who allows us to speak our language and worship our own gods. Now! Here is the armory, with all our weaponry." She led us to a large tent, where several people were hard at work crafting weapons and armor. The clang of metal against metal filled the air as they worked, and I marveled at their skill and speed. There was a wide variety of gear, including swords, shields, helms, bows, arrows—the list seemed endless.

Haddy approached a kind-faced young woman tinkering at a stone worktable at the corner of the tent and introduced me to her. "Liya, meet my sister," she said. "Aminata needs a dagger, and quickly."

Liya looked up from her workstation and smiled warmly at me. "Aminata, it is good to meet you." And then she took my hand, saying, "I'll craft your new dagger so that it fits perfectly into your palm."

Ousmane and Haddy stepped back to watch as my new dagger quickly took form under Liya's expert guidance. She worked much faster than any smith I had ever seen, her hands a skilled blur as she sang spells in a clear soprano that reminded me painfully of Jeneba. After only a few minutes of this work, I held a shining new blade. It was perfect: not too heavy but sturdy enough for fighting. Its hilt had been designed specifically for my small hands.

"Thank you," I told Liya, and I meant it. It was a thing of beauty.

"You are welcome," she replied, smiling over at my sister. "Haddy and I are dear friends, and I'll always help her kin."

Haddy smiled back at Liya and then at me. "I'm glad you like it."

Looking approvingly at the blade, Ousmane said, "Lieutenant General Liya leads our armory. She's an astounding talent."

I inhaled in shock. A woman was lieutenant general? I had never heard of such a thing ever occurring in the imperial army. I was beginning to understand why Haddy had chosen to align herself with such a precarious cause as the Scorpion Order. For her, it was not only about ousting the Malinke invaders and reinstating the Songhai rulers, language, and religion. The Order also provided her with a freedom and agency that she could not find anywhere else. In Timbuktu, she had been a nobleman's wife whose main purpose was to provide heirs to Lord Ayouta. But here in this camp in the desert, she was a powerful sorceress whose abilities could turn the tide of history. Haddy had always wanted to go to Sankoré University like our father and our male cousins, but the universities were closed to women. The Scorpion Order was very much like a university, I thought, but the pupils studied spells instead of scripture. Of course my sister loved it here.

Dawn turned into midday as I followed Haddy through the encampment, learning about each group of sorcerers and their contributions to the Order. We visited the herbalists, sorcerers of the planting goddess, Faran, who worked in a foul-smelling tent at the edge of camp grinding plants with stone and mortar, making medicine for their soldiers and poisons for their enemies. The sorcerers of Nyawri, god of the hunt, transformed pebbles and stones into fat flocks of goats and sheep for our meals. Liya and the other armory sorceresses of Hausakoy transformed pure iron ore into swords and shields with alarming speed. A few young sorcerers of Nyori held hands and chanted a small storm cloud into existence. The cloud emitted no rain, but tendrils of controlled lightning shot out from its depths and created several neat cooking fires, upon which the newly altered goats and sheep were promptly roasted. Another two rocks were turned into two horses for Haddy and me for when we embarked on our journey back to the city tomorrow.

Even after my meal that morning, I was still hungry, and the smells of meat made my mouth water. I was glad to take my place with Haddy and the other sorceresses to devour morsels of freshly cooked lamb. The men dined apart from the women, which reminded me of how things were in Timbuktu, but here the men helped just as much to clean up. Haddy was right to think that women were treated with more equality here than they were in the city.

After we'd finished eating, there was a series of announcements about the Order's internal operations. I did not listen very closely until a messenger came to report that Kader had arrived in Timbuktu and would be awaiting the Trials on Friday. Then the plain seemed to grow smaller around me, and I heard my blood whirring in my ears. My dread had grown into an awful pressure that threatened to crush me under its weight.

"Kader is awaiting the Trials," I repeated, feeling lightheaded. In my mind was an image of Kader, my Kader, stepping into the boiling heat of the suitor's kettle as ninety-nine men had before him. But unlike those men, Kader had Hausakoy's hammer and so he would survive, would triumph. And he was not *my* Kader, not anymore—my broken heart was proof of that—but I still wanted to have a conversation with him when he was not under an enchantment so that we could both have closure.

I wanted to ask him if he'd always planned to betray me or if the empress had planted that seed in his mind for the first time back in the forge house. He had never given me any reason to think that he had grand ambitions; he had never seemed to place very much importance on impressing his father and brothers—but perhaps I hadn't seen him clearly. And although I understood that I could no longer trust Kader, I still cared for him dearly and was relieved he wouldn't perish in the kettle in five days' time. I wanted him to live, just as I wanted Jeneba to live. Even if doing so put me in danger, I wanted to at least be able to say that I'd tried to rescue her—and that meant returning to Timbuktu and interrogating Mariama.

In that moment, I felt a surge of motivation to prepare for our trip. Taking Haddy by the hand, I asked her to lead me to the storerooms, where we packed away food, including dried dates, flatbread, and pounded yams. Haddy gave me fresh clothes for the journey, lovely wrappers of silk and linen that were so fine and clean that I felt guilty touching them in my unwashed state—I hadn't bathed since I'd left the palace. My skin was filthy with dust and sweat.

At my suggestion, Haddy and I went to fetch ourselves bath-water from the edge of camp. It was nearing dusk, and the plain was blue with shadows. As we drew water, I saw reflected in the depths not my own face but a rippling blue shape. I held my new dagger to the well, thinking of how it would feel to threaten the princess with it very soon. My stomach shifted as I tried to imagine the act; it made me feel uneasy.

"When you reach the palace, will you really be able to get Mari-ama to tell you the truth? And will you really be able to rescue Jen-eba?" I asked my reflection in a nervous whisper, too quietly for Haddy to hear. "When you reach the palace, what will you do?"

25

Haddy and I left camp the following day at sunset. We took two horses and five days' provisions.

We traveled by starlight each night like caravanners, following the road to Timbuktu. We slept in the heat of the day-time, and as evening approached, Haddy would show me how to sing simple spells as we saddled our horses for that night's jour-ney. And at night, I strained my eyes as we continued down the road, thinking of the drugged horsemen still in their saddlebags. I wondered if the horses still carried them at night, taking them aimlessly across the dimly moonlit dunes. Or—and this, I was be-ginning to see, was far more likely—perhaps the horses had grown too tired and thirsty to continue. And if the horses were already dead, that meant the horsemen would remain in those saddlebags even as flies and vultures descended upon the carrion. I wanted to find the men and give them the antidote and bring them back to their lives and families—but I knew it was impossible. Even if I somehow managed to find them in the vastness of the desert, the antidote was still with Jeneba, trapped with her in that wretched house beneath the sands.

We had known, of course, that we were on the road to Tim-buktu, but it still startled us to come upon the city—to see it seem to jump out of the plain, so flat and pale. The buildings looked, from a distance, like a series of little clay boxes, toys that could be picked up or perhaps broken to teach a child a lesson. We crossed a dark stretch of scrubland toward the herders' compounds at the edge of the city. No young herdsmen accosted us, no curious children watched us. It was after midnight, and everyone slept, even the animals.

"This is where we'll leave the horses," Haddy said, dismounting. I followed her lead, tying my horse alongside hers to the fence around the compound's small wooden stable. Whoever owned it would be overjoyed by the gift of two free animals. We'd always planned to get rid of our horses—we certainly couldn't bring them with us into the palace—and here seemed as good a place as any. Looking about the darkened livestock pens and thatched-roof huts, I thought of the last time I'd been to this place, when a young herdsman had sold me a Barb stallion with a yellow mane. I didn't like to remember that Amie, the girl who had been so determined to follow Kader into the desert and so unaware of the trap that awaited her within.

We continued on foot, tracing a path from the herdsmen's huts to the blacksmiths' quarter, past our parents' house in the merchants' district and the universities. Finally, we reached the dark and glittering river. No trading boats or fishing vessels glided down the currents; no women washed clothes in the shallows; no children played in the muddy bank. Haddy led me over the bridge, walking quickly with her graceful gait. I was a few steps behind. On the other side of the river, the market square was as still and silent as everywhere else, with only the bare tentpoles of merchants' stalls to suggest that by day it was a bustling center of trade. It seemed like a city built for ghosts.

The platform at its center was bare, save for the great clay kettle. I drew in a sharp breath when I saw that instrument of torture and death, and I immediately thought of its subterranean replica down in the depths of Hausakoy's forge house. Was there still a kettle underground? Did replicas of Mariama's deceased suitors still dwell in the great god's halls?

Today was Friday, and it frightened me half to death to think that Kader would step onto the platform and into the kettle later today, but I comforted myself with the knowledge that he would never join the ranks of those murdered young men in the smithing god's keep. After all, Kader had Hausakoy's hammer, the object Penda had died for so that he would live.

Each step brought us nearer to the palace. Its arches were white as palm wine against the cloudless sky, and most of its windows were dark. The palace seemed to watch us. I tipped back my head, letting the breeze sift through my hair. The night was warm and dry and windy; loose sand in the air made us cough as we neared the gates.

I allowed myself one backward glance at the black and gleaming river, at the kettle on the platform in the center of the market. I imagined Mariama atop it later this morning, standing alongside Emperor Suleyman and watching Kader step into the kettle. Would she again wear that smile of hers, the cold, practiced smile she showed to the world to hide the sensitive girl underneath? How would she react when he was the first suitor to survive? Would she be relieved?

No more Trials, no more dead suitors, and all it took was two girls' deaths.

Will Mariama be glad of it?

Now Haddy and I were at the palace's great iron gates. I remembered Issatou meeting me here on my first day of work. I remembered her authoritative manner, her crisp voice as she'd shown me how to perform my daily duties. I felt a flush of shame remembering, for I had been like a child then. I was embarrassed to think of that girl who had been so gullible, unable to see what awaited her in the desert. But I couldn't have known then that Issatou had once been Empress Cassi's nursemaid, that she was still unwaveringly loyal to her old mistress. And I also couldn't have known that when I'd come to Issatou for a sleeping draught to use on the emperor's horsemen, she had only been doing Mariama and the empress's bidding. I squared my shoulders as I peered past the gates, looking into the dark and silent yard.

It was empty save for the seven statues of the gods and a single guard who had a common face and was of a middling age. He greeted us with a nod and began to walk in our direction. "You're the girls sent by Lieutenant General Ousmane, aren't you?" he asked as he approached, and I knew he was the member of the Order who was supposed to be waiting for us. "One of you is Hadiza?"

My sister raised a hand to him in confirmation. "Thank you for helping us," she told him.

He lifted a key from his robes and unlocked the gates. We followed him beneath the archway, into an interior corridor lined with torches. The strong wind bent the flames and made the shadows skitter across the floor like rodents. Besides the three of us, the hall was empty. Still, I covered my face with my hand. I was wary of encountering servants who might remember me.

The guard gave us a replica of the key that opened Mariama's quarters and then left us in the hall of audience. It looked just as I remembered it: the gold leaf, the statues, the clear trickle of the fountains. I heard his retreating footsteps and then he was gone. I led my sister stealthily through the women's quarters, walking the many corridors and climbing the staircases I remembered so well. All was dark, but I did not mind: I knew my way by heart. Each silent courtyard I passed, each black and bubbling fountain, reminded me of my first day in the palace, when everything I'd seen had impressed me.

I felt torn between missing my old self and feeling embarrassed for her. It was painful to remember myself as I was, following Issa-tou through these halls for the very first time. I tried to remember that Amie. Would she recognize the person I was now, the girl with a dagger warming in her fist?

We used the guard's key to enter Mariama's dark quarters, climb-ing the staircase toward her bedchamber. The maids' room, when we passed it, seemed even smaller and plainer than I recalled. I glanced inside. Tears pricked my eyes when I saw that there were still three sleeping mats on the floor, but three girls I had never seen slept upon them.

Issatou had already found new servants to attend to the princess. I had tried not to think of Penda and Jeneba while I was traveling, but now I could not help myself. It felt wrong to see others in their places. Most of all, I was angry, furiously so, at Mariama and her mother for what they did to them.

We continued up the stairs until we reached Mariama's chamber. At Haddy's signal, I put my ear to the door and listened for voices. When I heard none, I pushed open the double doors slowly, bit by bit, my heart pounding furiously. Then Haddy pressed her hands upon the stone walls, whispering her spell to thicken them and muf-fle any sounds from within. Her fingers, delicate and nimble, danced through the air with a mesmerizing grace, tracing invisible patterns. Her eyes, normally a deep shade of brown, now glowed with an otherworldly intensity, reflecting the power coursing through her.

Soon, Haddy's concentration was absolute, her entire being fo-cused on the delicate balance of magic she wove. Beads of sweat glistened on her forehead, evidence of the immense effort required to maintain the enchantment. As she sang, a faint cerulean aura began to envelop her, radiating outward like a delicate web of light. It reached out to touch the stone walls, and the very air seemed to respond to her command.

"You can go in now," Haddy whispered. "You won't be over-heard."

"Thank you," I told her earnestly. What I was about to do would be impossible without Haddy's skills. I gave her a quick hug, but she could not return my embrace, so focused was she on her sorcery. I pushed the door another inch. It gave a low groan. I waited a long moment and heard nothing. Then came the steady hiss of Maria-ma's breathing.

With one final look at my sister, I stepped inside. Mariama's bedchamber seemed smaller and darker than I remembered. Usu-ally she kept an oil lamp burning all night because she feared the dark, but tonight there was no lamp, only moonlight and gray shadows. During the daytime, her room was rich with color—blue carpets and bright leather-bound books and linen wrappers in all hues—but night had bleached everything white and black, flat and colorless as words on a scroll. Mariama, too, seemed flat and sketch-like, devoid of color. The wind turned the coiled ends of her hair; that was all.

I'd imagined that the sight of her would fill me with rage, but when I looked at her, all I felt was longing. My heart was racing, my breathing shallow. I stood there a long moment, listening to her steady breaths and watching her frown at something in her dreams.

Three nights of desert travel had given me more than enough time to mentally prepare for this moment, but I still felt nervous about what I had to do next. I was meant to awaken Mariama, show her my dagger, and warn her that I would use it on her unless she showed me how to find Jeneba—and now that I was here with her in her bedchamber, I wondered if I really had the strength to do this. I had never threatened anyone before.

Taking a deep breath, I crept closer to Mariama until finally I knelt beside her sleeping mat. She did not stir. I pulled out my dagger and lifted it to the moonlight. I saw her reflected in the blade, and for a long moment I found myself watching the lines of moisture beneath her eyes, her rippling throat. I had to admit that she looked beautiful.

The herbalists at the Order taught Haddy that the throat was one of the most vulnerable parts of the anatomy, and if one memorized its delicate network of veins, one could administer medicine or poison within seconds. Remembering this, I placed my dagger at the hollow of Mariama's neck, silver against her dark, soft skin. The blade was hot in my palm. Its needle tip gleamed like jewelry in the moonlight.

Her chest expanded and contracted; I heard her sigh. The sound made me want to flee her chamber. Gripping the dagger tightly, I tried to urge myself on. *Amie, you can do this*, I told myself. *All you must do is frighten her with the dagger, and she will tell you how to find Jeneba. Maybe she'll even have another map. . . .*

Mariama's eyes fluttered abruptly open. She saw me, saw my dagger. My heartbeat quickened. I held her in place, thinking she might struggle or cry out.

She did not. She grew still as death and said, "Amie, it's you!" in an astonished whisper, her face contorted with disbelief. "But you cannot be Amie. Amie is dead, so you must be something sent by my mother's husband, some spirit conjured to frighten me," she continued. "She has refused to speak with me lately, so I knew she must be angry with me, but to send you in her place . . . ! Well, I am not frightened."

"I'm not dead, but your mother is," I pointed out, and held the dagger with an even more forceful grip. My fingers were sweating around the blade.

Her face showed shock and then disbelief. "She is not dead. She cannot be."

"Yes, she is." My voice trembled; I forced myself to speak more steadily. "I killed the empress in her husband's house. I plucked the vines that were keeping her alive. I even watched her draw her last breath."

"You're lying. Her husband is a great god, he would never let her perish." But I could tell that she was already beginning to believe me. Her eyes darted desperately across the chamber to the place on the wall where the looking glass shone gray as lead in the semi-darkness.

I watched the glass, too, thinking of all those times when she claimed to have had night terrors—until I grew so angry that I forgot myself. "You can speak into that mirror for the rest of your life, but your mother will never answer," I hissed. "You will never hear her voice again, just as you will never hear Penda's. Are you glad of it? Are you happy that you'll never again have to speak with the girl you killed?" My voice became shrill, accusatory. "Perhaps you are guilty and feel ashamed of what you did to her. Or perhaps not. She perished very far away. I imagine distance works wonders on your conscience."

Mariama smiled slightly—it was the most astonishing thing, to see a girl smile at knifepoint—and gazed up at me. Her look grew dark and fearless, as if she were the one who held the blade to my throat. "*Amie.* So you've escaped the great god's wrath and returned to the palace to kill me," she said, her eyes flashing. "Do it, then! Do it quickly. What have I to live for, anyway?"

"Kill y-you?" I stammered, loosening my grip upon the dagger in reflex. Her words had shocked me. "That is not my aim. I only want to find Jeneba." Kneeling here with my dagger to her neck, I thought about the last time I had been this close to her, during my last night in the palace. I remembered the feeling of her body against mine, the soft, sweet-smelling tendrils of her hair around my fingers. A sharp longing started up in my chest at the memory. I tried to ignore it.

"You want to find Jeneba?" Mariama shook her head in disbelief. "How would I know where she is? I haven't seen her since she left the palace, with you."

"She is in Hausakoy's forge house, and I intend to rescue her," I said firmly, holding my blade hand steadily against her skin. "Tell me quickly: How can I get there? Give me directions, now, to the best of your ability—otherwise, I'll slit your throat."

Her eyes widened at my threat. "So, you've just escaped Hausakoy's forge house, and now you want to return to it? Only a madwoman would do such a thing."

"Tell me how to reach the forge house, or you die," I repeated, making my voice as menacing as I possibly could. But I didn't really think I could kill her. I hoped she would comply so it wouldn't come to that.

"I cannot tell you, but I can show you—if you put away your blade." Mariama looked meaningfully at the point of my dagger.

I kept the blade in place. "You don't give me orders anymore. And what do you mean, *show* me?"

"My mother gave me two other versions of the map, in case you didn't find it where Issatou planted it," she explained. "If you hadn't found it in the kitchens, we would have tried another place where you commonly visited and placed a map there."

So there *were* other maps, just as I had hoped. Thank goodness! I sighed with relief, relaxing my dagger hand and, slowly, removing it from Mariama's neck. She gasped and started away from me, scrambling to her feet in seconds. Her eyes were large and her mouth was opened wide, like someone about to scream, but she made not a sound. Instead, she crossed over to her bookshelf and produced a scroll that rustled in her hands as she flattened it against the carpets next to me.

"Here is the map," she said, pointing down at the scroll, but it was dark in the room and I could not see it properly.

"Stay there," I told her, rising to my feet. "Don't move." I lit the oil lamps, one by one, bathing the chamber in yellow light. Then I knelt beside Mariama and looked again at the scroll. A triumphant feeling took hold of me when I saw that it was indeed identical to the map I'd lost in the caves, from the ink-and-dye ocean to the min-iature caravanners traversing the paper Sahara. I traced its surface with my fingers, resting my thumb upon Hausakoy's home.

"Amie, you cannot really mean that you're going to go back there?" She sounded genuinely concerned for me. "It isn't safe."

"Since when do you care if I'm safe?"

She lowered her eyes but did not answer.

I continued, "And when did you know your mother could end the Trials?" This was just one of the questions that swirled in my mind as densely as fog. How many of her night terrors had been real and how many had only been falsehoods designed to com-pel me to use a book of stories to calm her, a book from which an enchanted map had fallen conveniently into my lap like fruit dropping from a tree? And if Hausakoy had delivered the map to Issatou, how had the two of them known that I would find it while I peeled yams? For how long had she been planning to kill Penda and Jeneba? And what if I had been illiterate, what if I had not been able to read a map or a book of stories—would she still have chosen me to die?

"I knew a year before I met you," she admitted, looking uncom-fortable. She cast her eyes down. "My mother told me. She said, 'My divine husband and I can end this, but you'll have to send a sacrifice.' She wanted me to give her three people who wouldn't be missed. I knew I was sending Penda and Jeneba to their deaths, and I feel so guilty for it—the knowledge of what I did still keeps me awake with horror."

"You seemed to be sleeping just fine," I told her. "So, you sent the three of us into the desert already knowing what would become of us once we reached Hausakoy," I added, my mind reeling. My head throbbed, and I began to feel dizzy. Mariama might have been an object of her mother's designs, but she was still complicit. I felt a sharp contempt for her that nearly knocked me off-balance.

"I sent the two of *them*, Amie," she said. She swallowed. "Not you. Never you. I didn't want you to leave me."

This surprised me. "Why?"

She wrung her hands. "Because you're the only friend I've ever had."

"Friend?" I spat the word with contempt. How could she call me that? "I was your servant."

"You felt it, too," she whispered. "You cared for me. I could tell."

She was right, but I dared not admit it aloud. I said instead, "You have known for an entire year that Penda and Jeneba would have to die so that you could end the Trials. And you just needed a third person to go out into the desert with them. It could have been anyone at all. Why did you choose me?"

"Because you can read," she told me. "The map to Hausakoy has written instructions that the others would never have been able to follow."

"Ah," I said, cringing with the knowledge that my literacy, which I had thought made me special and put me somewhat above the other girls, had only made me an easier target. I kept waiting for her to scream, to call out for help, but she did not. She only seemed to relax against me.

"And also because you are ruined," she added. "The night when Lord Bagayogo ripped out your earring and announced to everyone at the banquet that you were a liar, I thought, *She is our third.* All while I was defending you, and later, when I was cleaning your wounds, I could hardly contain my excitement. I told my mother about you as soon as you had left my chamber. I said into the mirror, 'Mother, she is perfect. Young enough to withstand a desert journey, literate, and disinherited by her family.'"

I hated to hear her speak so callously of the first evening I had spent in her company, but it all made more sense now. Hadn't I wondered then why she had been so kind to me the night Lord Bagayogo ripped my ear? Hadn't I wanted to know why the princess was condescending to bandage the wound of a servant she had only just met? Now I had the answer.

I remembered with displeasure how privileged I once had felt to sit at her side during meals, how much I had liked wearing her clothes and jewels and being treated like her equal. How could I have been so easily tricked?

"And your night terrors, were they real?" I needed to know just how much of our time together had been a lie.

"Some of them were," she admitted. "I often dreamt of my suitors' deaths. Sometimes when you found me weeping, it was because I had lately spoken with my mother, and she'd had harsh words for me. And at other times, my mother visited my dreams and scolded me there, which was even more devastating. She kept saying I was weakhearted, that I was delaying things unnecessarily, preventing her from getting—"

"What was Issatou's role in all of this? How much did she know of your mother's plan?" I interrupted, remembering the night when I'd gone alone to her little room and used Mariama's money to purchase the sleeping draught for the emperor's horsemen. I had lied to Issatou then, saying that I sought a potion of drowsiness to cure my insomnia, and she had readily accepted my lie.

"More than I did," Mariama said bitterly. "Issatou has been quite devoted to my mother ever since she was her nursemaid. She uses the mirror to speak with her almost as much as I do."

"So the sleeping draught we bought from her . . ."

"I told Issatou that you would come asking for it. All of it was arranged ahead of time."

I imagined Issatou, Mariama, and the empress plotting against me and grimaced. Something else was still bothering me. "But you did not want all three of us to go into the desert at first," I pointed out. "You said that just one of us should go, and whoever volunteered would win her weight in gold. If you needed three lives to exchange for Hausakoy's hammer, then why wouldn't you have urged all of us to go in the first place?"

"Mother said that I should make going into the desert seem like a prize to be won, so the three of you would compete. She said I should dangle it like a reward and then sit back and let you bicker over which one of you deserved it the most." Her remorseful sigh filled me with angry indignation. How dared she feel sorry for the girls she'd harmed? It was like an executioner mourning the swing of his blade. "My mother can be ruthless," she continued. "She knows how to turn commoners' ambitions to her advantage."

Another spasm of white-hot anger blurred my vision. The princess and the empress had used their inherited gold to lure us into mortal danger. They thought we commoners were like birds, with tiny brains and a penchant for collecting coins and other shining objects. They certainly seemed to value our lives as little as they would have valued the life of a bird, or a fish, or any other animal. Fury bubbled in my belly as I let my free hand sink into the carpets.

"Amie, you must know I am sorry for what I did," she continued, her voice trembling. "I was only following my mother's instructions, only trying to end the Trials. You cannot know what a burden it was for me to have to watch all those suitors be murdered in my name. I thought it was more than worth it to sacrifice three lives, when ninety-nine had already been lost."

"But in the end, you did not sacrifice three lives," I corrected, my voice shaking with my contempt for her. "You tried to save mine, at the very last moment. You wanted me to remain with you at court. *Why?*"

For a moment, we said nothing. A thousand unspoken words hovered like soap bubbles in the air between us, ready to burst.

She tried to cup my face in her hands, but I shrank away from her. "Because I loved you," she said, looking wounded. "I thought you were the perfect target, but I also saw that you were beautiful, clever, and kind. I knew that my mother would be furious with me for disobeying her, for destroying our plans, but I did not care. I could not bring myself to put you to death like the others."

I exhaled my disgust, a new feeling settling about me—not pity but a kind of begrudging understanding. I still hated her for what she'd done, but with her words, my anger had begun to subside, like a fire burning itself out. After all the nights we had passed together, after all those lingering glances and moments of tension—she had finally admitted her feelings. She said she loved me. Did it matter? I knew I could never return her love, not after what she had done to the others. But I noticed that she was looking up at me expectantly, lovely and vulnerable. She wanted me to say it back.

"I might have loved you, once," I admitted. "But not anymore. I cannot. Do you know what it was like for me to watch Penda die? To leave Jeneba all alone with a cruel god?"

We looked at each other for a long moment, both of us unable to speak. A cloud crossed the moon, casting the room in shadow. All her windows were open. I could feel the rough, dry breeze on my skin and hear the rustle of mosquito netting on the ceiling. I heard the calling of larks in the trees—dawn was approaching.

"You cannot love me. I understand it. I don't deserve you," she said, swallowing back the last of her tears as if she had resigned herself to the knowledge that things could never again be as they once had been between us. Then, wiping her face, she said, "You'll still hate me after this, I am sure." Mariama stood before the looking glass and stared into it intently, saying, "Hausakoy," in a clear voice.

I did not expect that its silver surface would begin to move so immediately, rippling like pond water beneath my fingers. I stepped back from the wall in a panic, worried that the great god might reach out and seize me by the throat.

But when the mirror grew still again and a visage appeared upon it, I did not see Hausakoy—thankfully—only Jeneba's young and anxious face, looking at me as directly as if she stood in the chamber with me.

Mariama and I gasped out in unison, "Jeneba!" Relief and disbelief battled within me as I watched her nervous expression soften into recognition.

"Mariama, you would be wise not to call upon my husband," Jeneba said, and it was as if her voice were coming from the bottom of a well. But otherwise, she did sound like herself.

She lived! Could it really be her?

Bittersweet tears sprang to my eyes at the words *my husband*. I was so glad to see that she was not dead, but I hated to think that the great god had taken her for a bride. How had it happened? When last I'd spoken to Hausakoy, he'd said that he planned to torture and torment her. When had he changed tack, decided to marry her instead?

And when had she become his wife? For how long had he chased her through that horrible cave until she relented? Had he exchanged his last wife, the empress, so easily for a younger girl? In all the old tales of the seven gods, the smith was described as a lover of young girls, a predator who did not mind securing his brides through force.

"I'm not Mariama, I'm Amie," I told her hastily.

"What was that?" Jeneba asked, frowning. Her voice was even fainter now, muffled as if through wool. I realized she could not hear me. "Mariama, you must not contact me again."

"I am not Mariama! I only mean to ask—" I began to say, but her face was beginning to dissolve, the mirror's surface growing silvery once more.

"Wait!" My plea came in a desperate whisper.

Mariama said, "Do not go!"

But by then, we spoke only to our reflections. Jeneba was gone.

"Where did Jeneba go?" I demanded, wheeling on Mariama with narrowed eyes. "Bring her back!"

She said, "I can try," and said Jeneba's name, but the surface of the mirror did not stir. Mariama then called out Hausakoy's name, but still the silver surface did not move.

I tried it, too. "Jeneba," I said, touching the glass, but nothing happened. It occurred to me then that Haddy might be able to help with the mirror, that her skill for metal magic might help us speak with Jeneba. "Don't move," I told Mariama again, and I rushed to the hall, where Haddy was still focused on her spell, her eyes closed tightly with concentration.

"Haddy," I said, touching her arm gently so as not to startle her.

Her eyes flew open. "Amie, you're back! What happened? Did the princess give you a map?"

"Yes, but . . . please come with me. We need your help."

I took her by the hand and the two of us entered Mariama's

lamplit chamber. She looked up as we entered, seeming surprised that I'd brought someone with me.

"What's going on?" Mariama's eyes studied Haddy, as if determining whether she was a friend or a foe.

"You've met my sister, Haddy," I told her. "She is a sorceress."

26

ariama and Haddy had attended banquets and dances together in the palace and so knew each other's faces, but I doubted they had interacted meaningfully before tonight. It felt strange to be in that chamber with the both of them, as if the two halves of my world were at long last colliding. As Haddy sang spell after spell over the mirror, trying in vain to bring back Jeneba, Mariama watched with discomfort, her arms folded across her chest.

"Amie, you cannot really mean to go back to Hausakoy," she told me, raising her voice to be heard over Haddy's. "He will kill you where you stand."

"I have to find Jeneba," I said resolutely. "Now that I know she's still alive and Hausakoy has made her his bride, it is my duty to rescue her."

She pressed her lips together tightly, her eyes clouded over with worry for me. Then she said suddenly, "Let me come with you."

"Really?" I was shocked. "You would go with me to Hausakoy? But don't you have a wedding to attend, very soon? Kader will win the Trials today, you know that."

"So he will," she said. "But I won't marry him. How could I, when I'll be with you in the desert?"

Haddy turned her attention away from the mirror in surprise. "Princess, what are you saying?"

The worry was fading from Mariama's gaze, replaced with a clarity that almost frightened me. "I'm saying that Hausakoy knows me. When he married my mother, he promised never to harm her or any of her children. If I come with you to his forge house, I am certain I could convince him to spare both of your lives. But without me . . ." She shook her head sadly. "If you go without me, you'll both be dead women."

"Thank you for offering to join us, but I am not sure how we'd take you with us without anyone noticing," I told her, wondering why she would make such an offer. How did she feel about me now, after all that had passed between us? Was she really willing to defy her father and not marry Kader?

Haddy said, "I might have an idea." She told us her plan and we listened carefully, talking it over as the sky continued to lighten.

Dawn brought with it a renewed sense of purpose, sharp and defined, cutting through any lingering doubts I may have had about confronting Kader. Mariama, Haddy, and I had strategized quickly but effectively, plotting our course to uncover the truth about his betrayal. With determination etched on our faces, my sister and I wasted no time after leaving Mariama's chamber, our steps resolute as we approached the cells that were tucked away near the armory. I knew the way because Mariama had taken me before—back when I'd never left Timbuktu, before I'd ever survived a sandstorm or fought hyenas or met a god—but the last time I'd walked these corridors, there hadn't been any prisoners or guards, and all the cells had looked empty.

Now, however, a lone guard stood watch at what I assumed to be Kader's door, since it was the only one closed. Even with his back turned to us, I could still tell that the guard was tall and broad chested, not someone easy to bypass, but we had prepared for this obstacle. The corridor hung heavy with the scent of metal and dust, and the sound of our footfalls reverberated in the unsettling silence as we approached him from behind.

With a glance exchanged between us, Haddy moved forward, her movements fluid and calculated. The guard's protest was cut short as her magic ensnared him in a web of metal, his chain mail binding him to the wall, rendering him powerless to resist. He fell silent, trapped beneath the weight of her magic, and I could see the strain on my sister's face as she expended her strength into holding him in place.

She said with effort, "Let's see your traitor."

I hoped *traitor* wasn't the right word to describe Kader—but I was here to find out. With a lump in my throat, I began to follow my sister into his cell, but I hesitated on the threshold as I caught sight of him sprawled across the floor. There he was: once my reason for living, now a stranger wearing familiar flesh.

Haddy began to prod at him with cautious curiosity, her voice a soothing murmur of spells intended to break the empress's hold upon him. I felt the sting of his betrayal all over again as our eyes met. Betrayal, anger, distrust, attraction, affection, hope—the conflicting currents of emotions threatened to overwhelm my senses as Kader rose to his feet and reached for my arm. His touch sent sparks dancing along my skin, a reminder of the warmth we had once shared, now tainted by his deceit.

"Amie, thank the gods you're alive!" he breathed. His eyes looked clearer than they had in the forge house, less fogged over with enchantment, and I wondered if Haddy's spell had worked. Was he himself once again? "How did you escape? And what about your friend, is she safe, too?"

"She's not safe at all," I finally managed, flinching at my last memory of Jeneba frowning in the mirror. Then I brushed his hand aside; I did not want him to touch me. "You have a lot to answer for," I added, my voice trembling with pent-up emotion. "How much do you remember of the forge house?"

His expression darkened. "All of it, I suppose. I remember dining with the empress and falling asleep at her table after I'd agreed
to her terms. And I remember when you came and woke me up,
and I remember when Hausakoy took me through the sky over the
desert—"

Something he'd said concerned me. "What do you mean, you
agreed to her terms?" I demanded. Beside me, I was dimly aware
of Haddy exiting the cell—to give us some semblance of a private
conversation, I supposed, although I was sure she could hear us
from the corridor. I still drew comfort from her gesture.

"We've been intended for each other ever since we were children," he said slowly. "So of course I love you, Amie, and I will
always care for you, but I've made my choice. I'm going to step into
the kettle today, and I'm going to win." His words cut like a blade;
with each syllable, the chasm between us widened.

"So you meant what you said down there?" I asked as desperation caught hold in my chest. I didn't want to believe what he was
telling me. Was this really him? "You remember the empress's enchantment? You remember what it felt like? Do you feel it now?"

He looked regretful yet resigned to his words. "I haven't been
true to what we were trying to build together. When I told you I
wanted to win the Trials and impress my father, yes, I meant it. And
a conversation with the empress made me realize I wanted to win
the Trials more than I wanted to be with you. I'm sorry for it, and
I don't want to hurt you any more than I already have, but that's
the truth."

His words were like a blow; I had to catch my breath. I tried to
see if the enchantment was still in his eyes. Had Haddy managed
to disarm it? Was this really him? My bitterness overwhelmed me.
I turned my gaze away from him; he was still so beautiful and so

profoundly upsetting and disappointing. I was glad when Haddy said, "We have to go, I can't hold the guard in place much longer," and so we left.

I walked away feeling not entirely satisfied but still like I'd gotten the answers from Kader that I needed. He was so much of my life for so many years, and I was heartbroken, but now I saw his true loyalties. I knew now who he really was, and it left me deeply disheartened, but at least I knew. Haddy let us retreat mostly out of his way before we released the guard from his temporary imprisonment. We were so far down the hallway that even though he tried to chase after us, we outran him. We were lucky not to encounter anyone else on our trek back to Mariama's chamber, where she awaited us anxiously.

As soon as we walked through her door, Mariama asked us how things went with Kader and wondered if he seemed ready for the Trial. I told her that Kader helped me to understand why he had done what he did, but I wasn't able to forgive him, not yet. The morning sun climbed higher as Haddy, Mariama, and I finalized our plans. By then, it was time for Kader to face the kettle. Mariama had given the other maids the day off, so Haddy and I painted her face and plaited her hair with jewels. By noon, our preparations were finished. Mariama left the bedchamber in a swish of violet brocade, and Haddy and I followed her through the palace, finally accompanying her out of the palace yard and into the crowded market.

Then I was climbing the steps to the platform with Mariama once again, listening to the great din of spectators in the square below. Haddy and I gathered near the kettle alongside the emperor, his courtiers and advisers, and Mariama. I searched the crowd, hoping to catch a glimpse of our parents, and after a few moments I found them. Mother and Father were not too far from the front of the crowd, looking with relief at Haddy. They were glad to see her safe, I was sure. My parents watched only my sister and paid me little attention, but this no longer bothered me as it once had. I didn't need their approval, not anymore.

Once we had all taken our places, two foot soldiers led out Kader in chains. I inhaled sharply at the sight of him. I tried to hold his gaze, but he was clearly under the enchantment again—a realization that made me feel ill as the foot soldiers led Kader into the kettle. Then they lit the kindling beneath it and my stomach dropped at the familiar scent of smoke. The hot water was waist-deep and made his robes soaking wet, but he did not seem to react to the temperatures at all.

That's when I noticed that Kader held the air in a peculiar way, the fingers of his left hand curled as if around an invisible mallet, and realized that Hausakoy had made the hammer invisible so that the emperor wouldn't have it confiscated. I let out a sigh of relief that Kader had what he needed to survive. After they placed the lid over the kettle, the foot soldiers looked curiously at each other, confused by the absence of screams of pain.

An eternity seemed to pass before the foot soldiers lifted the lid on the kettle and Kader slowly emerged, unhurt and unscathed. His eyes were wide with the daze of the enchantment, but he seemed otherwise unchanged. I felt a surge of relief that Kader had come out unharmed—my hope had been rewarded. It had taken a lot to get to this moment.

The emperor stood in stunned silence, while the courtiers and foot soldiers looked on with mouths agape and the crowds fell quiet with discomfort and disbelief.

The sun was hot, the platform warm enough that I felt the heat through my sandals. Beside me, Haddy stepped forward and sang a low, melodic spell to Kader's chains. The metal seemed to hum and pulse with energy, and soon the chains began to shift and grow. As I watched in amazement, the chains transformed into three iron horses. They whickered and shuffled like normal horses, but their skin was the same metallic gray as the chains.

At first, the emperor was slow to react. He could only watch as Haddy mounted the first horse. Mariama and I quickly climbed atop our own horses as the silent crowd reacted in horror, screaming, "Sorceress!" This seemed to awaken the emperor, who called out for his guards to seize Haddy. But it was too late: she was already spurring her iron horse forward. She galloped away from the platform, and Mariama and I followed, leaving Kader behind.

We rode madly, trying to escape the emperor's guards. The horses' metal hooves clattered on the ground, making a racket that echoed throughout the streets. As we raced through Timbuktu, we were met with a strange silence; people stopped what they were doing to watch us fly past on our iron horses. At last, we made it across the bridge and into the merchants' district. We continued our hurried pace as we traveled through winding roads and side streets.

I glanced behind me to see that our pursuers were drawing closer. We passed the merchants' district and the riverbank and the universities, but the emperor's men still drew nearer, crying, "Return the princess!" It occurred to me then that they thought we were kidnapping Mariama.

We were now galloping across the terrain at a frantic pace, the horses' hooves pounding into the dry earth. Looking more closely, I saw that one of the men in hot pursuit of us was Haddy's husband, Lord Ayouta. "Wife! Come back, wife," he shouted, urging his horse onward as the other horses grew tired and began to lag behind. He was an excellent horseman: each movement of his body and every tug of his reins showed how expertly he could control the massive animal beneath him. Charging forth with alarming speed, he gained ground on us quickly.

We were nearing the compounds at the edge of the desert, drawing closer to the sandy expanse of dunes. The emperor's other men
had fallen back, exhausted, but Lord Ayouta continued, screaming,
"Wife! Come back, wife!" He spurred his horse forward with a feroc-
ity that made it seem as though he were possessed. "Wife!" he cried
again. His voice was carried away on the wind; it was clear he would
stop at nothing to catch up to Haddy.

I heard Lord Ayouta shouting behind us as he pushed his horse
faster and faster, gaining on her. His voice rang out, growing triumphant. "Hadiza!"

I watched in horror as he pushed Haddy's iron horse. It was
thrown off course and she was sent flying. She hit the ground hard,
a cloud of dust rising with the impact. Her horse kept running without her. Panic shot through me at the sight of Haddy sprawled on
the ground while Lord Ayouta circled her menacingly on his own
steed.

His sword was drawn, and he sneered down at her as she shouted,
"Keep going, Amie! I can protect myself!"

"No!" I cried. I pulled on the reins of my own horse, but nothing
happened; it didn't respond to me at all. It was one of Haddy's enchanted creatures, created to run until sunset. "Haddy!" I screamed,
turning back even as my horse continued onward with a mind of
its own.

I can protect myself, she'd said. I hoped that she could. She had
sorcery on her side—but still I shouted her name over and over
until my throat was raw, aching for answers. Mariama's iron horse
galloped beside mine as Haddy and her husband grew smaller and
smaller.

The city fell away, shrinking behind us. Tears pricked my eyes
as I thought of everything I was leaving behind with it—my sister,
Kader, my parents. But although my heart still ached for Haddy's

presence, I sensed a shift within me, a dimming of the flame I once carried for Kader, replaced by a blaze of determination to find and rescue Jeneba.

The person I had been when last I left the city, the girl whose goal had been to marry Kader and live peacefully with him ever after, seemed like a stranger to me. The last of Timbuktu receded in the distance along with my remaining trepidation. And then Mariama and I were alone in an expanse of rolling sand, borne swiftly forward toward the forge house and Hausakoy. I was resolute and fearless, intent on rescuing my friend from the smithing god's lair— and with Mariama's strength bolstering mine, I felt ready to brave any danger that crossed our path, even if it meant risking everything, including my own life.

I glanced at her when I could, watching her on her horse and wondering: *Can I trust her?* In the stories I had loved growing up, there would come a time when the hero had to take a leap of faith, trusting against his better judgment to move his aims forward. I felt conflicted about Mariama, but now that we were partnered, I had to do the same. I had to trust her enough for us to work together and find Jeneba.

Looking up at the expanse of pure blue sky above the dunes, I saw a sudden flash of color—a dark red shape flying against the cerulean backdrop. A fire finch. My heart lurched at the sight. Its wings shone scarlet as it made its way closer to the horizon until, finally, it disappeared into the infinite line joining desert and sky.

ACKNOWLEDGMENTS

There are so many people who made this dream possible!

First, I'd like to thank my parents for their longtime support.

Thank you to my agent, Jenny Bent, for believing in my first draft and for your invaluable feedback.

Thanks to my editors, Maxine Charles, Sarah Barley, and Emma Jones, and thanks also to the wider Flatiron Books team for your thoughtfulness and encouragement.

Thanks to my sister, Delmar, for being my first reader and inspiring me to write a sibling story.

To my godmother, Carol Saffold, thanks for letting me use your home as a writer's studio.

Thanks to the Mallebay-Vacquer family for guiding my research on Francophone West Africa.

Thanks to the Diakité family for their insights about present-day Mali.

Thank you to my beta readers and writer friends, Alison McKenzie and Meridith Viguet, for your early support, industry advice, and friendship. Melissa Albert, your kind words and advice were crucial during my revisions. Thank you for helping me complete this manuscript!

Thank you to Columbia University professor and historian Gregory Mann for teaching West African history and sparking the seeds of this book when I was still an undergraduate. To my undergraduate and graduate creative writing professors Dorla McIntosh, Paul Beatty, Gary Shteyngart, Alena Graedon, Alexandra Kleeman, Heidi

Julavits, and Sam Lipsyte, thank you for encouraging my studies and supporting my work.

Finally, a special thanks to historians Baz Lecocq, Augustus Casely-Hayford, Fatima Sadiqi, and Nick Jubber for answering my many, many questions about fourteenth-century West Africa. One of the most thoughtful and helpful resources on the region is Ousmane Oumar Kane's *Beyond Timbuktu: An Intellectual History of Muslim West Africa* (2016), which heavily informed my work.

1 Rabi al-Awwal 1359 | The First Day of the First Month of Spring 1359

Her Imperial Highness Mariama Keita shall please find enclosed her spring 1359 lesson plans, as approved by her father, His Imperial Highness Suleyman I.

With God's grace,

Lord Abu al-Fazanni,
Senior Master of the Madrasa Djinguereber in Timbuktu

Her Imperial Highness's plan of study for Rabi al-Awwal, the first month of spring:

- Afternoons:
  - Arabic grammar and syntax, one hour. Her Highness will kindly bring her copy of Ibn Malik's *Alfiya*.
  - Principles of Islamic jurisprudence, two hours.
  - Geometry and arithmetic, one hour. Her Highness will kindly bring her copy of Avicenna's *The Book of Healing*.

- Evenings:
  - Qur'anic recitation, one hour. Her Highness will kindly bring her Holy Book.
  - Astronomy, one hour. Her Highness will kindly bring her copy of Muhammad ibn Musa al-Khwarizmi's *Zij al-Sindhind*.

Her Imperial Highness's plan of study for Rabi al-Thani, the second month of spring:

- Afternoons:
  * Anatomy and medicine, one hour. Her Highness will kindly bring her copy of Avicenna's *The Book of Healing*.
  * Logic and rhetoric, one hour.
  * Arabic grammar and syntax, two hours. Her Highness will kindly bring her copy of Ibn Malik's *Alfiya*.

- Evenings:
  * Qur'anic interpretation and exegesis, two hours. Her Highness will kindly bring her Holy Book.

Her Imperial Highness's plan of study for Jumada al-Awwal, the final month of spring:

- Afternoons:
  * Principles of Islamic jurisprudence, two hours.
  * Astronomy, one hour. Her Highness will kindly bring her copy of al-Battani's *Kitab az-Zij*.
  * Qur'anic recitation, one hour. Her Highness will kindly bring her Holy Book.

- Evenings:
  * Anatomy and medicine, two hours. Her Highness will kindly bring her copy of Avicenna's *The Book of Healing*.

5 Shawwal 1355 | *The Fifth Day of the Tenth Month of 1355*

Timbuktu Palace

Although the omnipotent God has, for the benefit of the populace, given me charge of the empire of Mali and has delivered the governance of not a few peoples into my imperial stewardship, nevertheless I remember that I, too, am of mortal condition. And it is with a keen understanding of my mortality that I have developed a decree regarding the eventual marriage of my only daughter, the imperial princess Mariama Keita. On her behalf, I make the following sacred decree and have signed it, with God as my witness.

My daughter, Mariama, may wed a Malinke man of noble or royal lineage who can provide the full sum of her brideprice after successfully completing a Trial of my own design. To attempt the Trial, venture into the desert for three nights with three of my best horsemen. On the third evening, you shall come across a grove of date palms with bark as blue as a summer sky. Split the largest tree with an ax, and you will see that its wood is dark red, like blood. Return to my palace, present me with three planks of this wood, and I will permit you to wed my daughter. But if you fail this first Trial, if my horsemen bring you back to the palace empty-handed, you must attempt a second Trial—a bath in boiling water. The suitor who leaves the bath with air still in his lungs and blood still in his veins may marry the princess.

By the grace of God,

His Imperial Highness Emperor Suleyman Keita I of Mali

ABOUT THE AUTHOR

Mina Fears earned her BA and MFA in fiction from Columbia University. Originally from Michigan, she remains in New York City to support corporate communications for tech and finance brands. *The Scorpion Queen* is her first novel.